Ham Helsing: Raising the Stakes was illustrated in Clip Studio Pro and Photoshop.

 Published in the United States by
RH Graphic, an imprint of Random House Children's Books,
a division of Penguin Random House LLC, New York.

RH Graphic with the book design is a trademark of Penguin Random House LLC.

Visit us on the Web! RHKidsGraphic.com
@RHKidsGraphic

Educators and librarians, for a variety of teaching tools,
visit us at RHTeachersLibrarians.com

Library of Congress Cataloging-in-Publication Data is available upon request.
ISBN 978-0-593-30899-8 (hardcover)
ISBN 978-0-593-30901-8 (ebook)

Cover design, logo, and interior colors by Josh Lewis

MANUFACTURED IN CHINA
10 9 8 7 6 5 4 3 2 1
First Edition

RH GRAPHIC
A comic on every bookshelf.

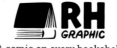

For my girls.
Thank you for the gift of seeing
the world through your eyes.
I'm eternally in your debt.

PROLOGUE

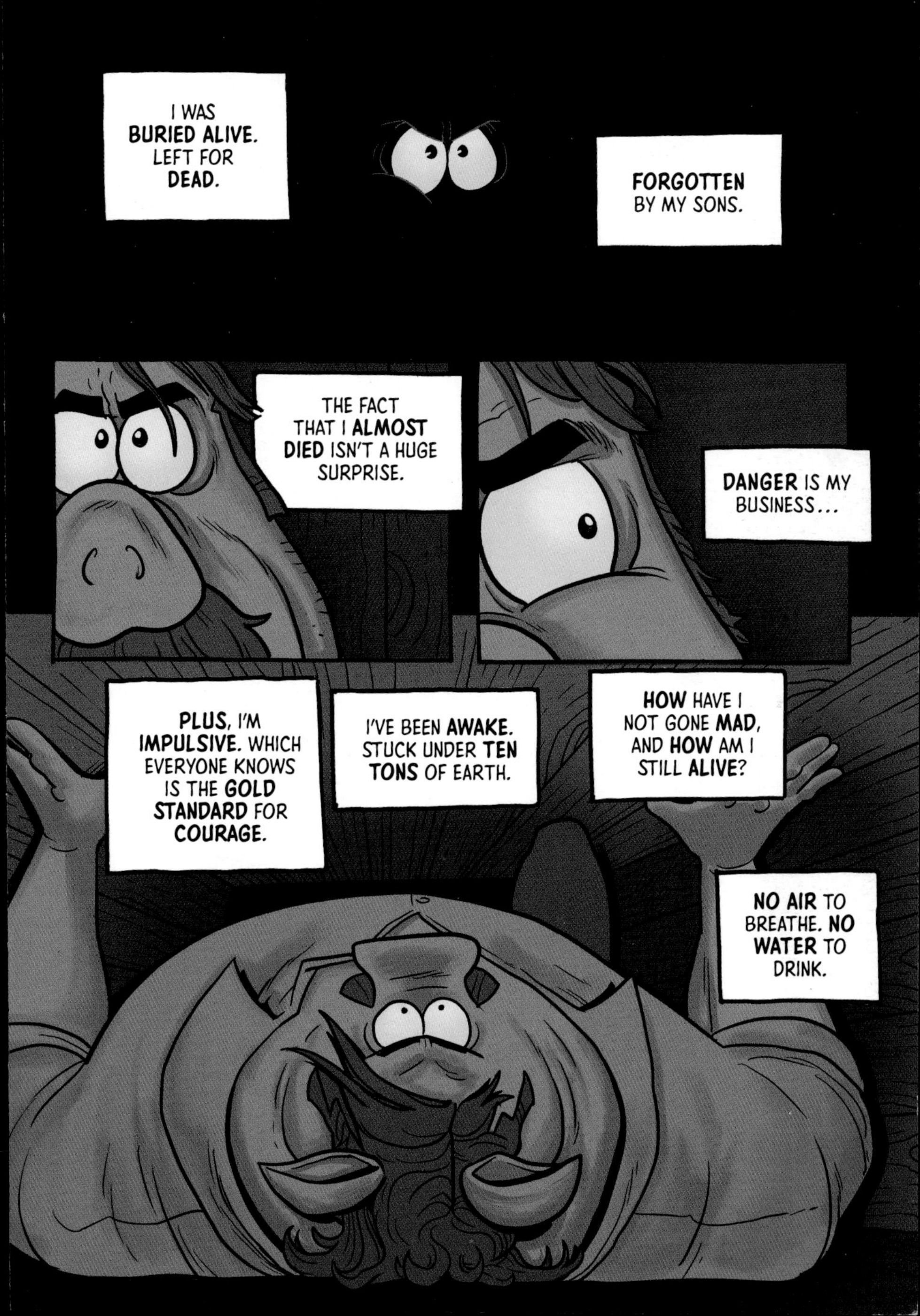

I WAS BURIED ALIVE. LEFT FOR DEAD.
FORGOTTEN BY MY SONS.
THE FACT THAT I ALMOST DIED ISN'T A HUGE SURPRISE.
DANGER IS MY BUSINESS...
PLUS, I'M IMPULSIVE. WHICH EVERYONE KNOWS IS THE GOLD STANDARD FOR COURAGE.
I'VE BEEN AWAKE. STUCK UNDER TEN TONS OF EARTH.
HOW HAVE I NOT GONE MAD, AND HOW AM I STILL ALIVE?
NO AIR TO BREATHE. NO WATER TO DRINK.

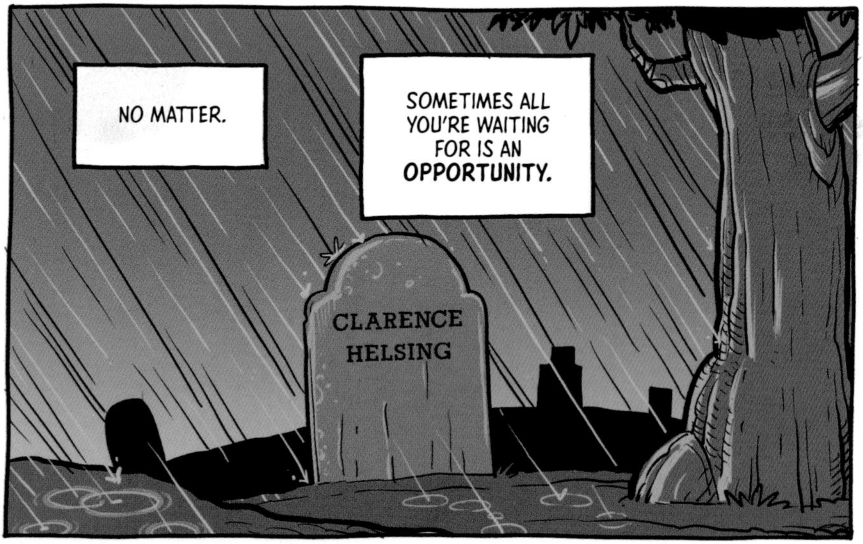
NO MATTER.
SOMETIMES ALL YOU'RE WAITING FOR IS AN **OPPORTUNITY.**
CLARENCE HELSING

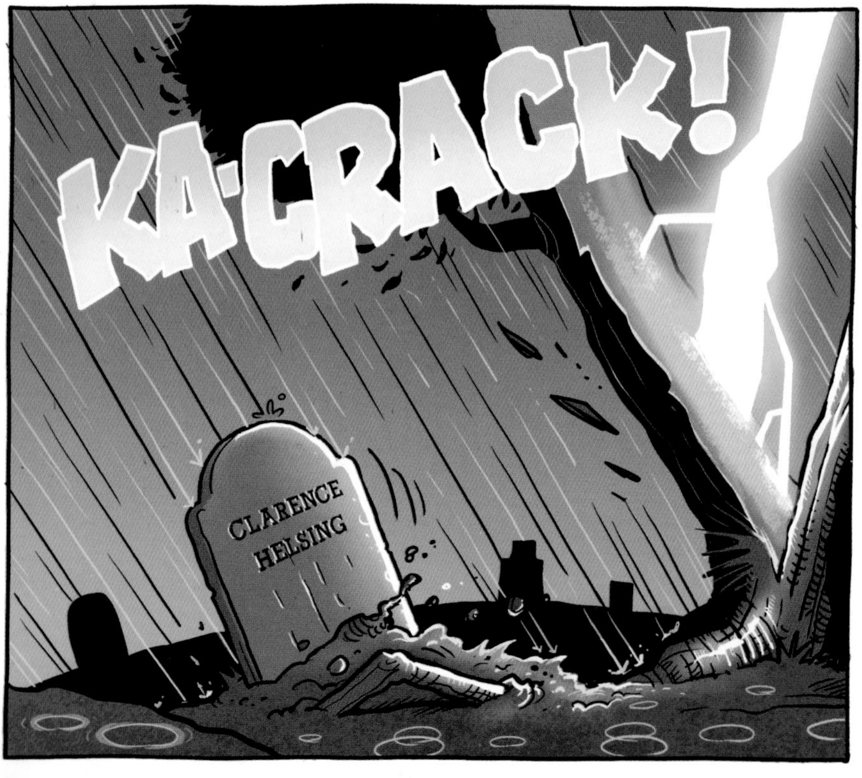
KA-CRACK!
CLARENCE HELSING

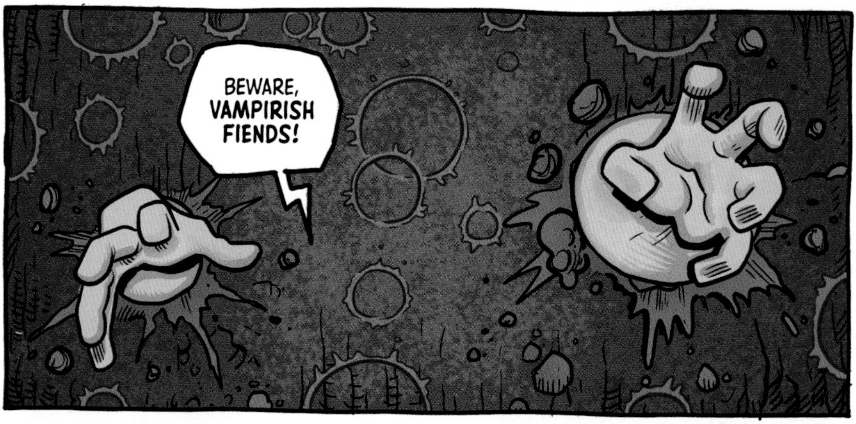
BEWARE, VAMPIRISH FIENDS!

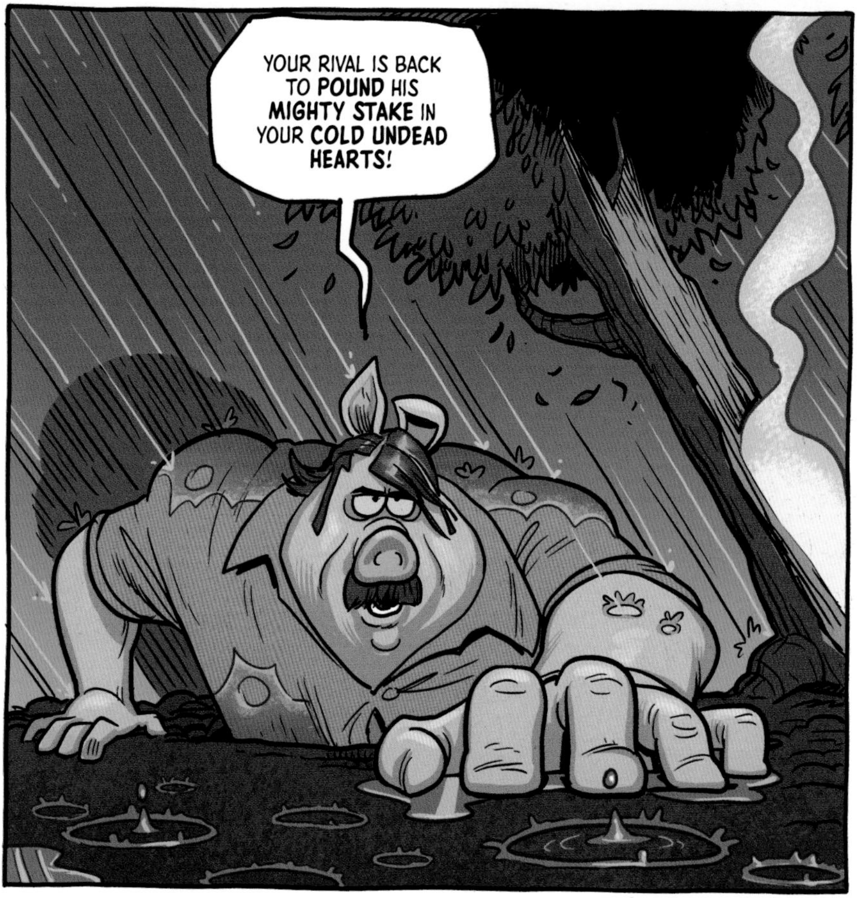
YOUR RIVAL IS BACK TO POUND HIS MIGHTY STAKE IN YOUR COLD UNDEAD HEARTS!

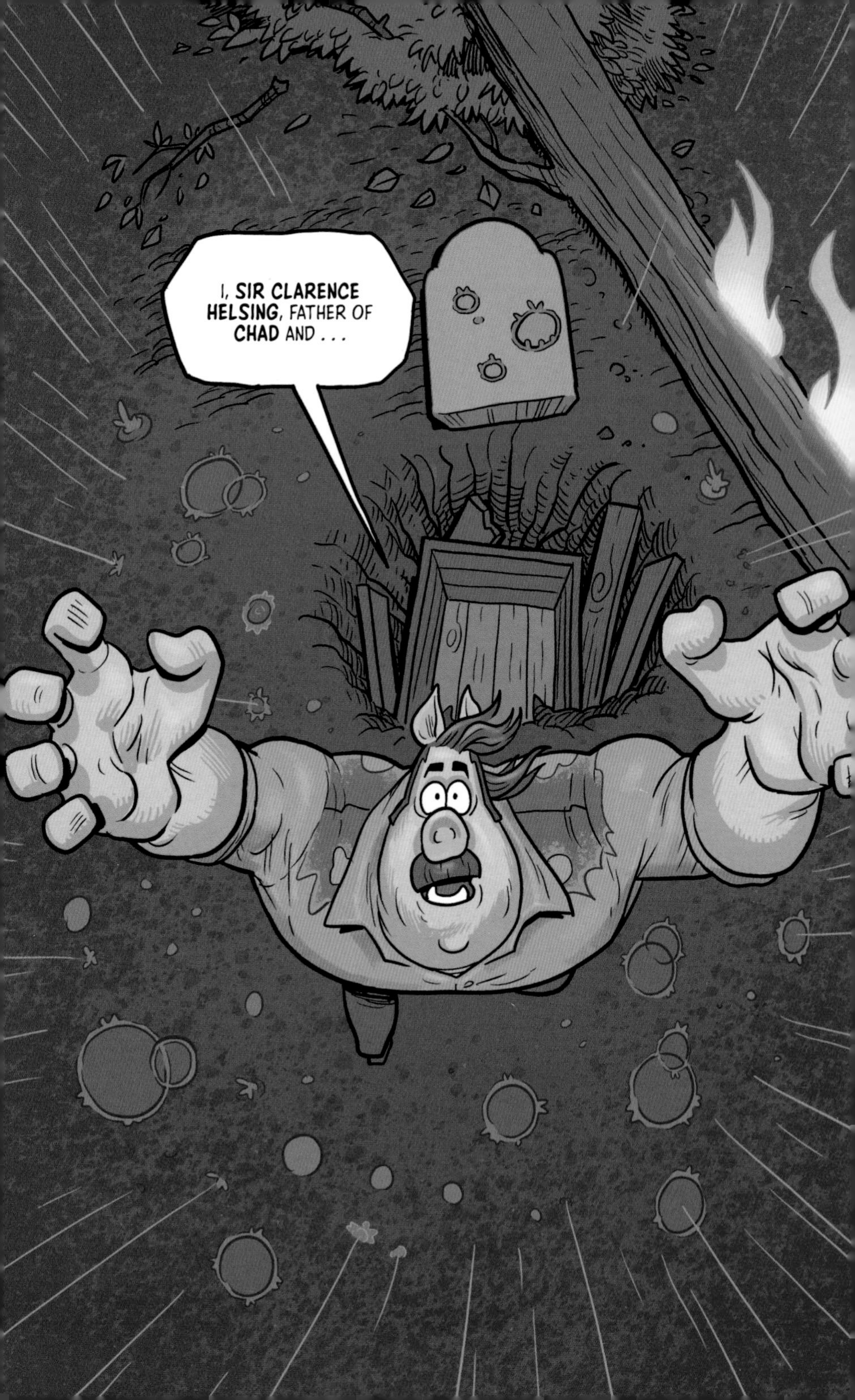
I, SIR CLARENCE HELSING, FATHER OF CHAD AND . . .

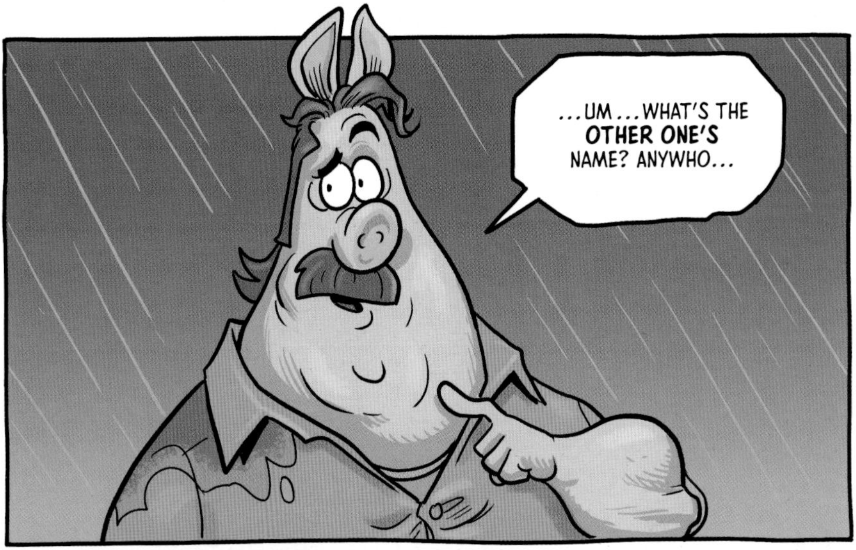
...UM...WHAT'S THE OTHER ONE'S NAME? ANYWHO...

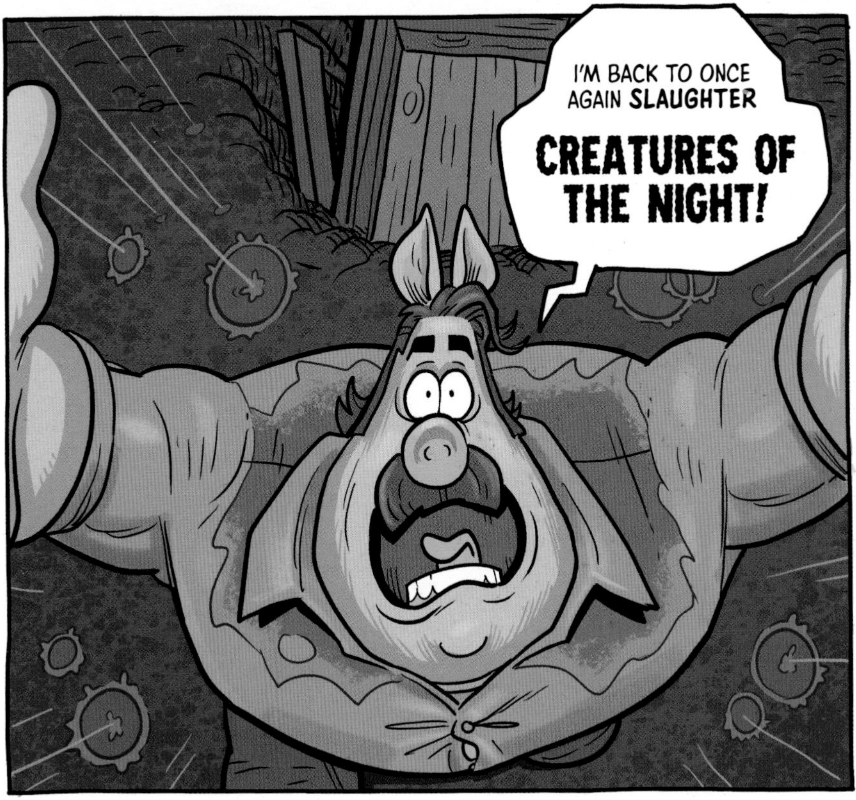
I'M BACK TO ONCE AGAIN SLAUGHTER
CREATURES OF THE NIGHT!

CHAPTER ONE

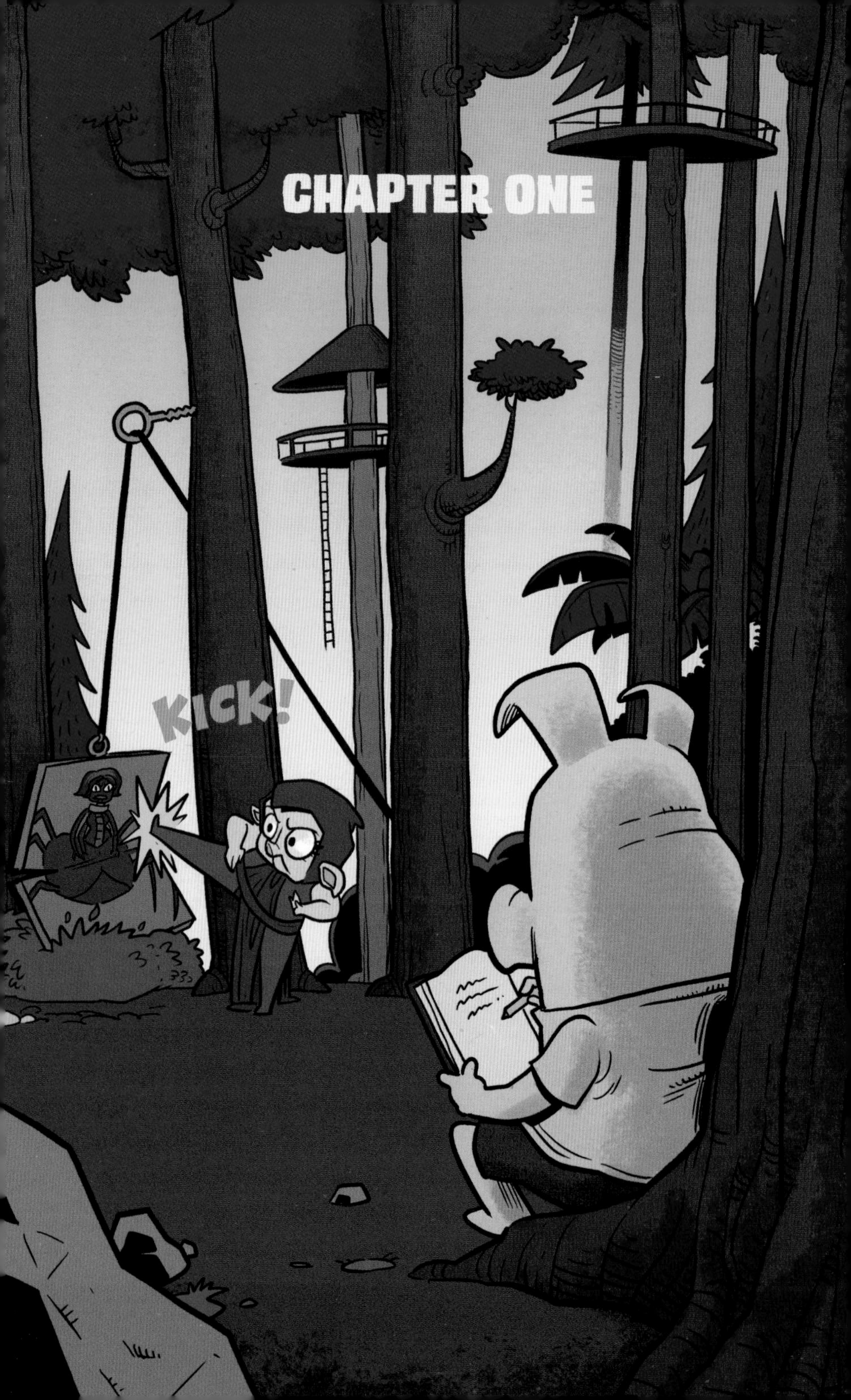
KICK!

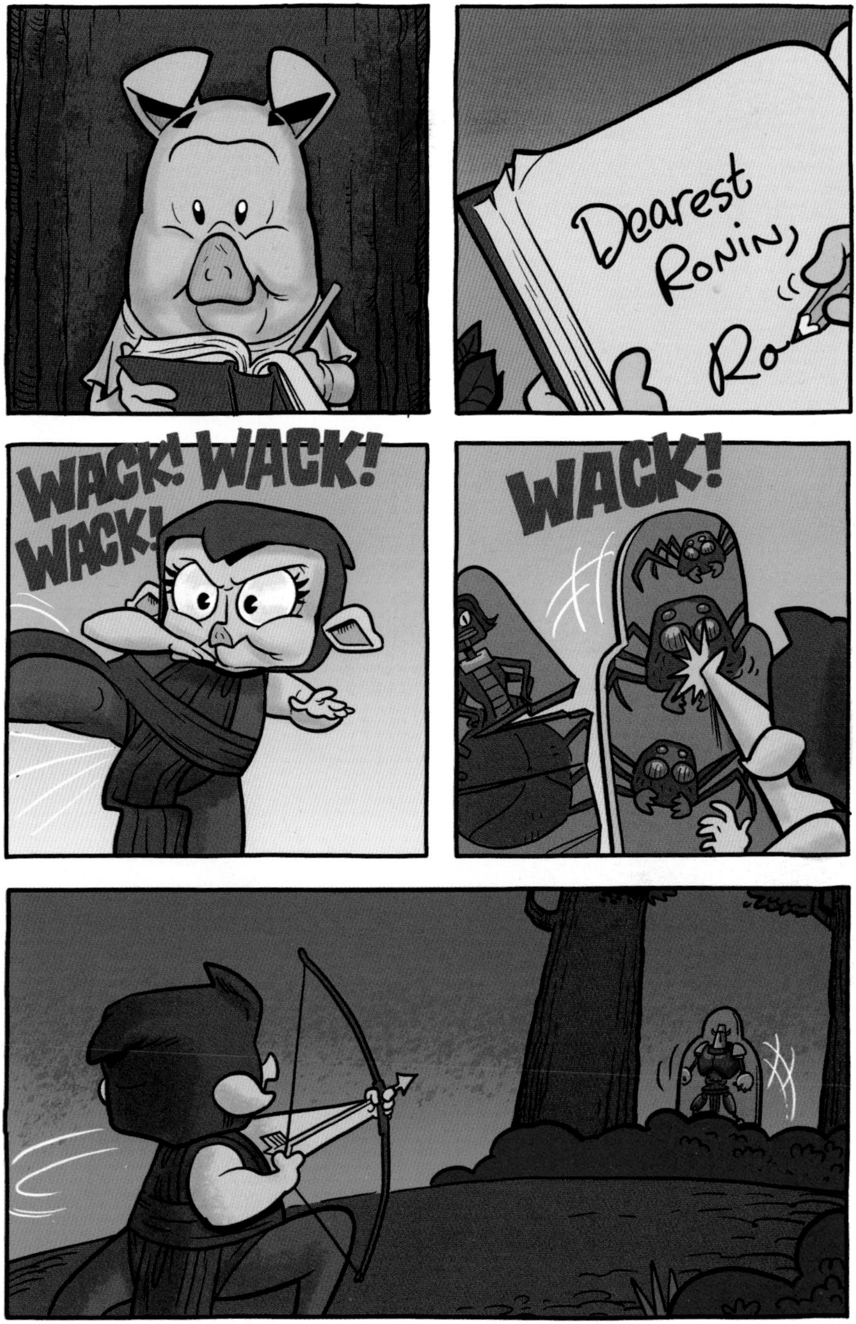
Dearest
Ronin,
Ro
WACK! WACK!
WACK!
WACK!

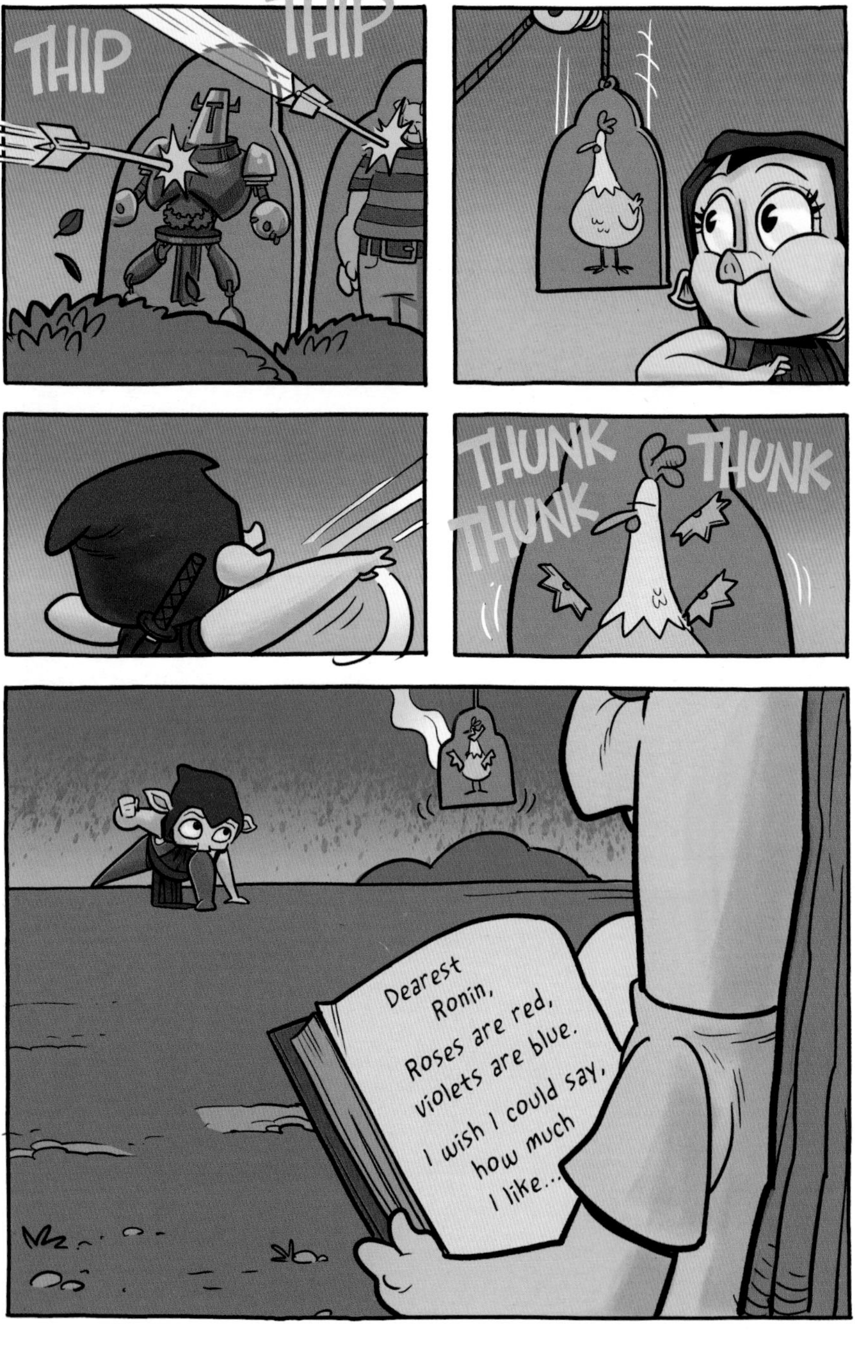
THIP
THIP
THUNK
THUNK
THUNK
Dearest
Ronin,
Roses are red,
violets are blue.
I wish I could say,
how much
I like...

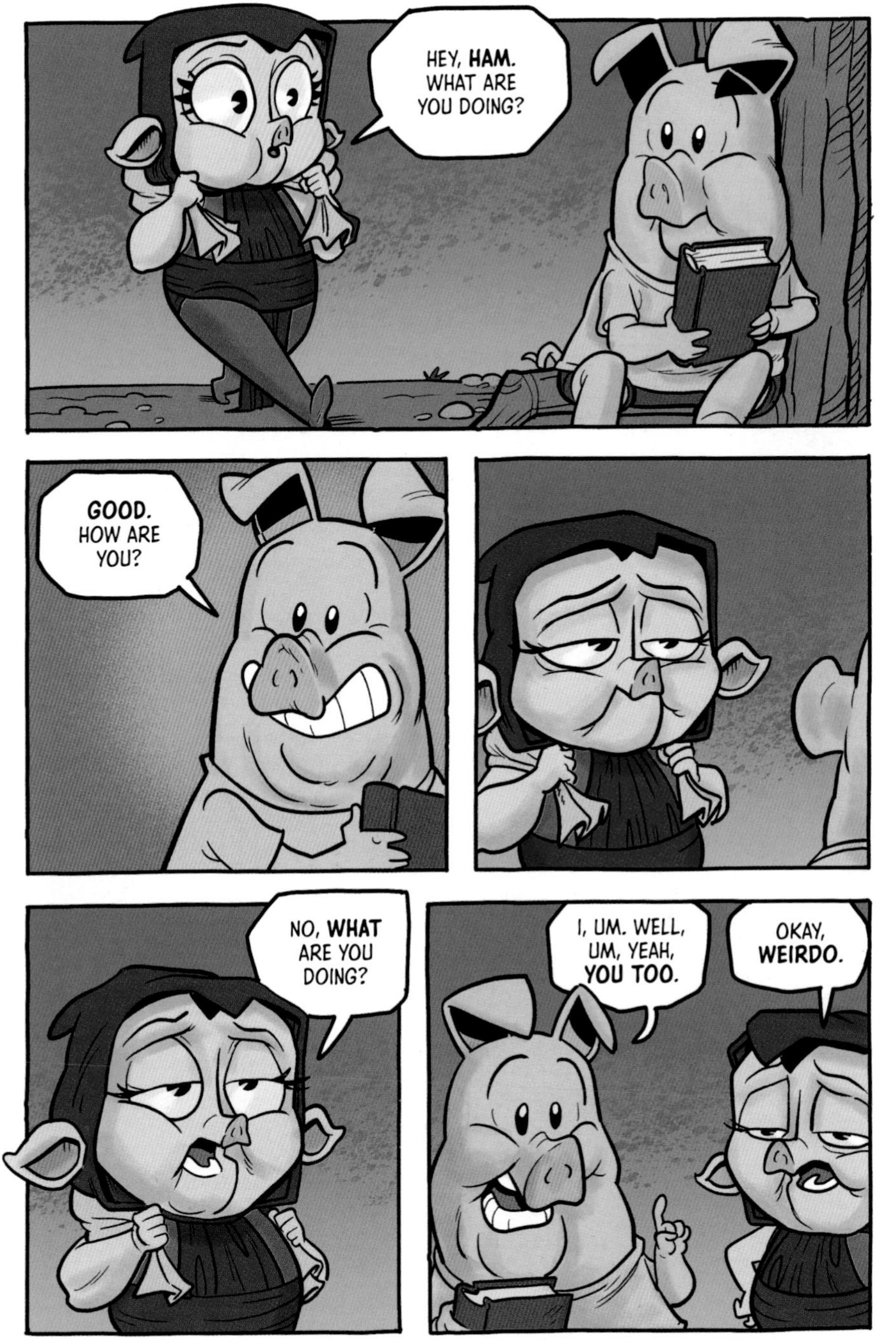
HEY, HAM. WHAT ARE YOU DOING?
GOOD. HOW ARE YOU?
NO, WHAT ARE YOU DOING?
I, UM. WELL, UM, YEAH, YOU TOO.
OKAY, WEIRDO.

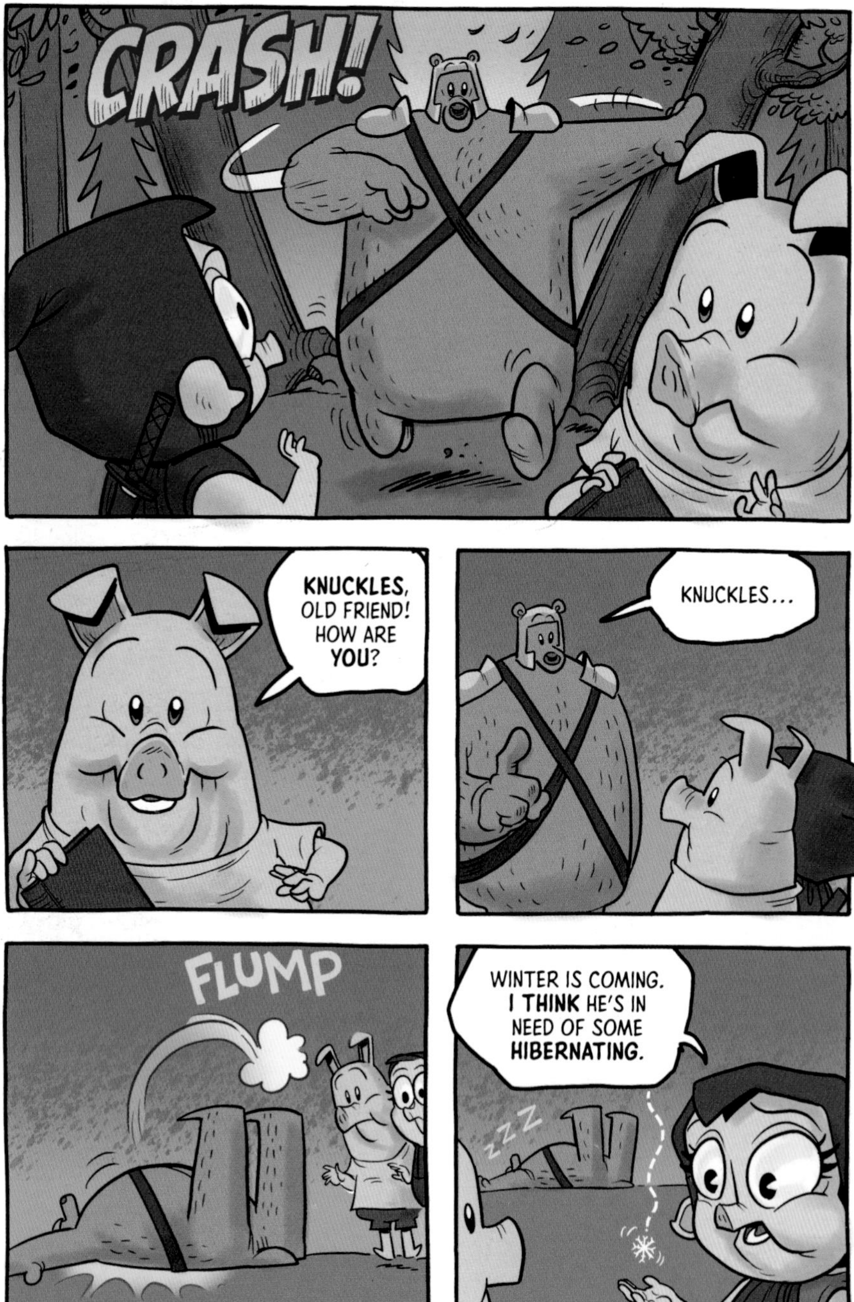
CRASH!
KNUCKLES, OLD FRIEND! HOW ARE YOU?
KNUCKLES...
FLUMP
ZZZ
WINTER IS COMING. I THINK HE'S IN NEED OF SOME HIBERNATING.

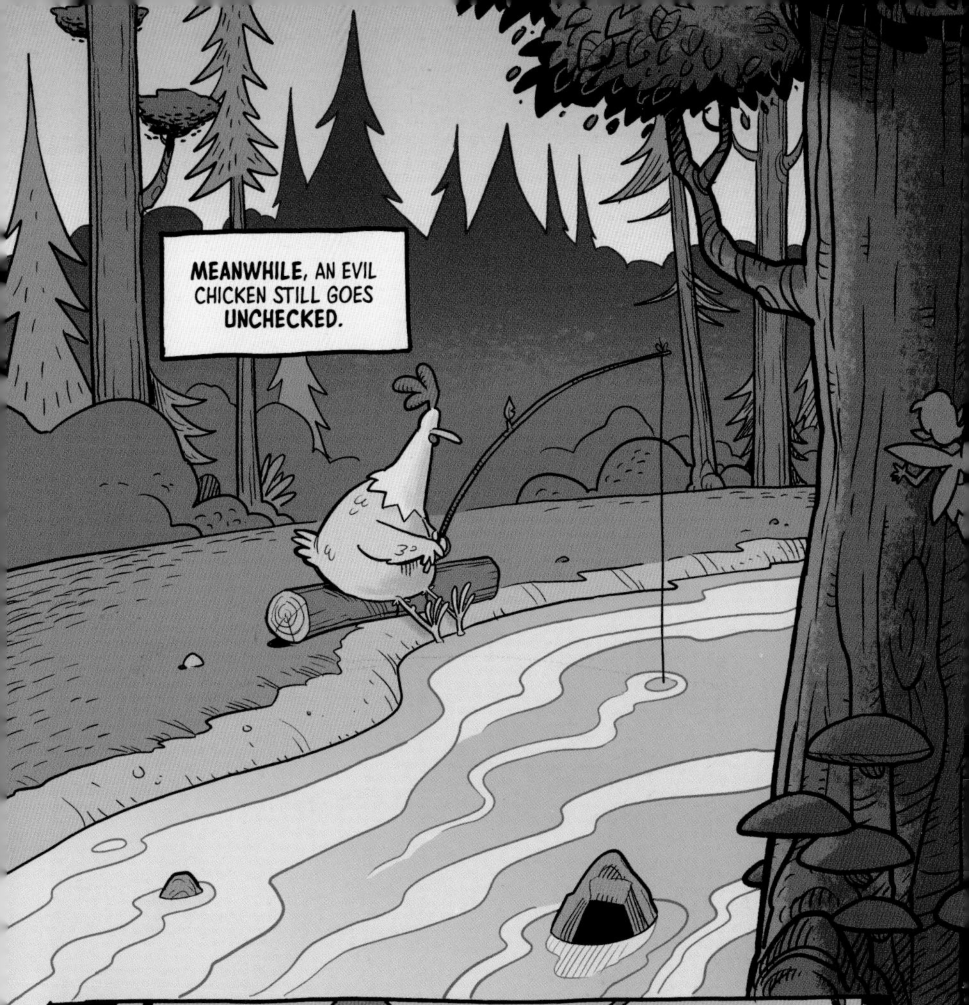
MEANWHILE, AN EVIL CHICKEN STILL GOES UNCHECKED.

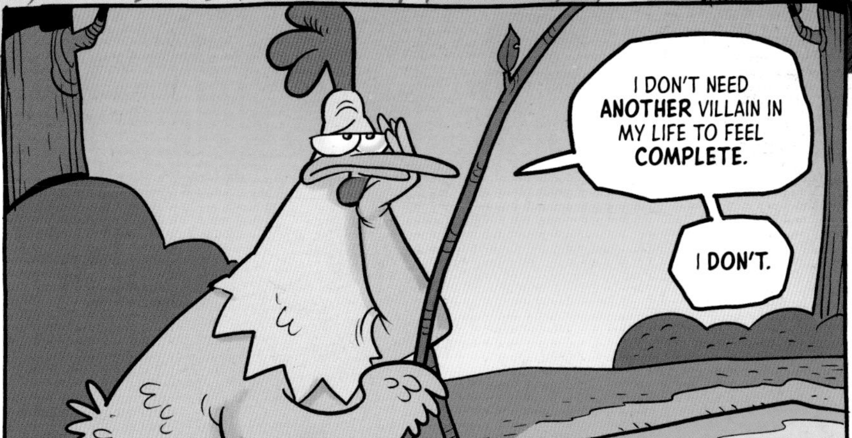
I DON'T NEED ANOTHER VILLAIN IN MY LIFE TO FEEL COMPLETE.
I DON'T.

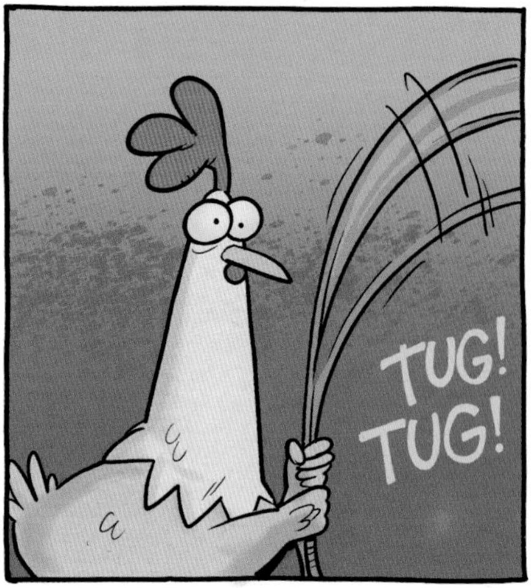
TUG!
TUG!

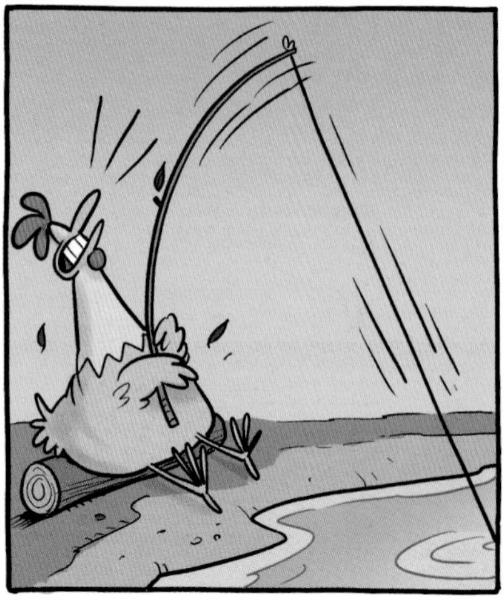

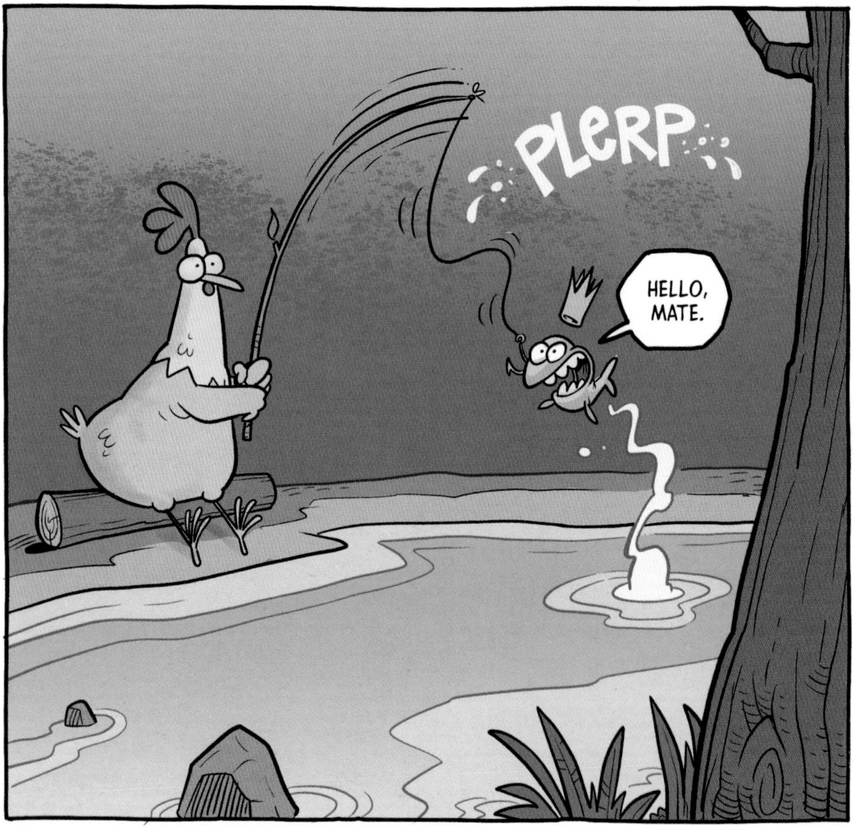
PLERP
HELLO, MATE.

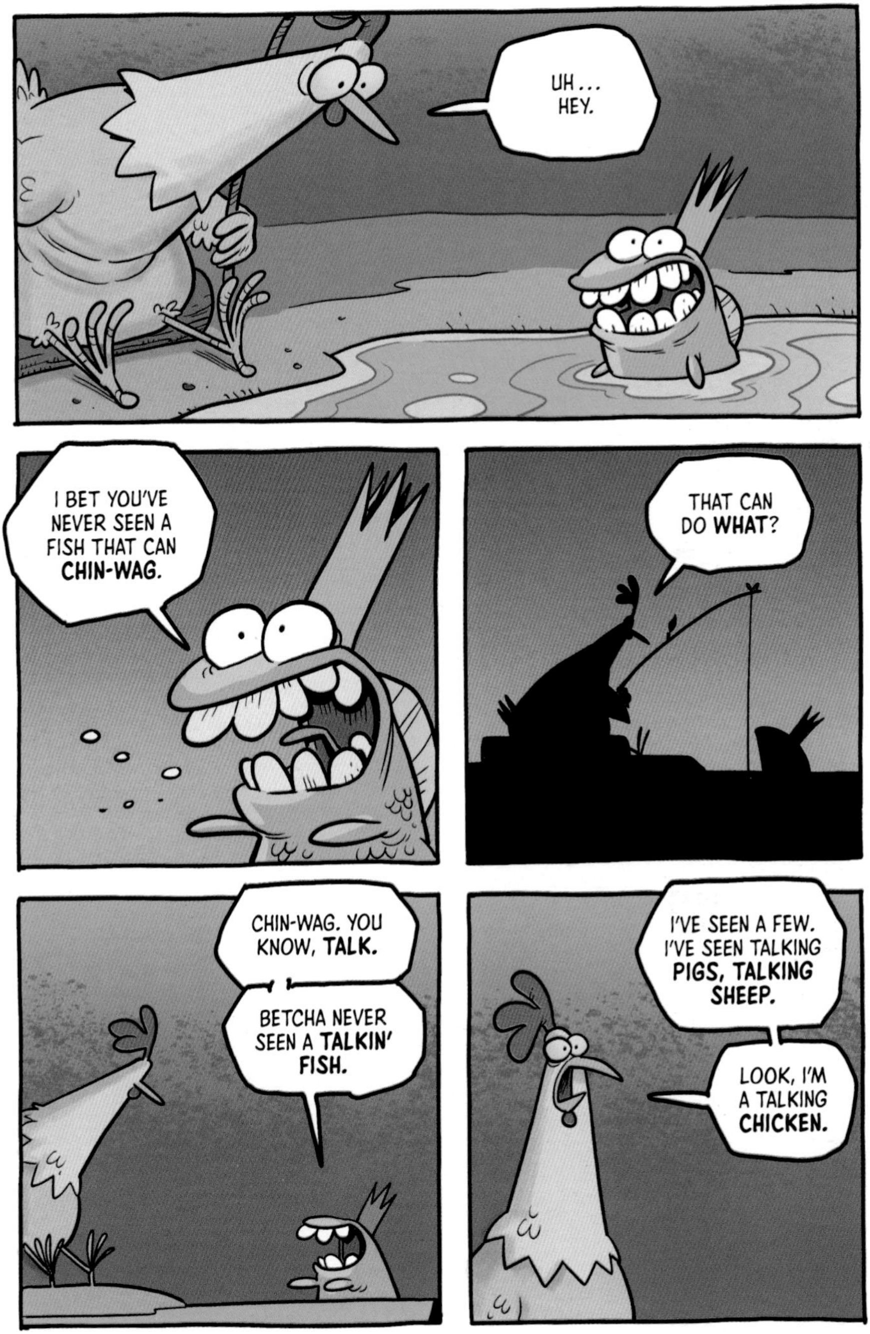
UH... HEY.
I BET YOU'VE NEVER SEEN A FISH THAT CAN **CHIN-WAG.**
THAT CAN DO **WHAT**?
CHIN-WAG. YOU KNOW, **TALK.**
BETCHA NEVER SEEN A **TALKIN' FISH.**
I'VE SEEN A FEW. I'VE SEEN TALKING **PIGS, TALKING SHEEP.**
LOOK, I'M A TALKING **CHICKEN.**

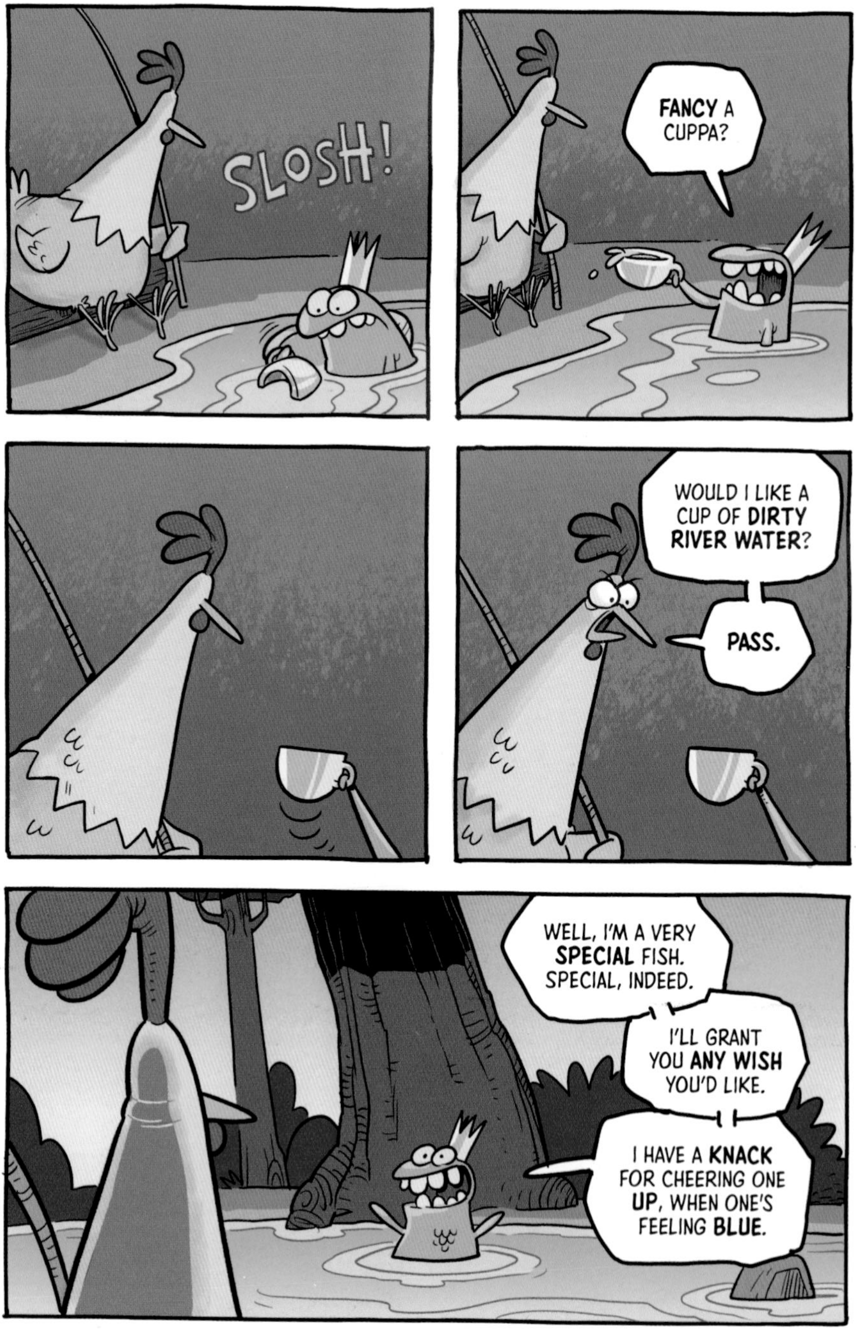
SLOSH!
FANCY A CUPPA?
WOULD I LIKE A CUP OF DIRTY RIVER WATER?
PASS.
WELL, I'M A VERY SPECIAL FISH. SPECIAL, INDEED.
I'LL GRANT YOU ANY WISH YOU'D LIKE.
I HAVE A KNACK FOR CHEERING ONE UP, WHEN ONE'S FEELING BLUE.

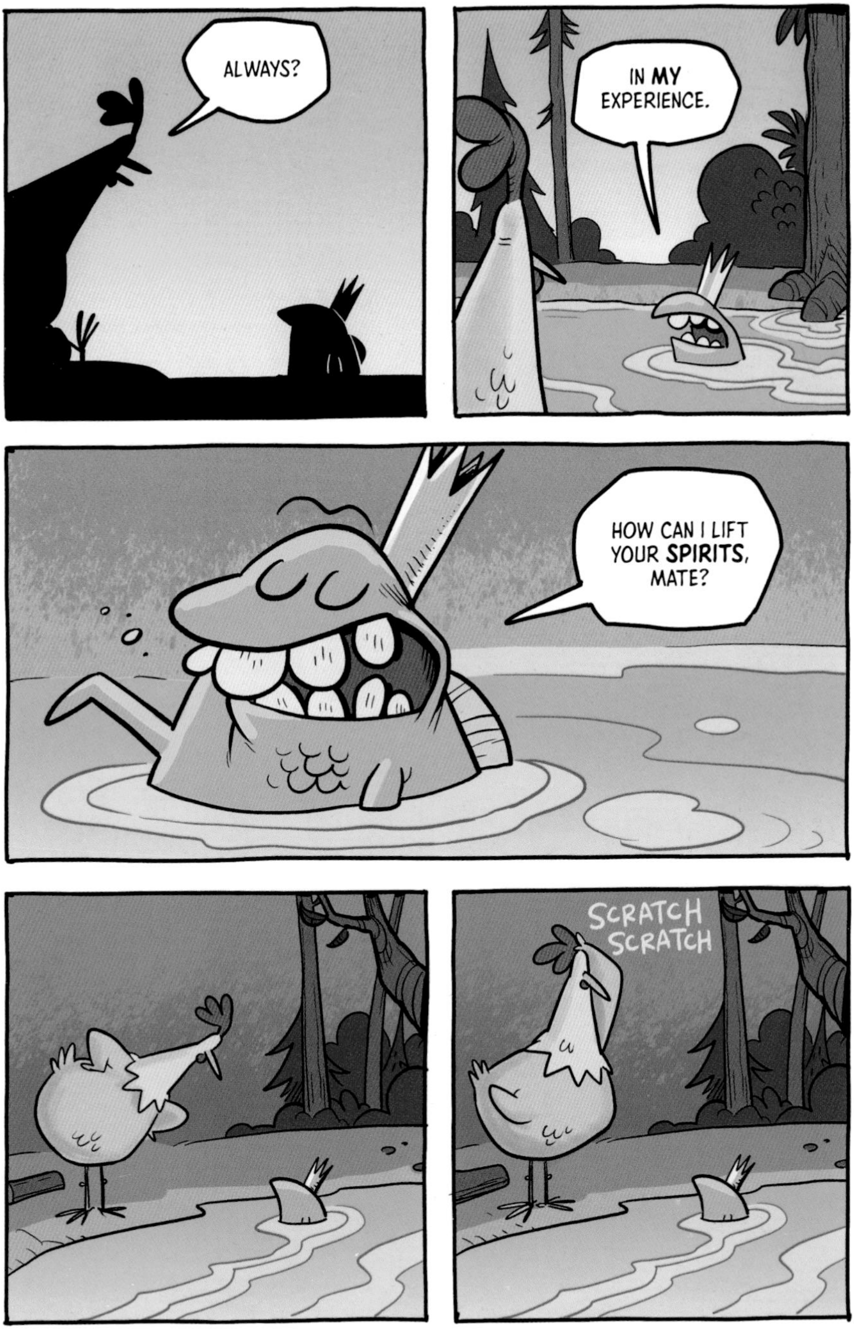
ALWAYS?
IN MY EXPERIENCE.
HOW CAN I LIFT YOUR SPIRITS, MATE?
SCRATCH SCRATCH

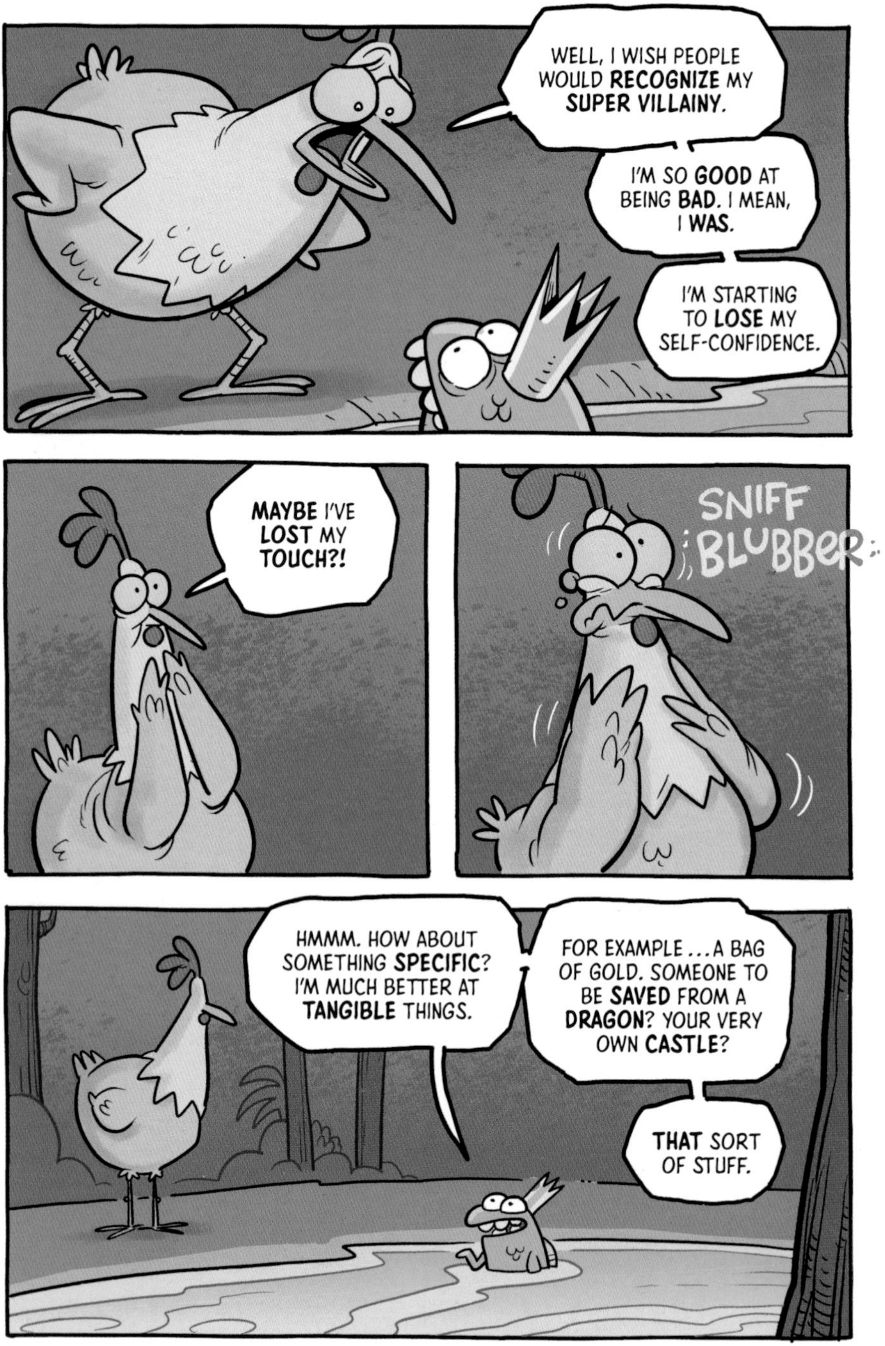
WELL, I WISH PEOPLE WOULD **RECOGNIZE** MY **SUPER VILLAINY.**
I'M SO **GOOD** AT BEING **BAD.** I MEAN, I **WAS.**
I'M STARTING TO **LOSE** MY SELF-CONFIDENCE.
MAYBE I'VE **LOST** MY **TOUCH?!**
SNIFF
BLUBBER
HMMM. HOW ABOUT SOMETHING **SPECIFIC**? I'M MUCH BETTER AT **TANGIBLE** THINGS.
FOR EXAMPLE . . . A BAG OF GOLD. SOMEONE TO BE **SAVED** FROM A **DRAGON**? YOUR VERY OWN **CASTLE**?
THAT SORT OF STUFF.

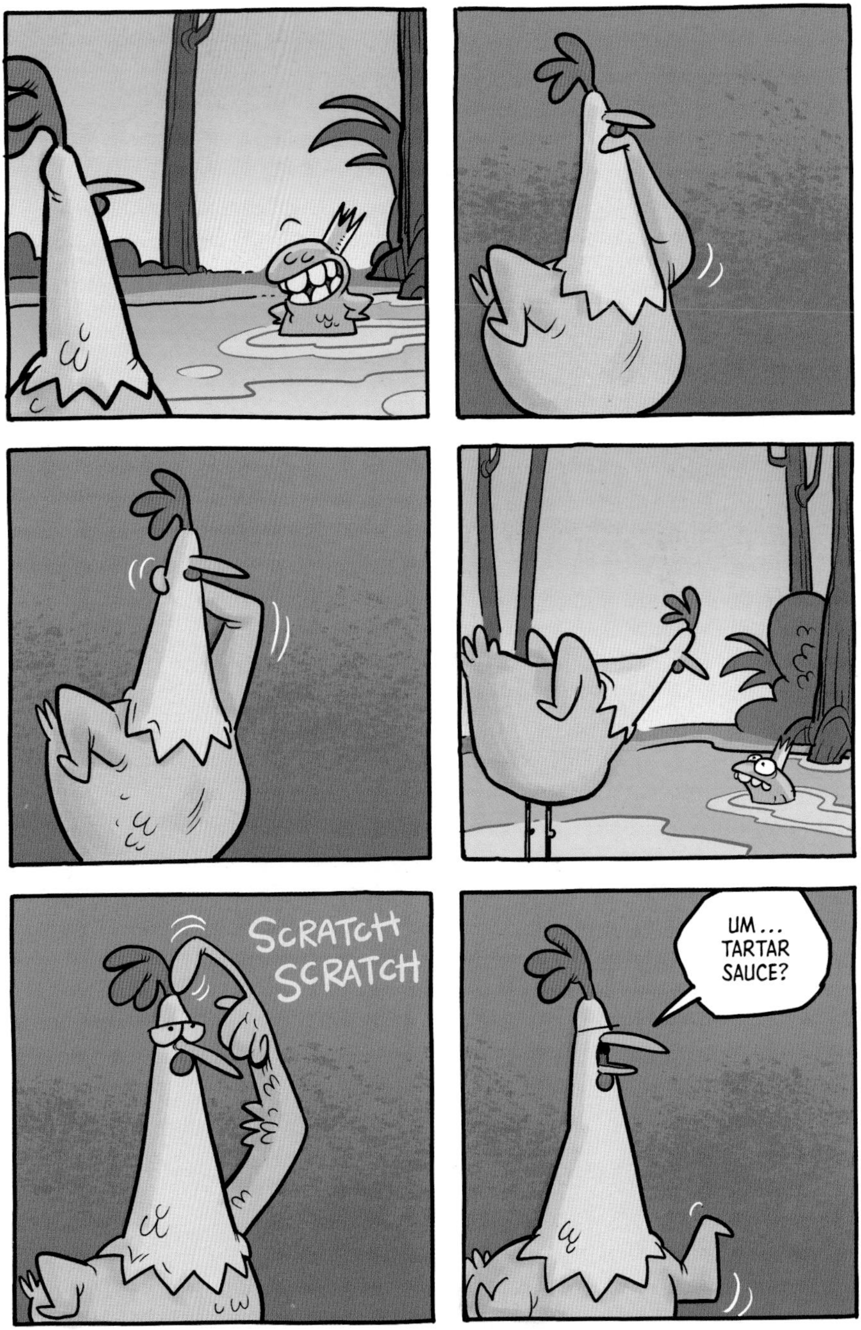
SCRATCH
SCRATCH
UM...
TARTAR
SAUCE?

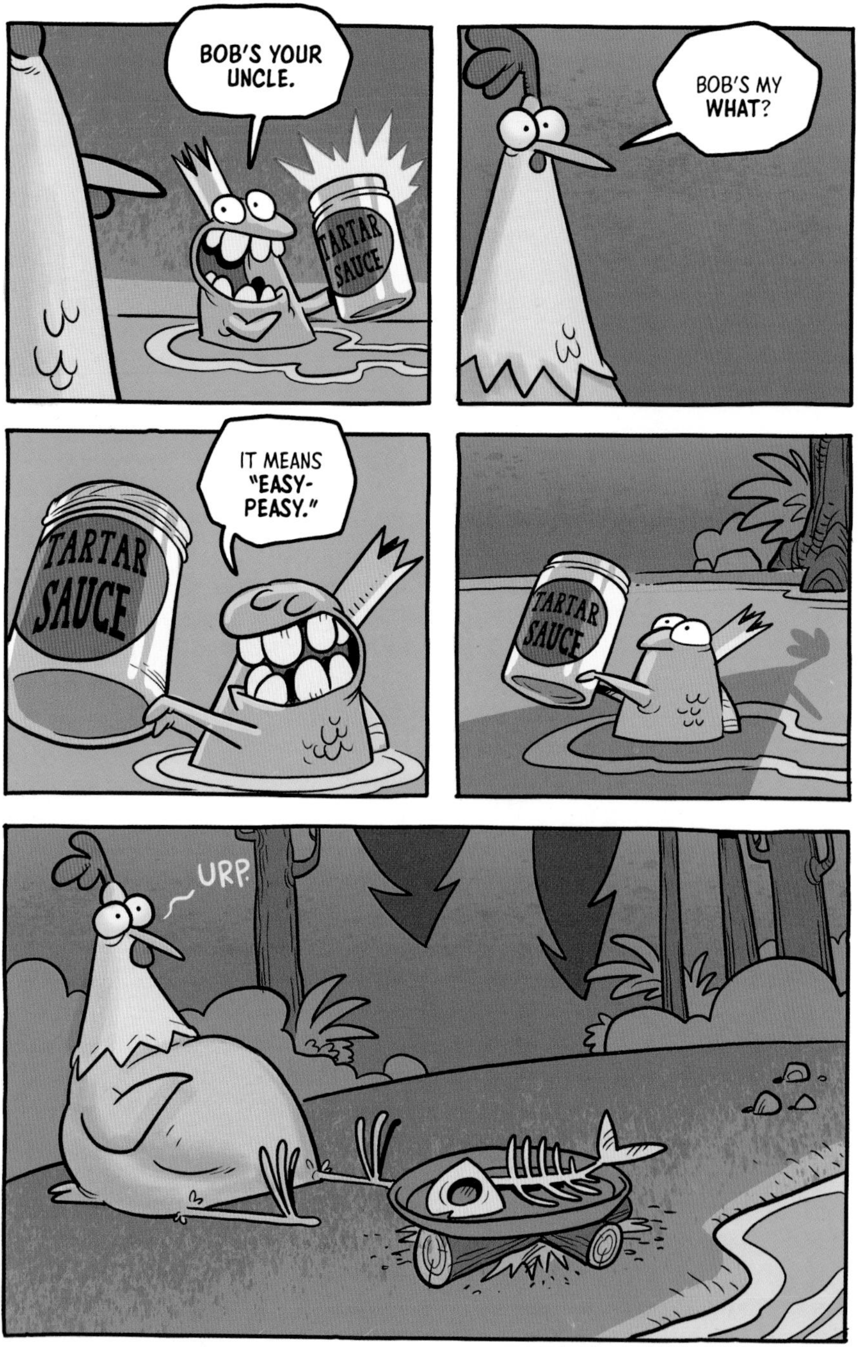
BOB'S YOUR UNCLE.
TARTAR SAUCE
BOB'S MY WHAT?
IT MEANS "EASY-PEASY."
TARTAR SAUCE
TARTAR SAUCE
URP.

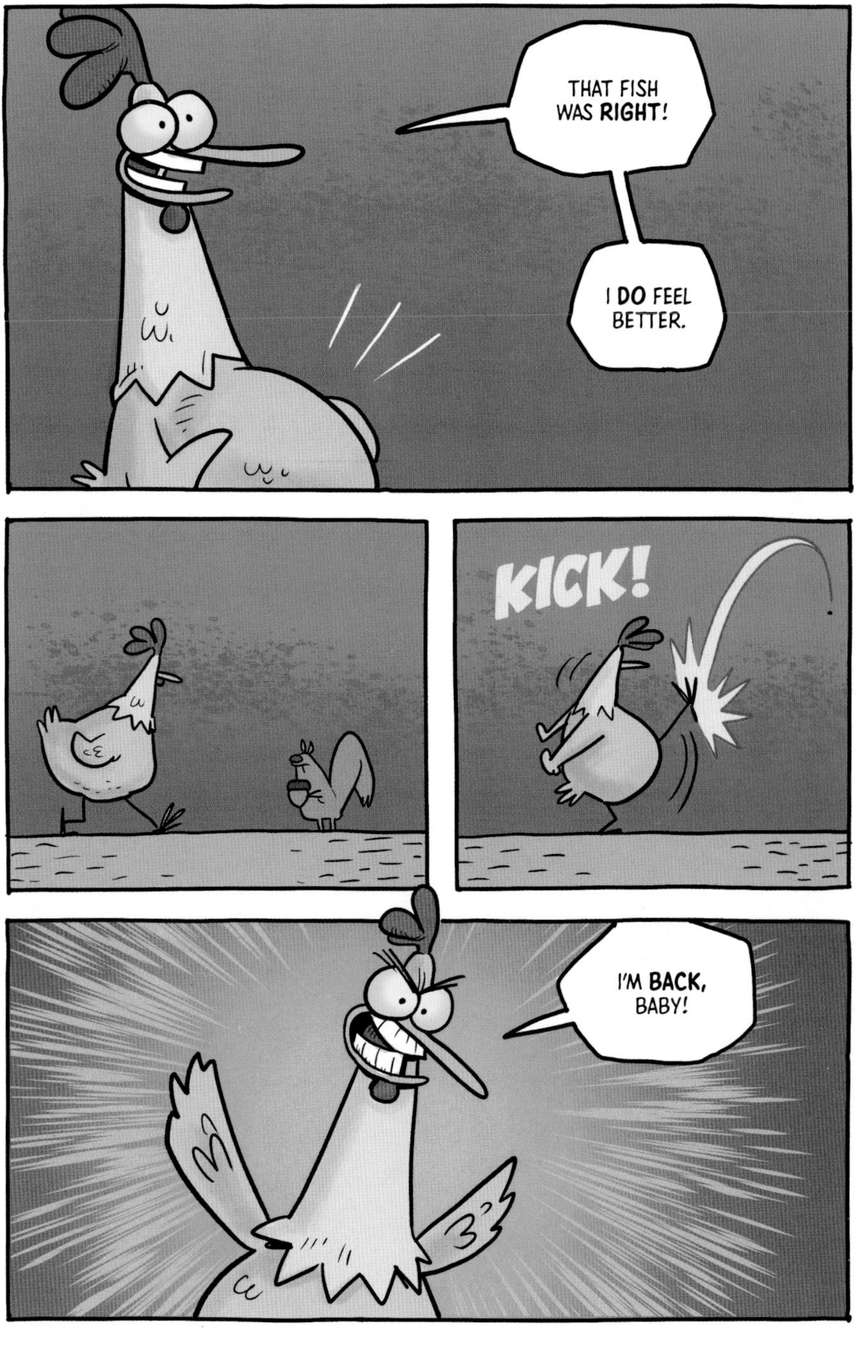
THAT FISH WAS **RIGHT**!
I **DO** FEEL BETTER.
KICK!
I'M **BACK**, BABY!

CHAPTER TWO

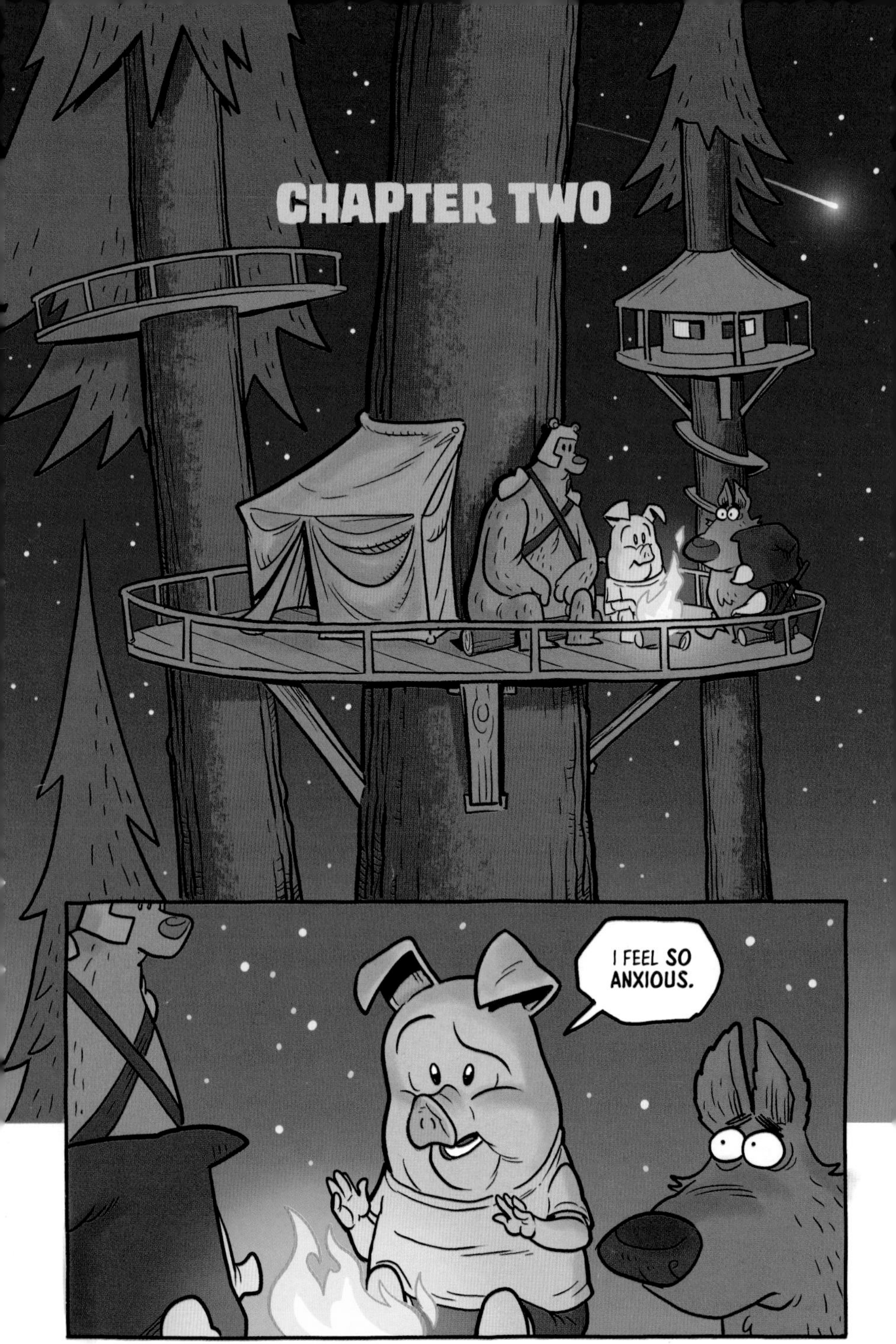
I FEEL SO ANXIOUS.

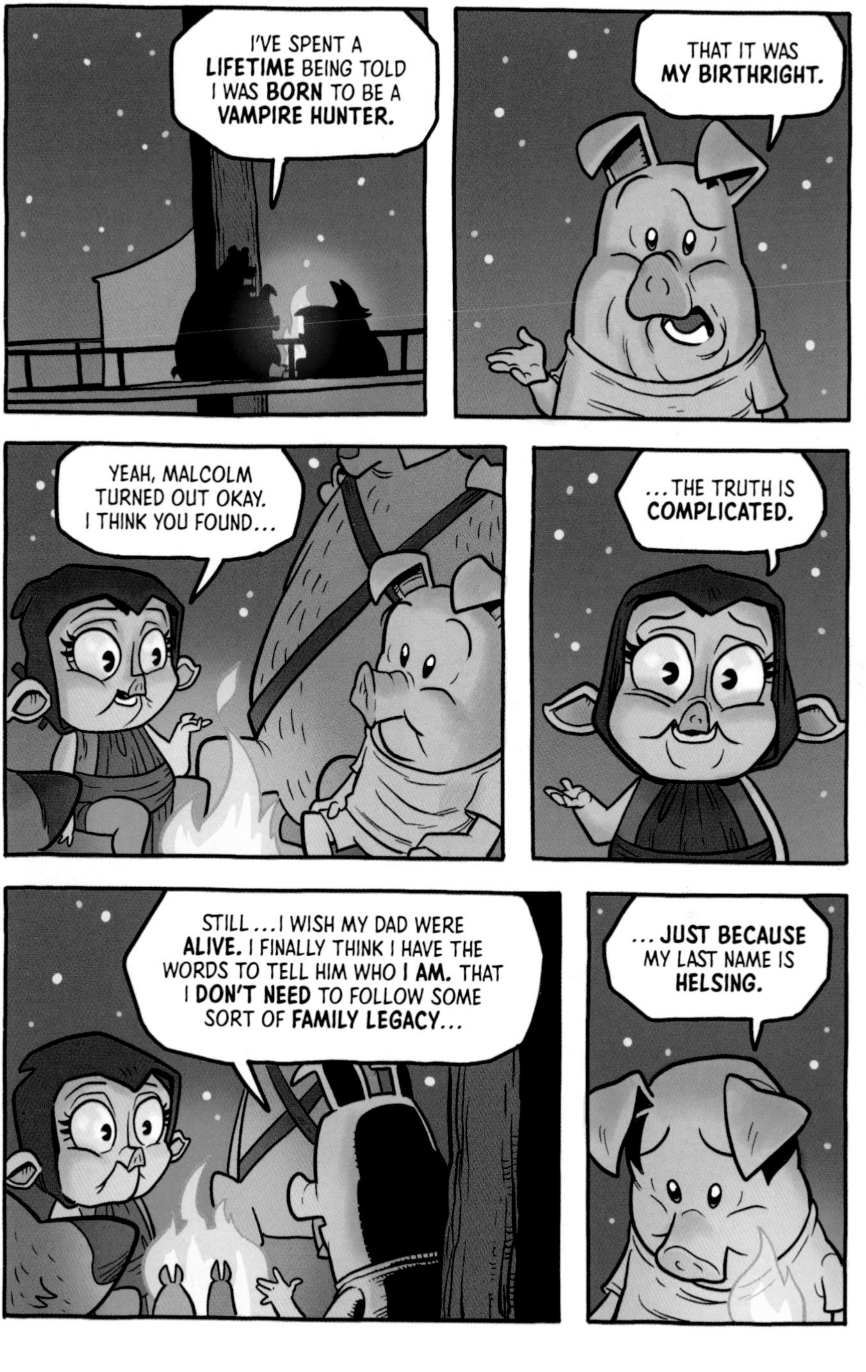
I'VE SPENT A LIFETIME BEING TOLD I WAS BORN TO BE A VAMPIRE HUNTER.
THAT IT WAS MY BIRTHRIGHT.
YEAH, MALCOLM TURNED OUT OKAY. I THINK YOU FOUND...
...THE TRUTH IS COMPLICATED.
STILL...I WISH MY DAD WERE ALIVE. I FINALLY THINK I HAVE THE WORDS TO TELL HIM WHO I AM. THAT I DON'T NEED TO FOLLOW SOME SORT OF FAMILY LEGACY...
...JUST BECAUSE MY LAST NAME IS HELSING.

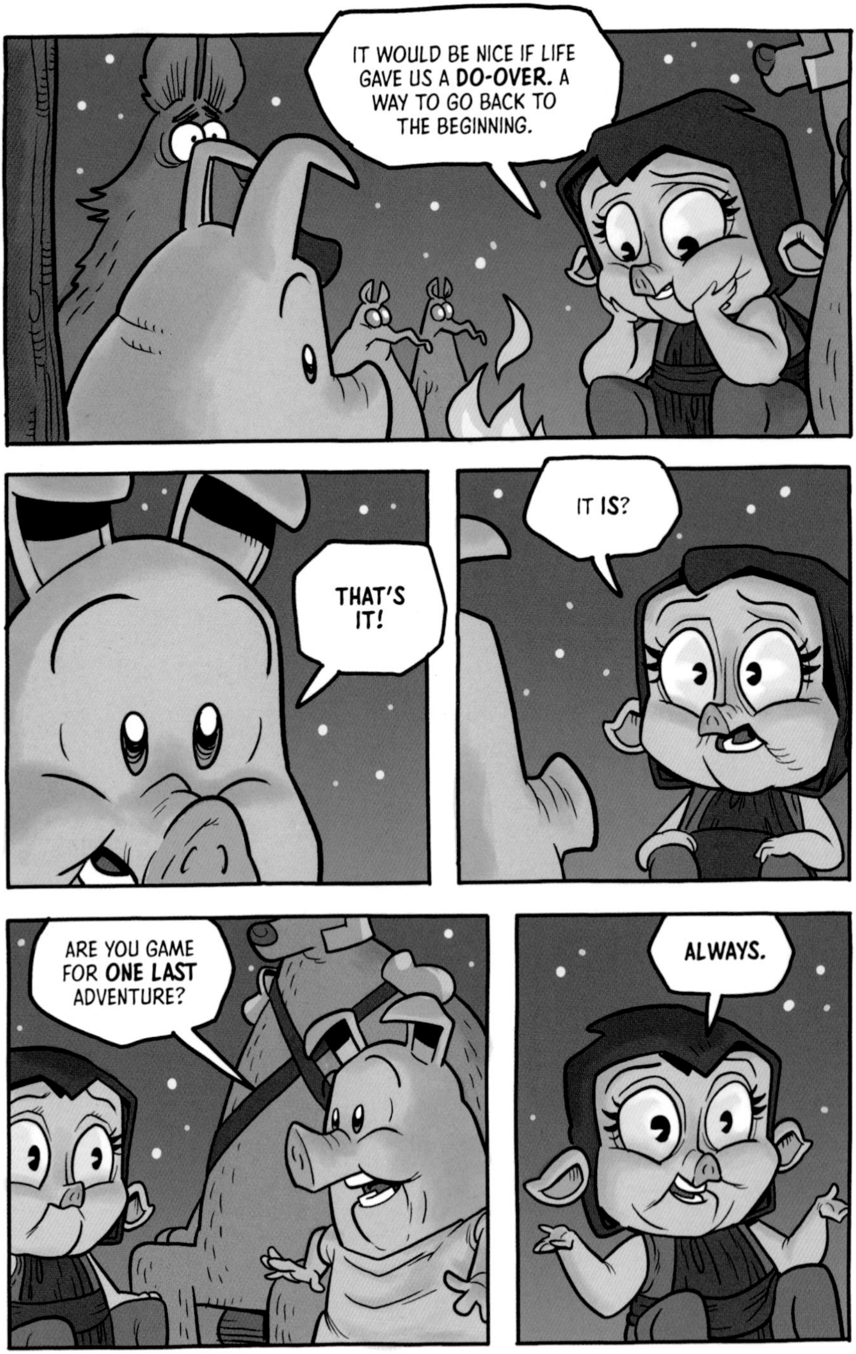
IT WOULD BE NICE IF LIFE GAVE US A **DO-OVER.** A WAY TO GO BACK TO THE BEGINNING.
THAT'S IT!
IT **IS?**
ARE YOU GAME FOR **ONE LAST** ADVENTURE?
ALWAYS.

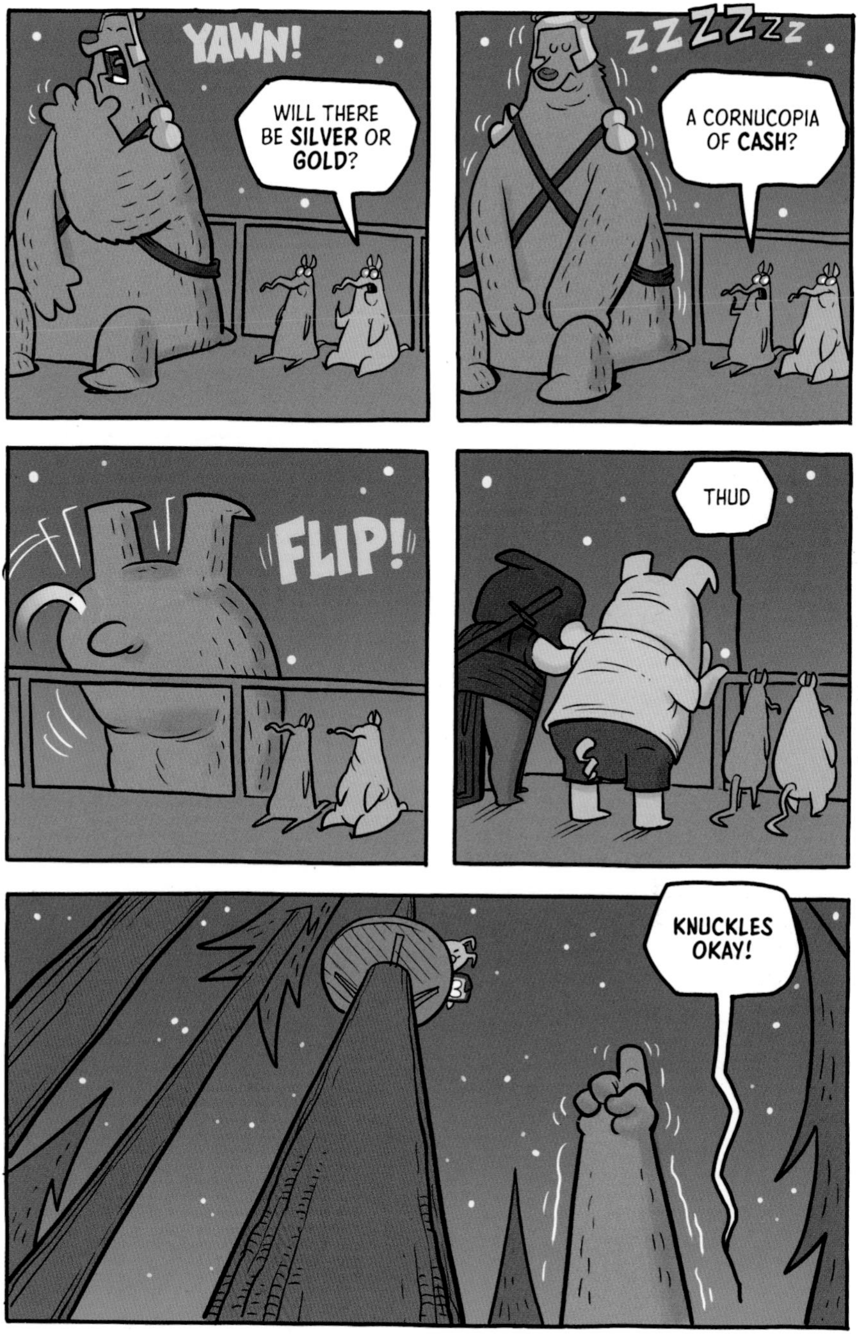
YAWN!
WILL THERE BE SILVER OR GOLD?
zZZZZzz
A CORNUCOPIA OF CASH?
FLIP!
THUD
KNUCKLES OKAY!

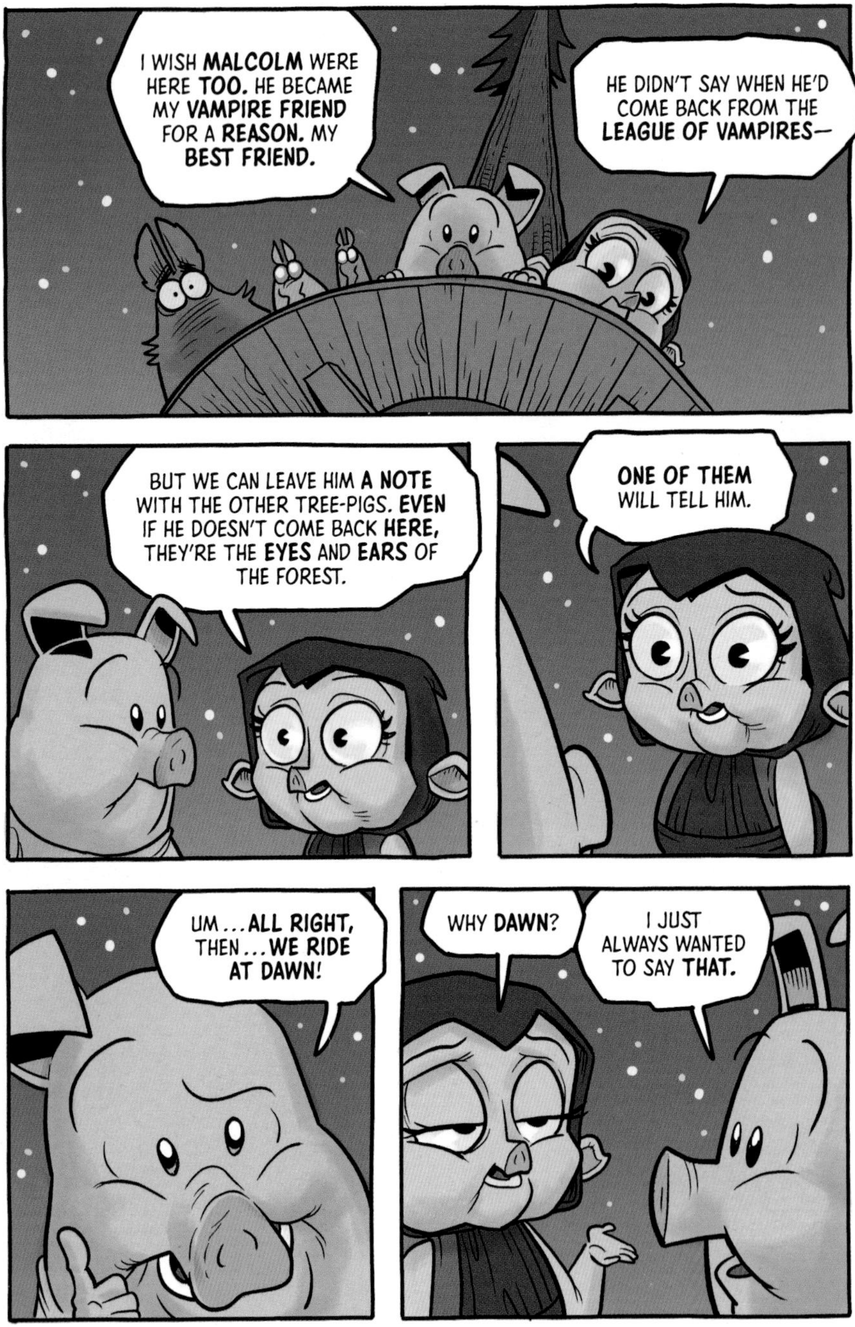
I WISH MALCOLM WERE HERE TOO. HE BECAME MY VAMPIRE FRIEND FOR A REASON. MY BEST FRIEND.
HE DIDN'T SAY WHEN HE'D COME BACK FROM THE LEAGUE OF VAMPIRES—
BUT WE CAN LEAVE HIM A NOTE WITH THE OTHER TREE-PIGS. EVEN IF HE DOESN'T COME BACK HERE, THEY'RE THE EYES AND EARS OF THE FOREST.
ONE OF THEM WILL TELL HIM.
UM...ALL RIGHT, THEN...WE RIDE AT DAWN!
WHY DAWN?
I JUST ALWAYS WANTED TO SAY THAT.

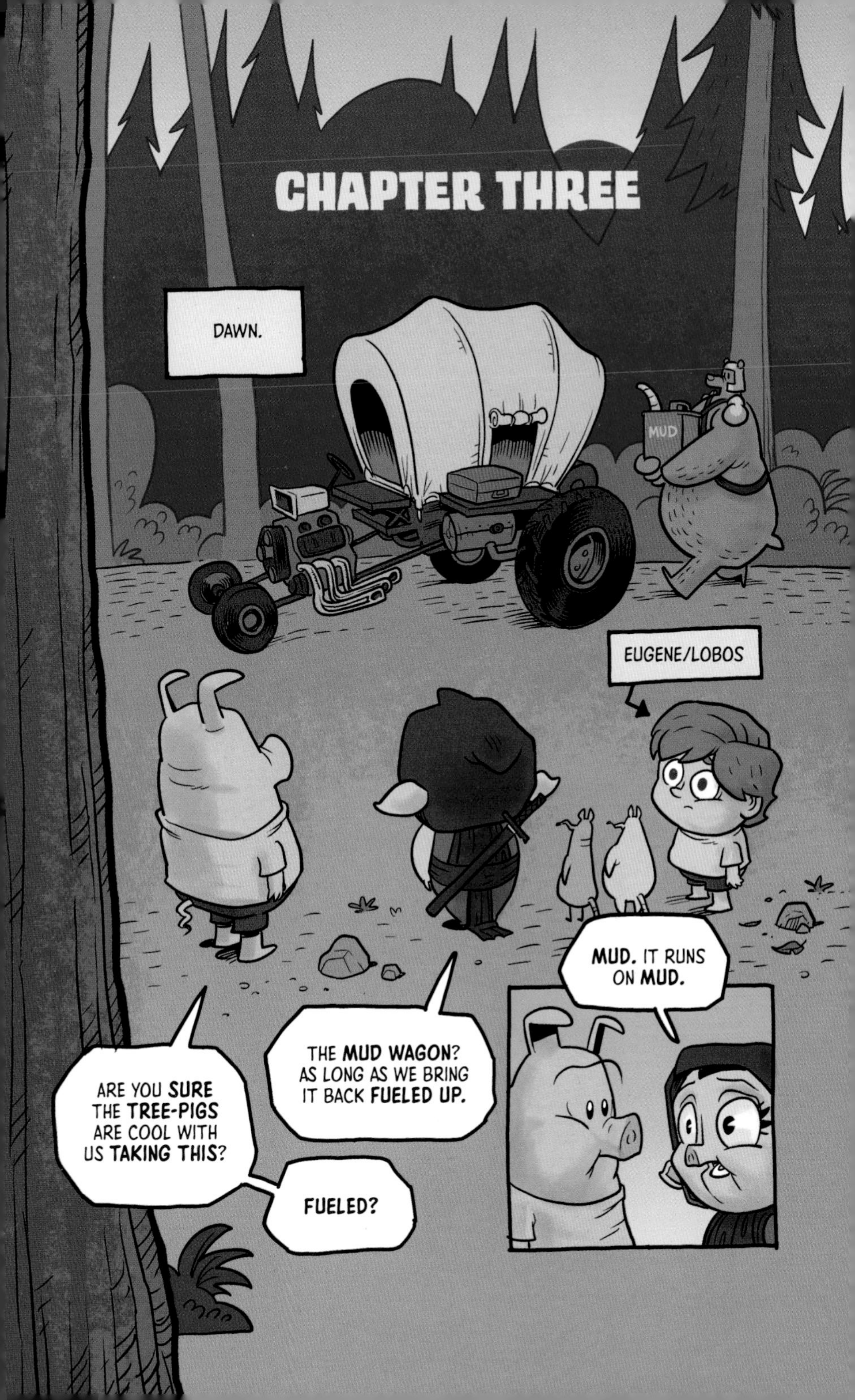
CHAPTER THREE
DAWN.
MUD
EUGENE/LOBOS
ARE YOU SURE THE TREE-PIGS ARE COOL WITH US TAKING THIS?
THE MUD WAGON? AS LONG AS WE BRING IT BACK FUELED UP.
FUELED?
MUD. IT RUNS ON MUD.

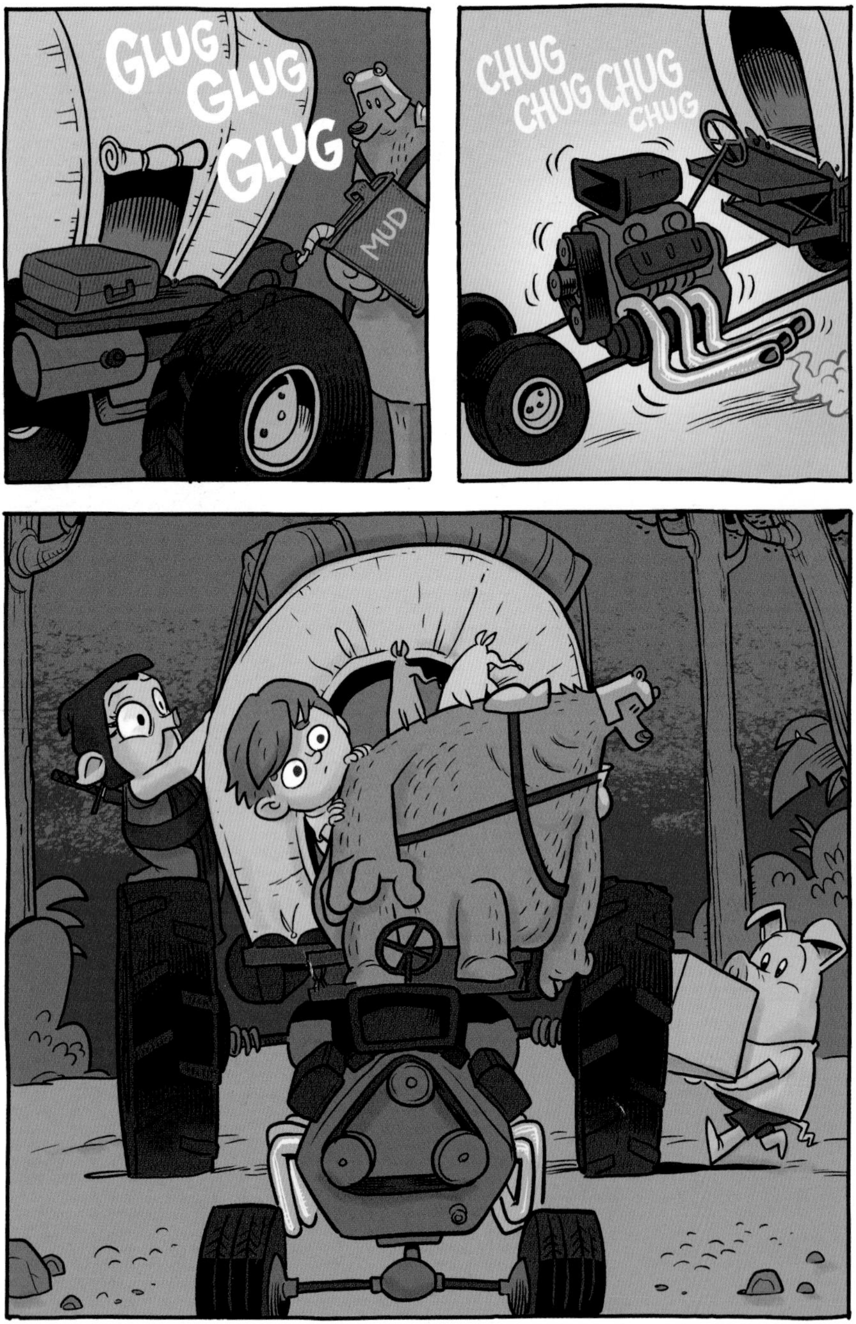
GLUG
GLUG
GLUG
MUD
CHUG
CHUG CHUG
CHUG

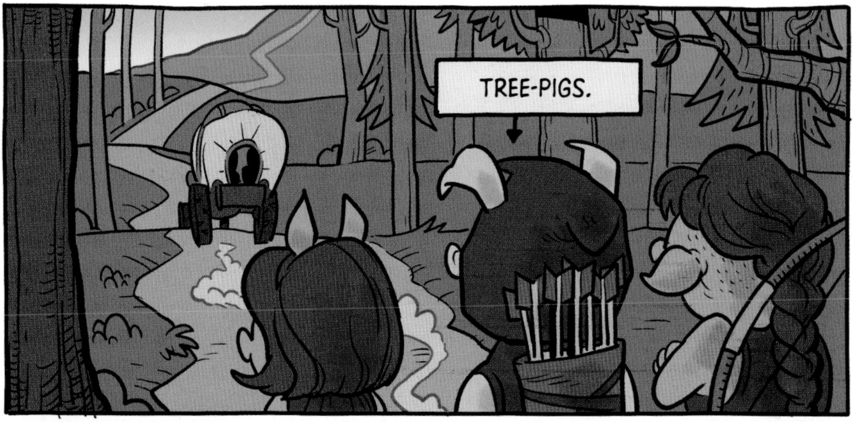
TREE-PIGS.

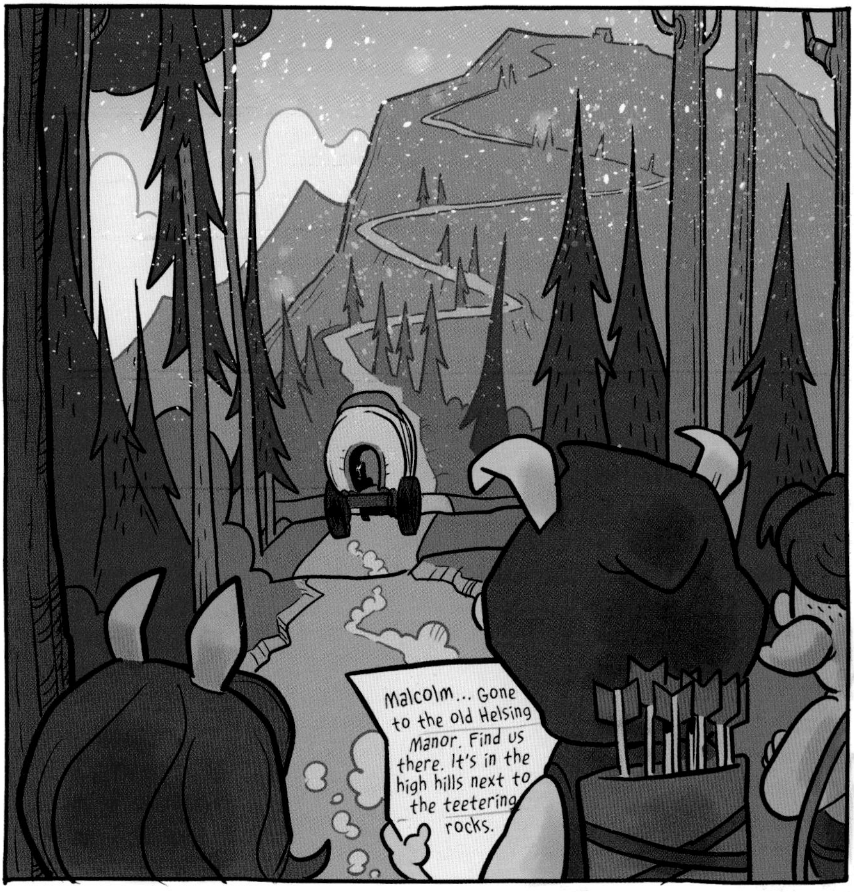
Malcolm... Gone to the old Helsing Manor. Find us there. It's in the high hills next to the teetering rocks.

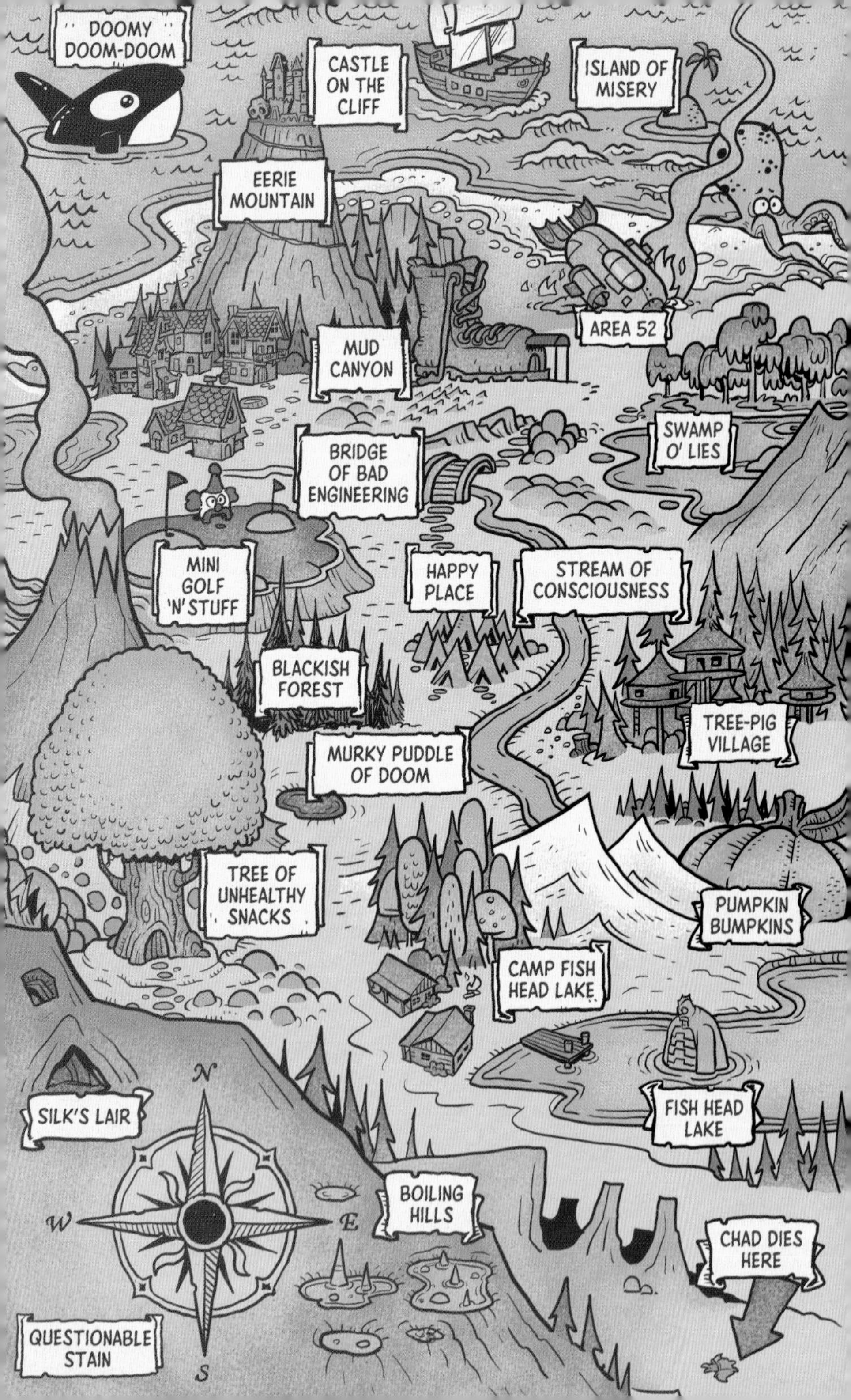
DOOMY DOOM-DOOM
CASTLE ON THE CLIFF
ISLAND OF MISERY
EERIE MOUNTAIN
AREA 52
MUD CANYON
SWAMP O' LIES
BRIDGE OF BAD ENGINEERING
MINI GOLF 'N' STUFF
HAPPY PLACE
STREAM OF CONSCIOUSNESS
BLACKISH FOREST
TREE-PIG VILLAGE
MURKY PUDDLE OF DOOM
TREE OF UNHEALTHY SNACKS
PUMPKIN BUMPKINS
CAMP FISH HEAD LAKE
N
SILK'S LAIR
FISH HEAD LAKE
W
E
BOILING HILLS
CHAD DIES HERE
QUESTIONABLE STAIN
S

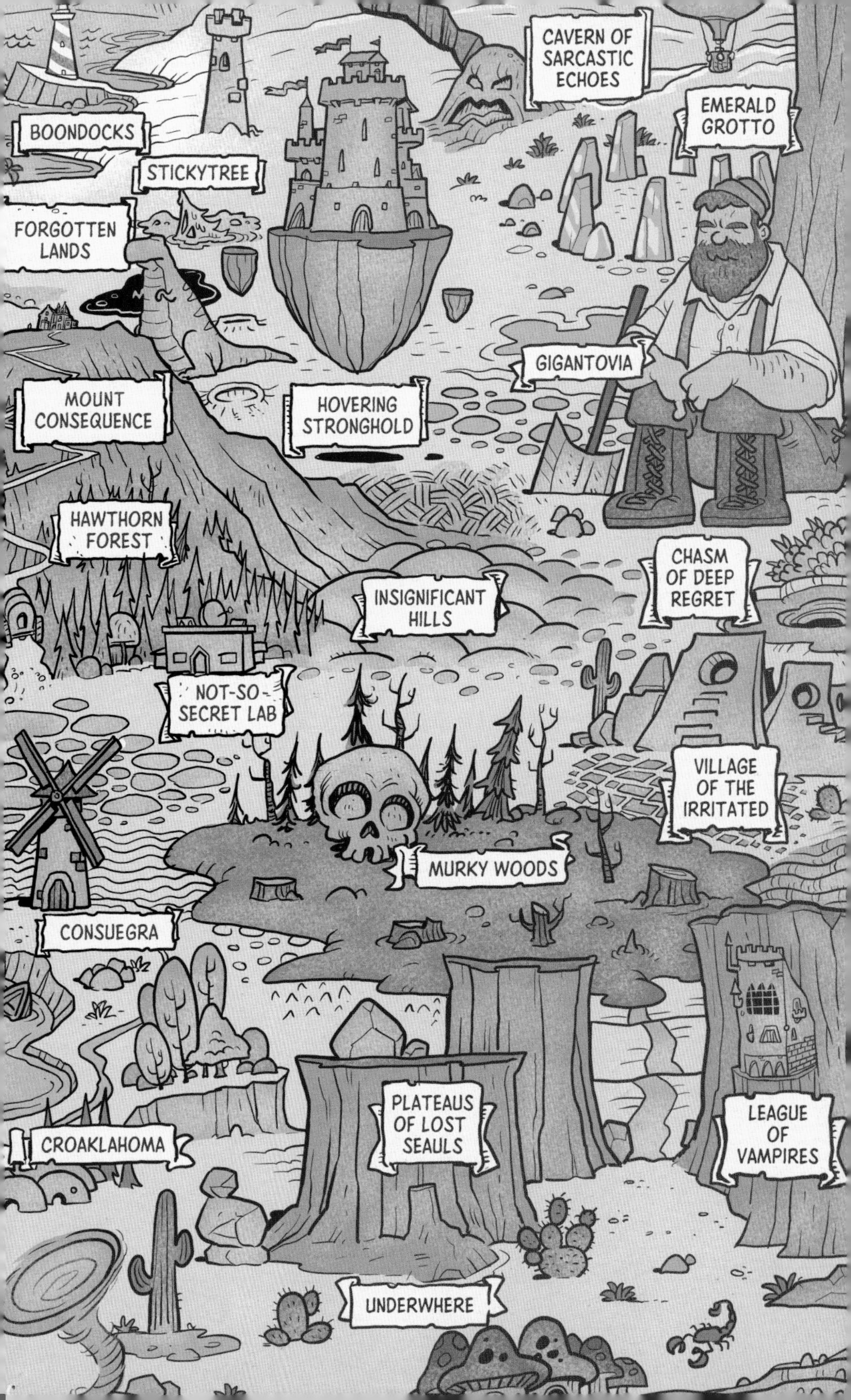
CAVERN OF SARCASTIC ECHOES
EMERALD GROTTO
BOONDOCKS
STICKYTREE
FORGOTTEN LANDS
GIGANTOVIA
MOUNT CONSEQUENCE
HOVERING STRONGHOLD
HAWTHORN FOREST
CHASM OF DEEP REGRET
INSIGNIFICANT HILLS
NOT-SO-SECRET LAB
VILLAGE OF THE IRRITATED
MURKY WOODS
CONSUEGRA
PLATEAUS OF LOST SEAULS
LEAGUE OF VAMPIRES
CROAKLAHOMA
UNDERWHERE

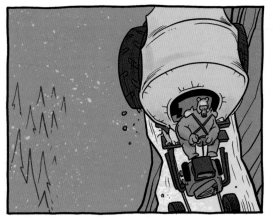

ONCE WE GET **THERE**, THIS WILL **ALL** BE WORTH **IT**.

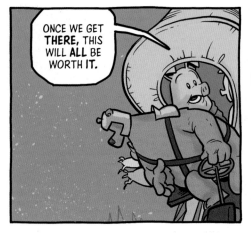

WHAT'S "**IT**"?

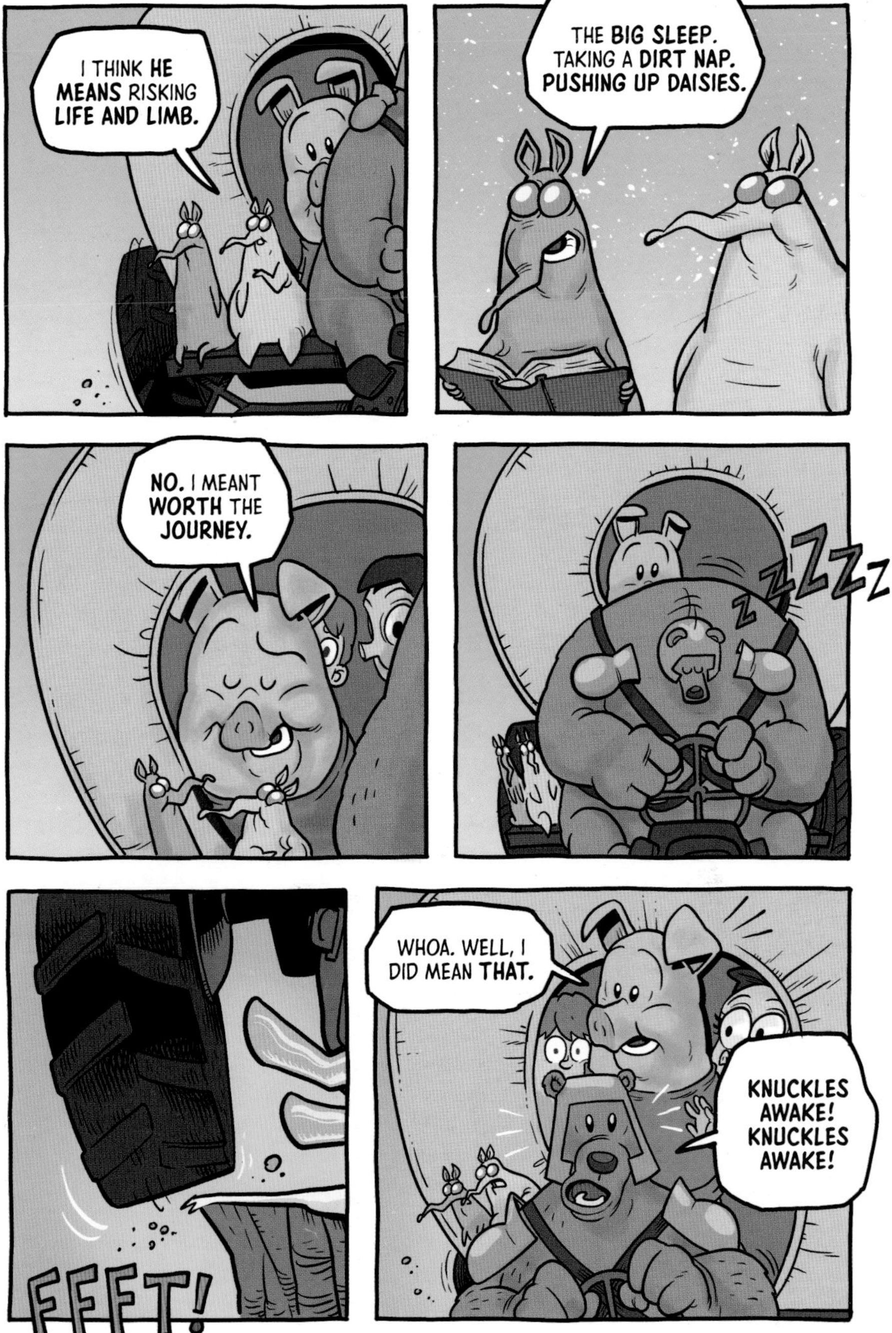
I THINK HE MEANS RISKING LIFE AND LIMB.
THE BIG SLEEP. TAKING A DIRT NAP. PUSHING UP DAISIES.
NO. I MEANT WORTH THE JOURNEY.
ZZZZZZ
FFFT!
WHOA. WELL, I DID MEAN THAT.
KNUCKLES AWAKE! KNUCKLES AWAKE!

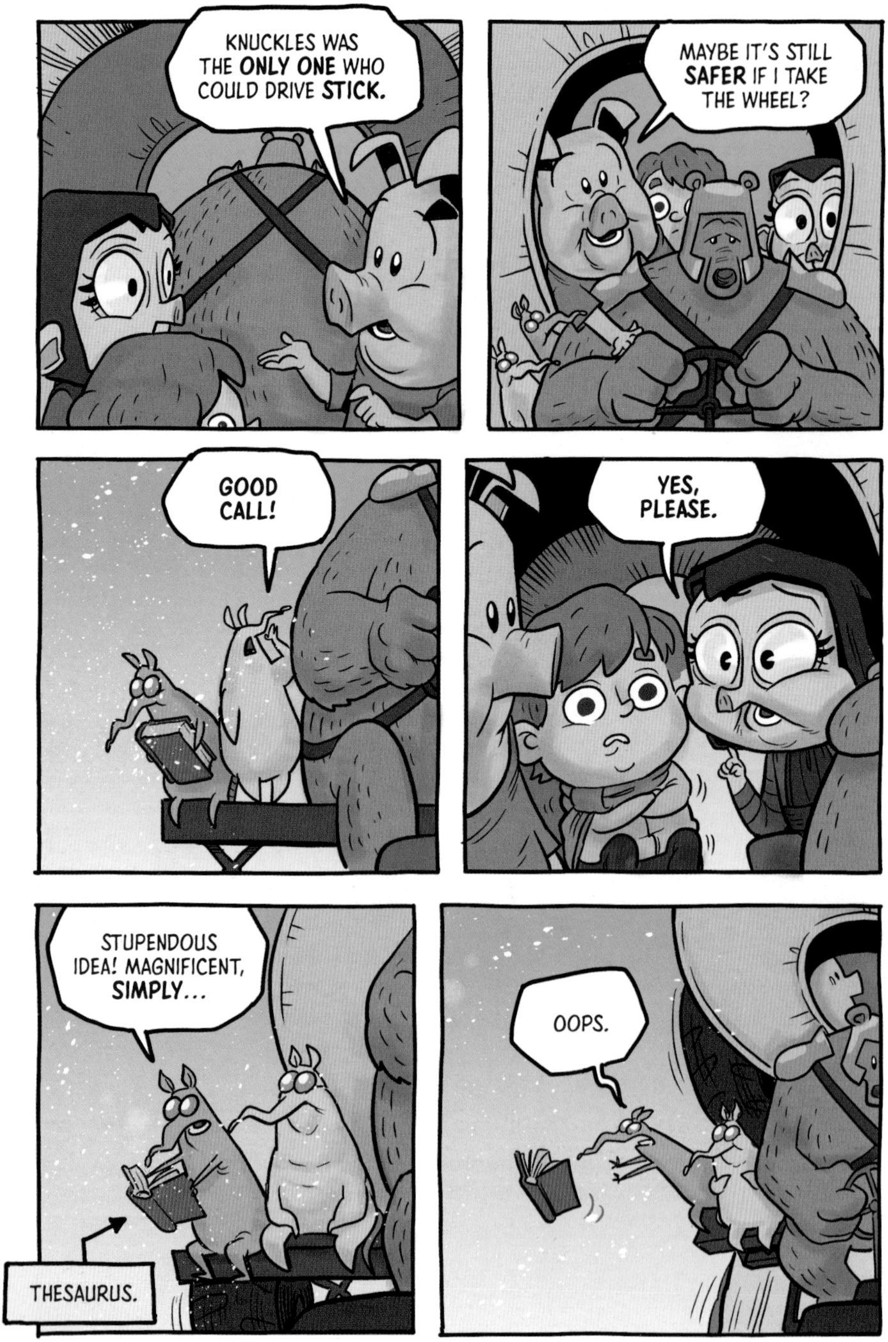
KNUCKLES WAS THE ONLY ONE WHO COULD DRIVE STICK.
MAYBE IT'S STILL SAFER IF I TAKE THE WHEEL?
GOOD CALL!
YES, PLEASE.
STUPENDOUS IDEA! MAGNIFICENT, SIMPLY...
THESAURUS.
OOPS.

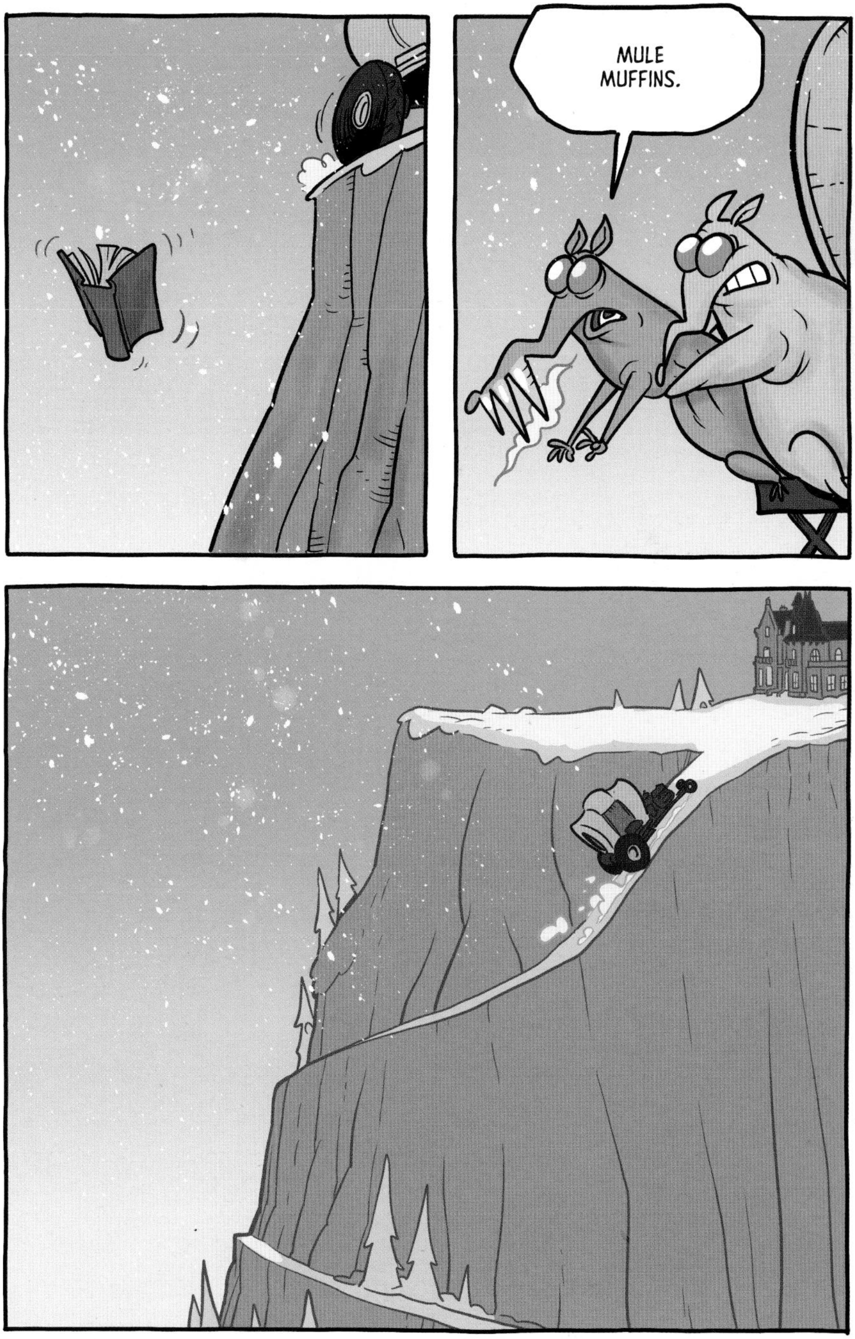
MULE MUFFINS.

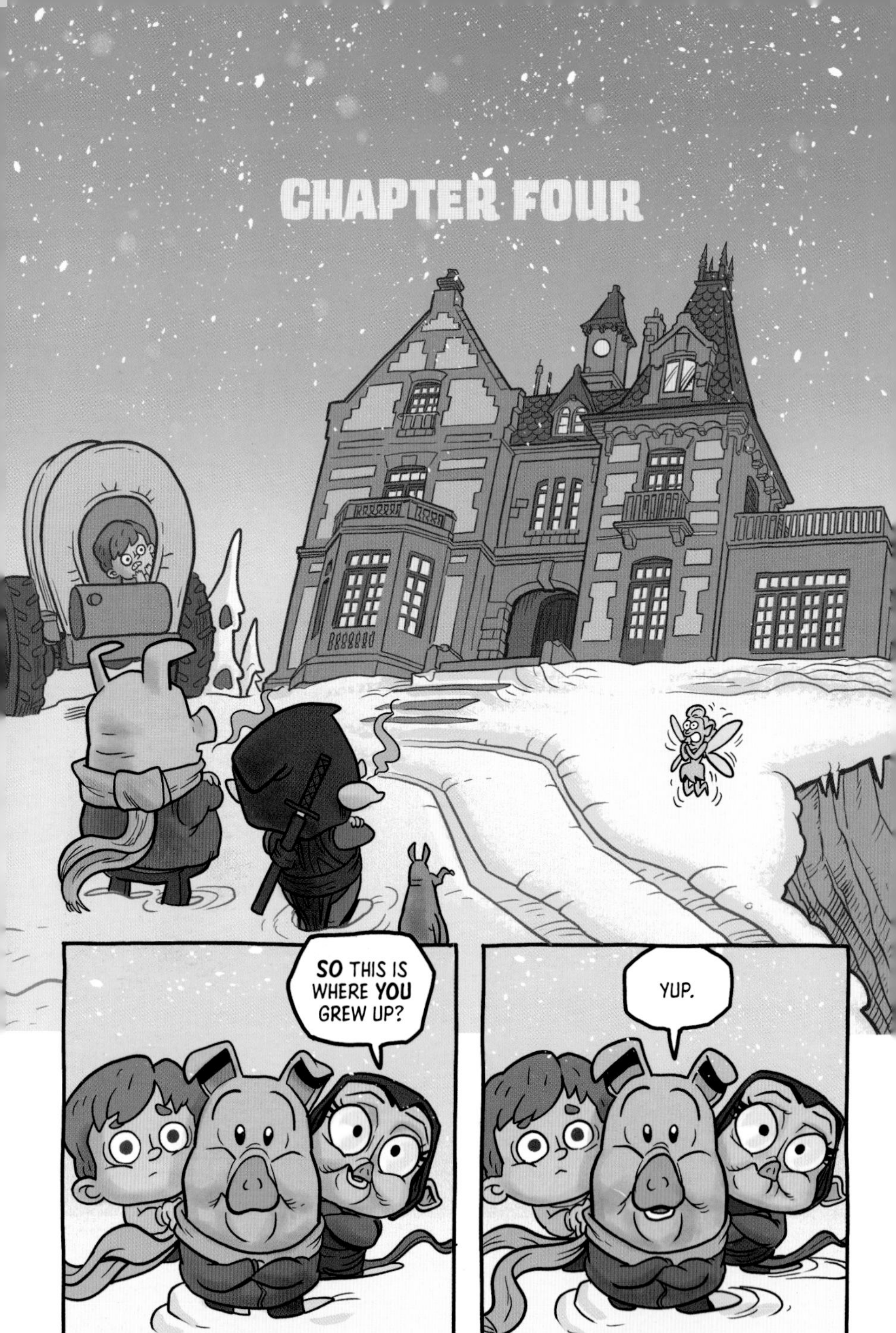
CHAPTER FOUR
SO THIS IS WHERE YOU GREW UP?
YUP.

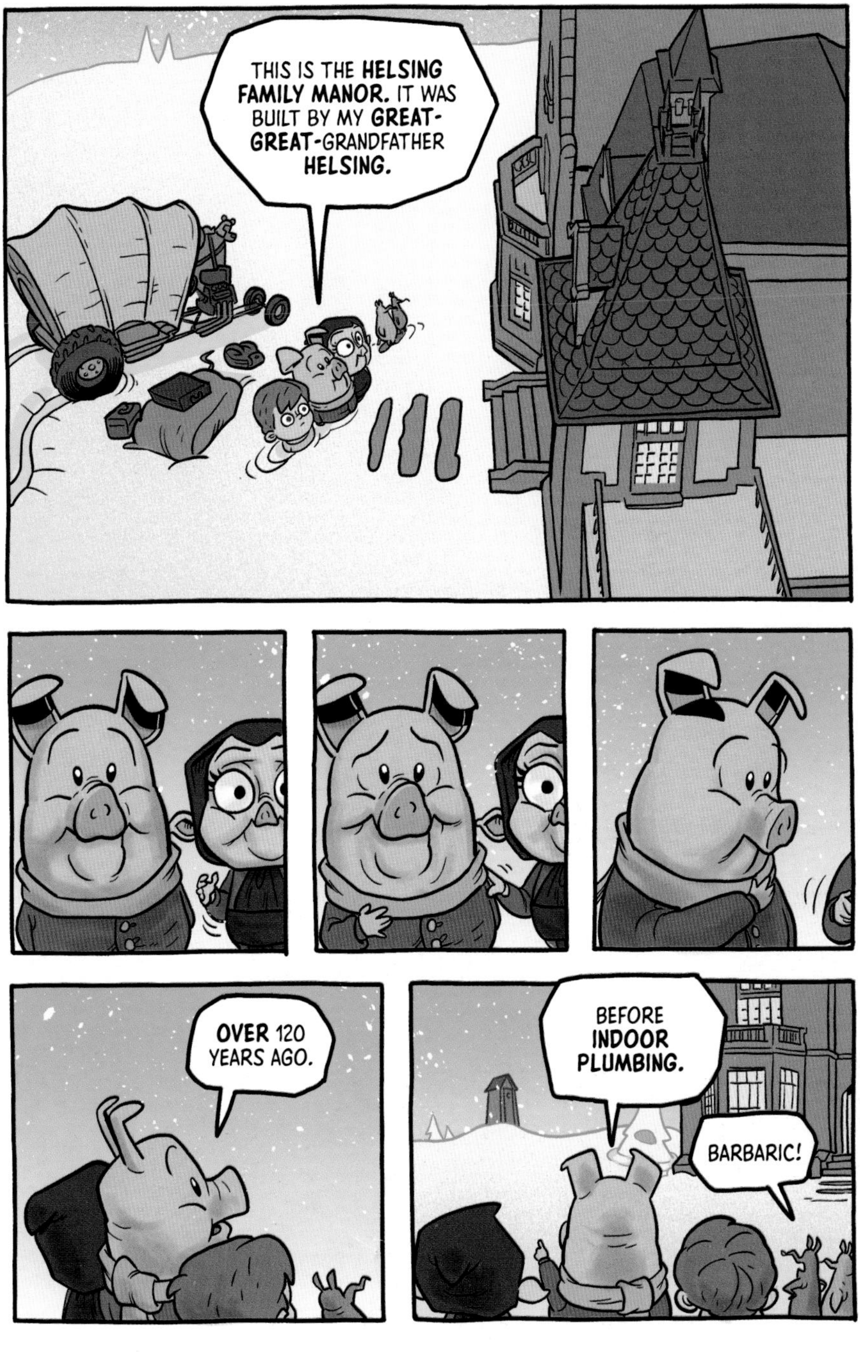

THIS IS THE HELSING FAMILY MANOR. IT WAS BUILT BY MY GREAT-GREAT-GRANDFATHER HELSING.
OVER 120 YEARS AGO.
BEFORE INDOOR PLUMBING.
BARBARIC!

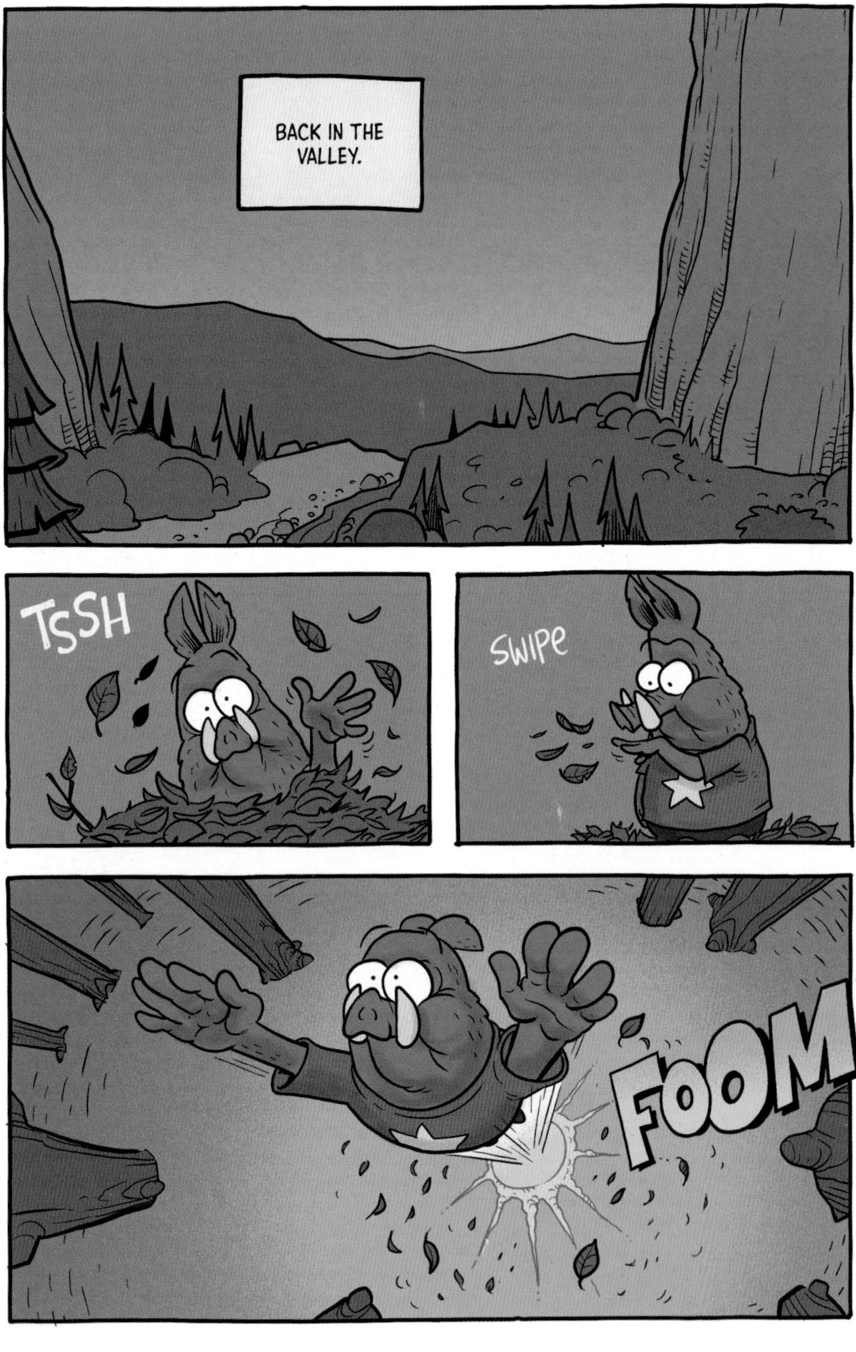
BACK IN THE VALLEY.
TSSH
SWIPE
FOOM!

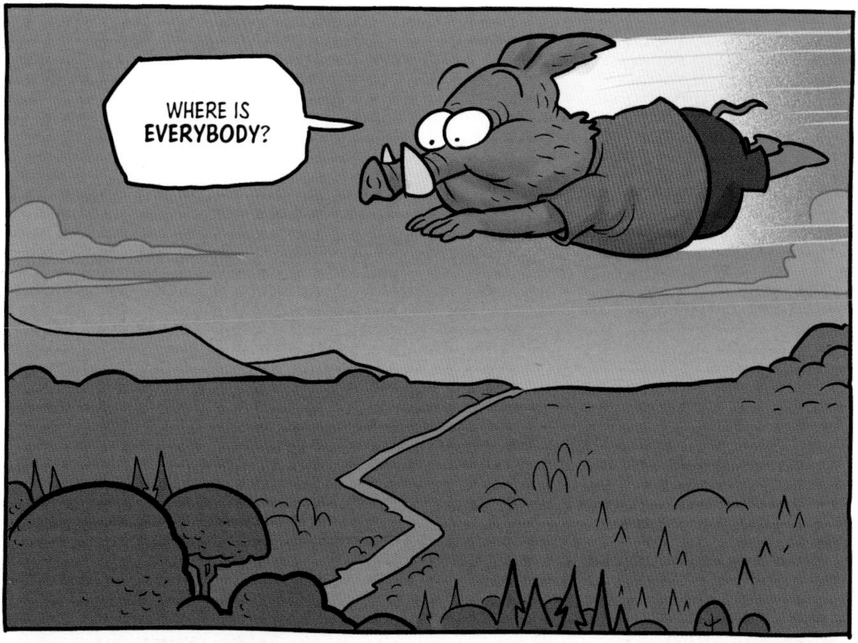
WHERE IS EVERYBODY?

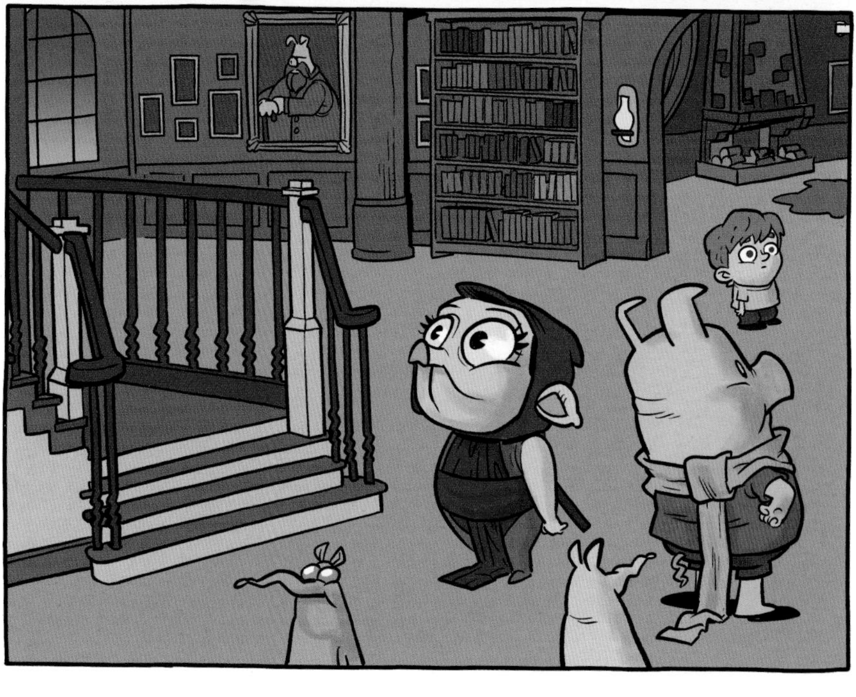

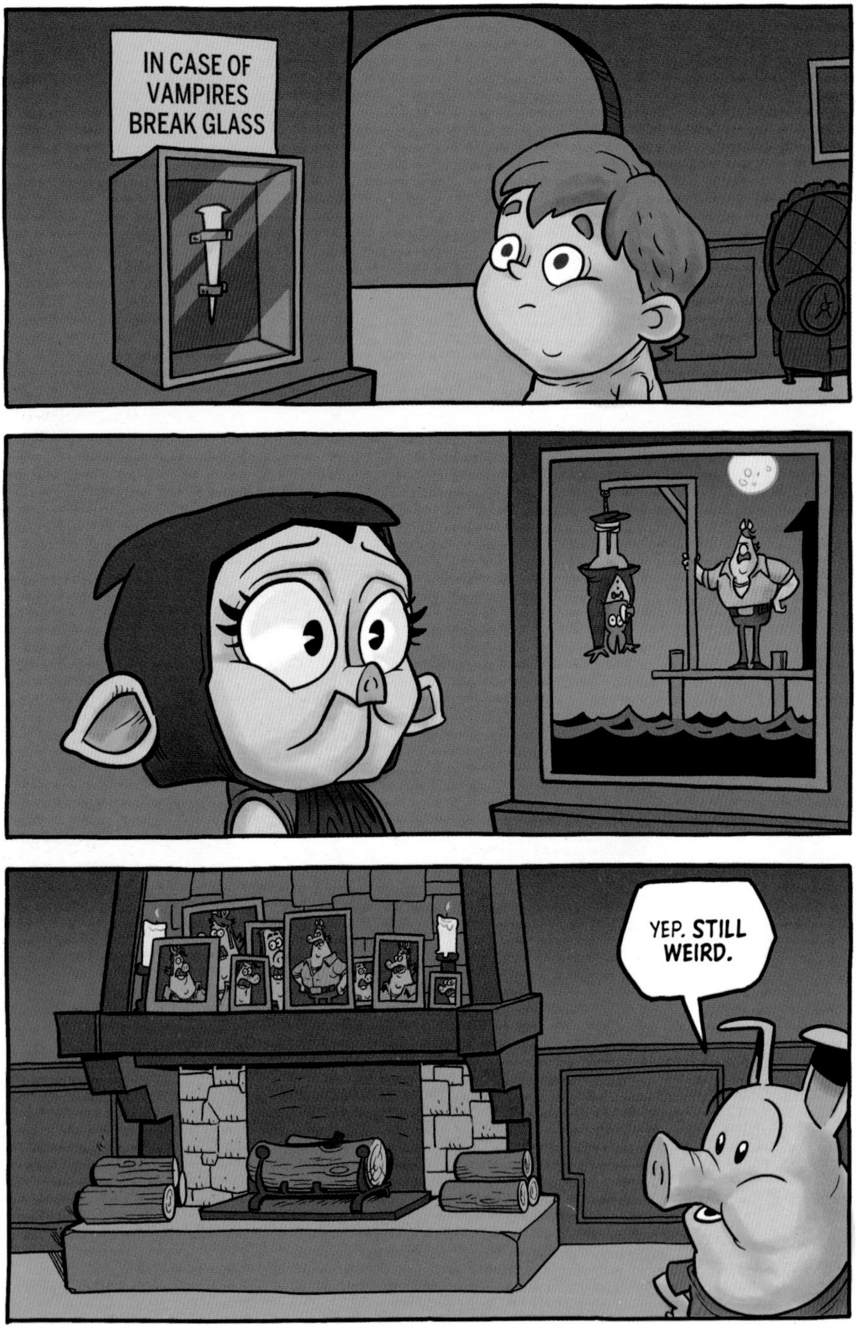
IN CASE OF
VAMPIRES
BREAK GLASS
YEP. **STILL WEIRD.**

CHAPTER FIVE

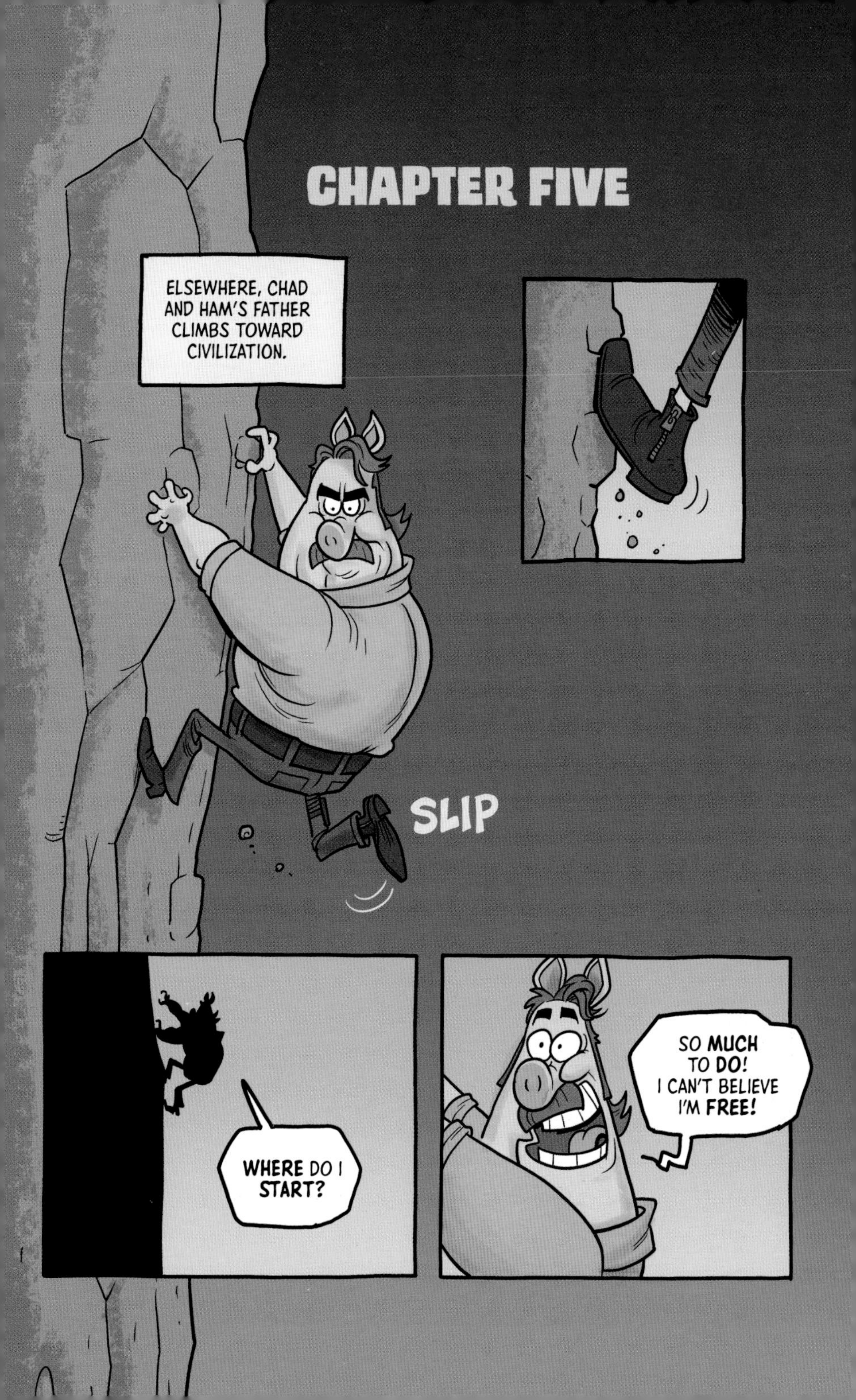
ELSEWHERE, CHAD AND HAM'S FATHER CLIMBS TOWARD CIVILIZATION.
SLIP
WHERE DO I START?
SO MUCH TO DO! I CAN'T BELIEVE I'M FREE!

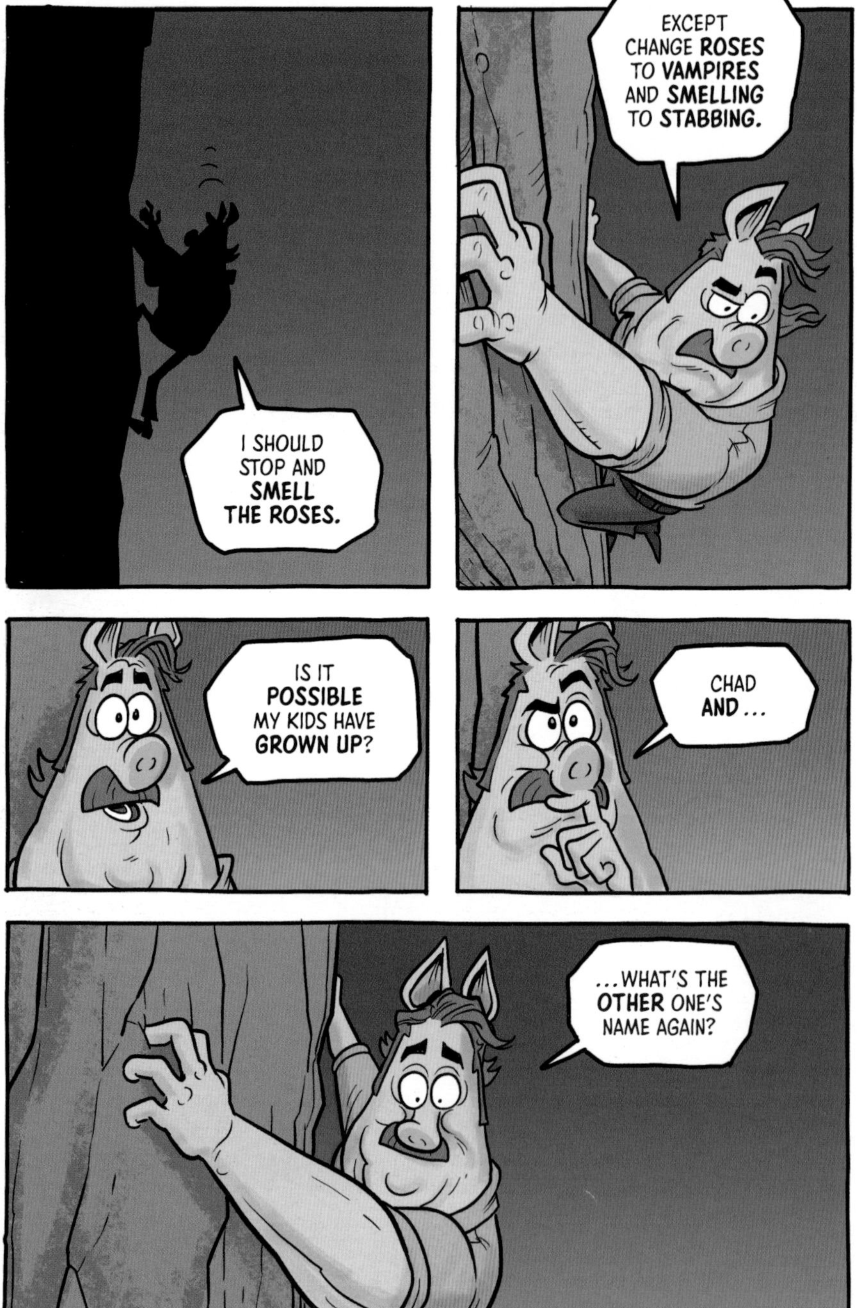
I SHOULD STOP AND SMELL THE ROSES.
EXCEPT CHANGE ROSES TO VAMPIRES AND SMELLING TO STABBING.
IS IT POSSIBLE MY KIDS HAVE GROWN UP?
CHAD AND . . .
. . . WHAT'S THE OTHER ONE'S NAME AGAIN?

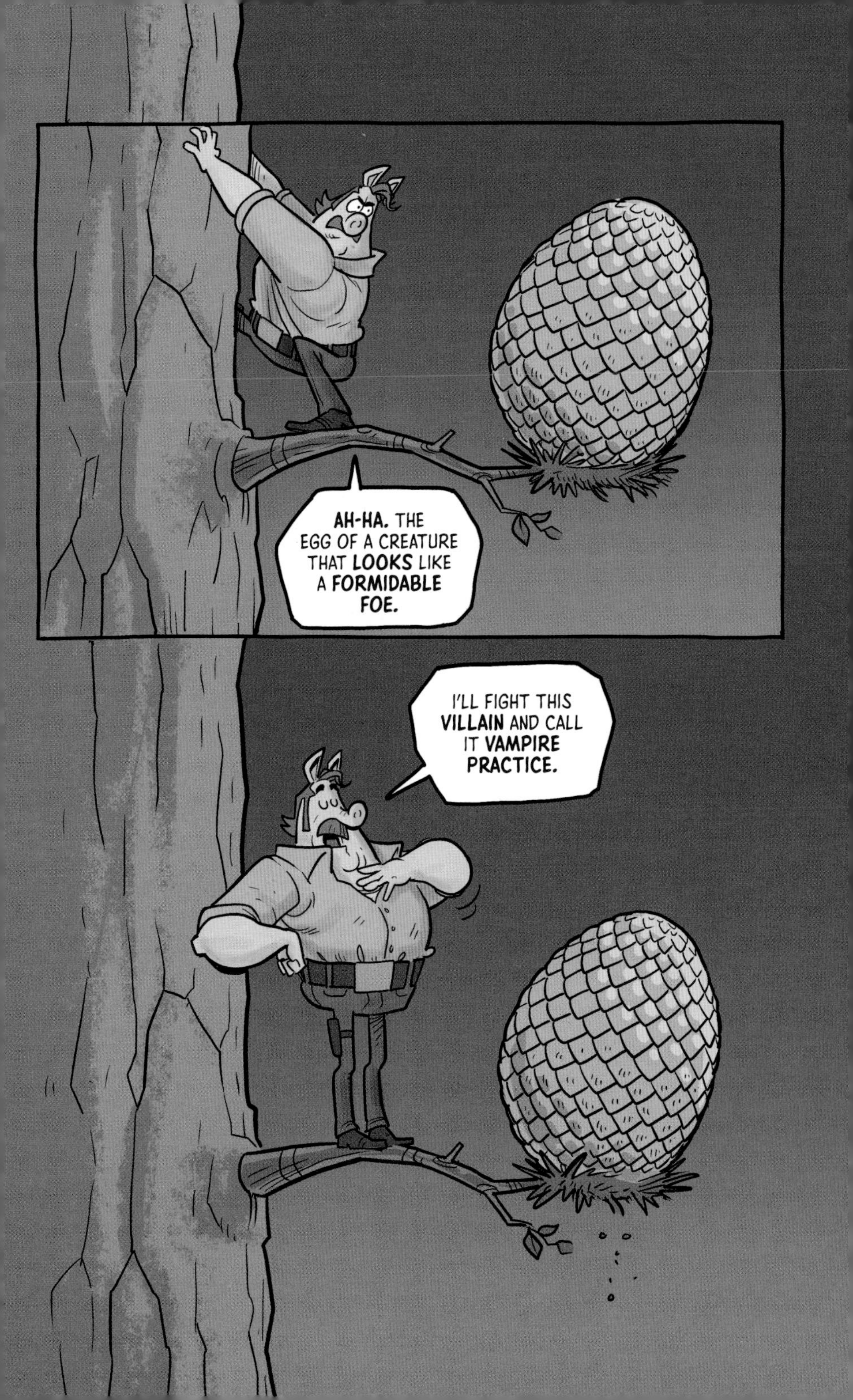
AH-HA. THE EGG OF A CREATURE THAT **LOOKS** LIKE A **FORMIDABLE FOE.**
I'LL FIGHT THIS **VILLAIN** AND CALL IT **VAMPIRE PRACTICE.**

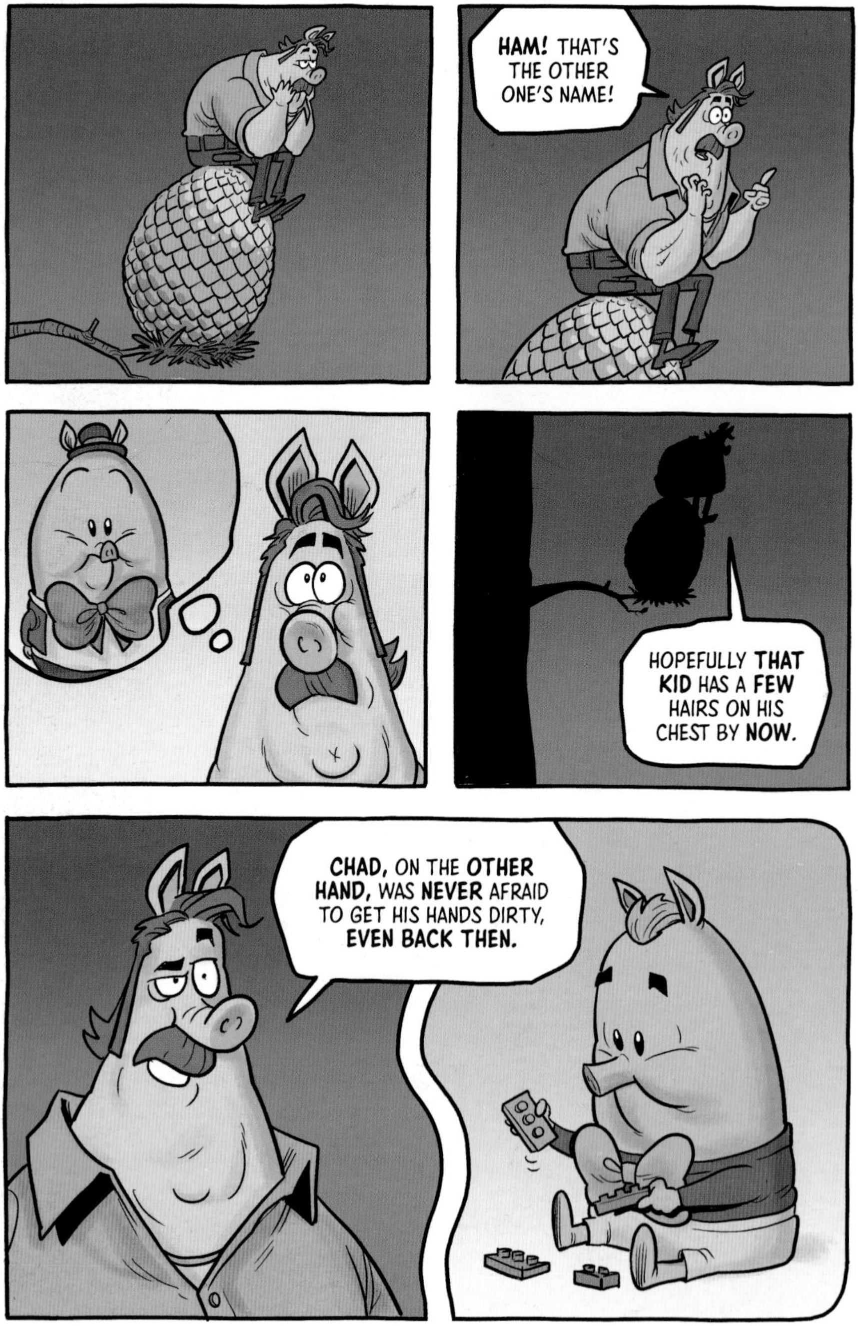
HAM! THAT'S THE OTHER ONE'S NAME!
HOPEFULLY THAT KID HAS A FEW HAIRS ON HIS CHEST BY NOW.
CHAD, ON THE OTHER HAND, WAS NEVER AFRAID TO GET HIS HANDS DIRTY, EVEN BACK THEN.

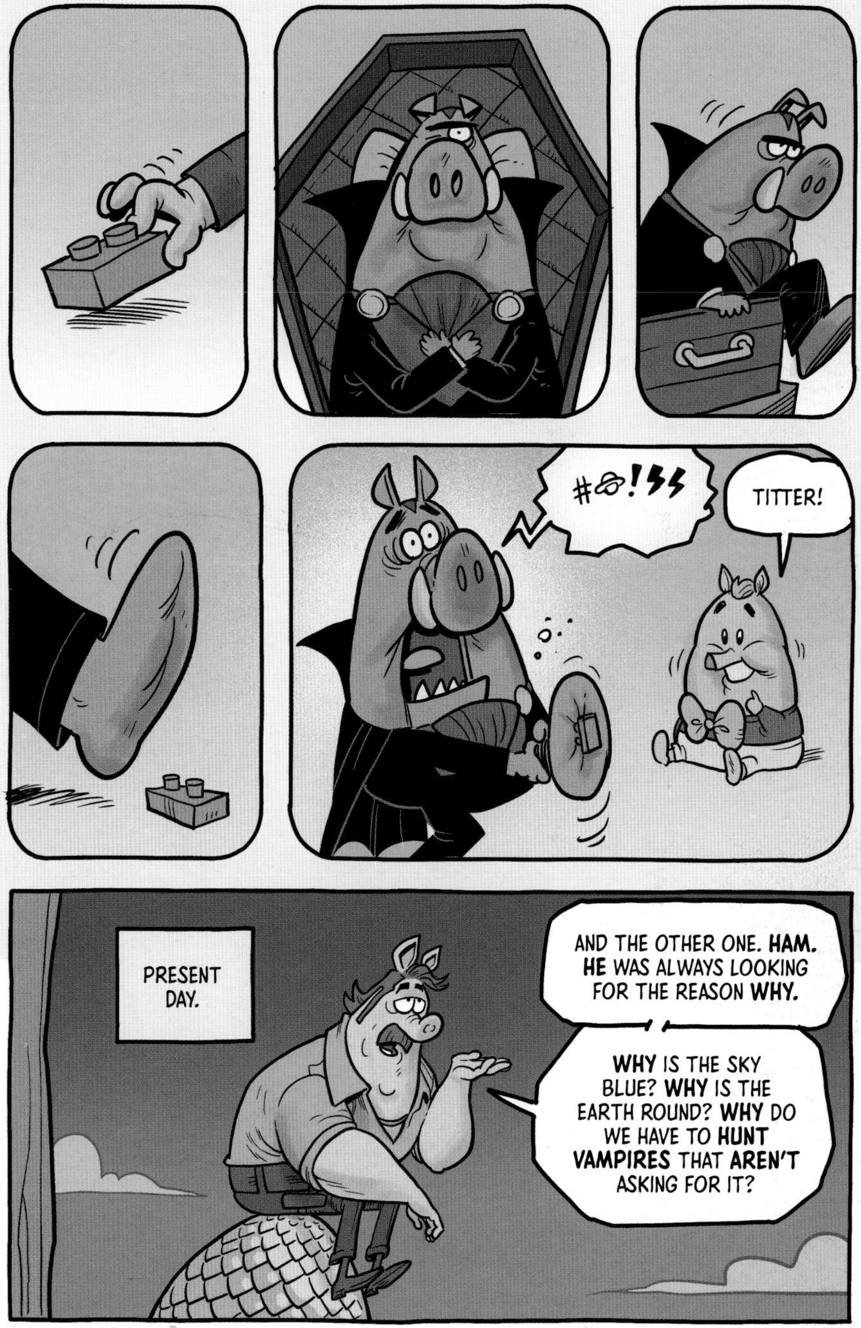
#@!$$
TITTER!
PRESENT DAY.
AND THE OTHER ONE. HAM. HE WAS ALWAYS LOOKING FOR THE REASON WHY.
WHY IS THE SKY BLUE? WHY IS THE EARTH ROUND? WHY DO WE HAVE TO HUNT VAMPIRES THAT AREN'T ASKING FOR IT?

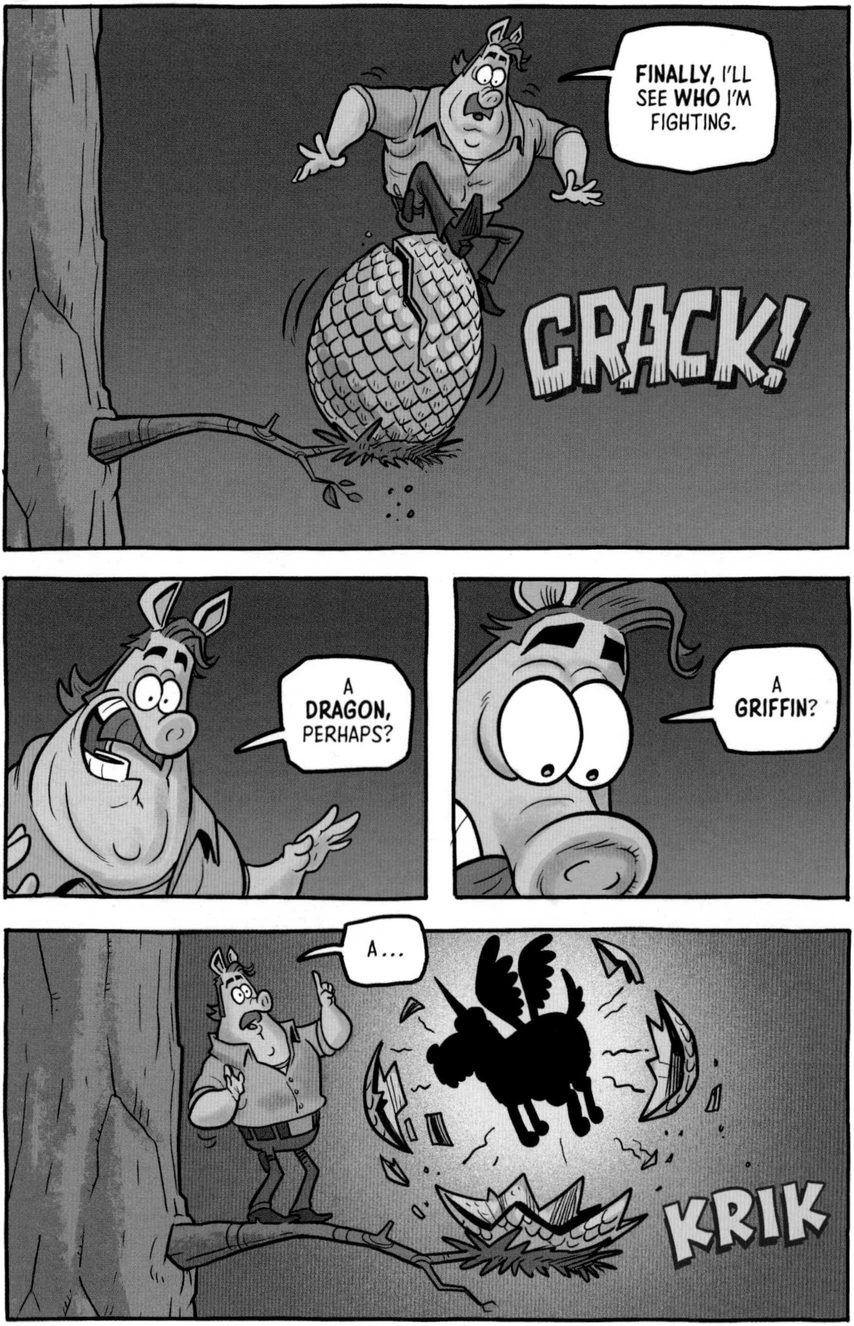
FINALLY, I'LL SEE WHO I'M FIGHTING.
CRACK!
A DRAGON, PERHAPS?
A GRIFFIN?
A...
KRIK

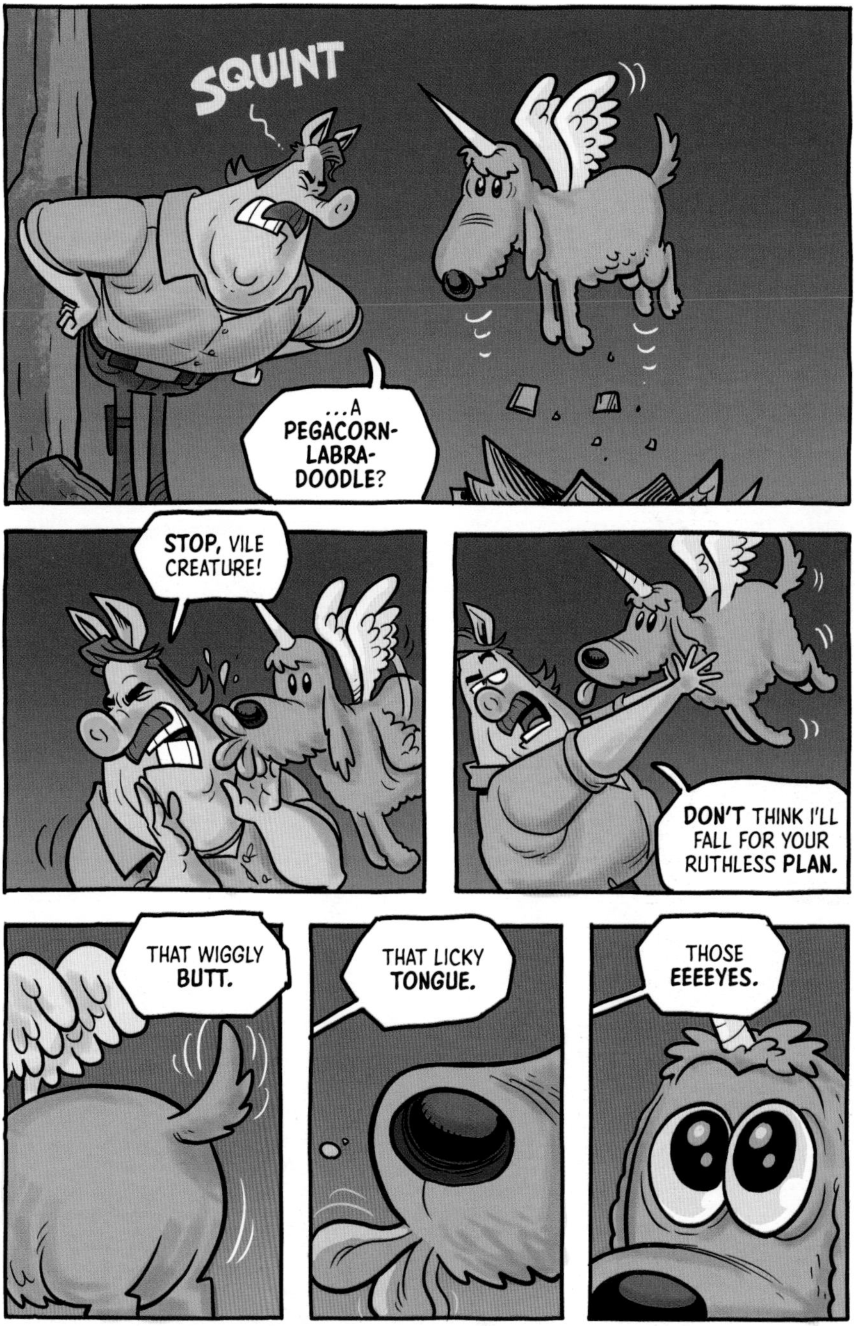
SQUINT
...A PEGACORN-LABRA-DOODLE?
STOP, VILE CREATURE!
DON'T THINK I'LL FALL FOR YOUR RUTHLESS PLAN.
THAT WIGGLY BUTT.
THAT LICKY TONGUE.
THOSE EEEEYES.

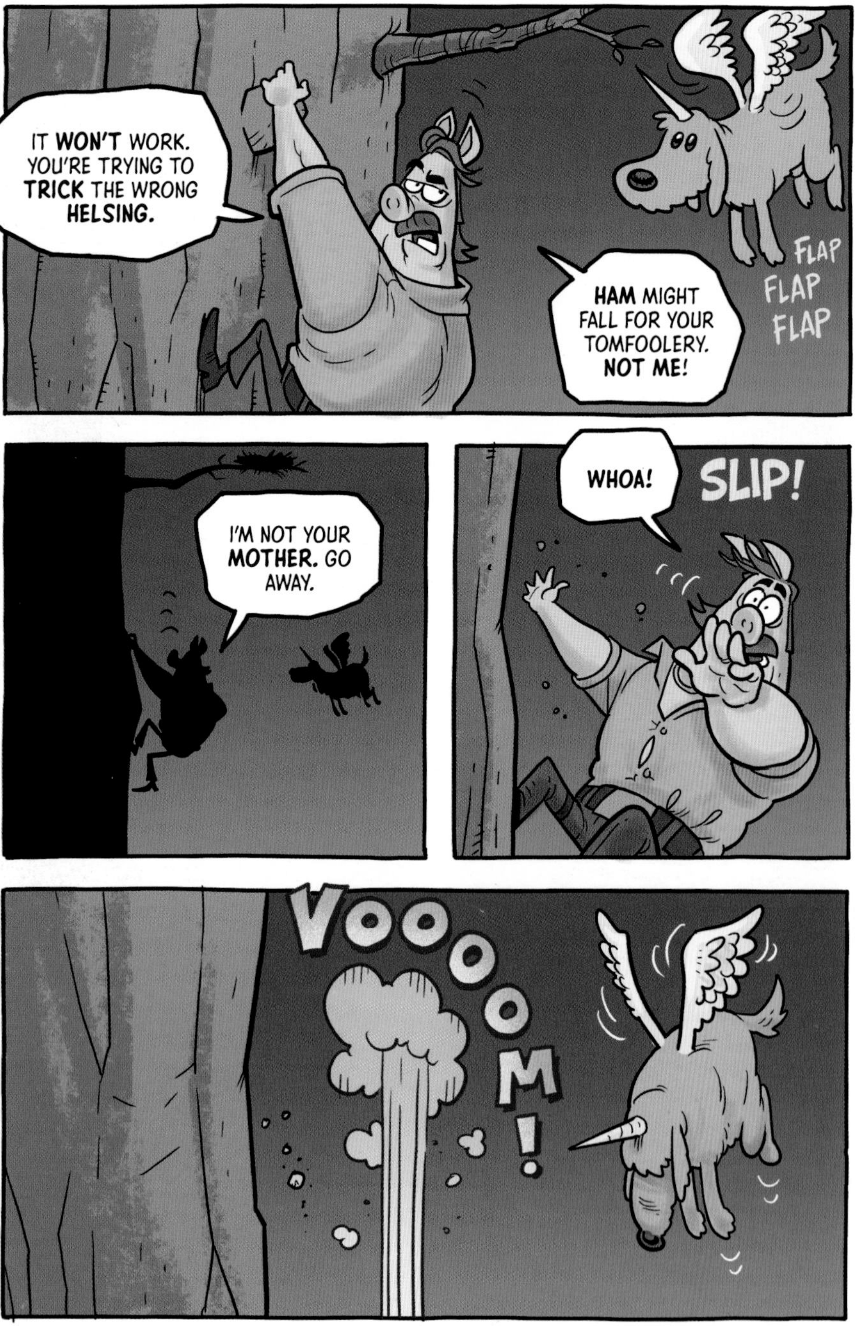
IT WON'T WORK. YOU'RE TRYING TO TRICK THE WRONG HELSING.
HAM MIGHT FALL FOR YOUR TOMFOOLERY. NOT ME!
FLAP FLAP FLAP
I'M NOT YOUR MOTHER. GO AWAY.
WHOA!
SLIP!
VOOOOOM!

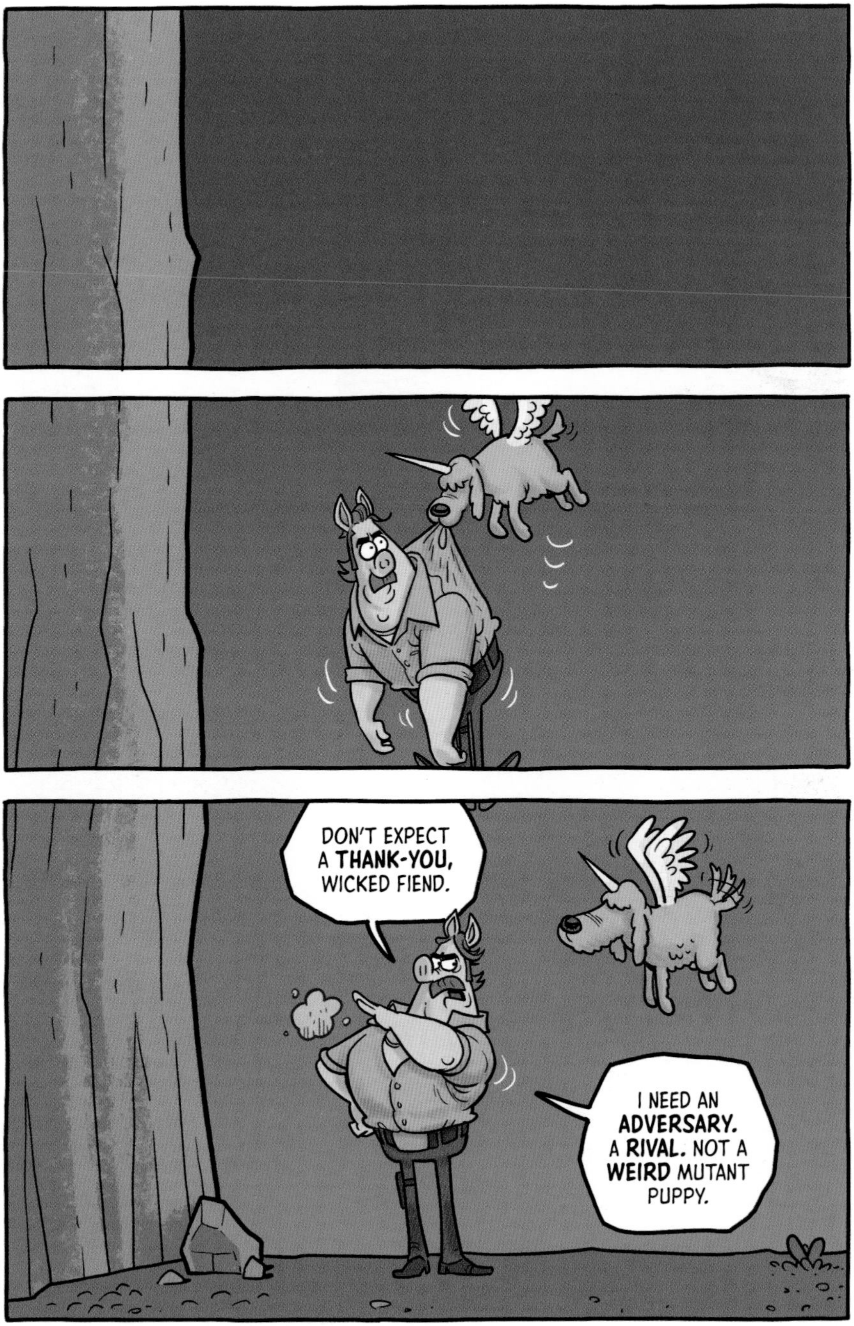
DON'T EXPECT A **THANK-YOU,** WICKED FIEND.
I NEED AN **ADVERSARY.** A **RIVAL.** NOT A **WEIRD** MUTANT PUPPY.

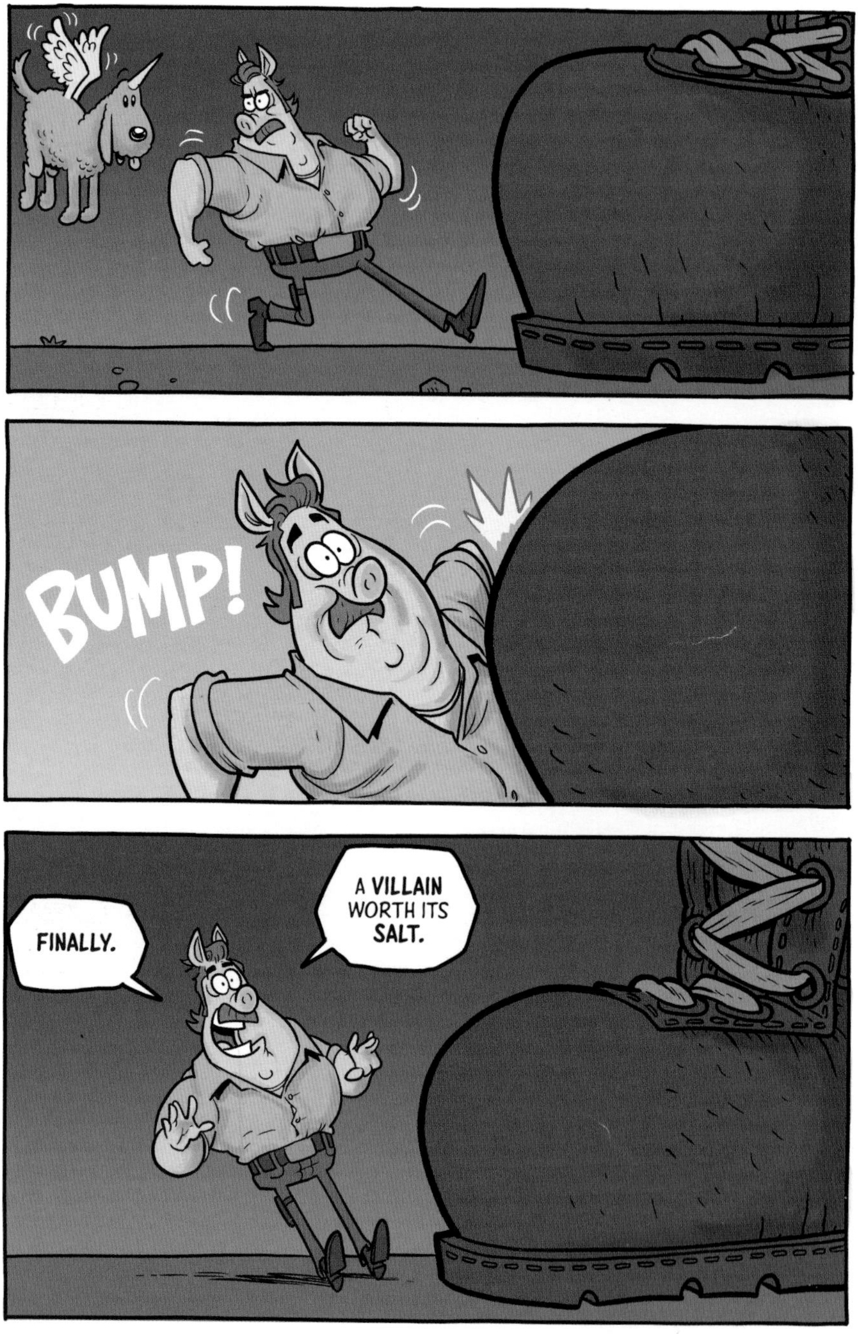
BUMP!
FINALLY.
A VILLAIN WORTH ITS SALT.

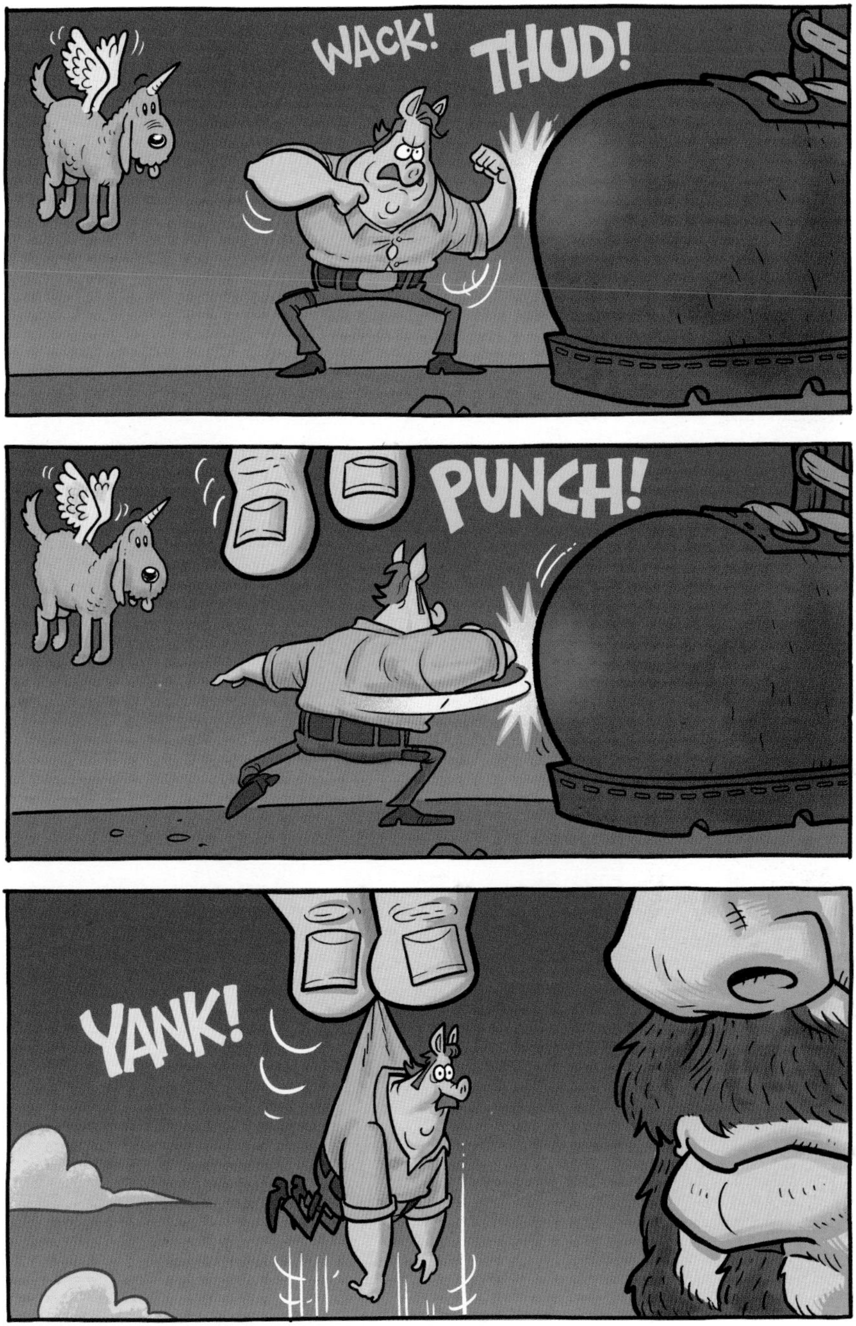
WACK!
THUD!
PUNCH!
YANK!

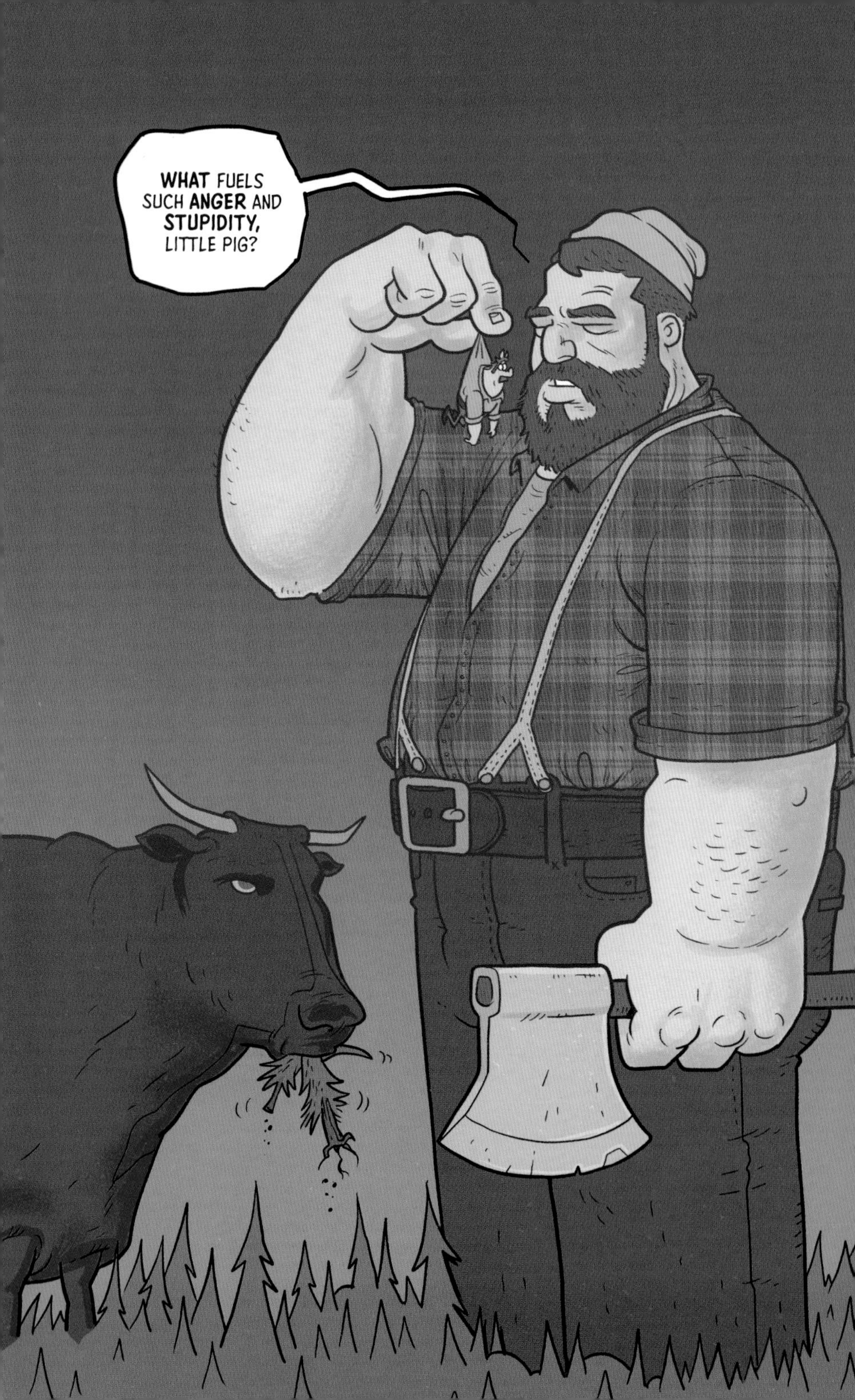
WHAT FUELS SUCH **ANGER** AND **STUPIDITY,** LITTLE PIG?

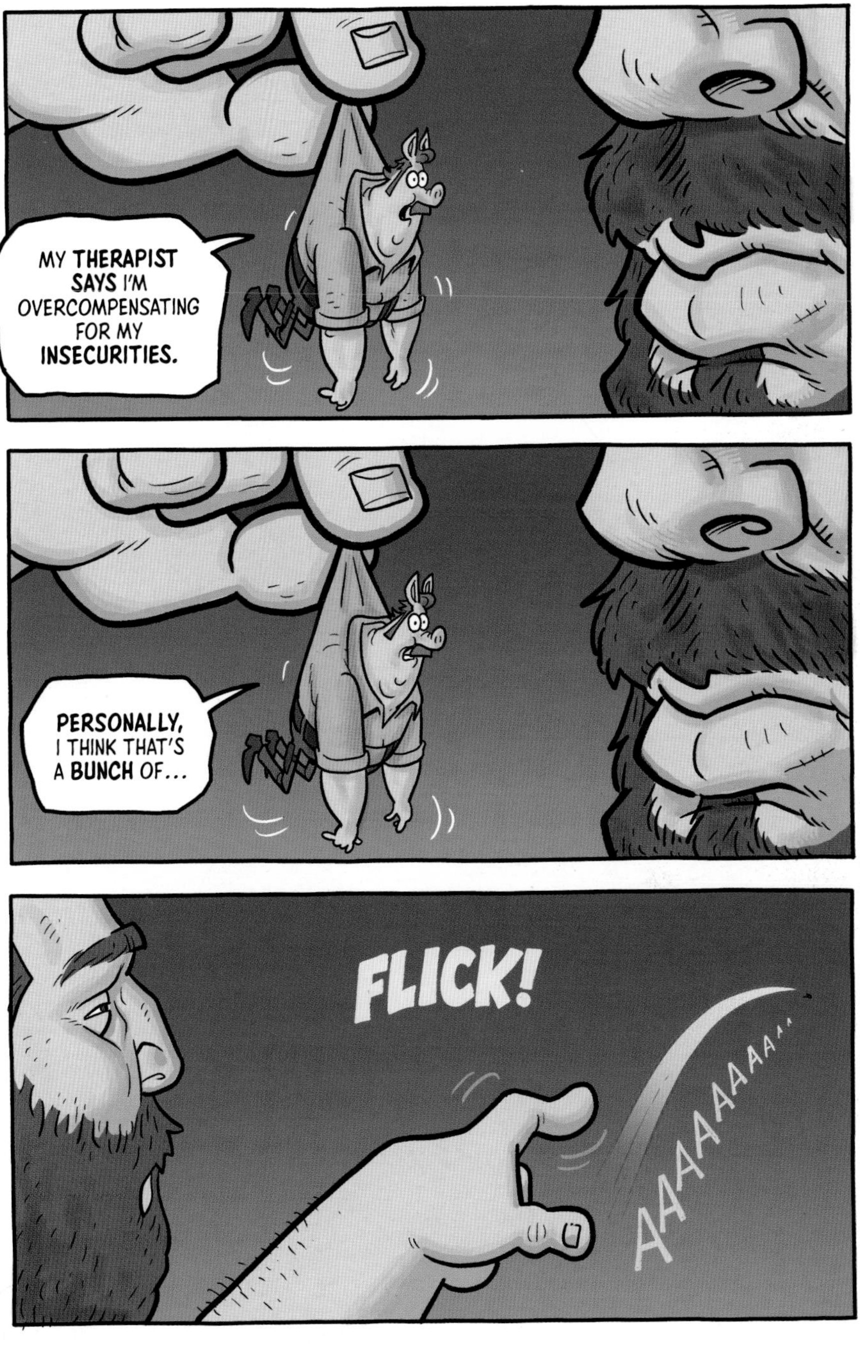
MY **THERAPIST** **SAYS** I'M OVERCOMPENSATING FOR MY **INSECURITIES.**
PERSONALLY, I THINK THAT'S A **BUNCH** OF...
FLICK!
AAAAAAAAAA

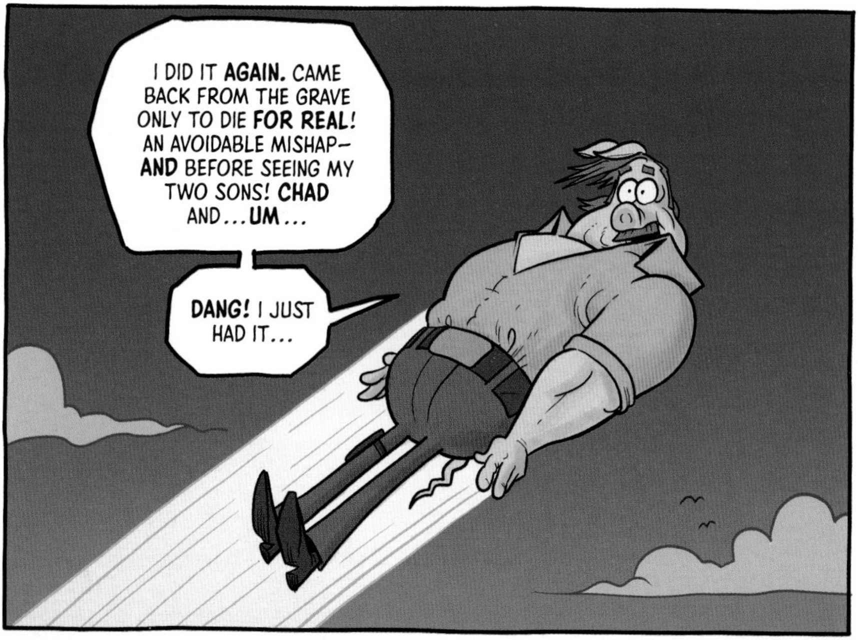
I DID IT **AGAIN.** CAME BACK FROM THE GRAVE ONLY TO DIE **FOR REAL!** AN AVOIDABLE MISHAP—**AND** BEFORE SEEING MY TWO SONS! **CHAD** AND . . . **UM** . . .
DANG! I JUST HAD IT . . .

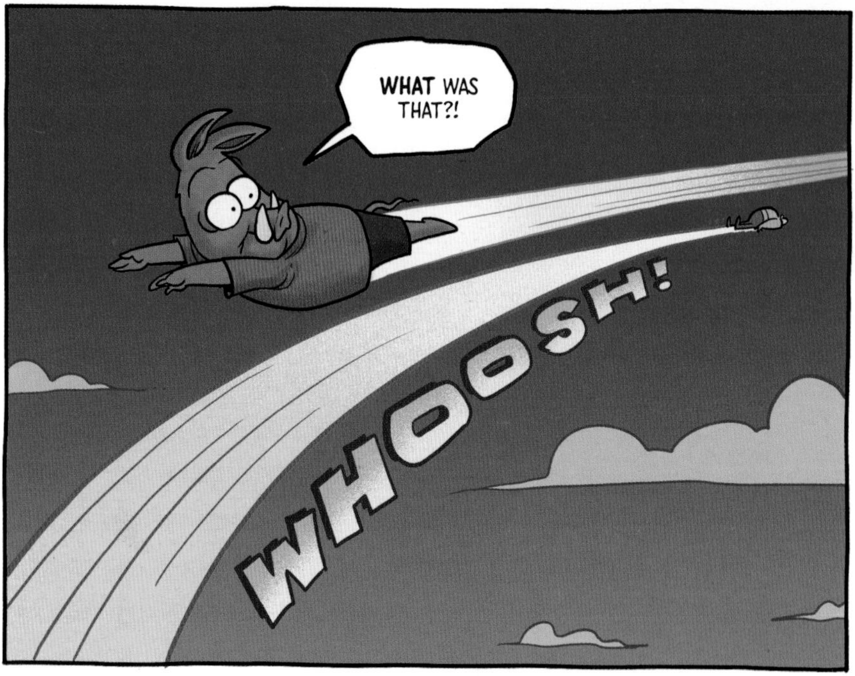
WHAT WAS THAT?!
WHOOSH!

CHAPTER SIX

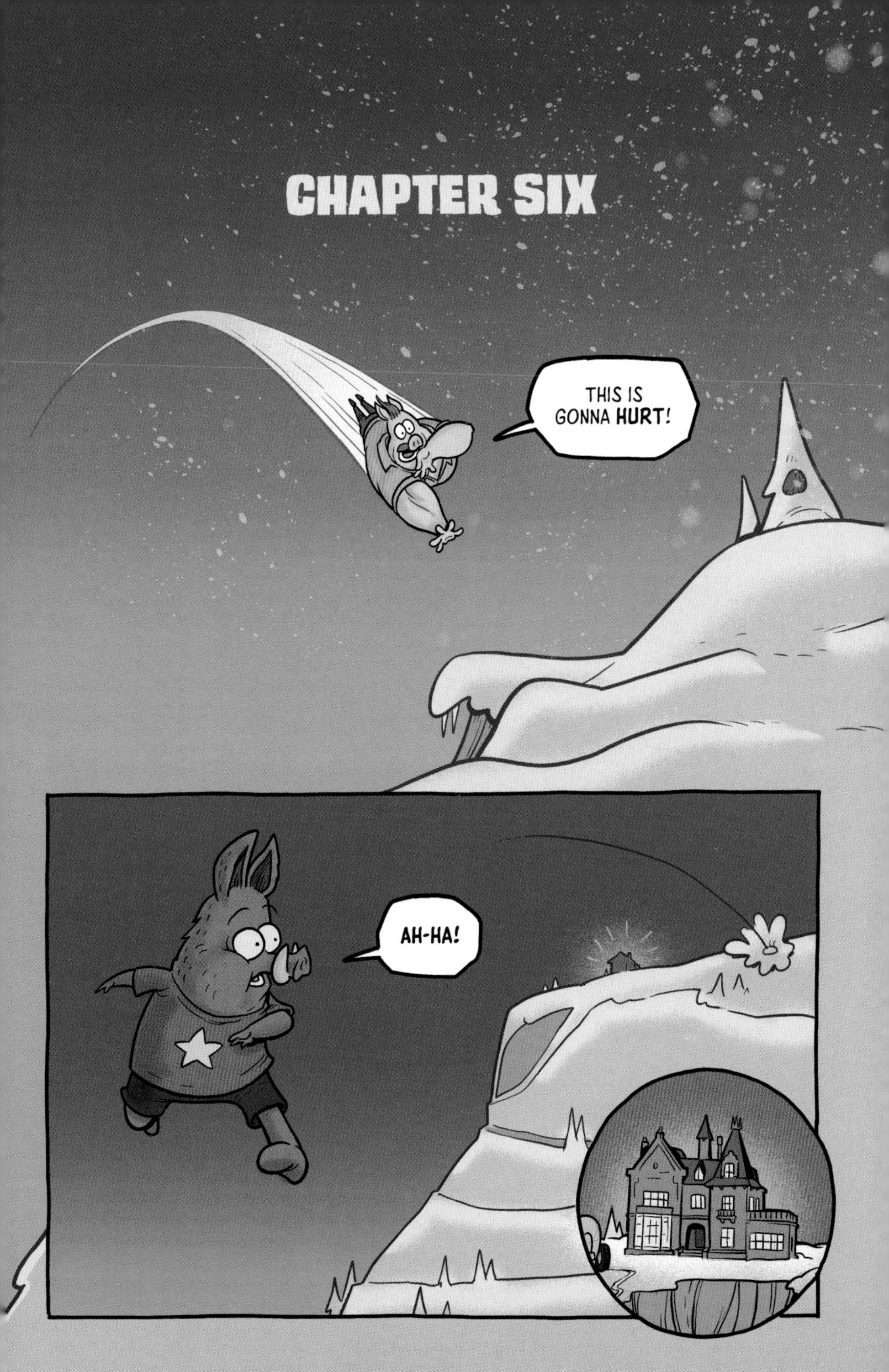
THIS IS GONNA HURT!
AH-HA!

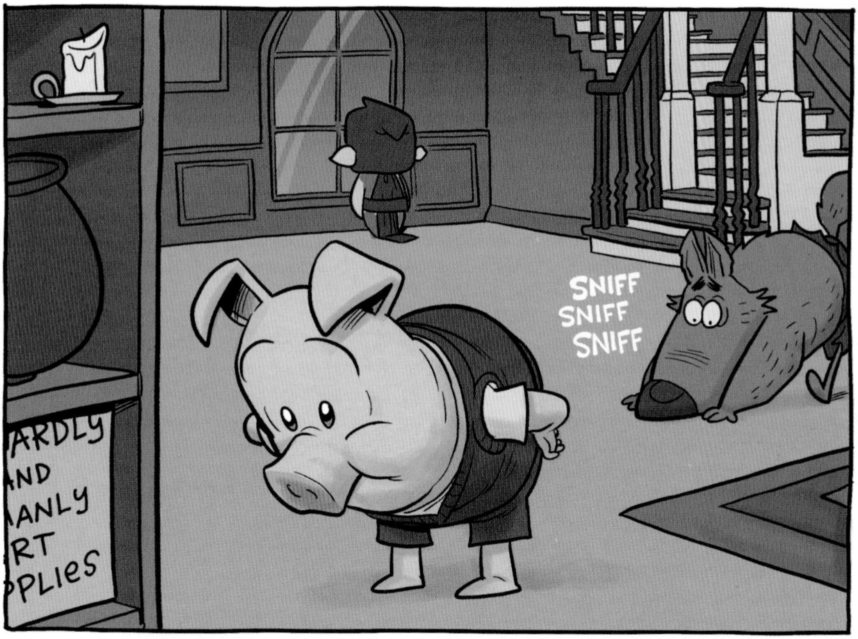
SNIFF
SNIFF
SNIFF

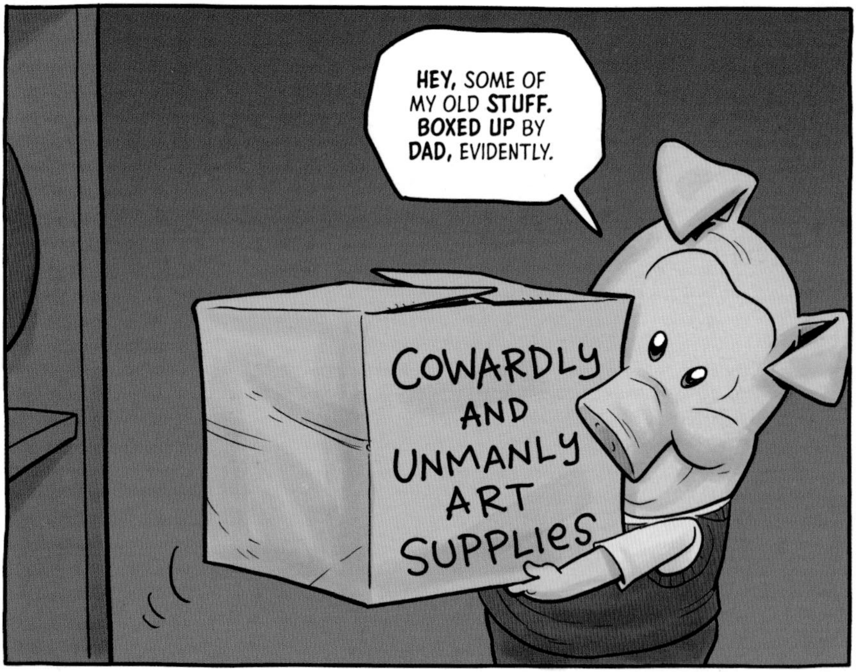
HEY, SOME OF MY OLD STUFF. BOXED UP BY DAD, EVIDENTLY.
COWARDLY AND UNMANLY ART SUPPLIES

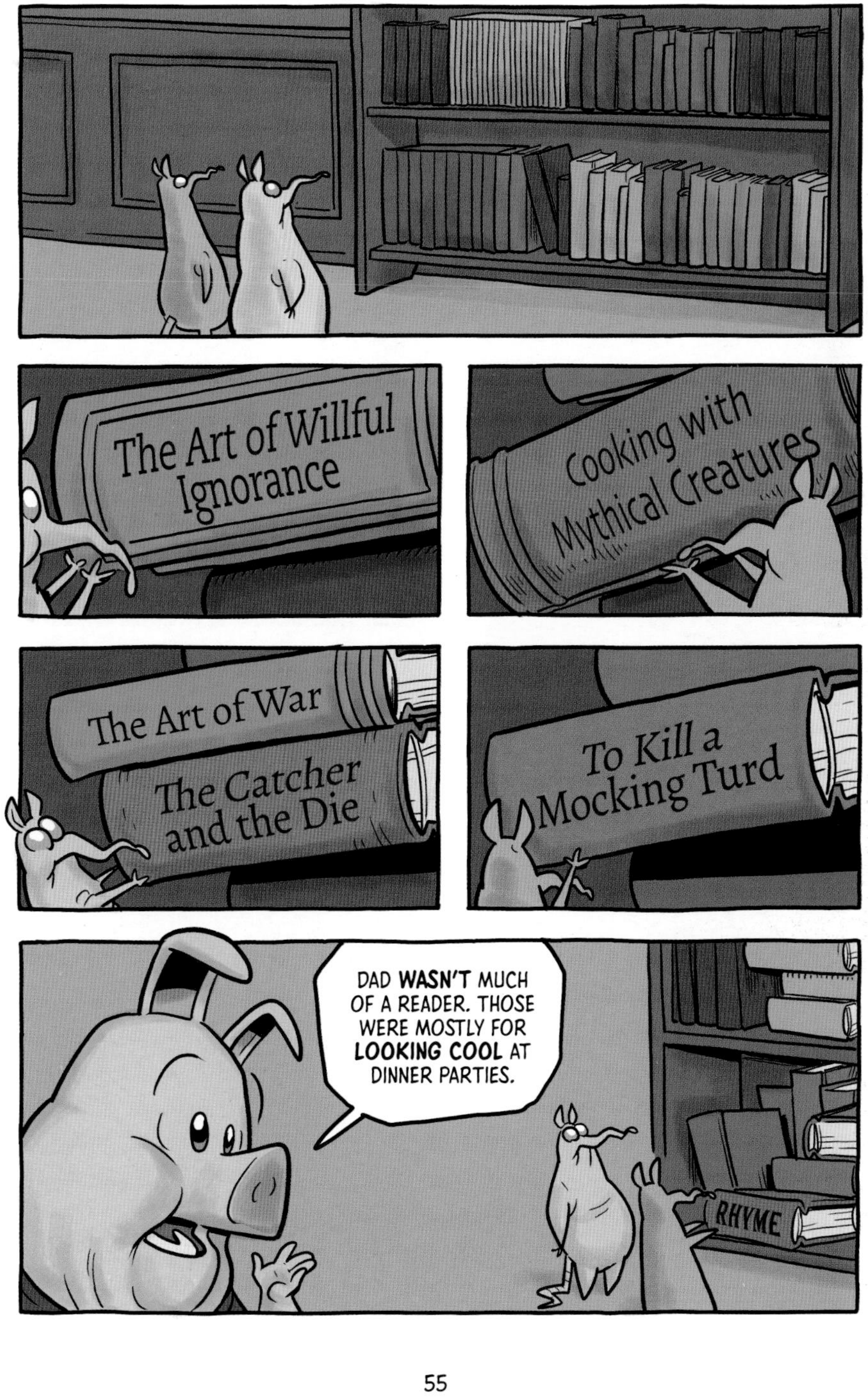
The Art of Willful Ignorance
Cooking with Mythical Creatures
The Art of War
The Catcher and the Die
To Kill a Mocking Turd
DAD WASN'T MUCH OF A READER. THOSE WERE MOSTLY FOR LOOKING COOL AT DINNER PARTIES.
RHYME

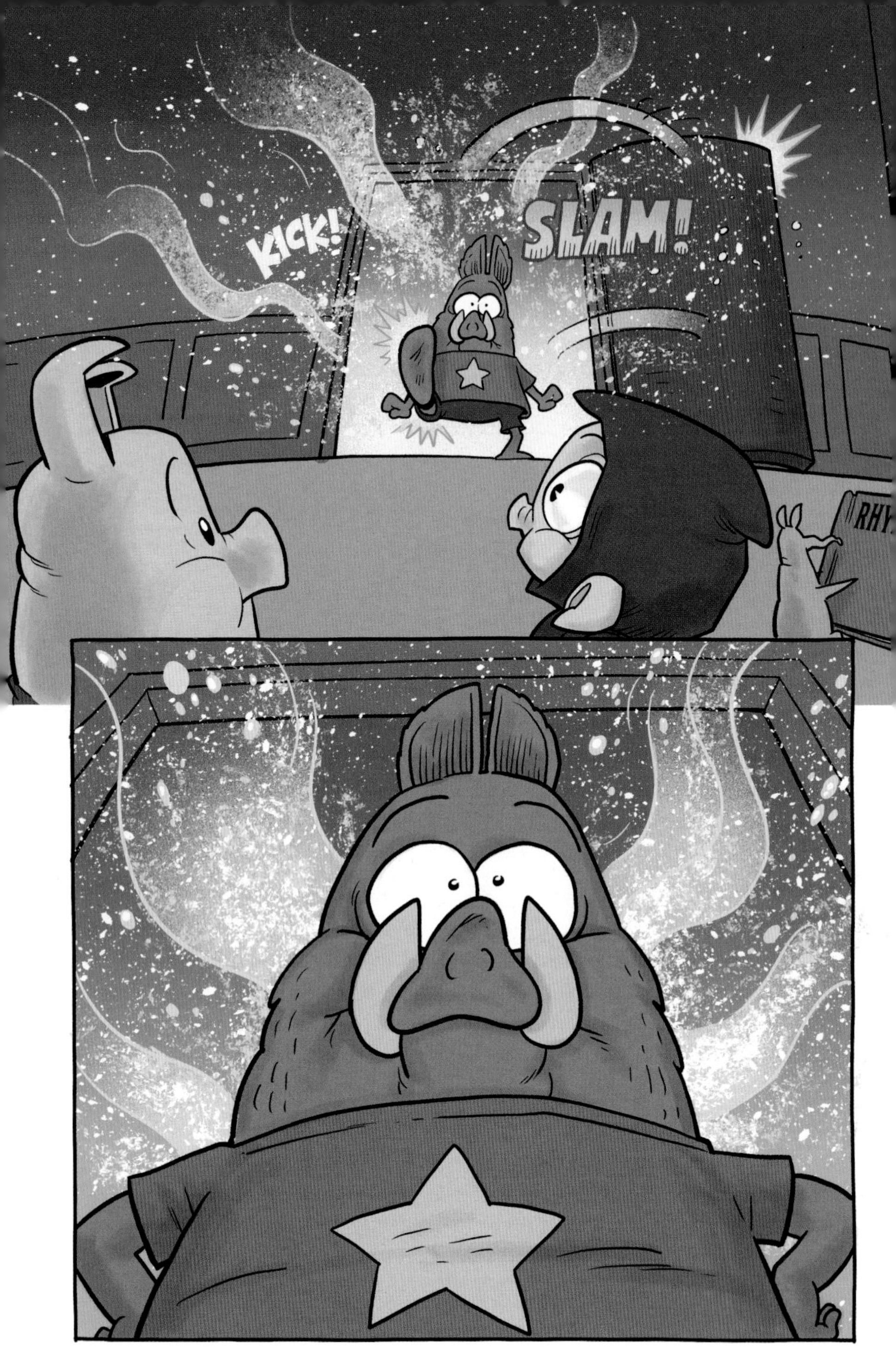
KICK!
SLAM!
RHY

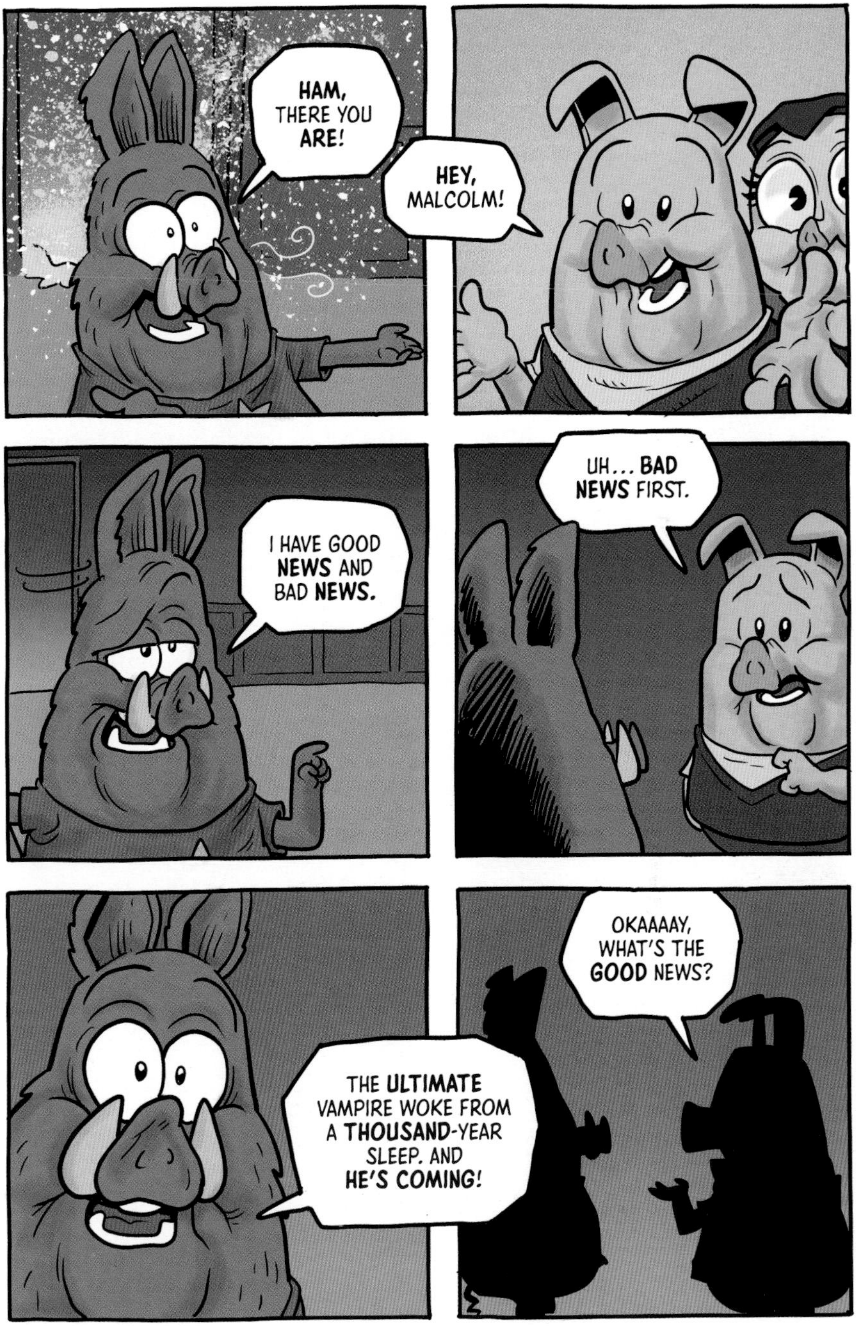
HAM, THERE YOU ARE!
HEY, MALCOLM!
I HAVE GOOD NEWS AND BAD NEWS.
UH... BAD NEWS FIRST.
THE ULTIMATE VAMPIRE WOKE FROM A THOUSAND-YEAR SLEEP. AND HE'S COMING!
OKAAAAY, WHAT'S THE GOOD NEWS?

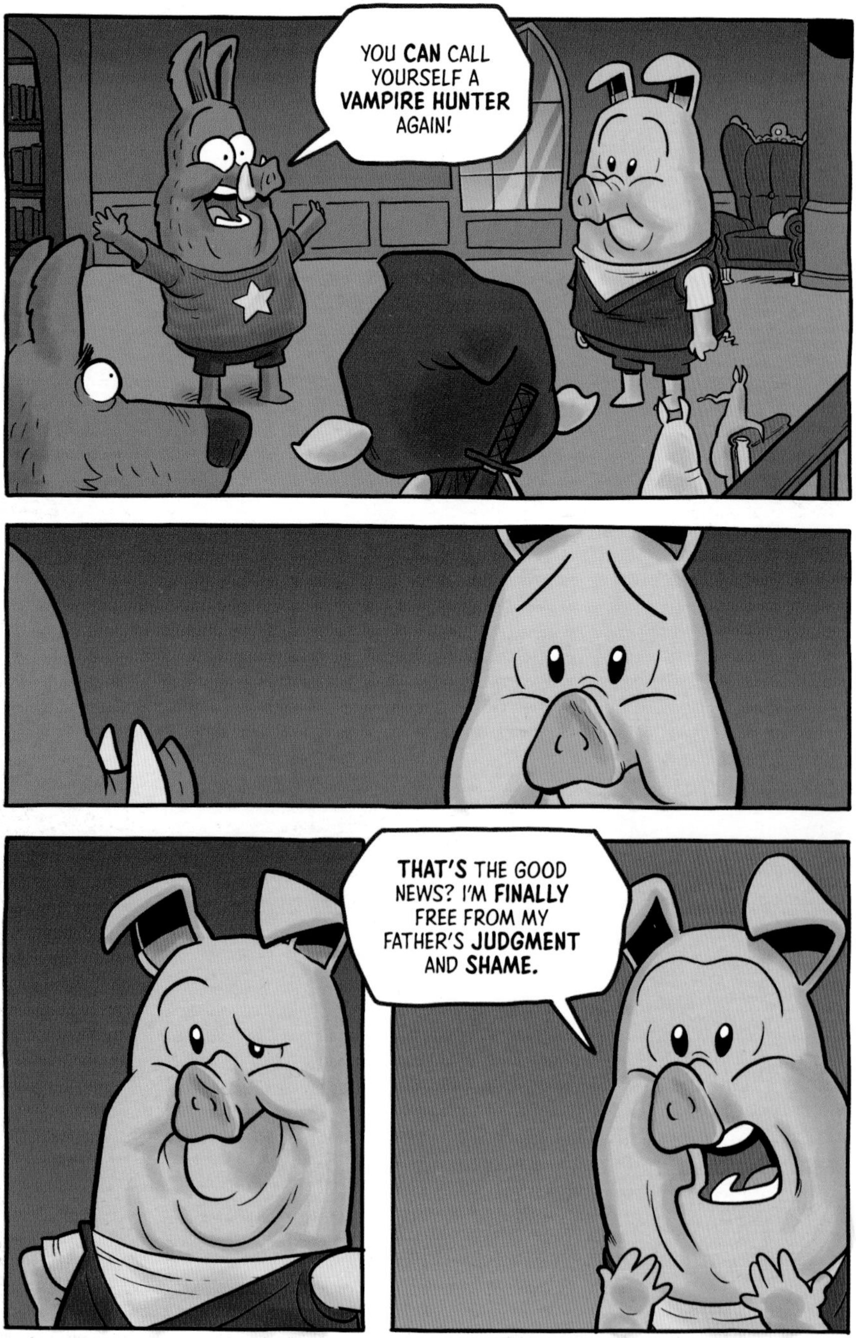
YOU CAN CALL YOURSELF A VAMPIRE HUNTER AGAIN!
THAT'S THE GOOD NEWS? I'M FINALLY FREE FROM MY FATHER'S JUDGMENT AND SHAME.

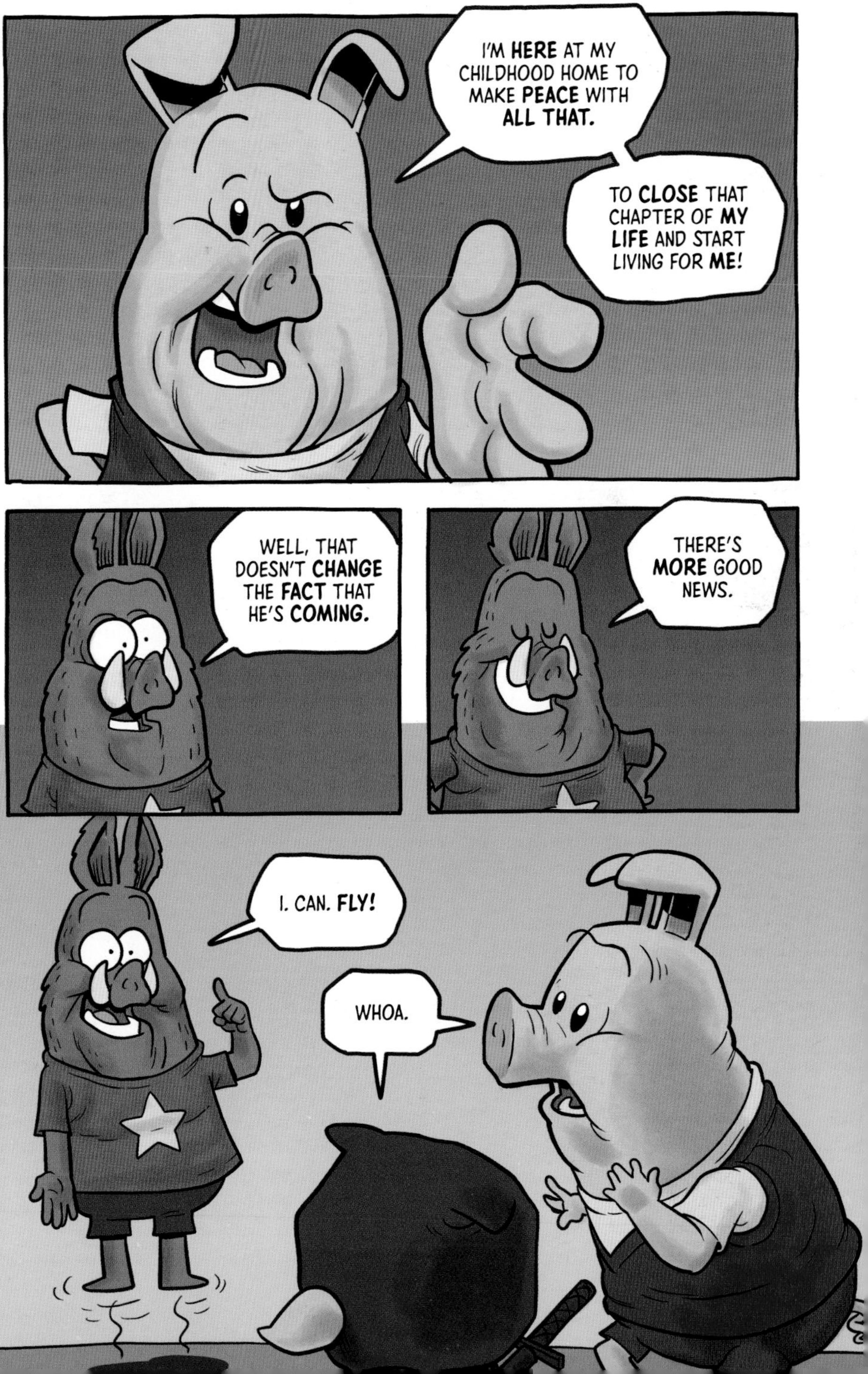
I'M HERE AT MY CHILDHOOD HOME TO MAKE PEACE WITH ALL THAT.
TO CLOSE THAT CHAPTER OF MY LIFE AND START LIVING FOR ME!
WELL, THAT DOESN'T CHANGE THE FACT THAT HE'S COMING.
THERE'S MORE GOOD NEWS.
I. CAN. FLY!
WHOA.

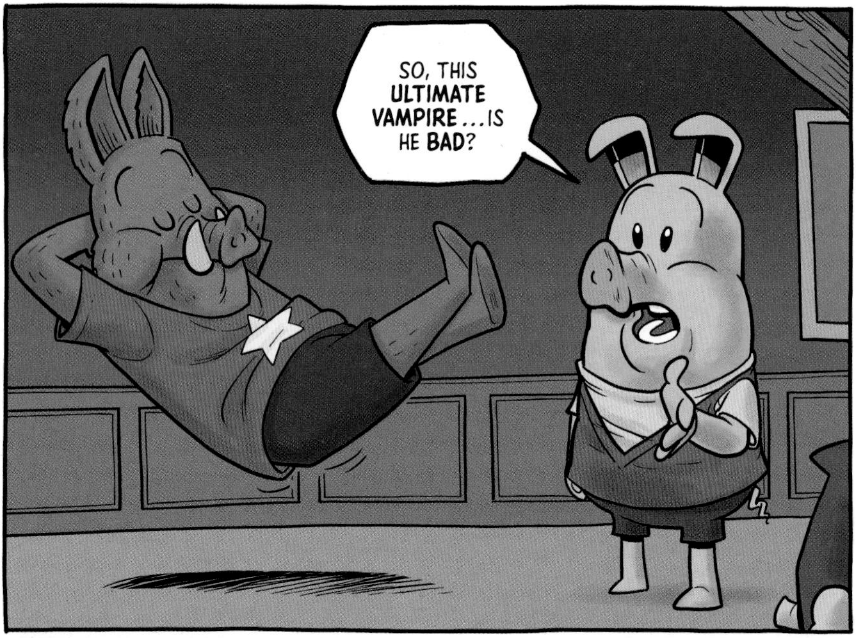
SO, THIS ULTIMATE VAMPIRE...IS HE BAD?

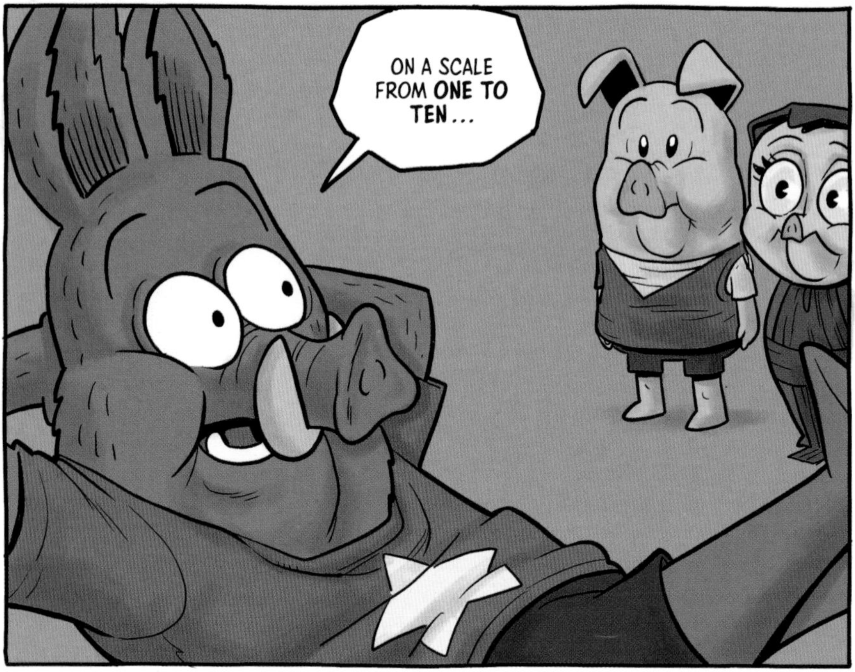
ON A SCALE FROM ONE TO TEN...

...HE'S AN ELEVEN.

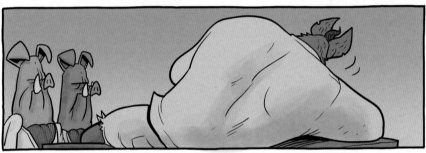

CHAPTER SEVEN

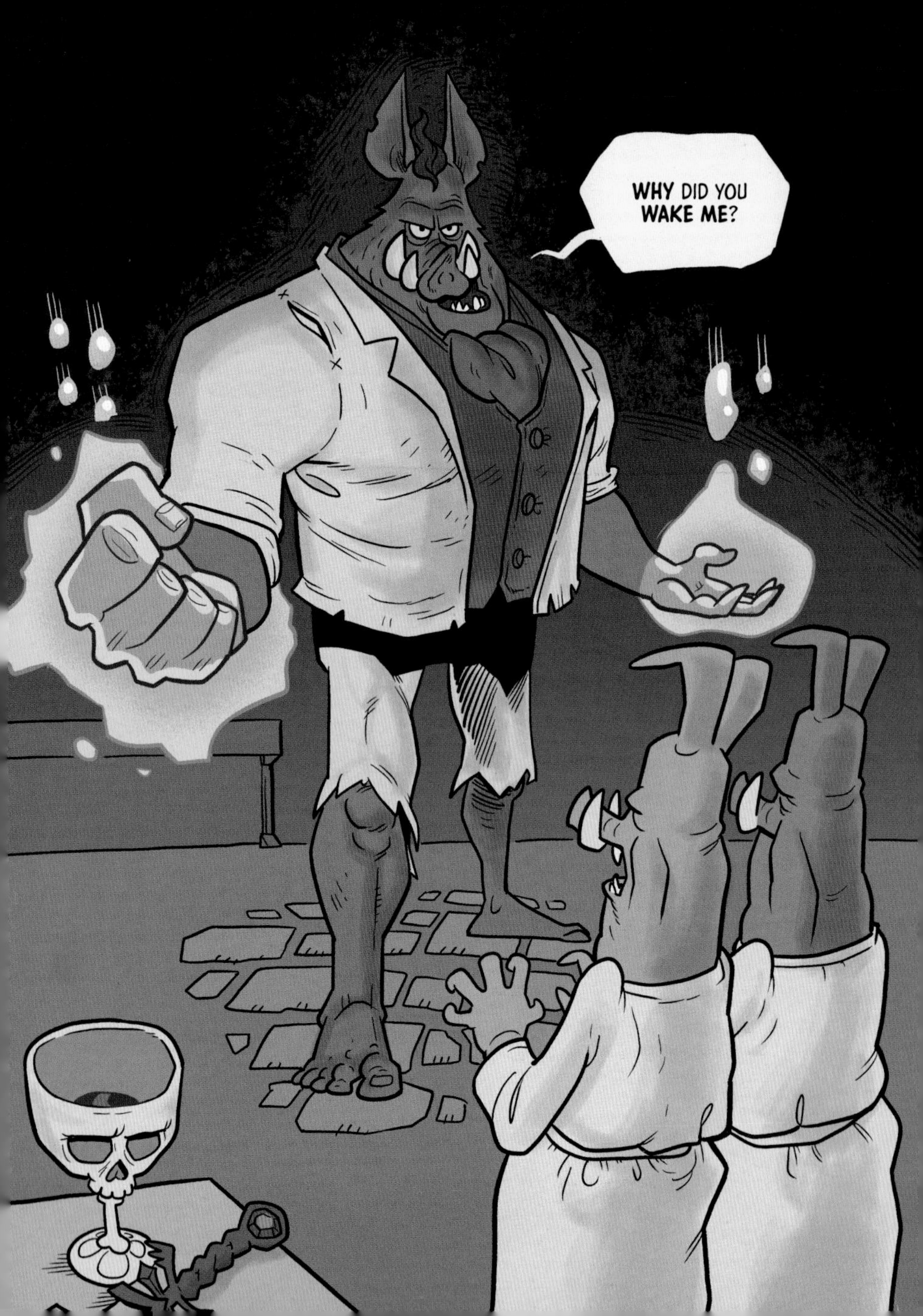
WHY DID YOU WAKE ME?

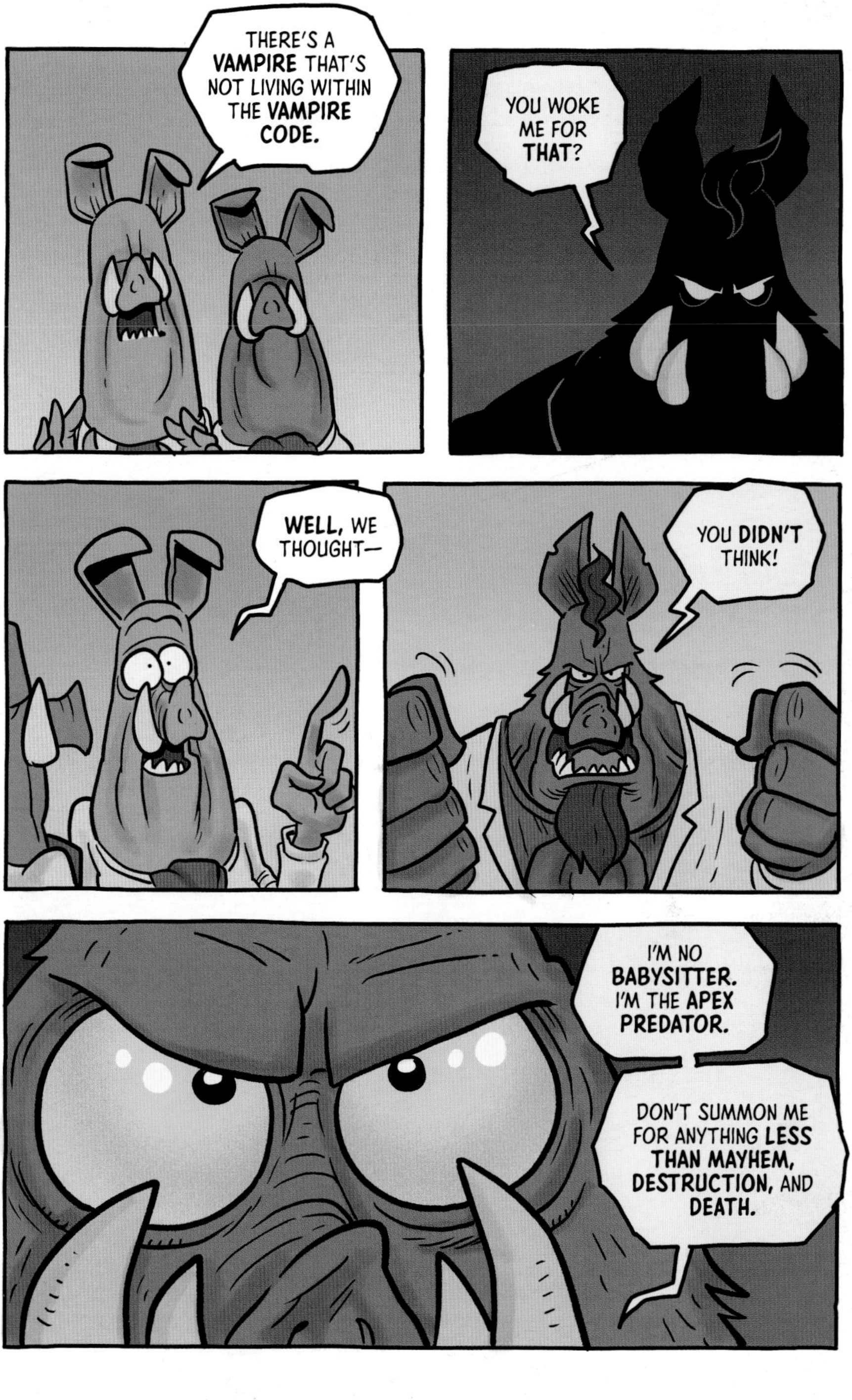
THERE'S A VAMPIRE THAT'S NOT LIVING WITHIN THE VAMPIRE CODE.
YOU WOKE ME FOR THAT?
WELL, WE THOUGHT—
YOU DIDN'T THINK!
I'M NO BABYSITTER. I'M THE APEX PREDATOR.
DON'T SUMMON ME FOR ANYTHING LESS THAN MAYHEM, DESTRUCTION, AND DEATH.

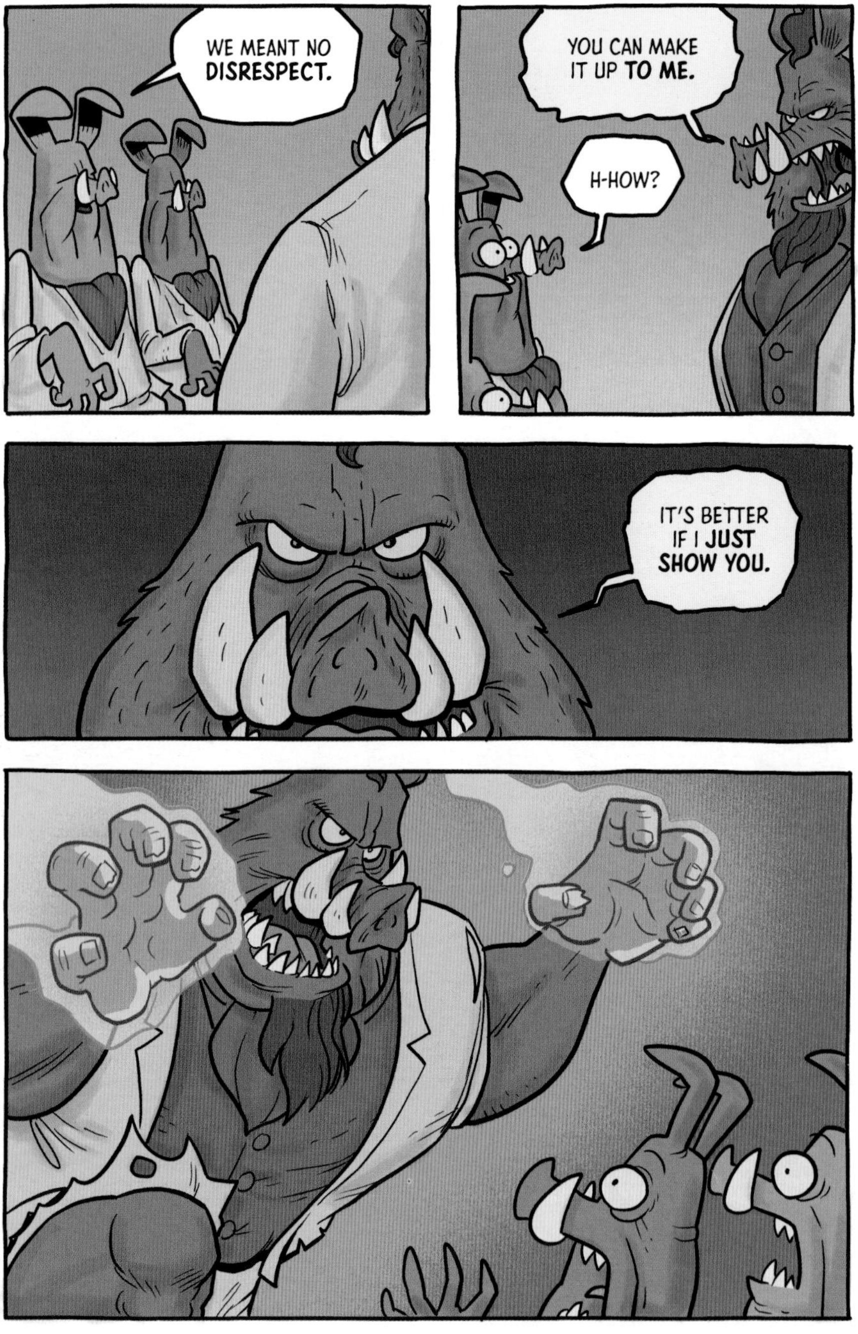
WE MEANT NO **DISRESPECT.**
YOU CAN MAKE IT UP **TO ME.**
H-HOW?
IT'S BETTER IF I **JUST SHOW YOU.**

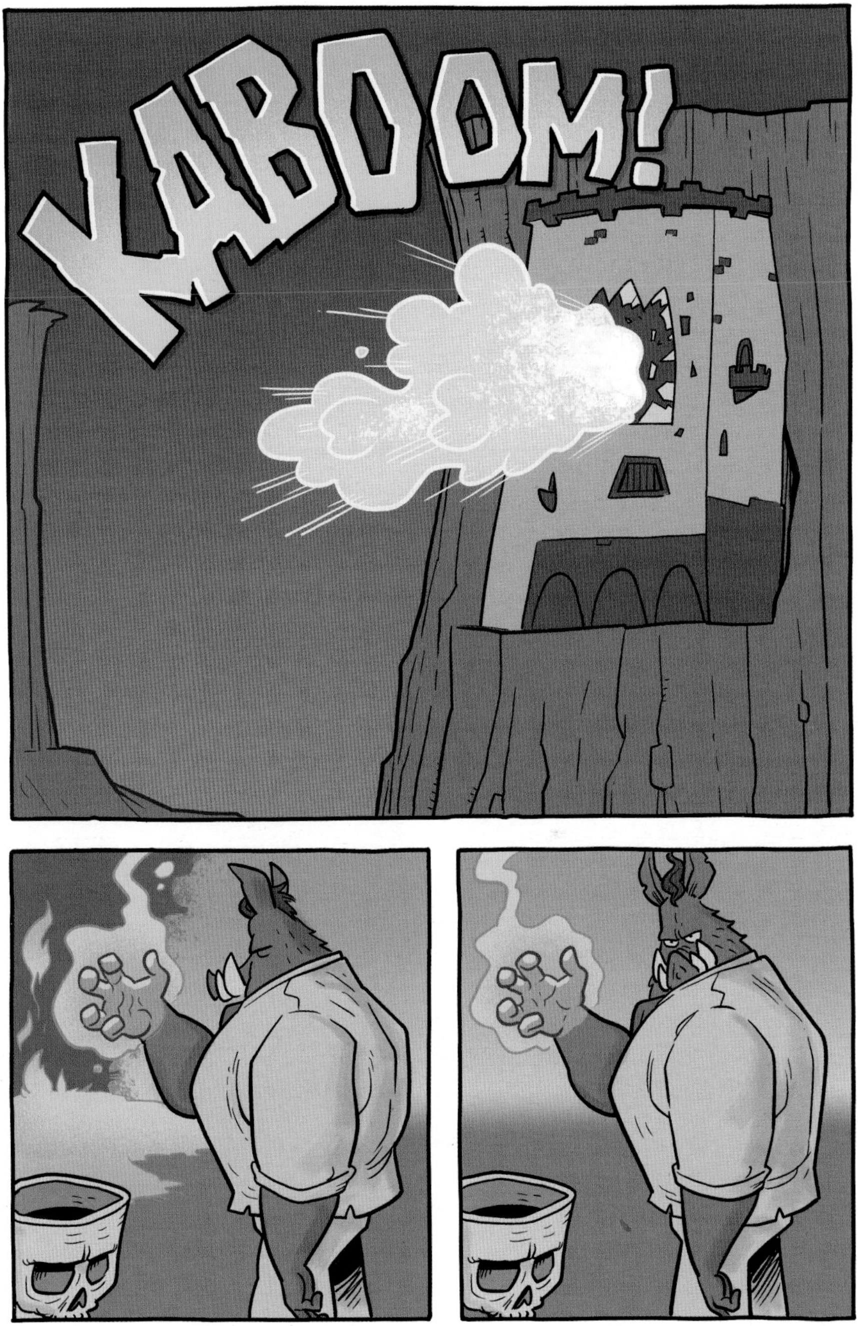
KABOOM!

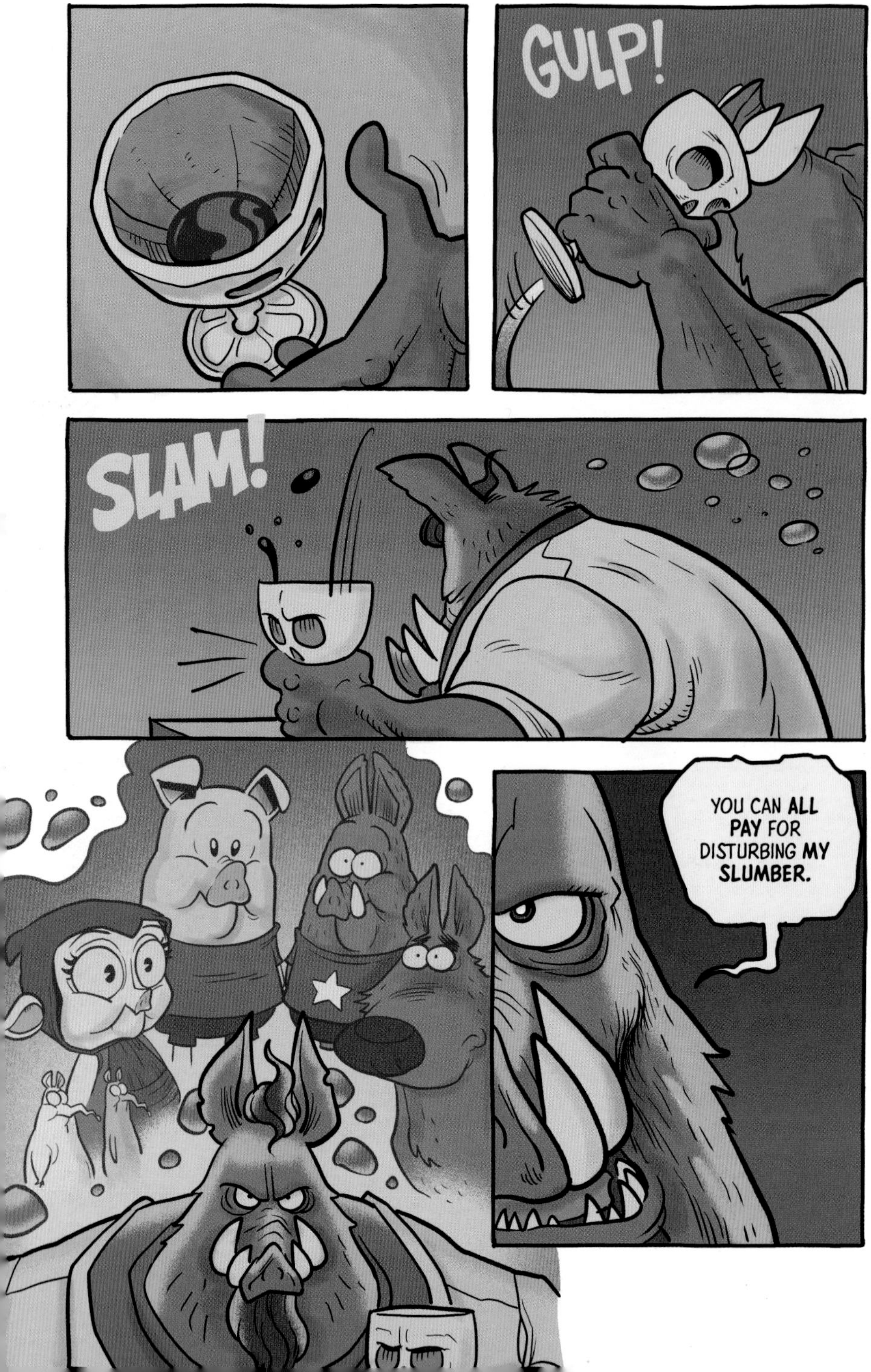
GULP!
SLAM!
YOU CAN ALL PAY FOR DISTURBING MY SLUMBER.

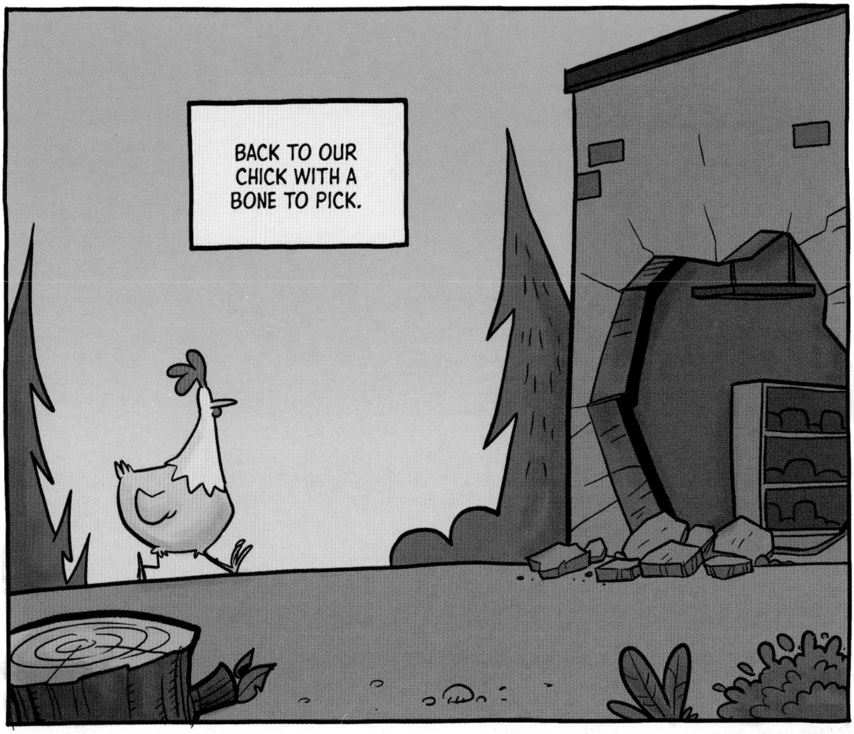
BACK TO OUR CHICK WITH A BONE TO PICK.

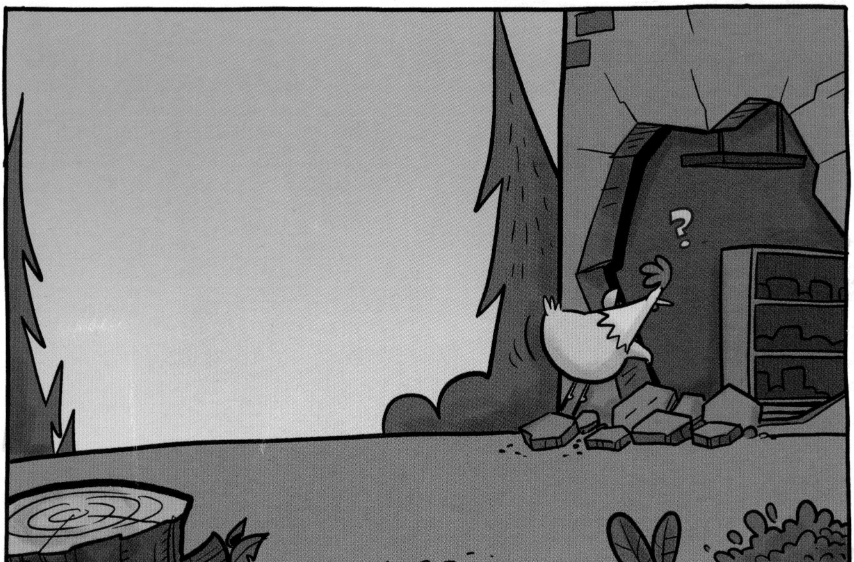
?

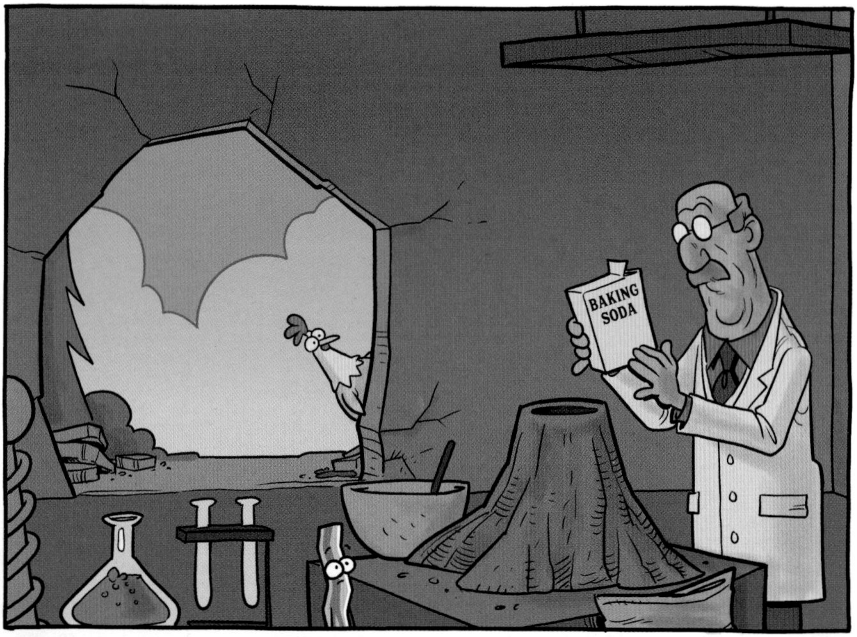
BAKING SODA

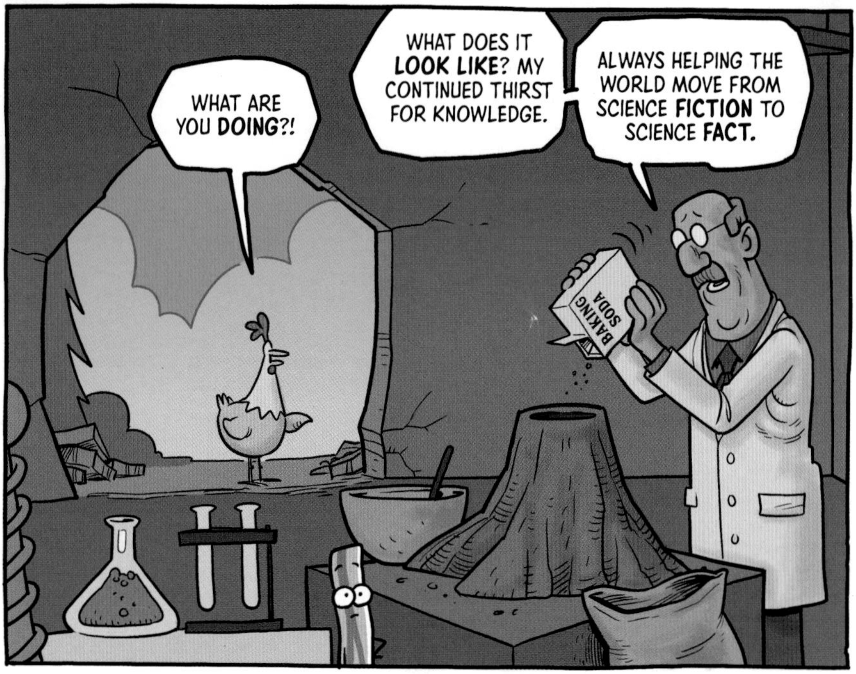
WHAT ARE YOU DOING?!
WHAT DOES IT LOOK LIKE? MY CONTINUED THIRST FOR KNOWLEDGE.
ALWAYS HELPING THE WORLD MOVE FROM SCIENCE FICTION TO SCIENCE FACT.
BAKING SODA

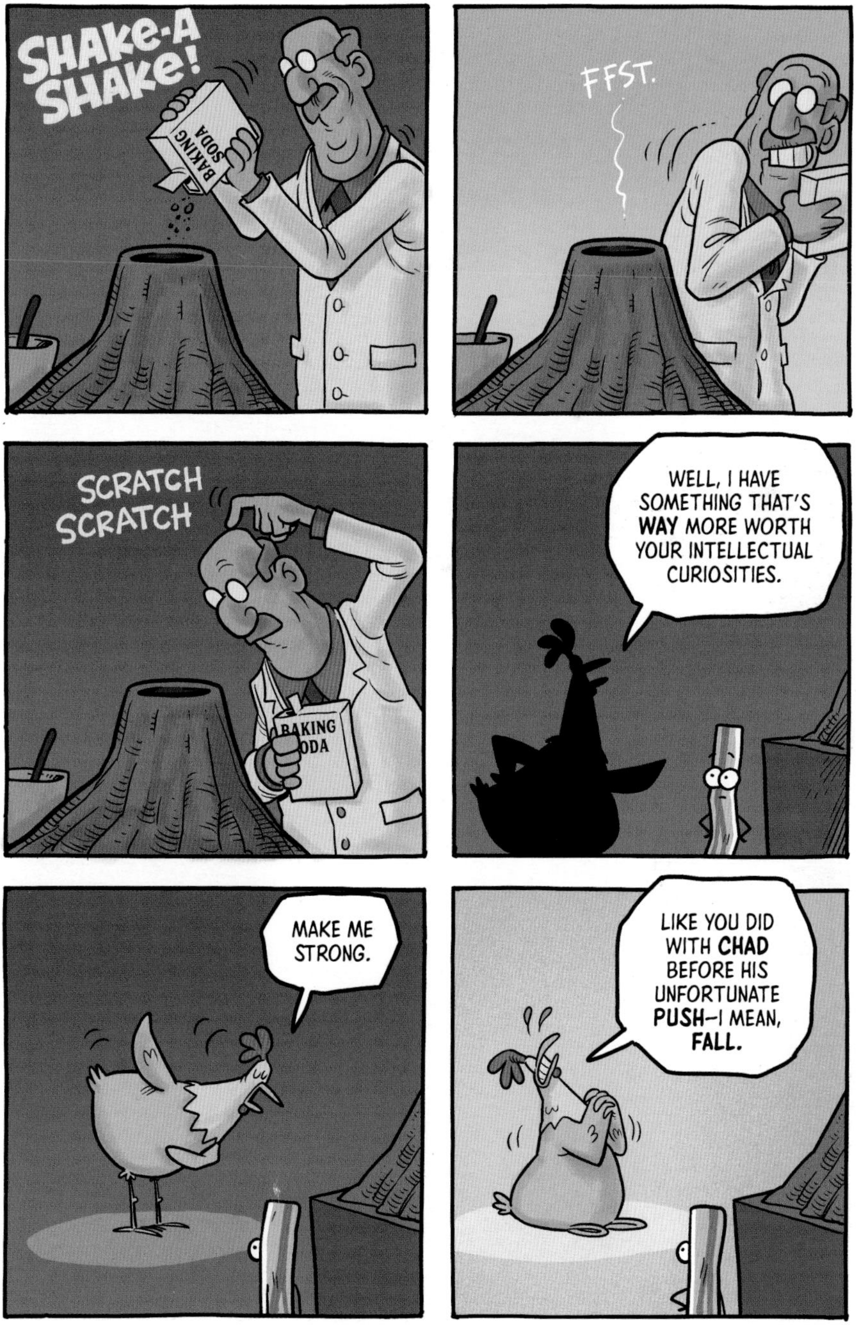
SHAKE-A SHAKE!
BAKING SODA
FFST.
SCRATCH SCRATCH
BAKING SODA
WELL, I HAVE SOMETHING THAT'S WAY MORE WORTH YOUR INTELLECTUAL CURIOSITIES.
MAKE ME STRONG.
LIKE YOU DID WITH CHAD BEFORE HIS UNFORTUNATE PUSH—I MEAN, FALL.

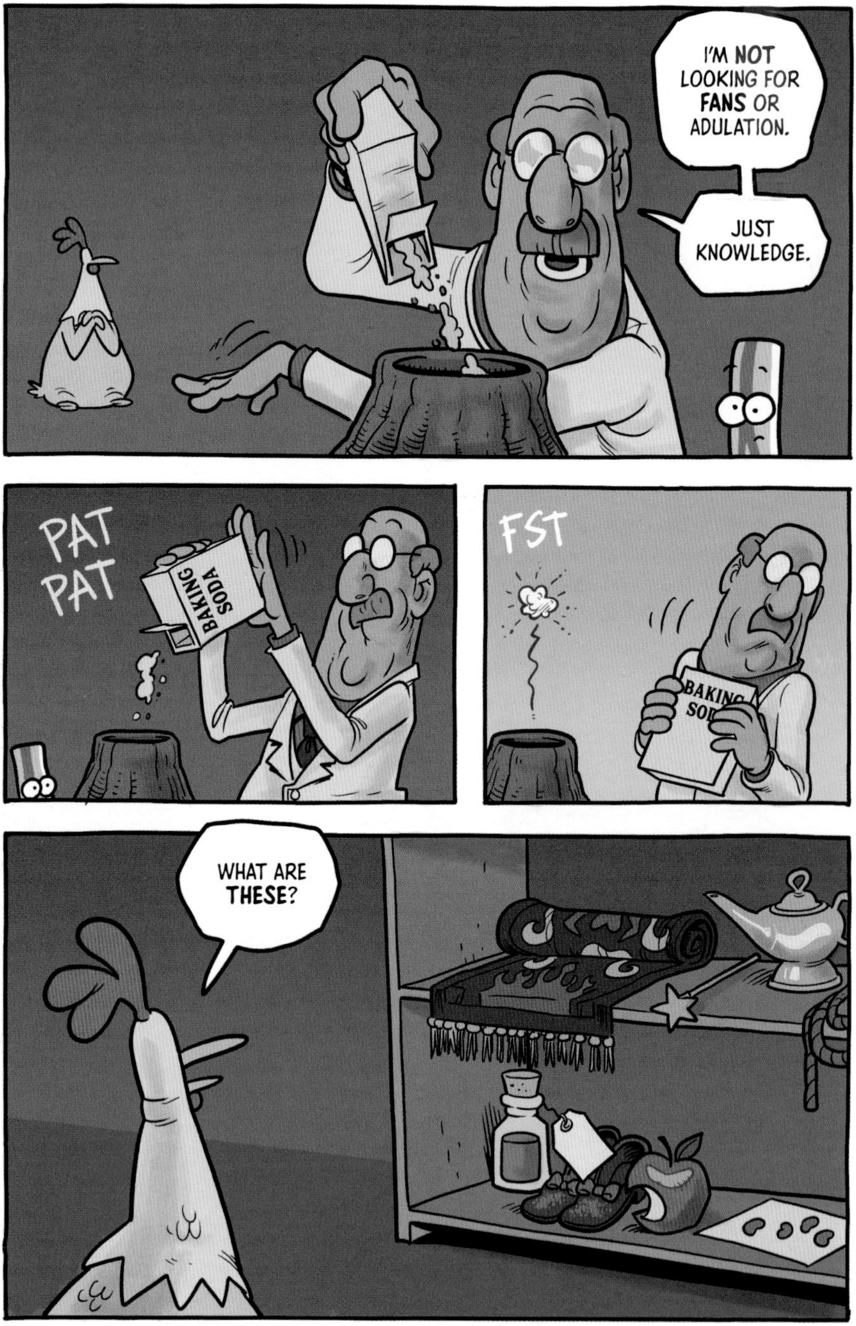
I'M NOT LOOKING FOR FANS OR ADULATION.
JUST KNOWLEDGE.
PAT PAT
BAKING SODA
FST
WHAT ARE THESE?

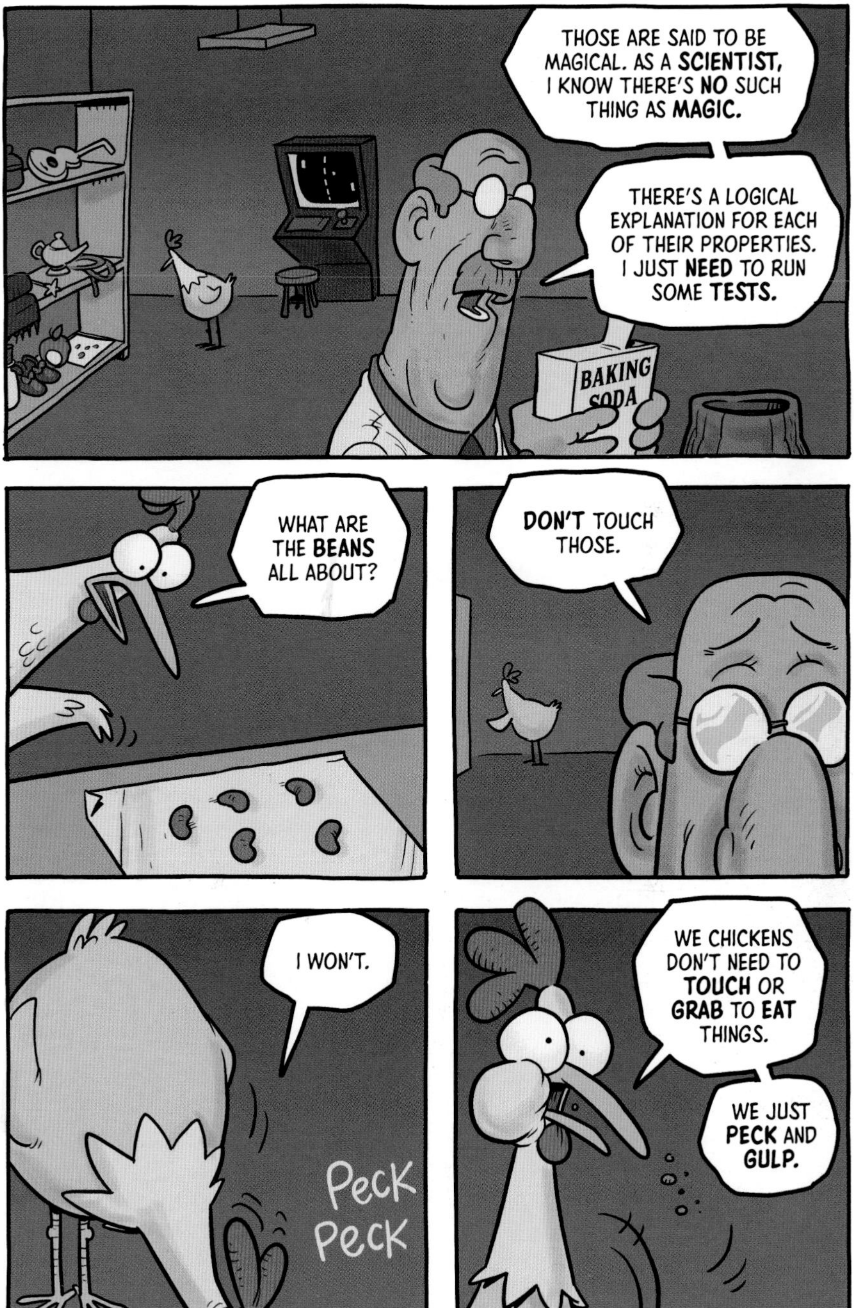
THOSE ARE SAID TO BE MAGICAL. AS A SCIENTIST, I KNOW THERE'S NO SUCH THING AS MAGIC.
THERE'S A LOGICAL EXPLANATION FOR EACH OF THEIR PROPERTIES. I JUST NEED TO RUN SOME TESTS.
BAKING SODA
WHAT ARE THE BEANS ALL ABOUT?
DON'T TOUCH THOSE.
I WON'T.
Peck Peck
WE CHICKENS DON'T NEED TO TOUCH OR GRAB TO EAT THINGS.
WE JUST PECK AND GULP.

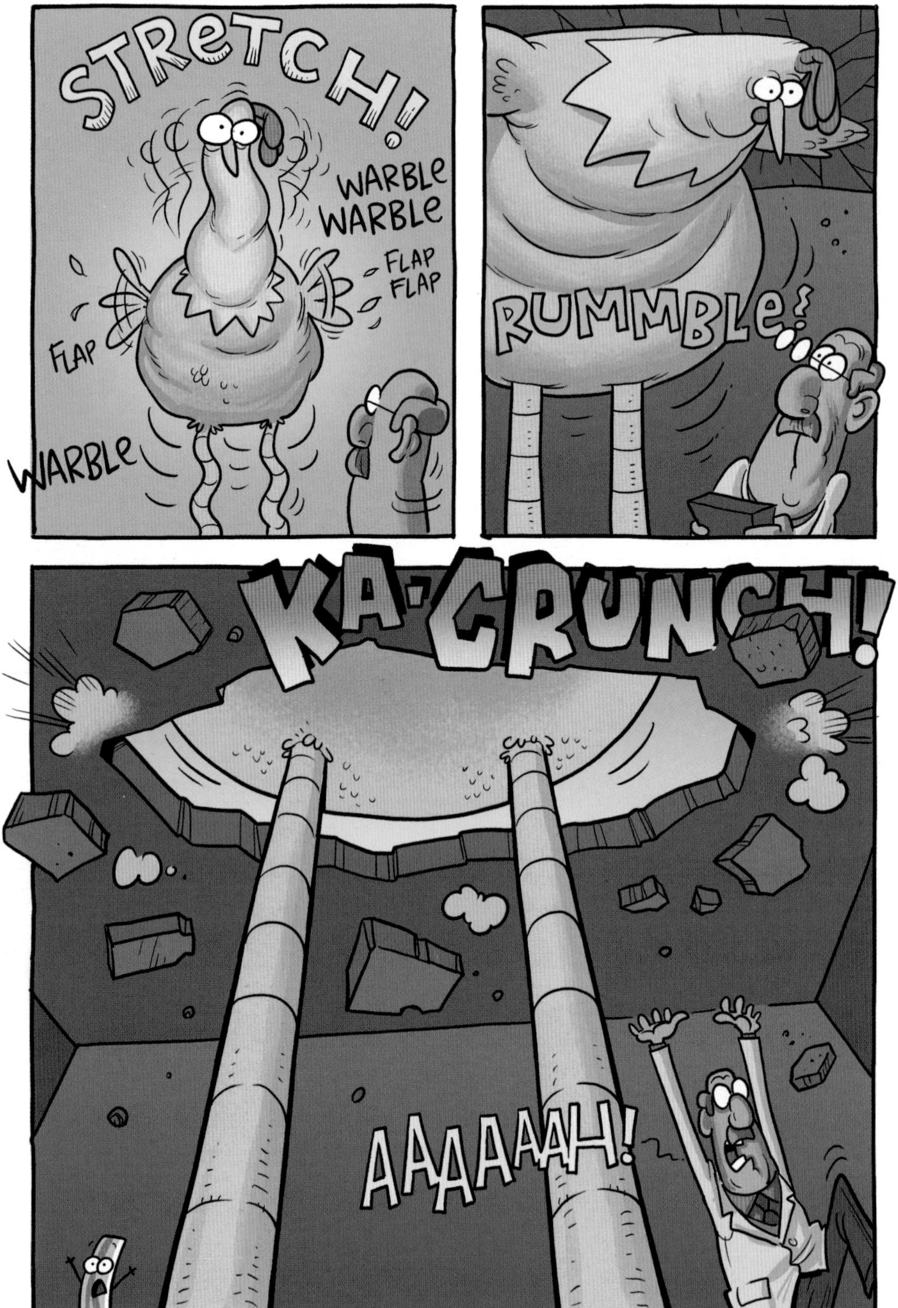
STRETCH!
WARBLE WARBLE
FLAP FLAP
FLAP
WARBLE
RUMMBLE!
KA-CRUNCH!
AAAAAAH!

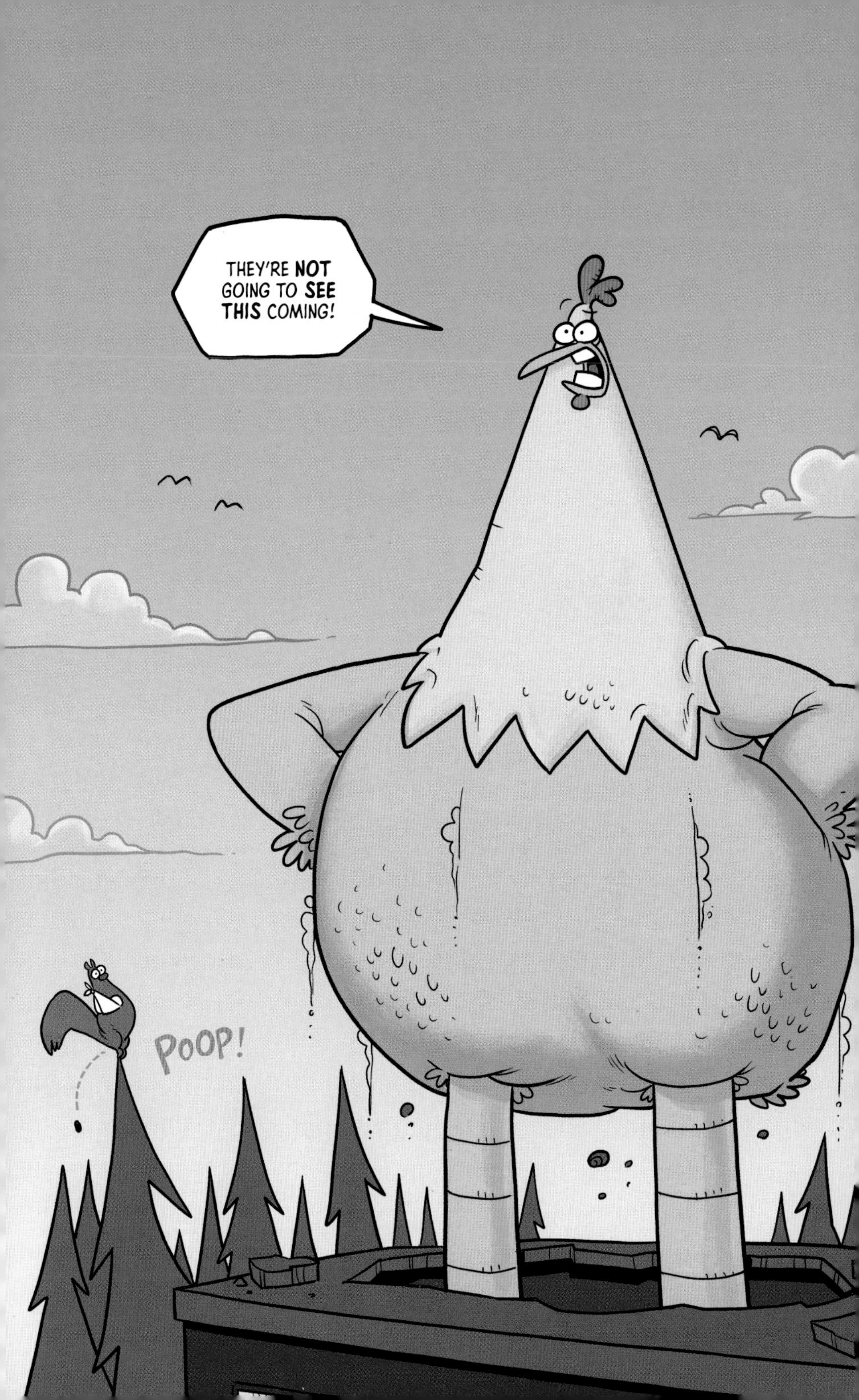
THEY'RE NOT GOING TO SEE THIS COMING!
POOP!

CHAPTER EIGHT

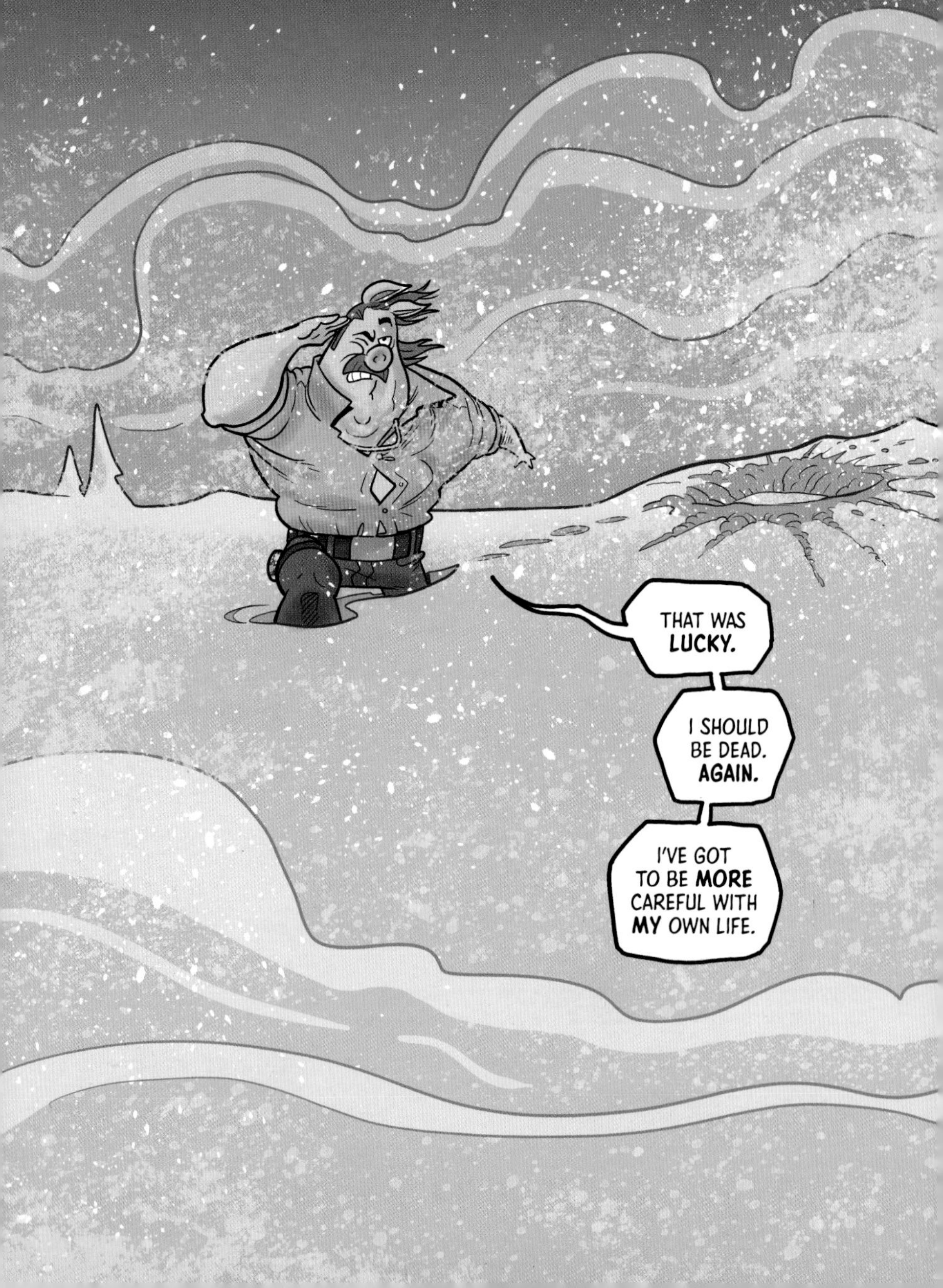
THAT WAS LUCKY.
I SHOULD BE DEAD. AGAIN.
I'VE GOT TO BE MORE CAREFUL WITH MY OWN LIFE.

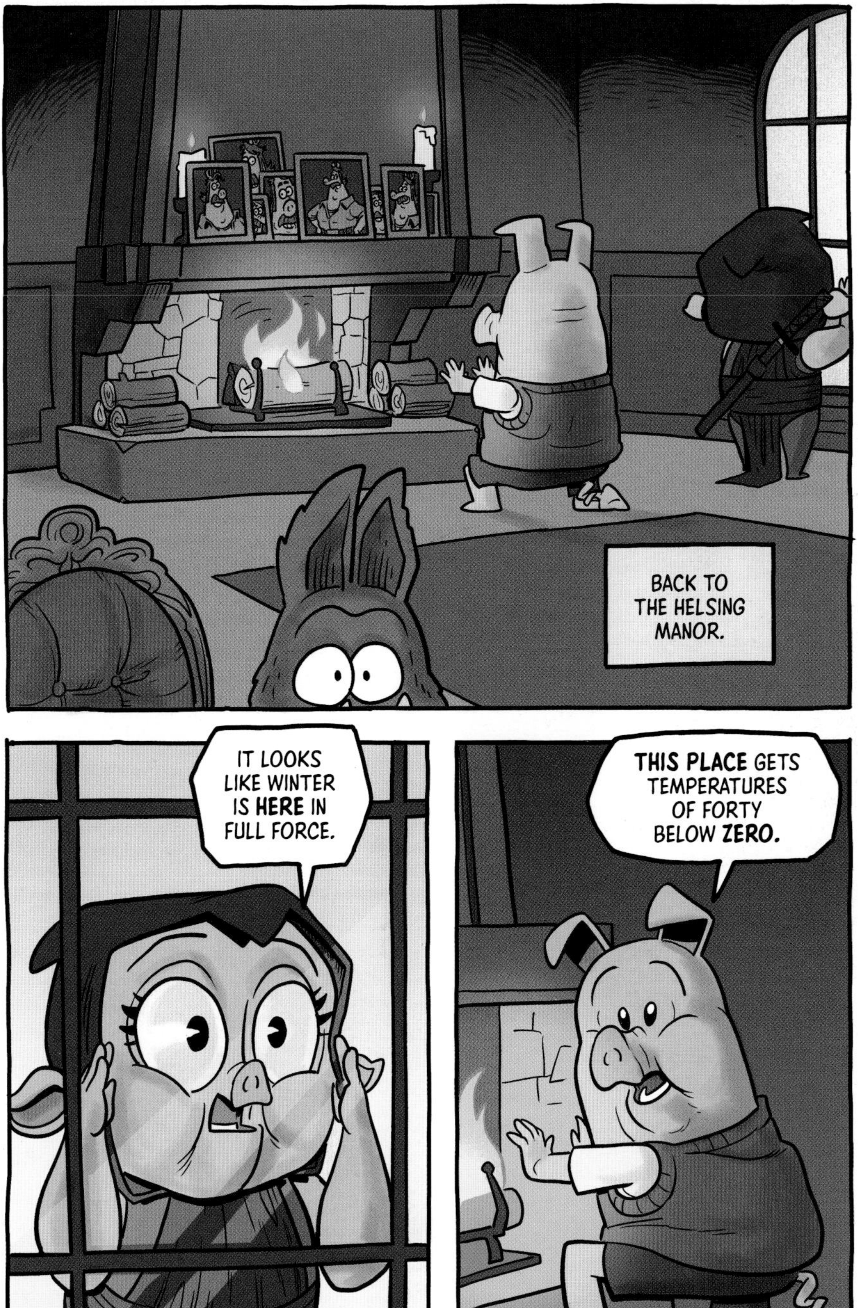
BACK TO THE HELSING MANOR.
IT LOOKS LIKE WINTER IS **HERE** IN FULL FORCE.
THIS PLACE GETS TEMPERATURES OF FORTY BELOW **ZERO.**

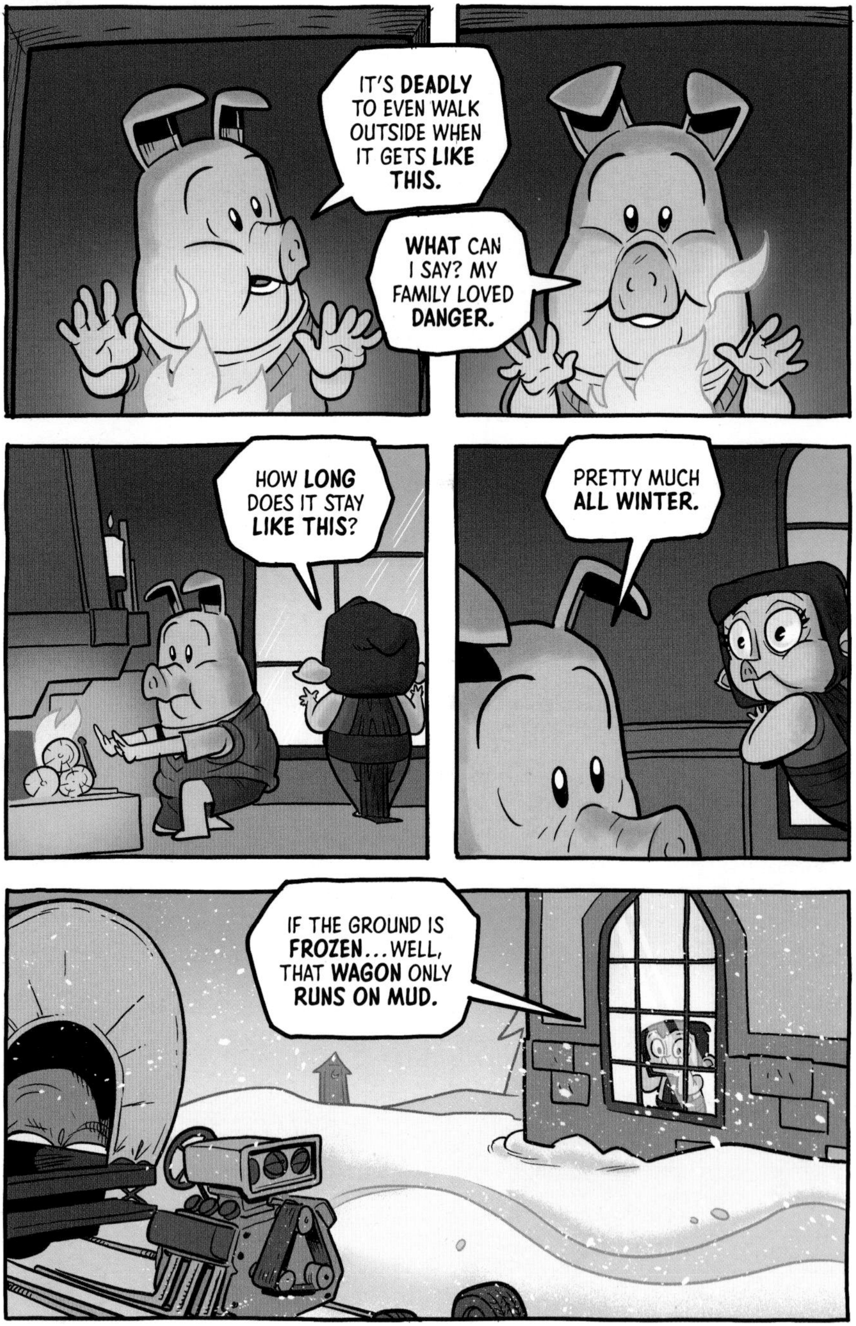
IT'S **DEADLY** TO EVEN WALK OUTSIDE WHEN IT GETS **LIKE THIS.**
WHAT CAN I SAY? MY FAMILY LOVED **DANGER.**
HOW **LONG** DOES IT STAY **LIKE THIS**?
PRETTY MUCH **ALL WINTER.**
IF THE GROUND IS **FROZEN**...WELL, THAT **WAGON** ONLY **RUNS ON MUD.**

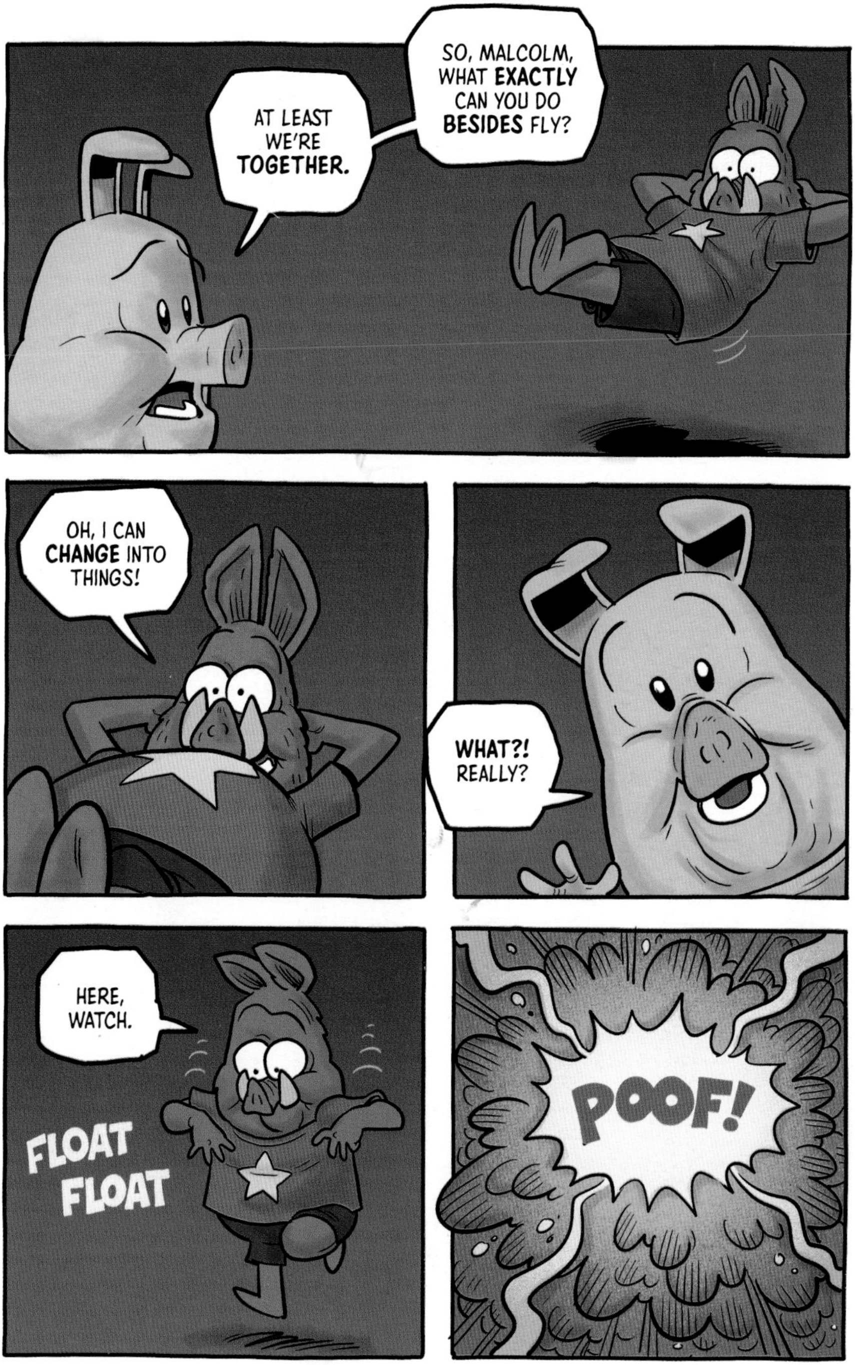

AT LEAST WE'RE TOGETHER.
SO, MALCOLM, WHAT EXACTLY CAN YOU DO BESIDES FLY?
OH, I CAN CHANGE INTO THINGS!
WHAT?! REALLY?
HERE, WATCH.
FLOAT FLOAT
POOF!

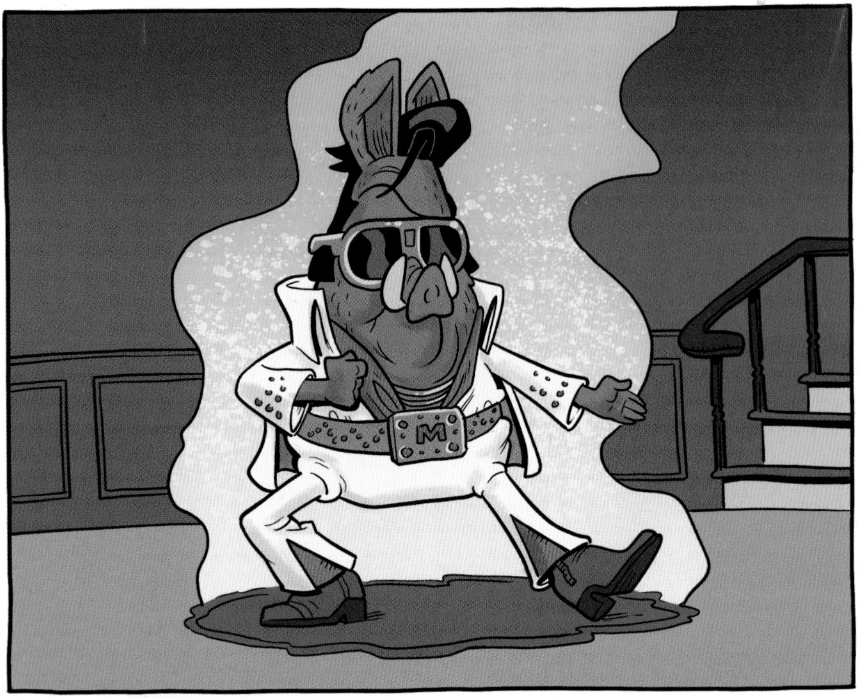

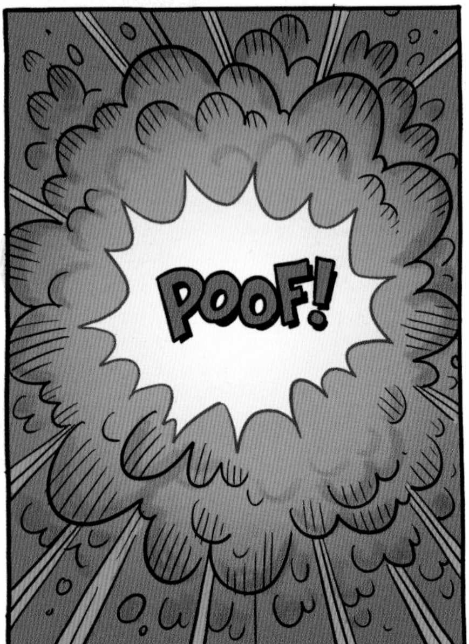
POOF!

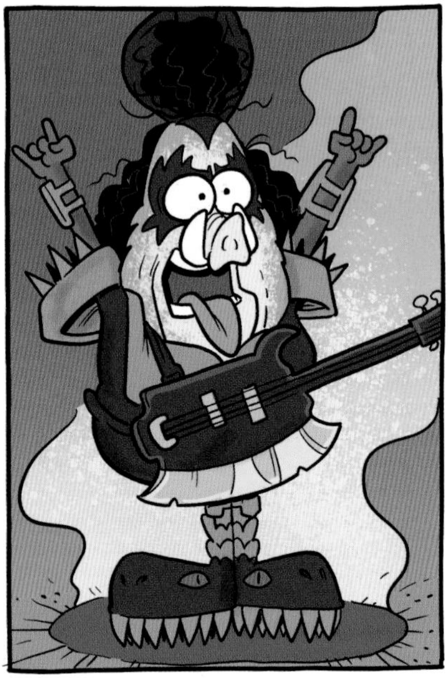

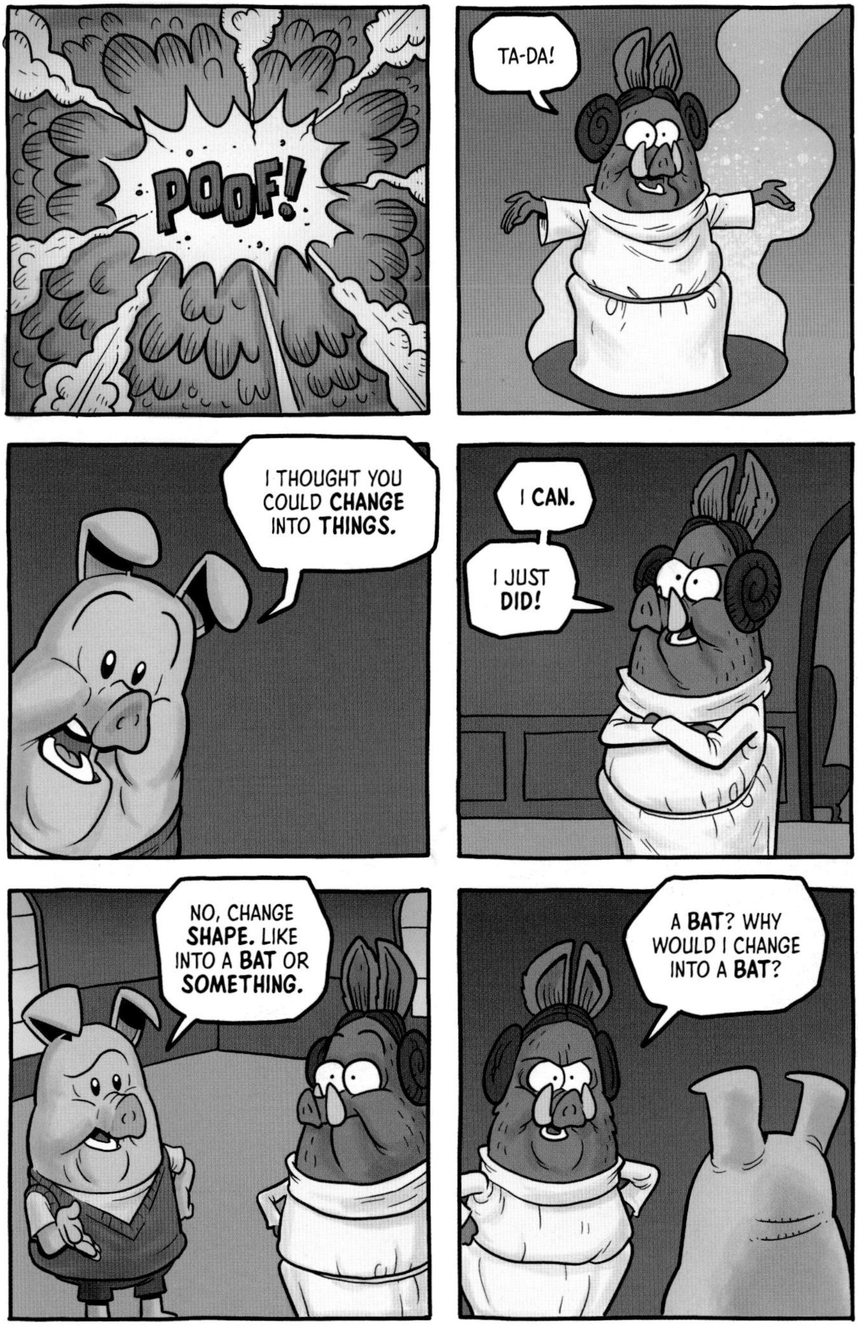
POOF!
TA-DA!
I THOUGHT YOU COULD CHANGE INTO THINGS.
I CAN.
I JUST DID!
NO, CHANGE SHAPE. LIKE INTO A BAT OR SOMETHING.
A BAT? WHY WOULD I CHANGE INTO A BAT?

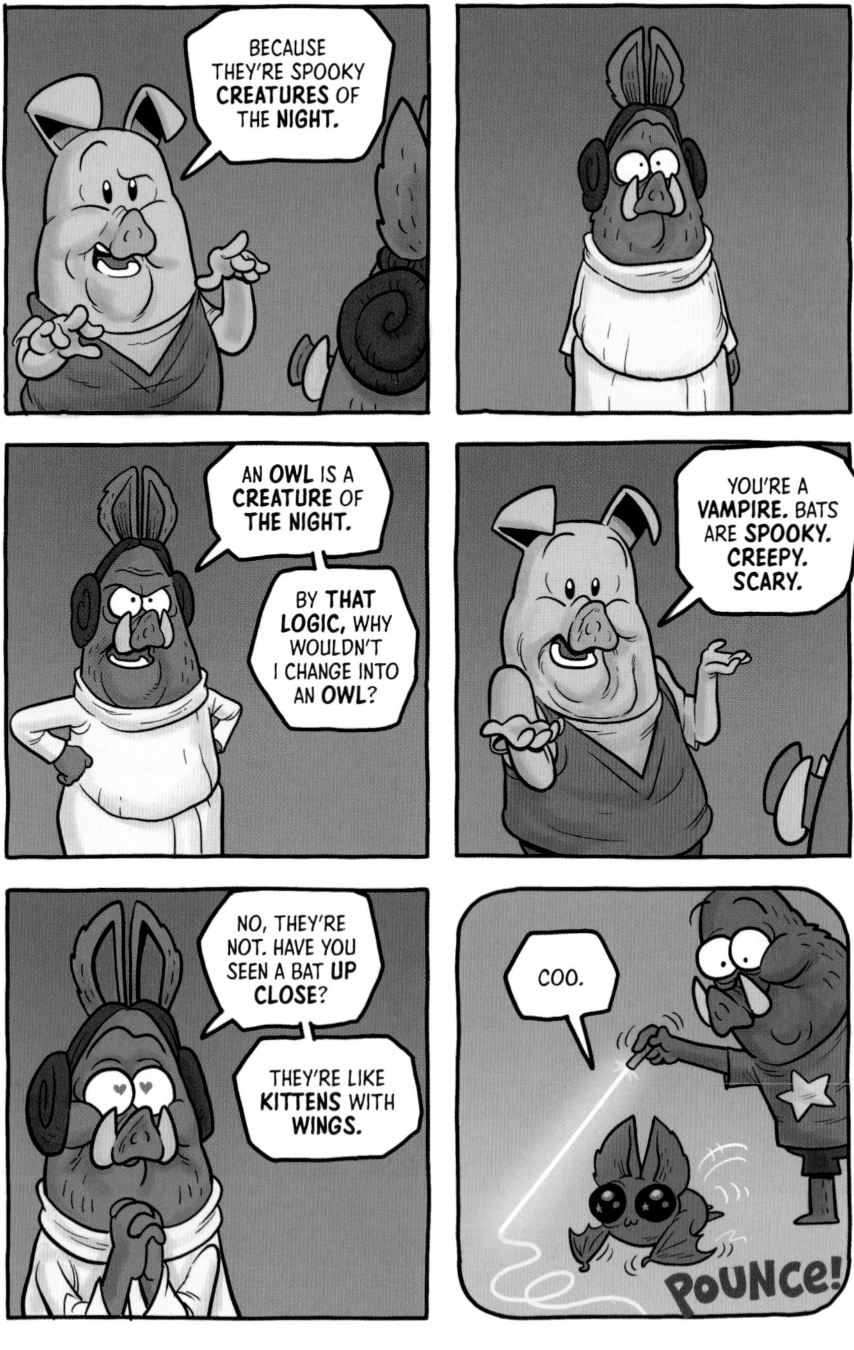
BECAUSE THEY'RE SPOOKY CREATURES OF THE NIGHT.
AN OWL IS A CREATURE OF THE NIGHT.
BY THAT LOGIC, WHY WOULDN'T I CHANGE INTO AN OWL?
YOU'RE A VAMPIRE. BATS ARE SPOOKY. CREEPY. SCARY.
NO, THEY'RE NOT. HAVE YOU SEEN A BAT UP CLOSE?
THEY'RE LIKE KITTENS WITH WINGS.
COO.
POUNCE!

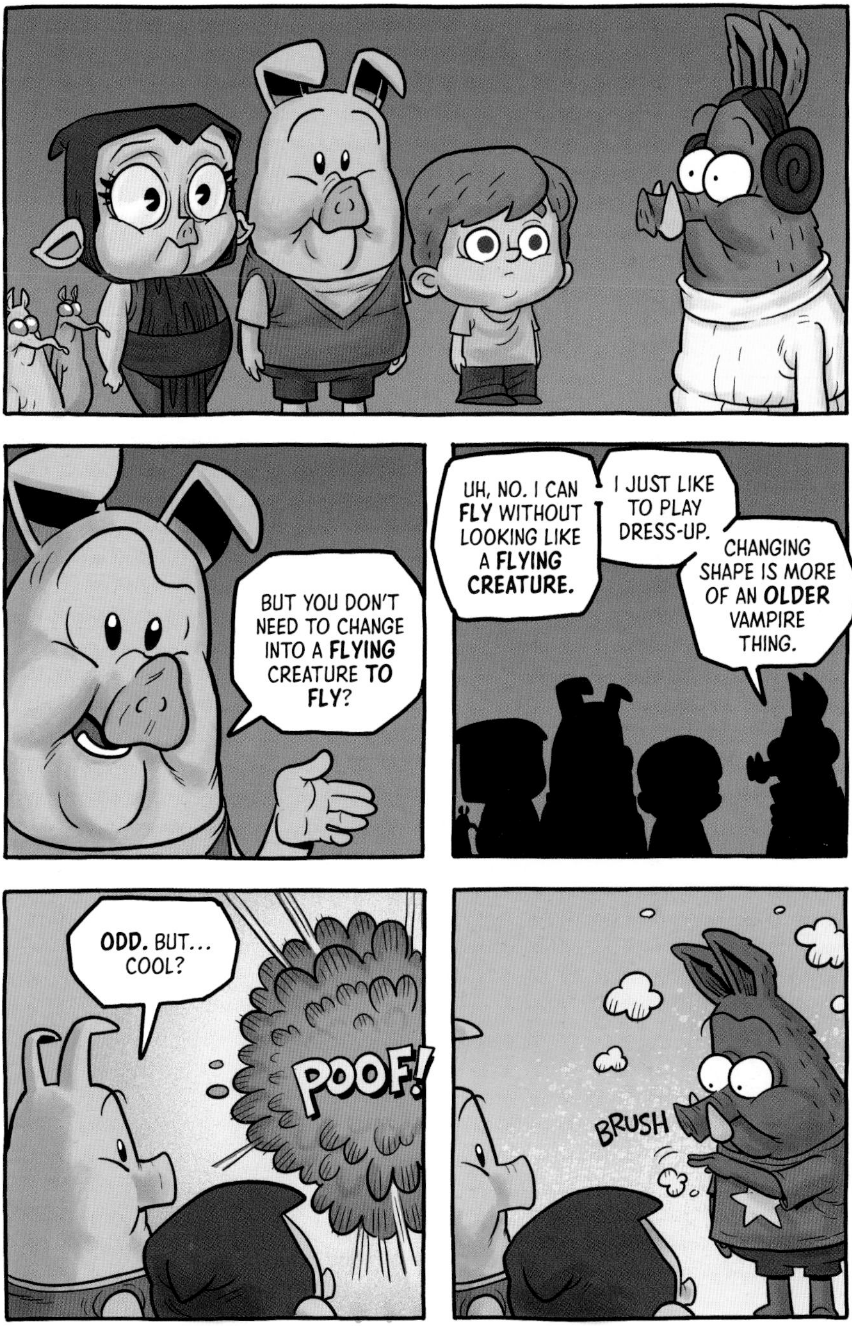
BUT YOU DON'T NEED TO CHANGE INTO A FLYING CREATURE TO FLY?
UH, NO. I CAN FLY WITHOUT LOOKING LIKE A FLYING CREATURE.
I JUST LIKE TO PLAY DRESS-UP.
CHANGING SHAPE IS MORE OF AN OLDER VAMPIRE THING.
ODD. BUT... COOL?
POOF!
BRUSH

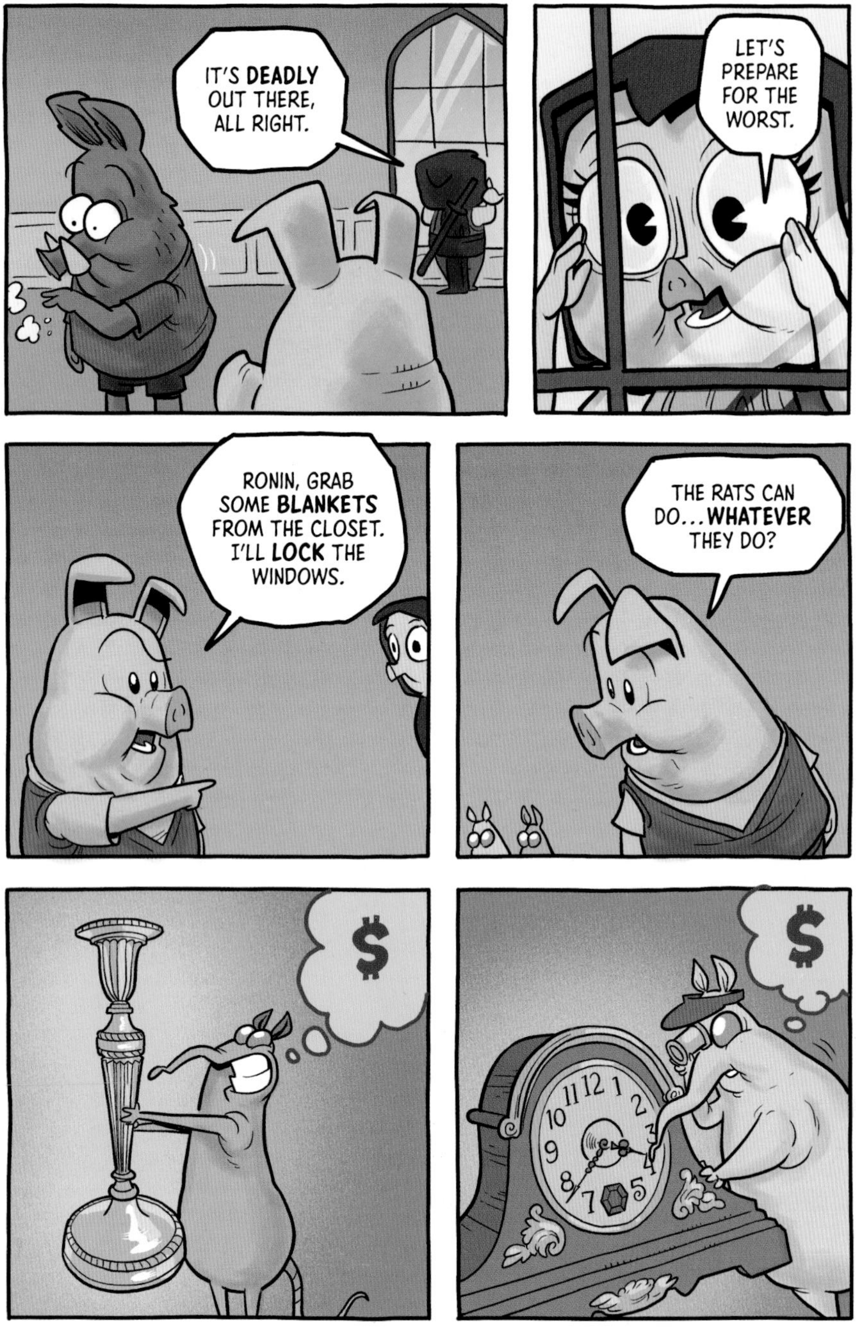
IT'S DEADLY OUT THERE, ALL RIGHT.
LET'S PREPARE FOR THE WORST.
RONIN, GRAB SOME BLANKETS FROM THE CLOSET. I'LL LOCK THE WINDOWS.
THE RATS CAN DO...WHATEVER THEY DO?
$
$

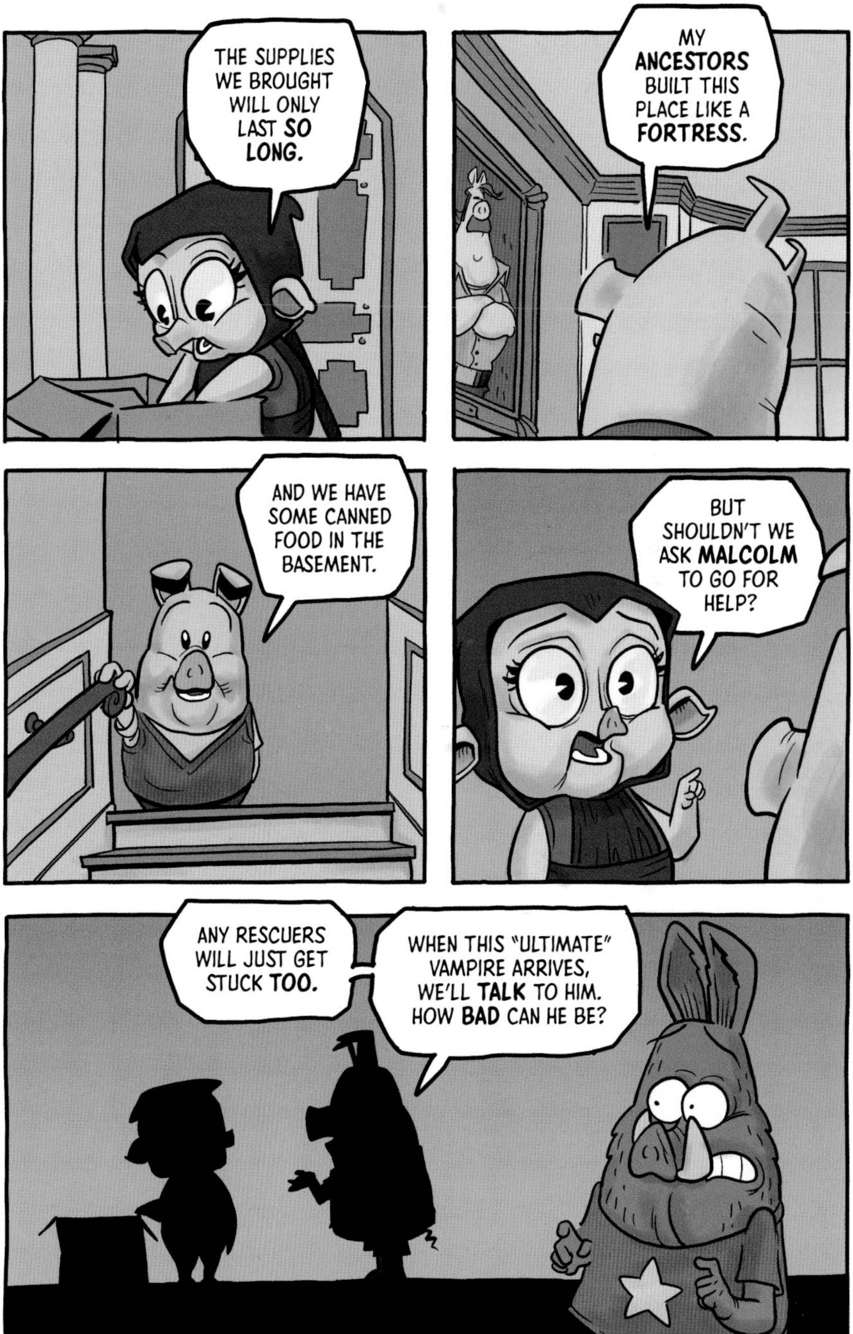
THE SUPPLIES WE BROUGHT WILL ONLY LAST **SO LONG.**
MY **ANCESTORS** BUILT THIS PLACE LIKE A **FORTRESS.**
AND WE HAVE SOME CANNED FOOD IN THE BASEMENT.
BUT SHOULDN'T WE ASK **MALCOLM** TO GO FOR HELP?
ANY RESCUERS WILL JUST GET STUCK **TOO.**
WHEN THIS "ULTIMATE" VAMPIRE ARRIVES, WE'LL **TALK** TO HIM. HOW **BAD** CAN HE BE?

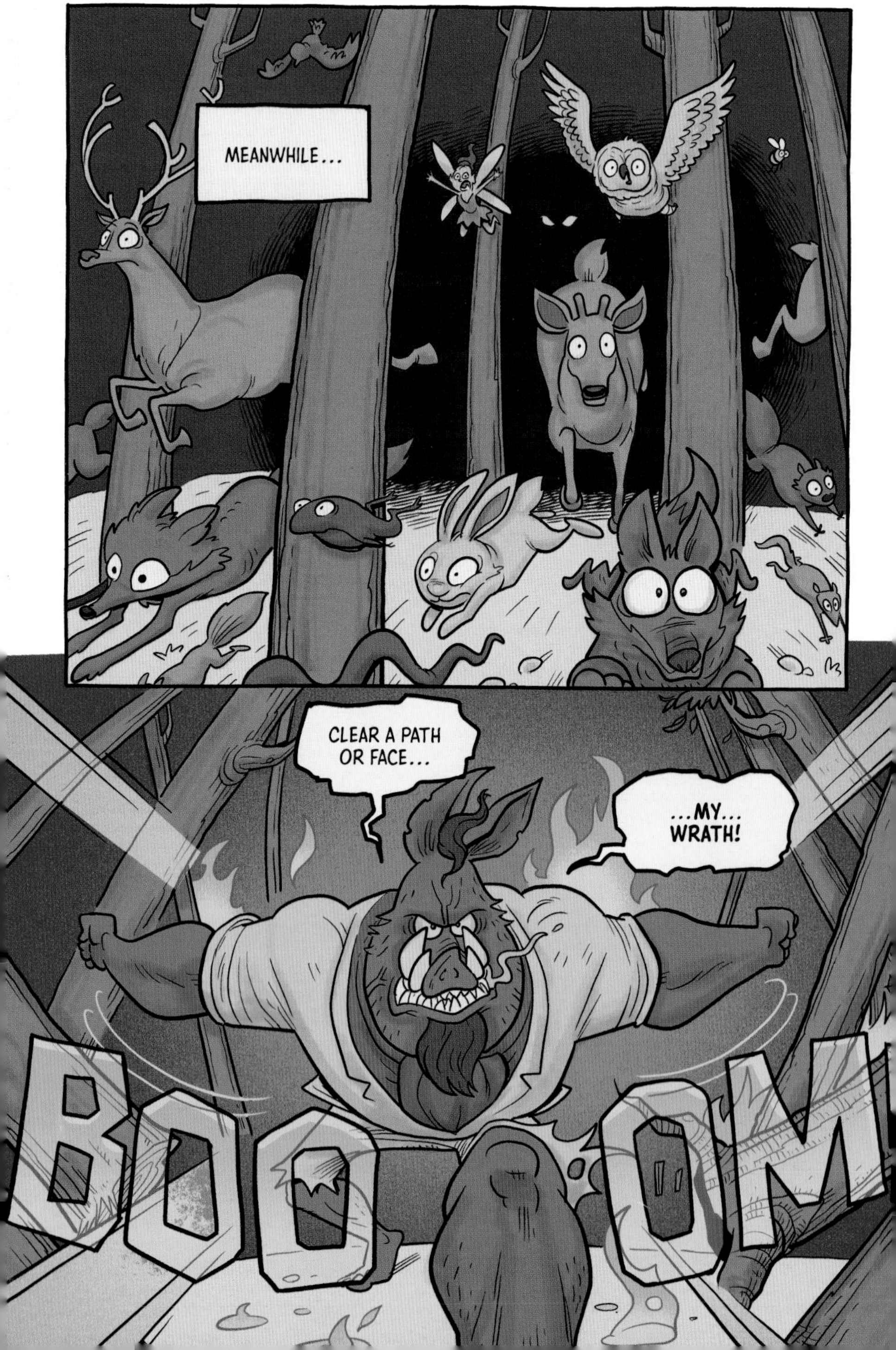
MEANWHILE...
CLEAR A PATH OR FACE...
...MY... WRATH!
BOOOM

CHAPTER NINE

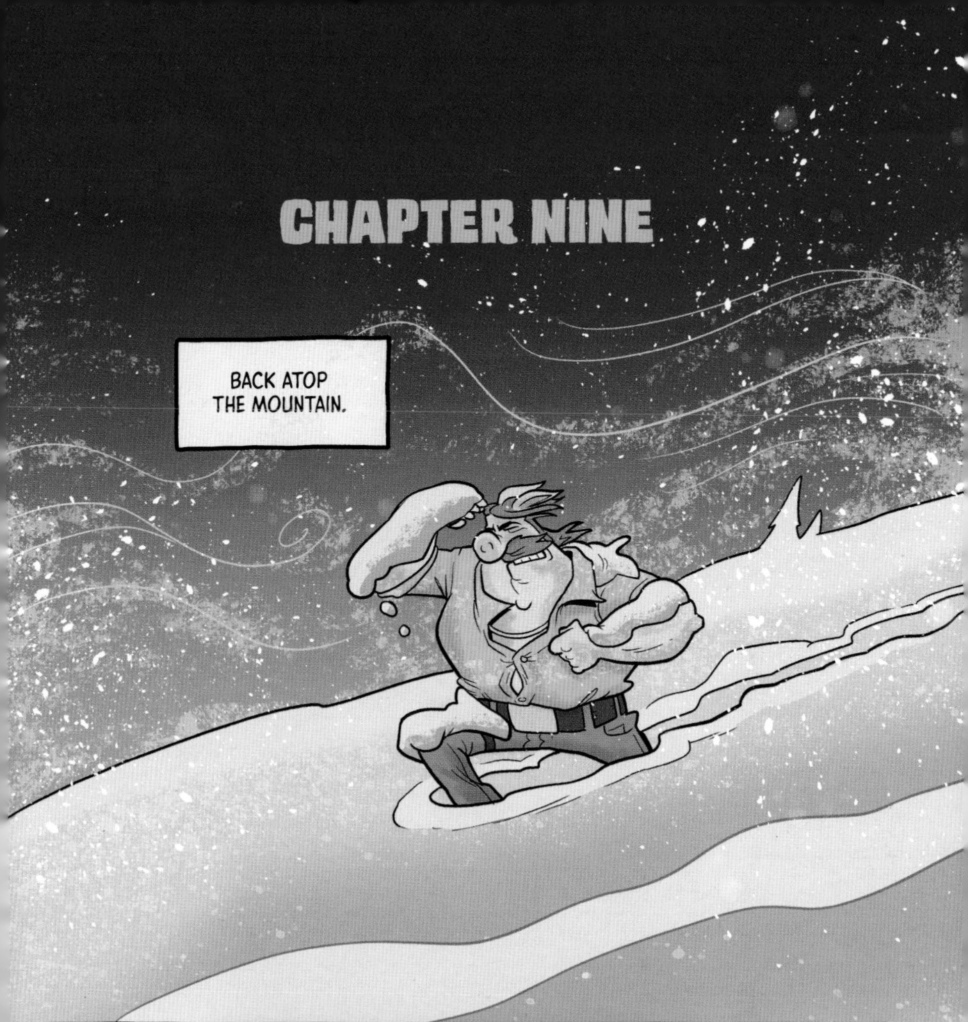
BACK ATOP THE MOUNTAIN.

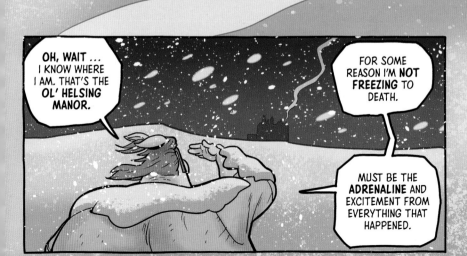

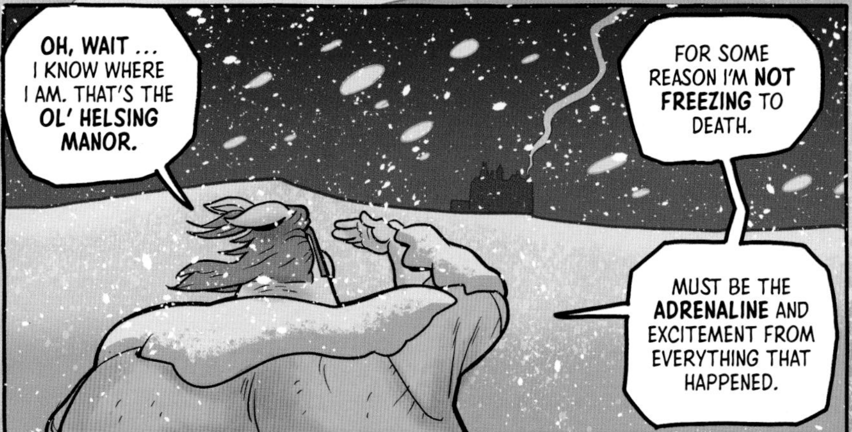
OH, WAIT ... I KNOW WHERE I AM. THAT'S THE OL' HELSING MANOR.
FOR SOME REASON I'M NOT FREEZING TO DEATH.
MUST BE THE ADRENALINE AND EXCITEMENT FROM EVERYTHING THAT HAPPENED.

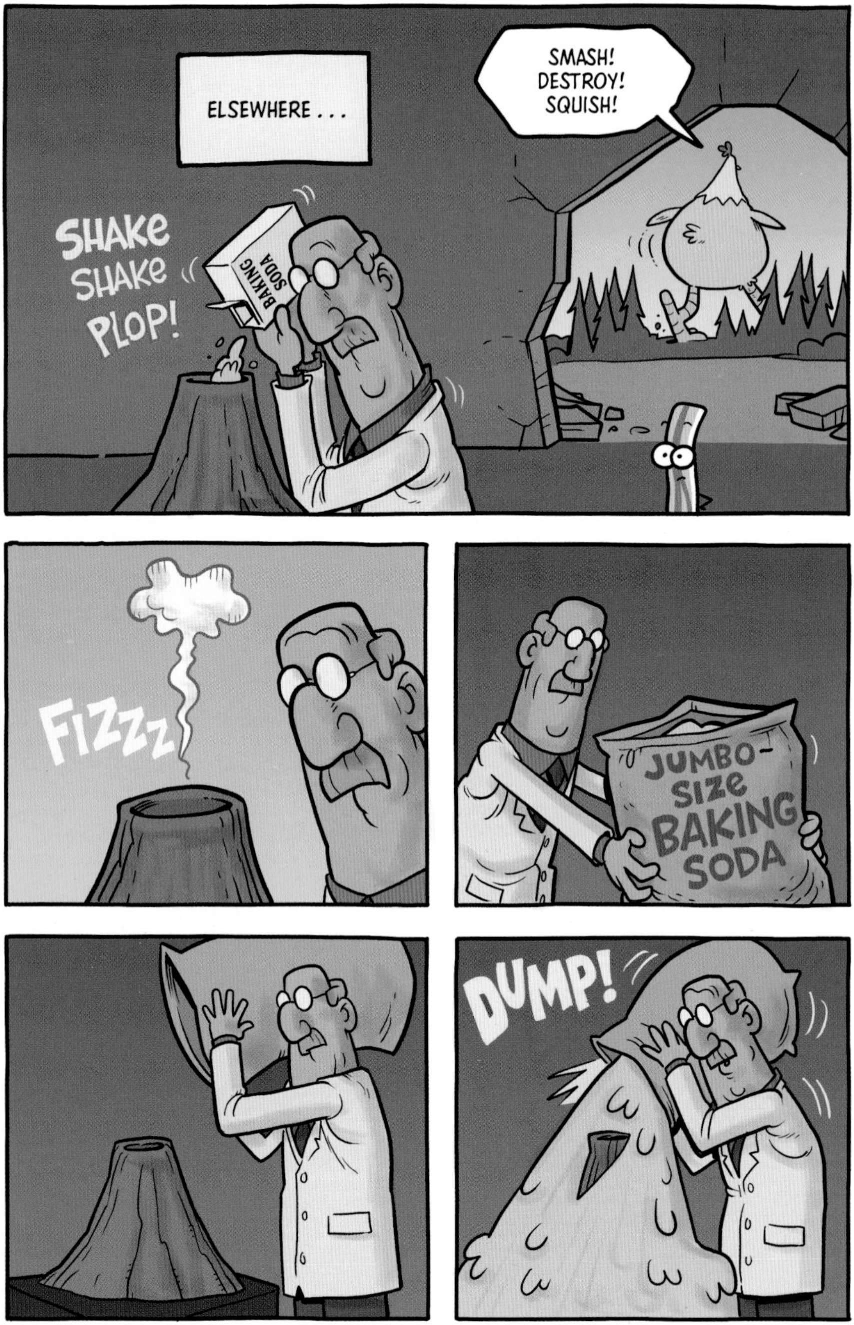
ELSEWHERE . . .
SMASH! DESTROY! SQUISH!
SHAKE SHAKE PLOP!
BAKING SODA
FIZZZ
JUMBO-SIZE BAKING SODA
DUMP!

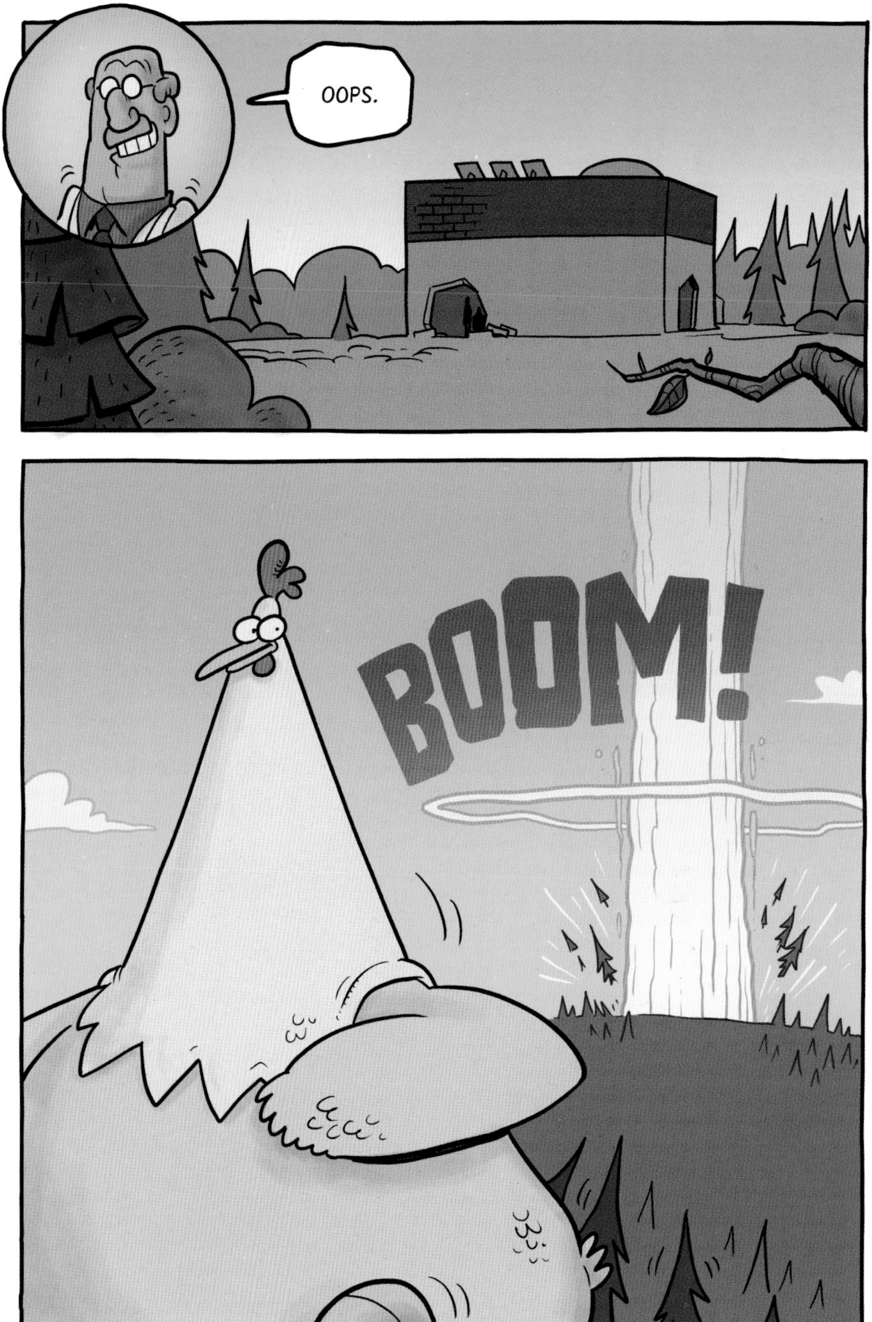
OOPS.
BOOM!

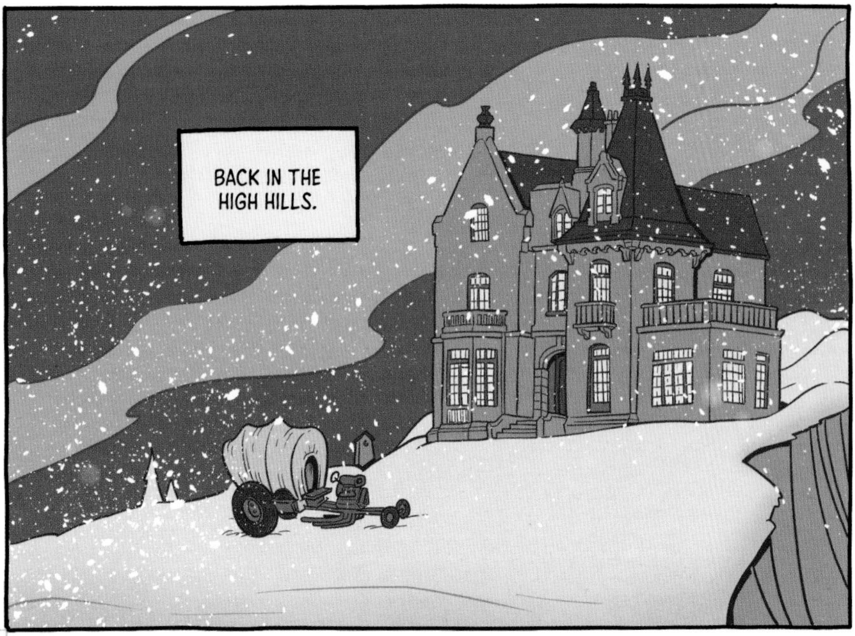
BACK IN THE HIGH HILLS.

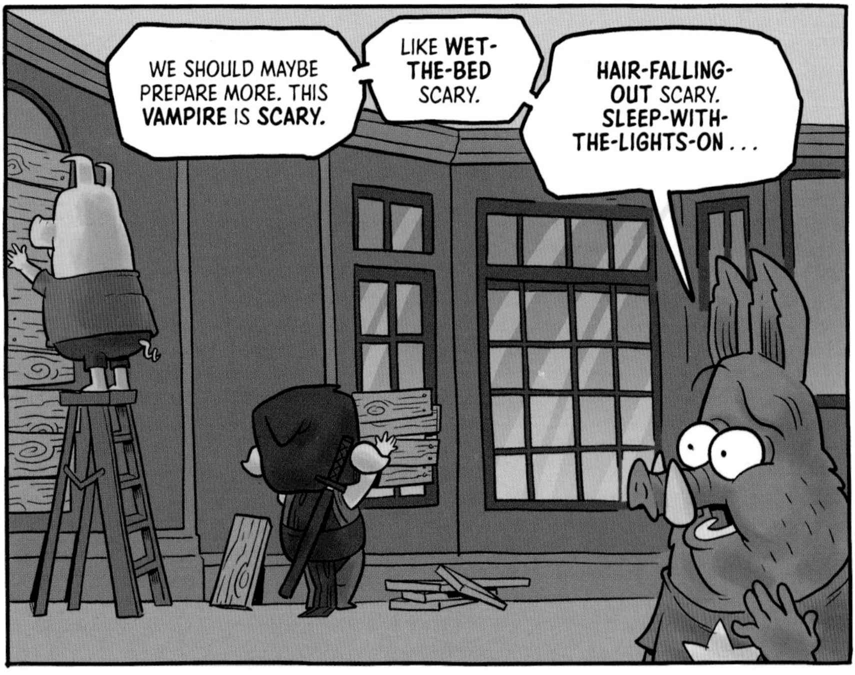
WE SHOULD MAYBE PREPARE MORE. THIS VAMPIRE IS SCARY.
LIKE WET-THE-BED SCARY.
HAIR-FALLING-OUT SCARY. SLEEP-WITH-THE-LIGHTS-ON . . .

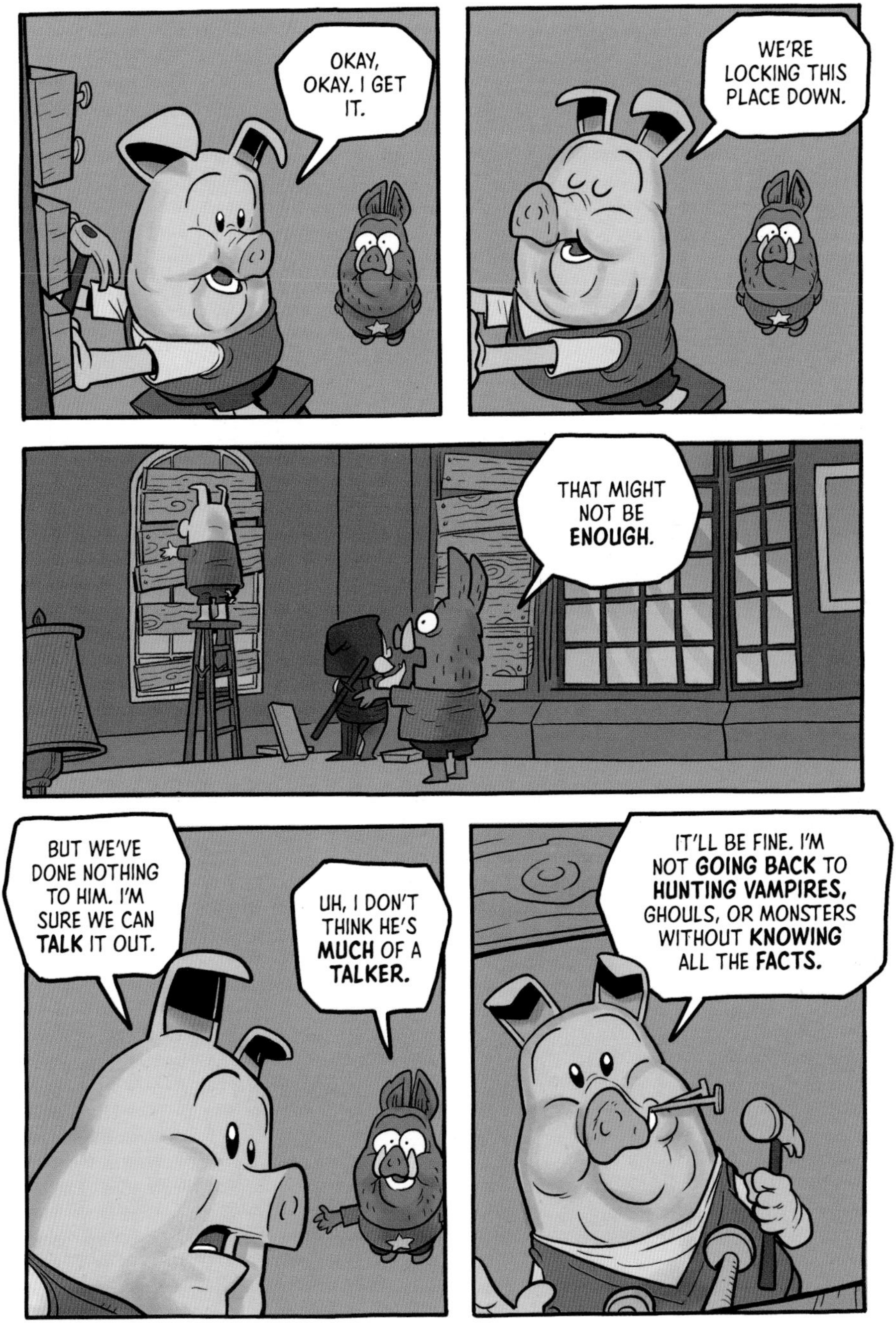
OKAY, OKAY. I GET IT.
WE'RE LOCKING THIS PLACE DOWN.
THAT MIGHT NOT BE ENOUGH.
BUT WE'VE DONE NOTHING TO HIM. I'M SURE WE CAN TALK IT OUT.
UH, I DON'T THINK HE'S MUCH OF A TALKER.
IT'LL BE FINE. I'M NOT GOING BACK TO HUNTING VAMPIRES, GHOULS, OR MONSTERS WITHOUT KNOWING ALL THE FACTS.

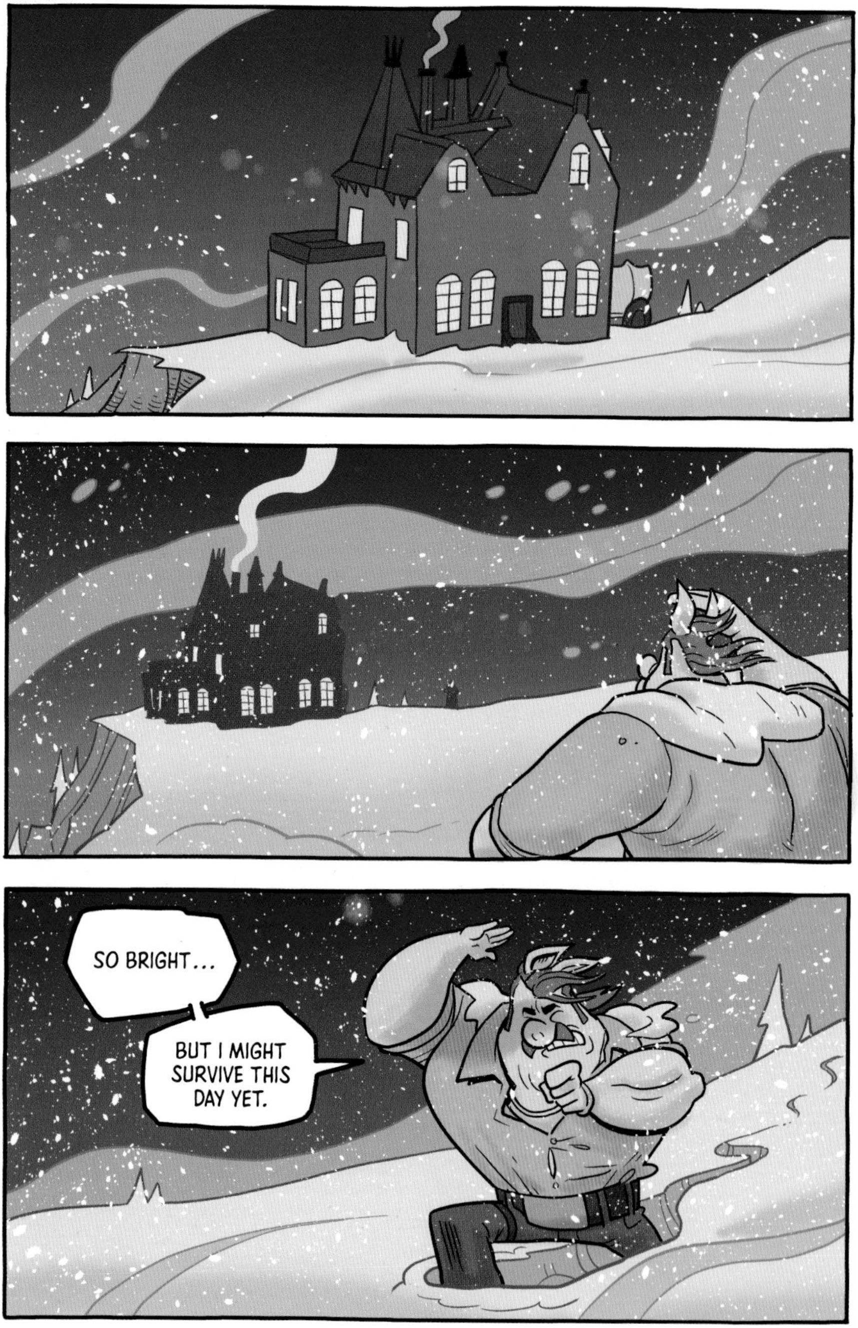
SO BRIGHT...
BUT I MIGHT SURVIVE THIS DAY YET.

CHAPTER TEN

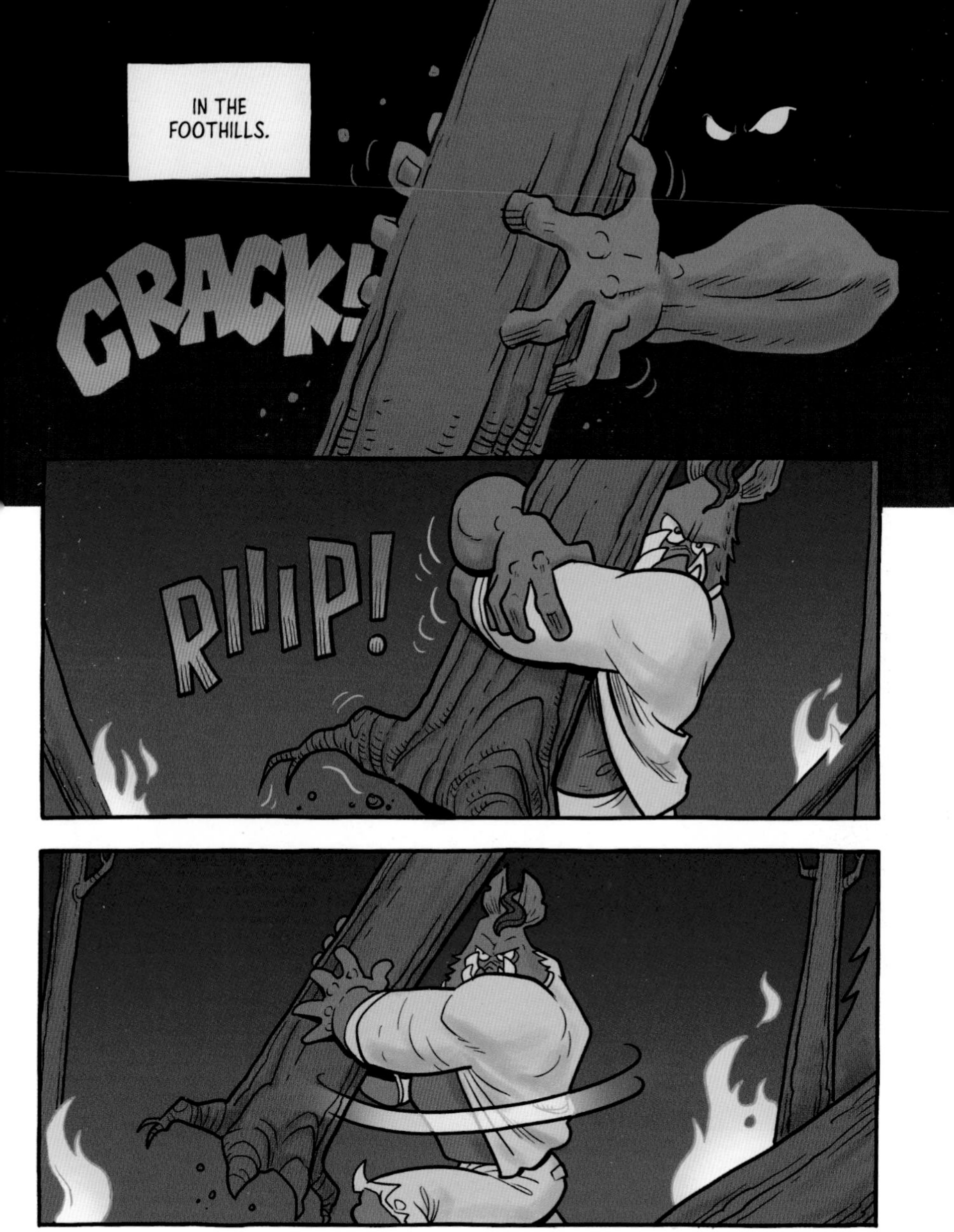
IN THE FOOTHILLS.
CRACK!
RIIIP!

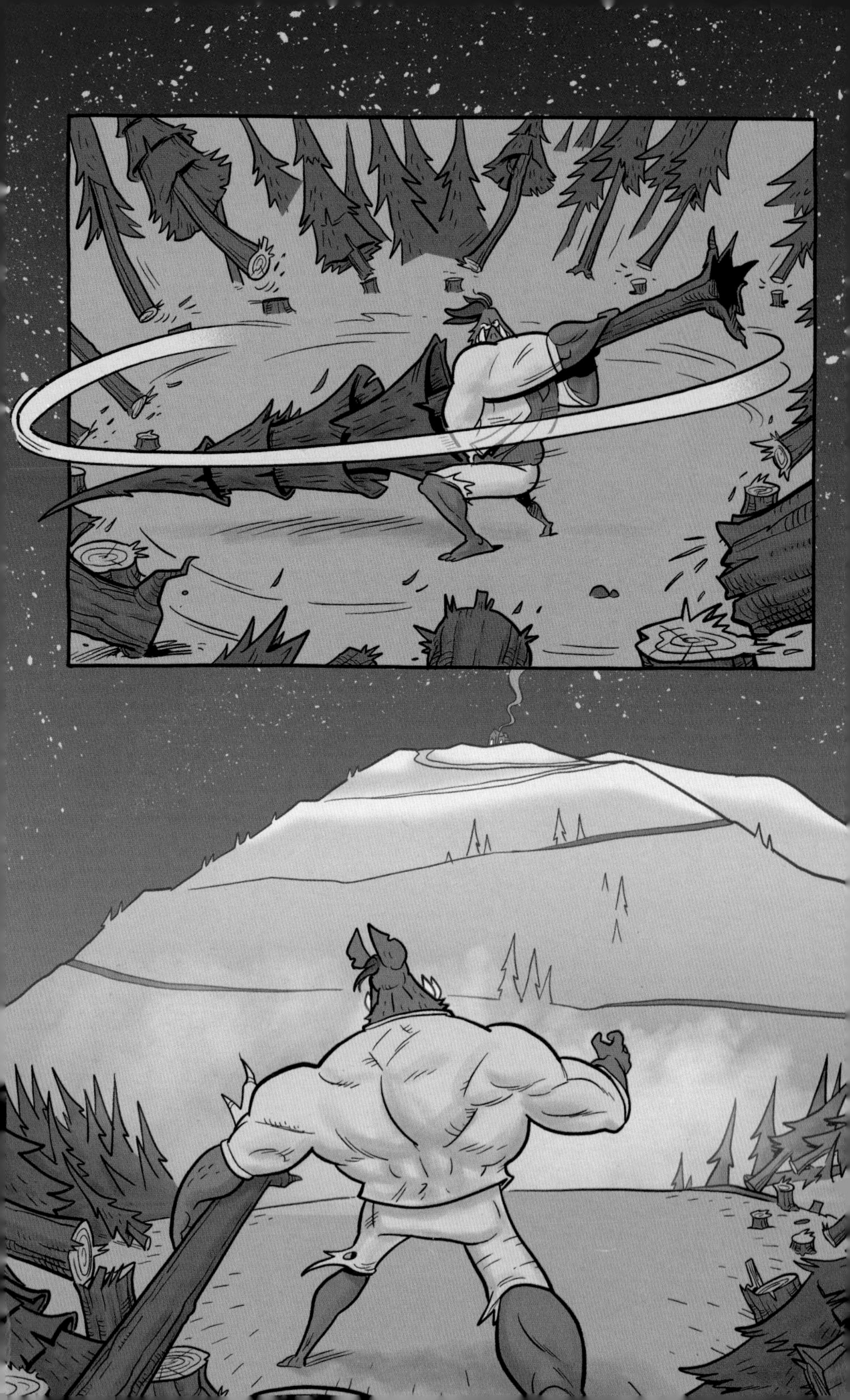

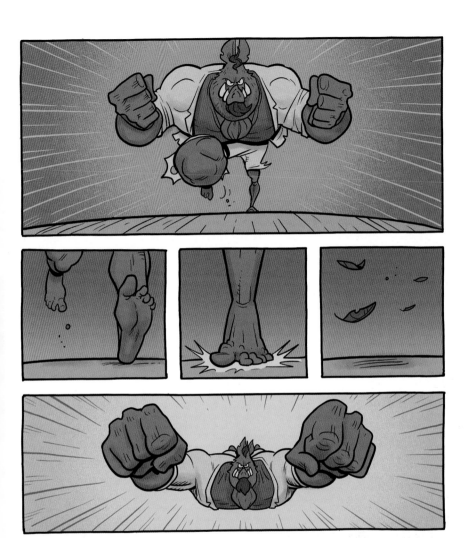

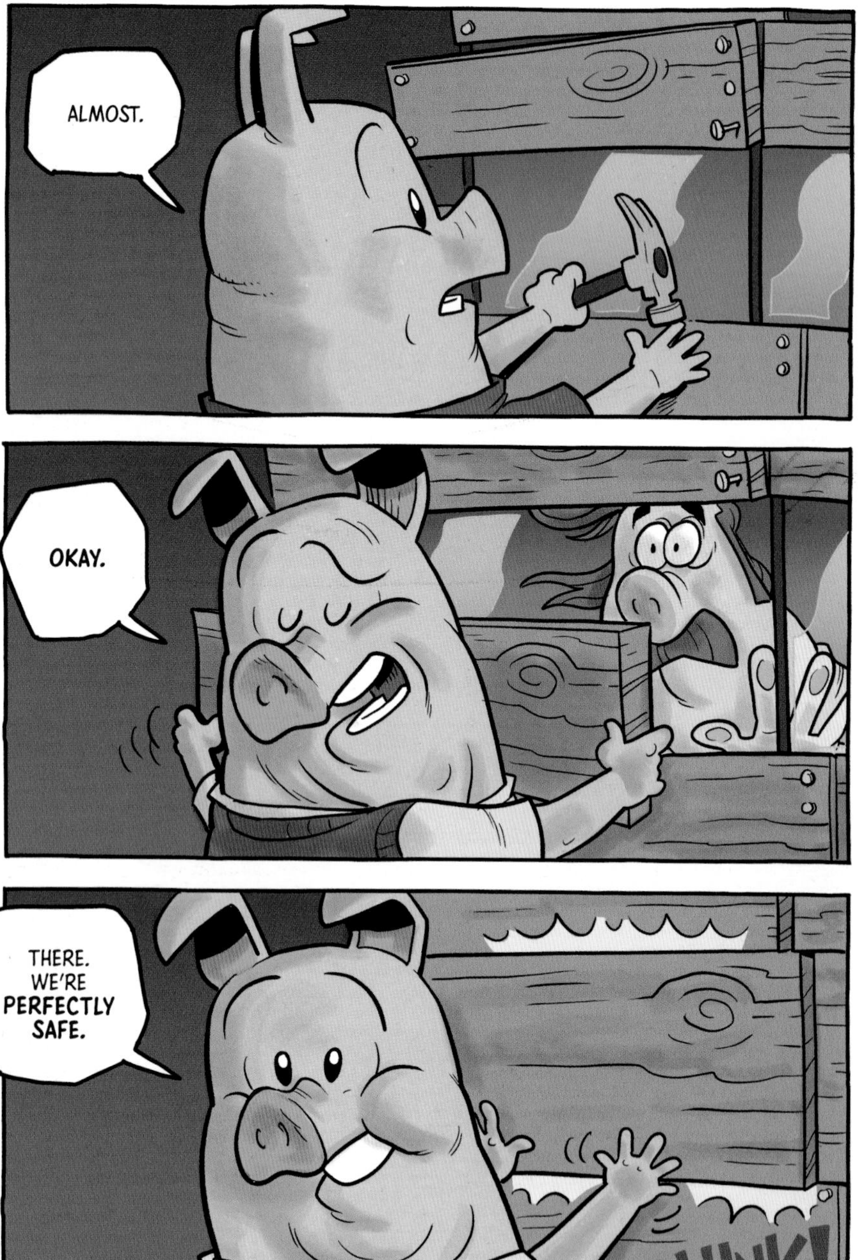
ALMOST.
OKAY.
THERE. WE'RE PERFECTLY SAFE.
PLUNK!

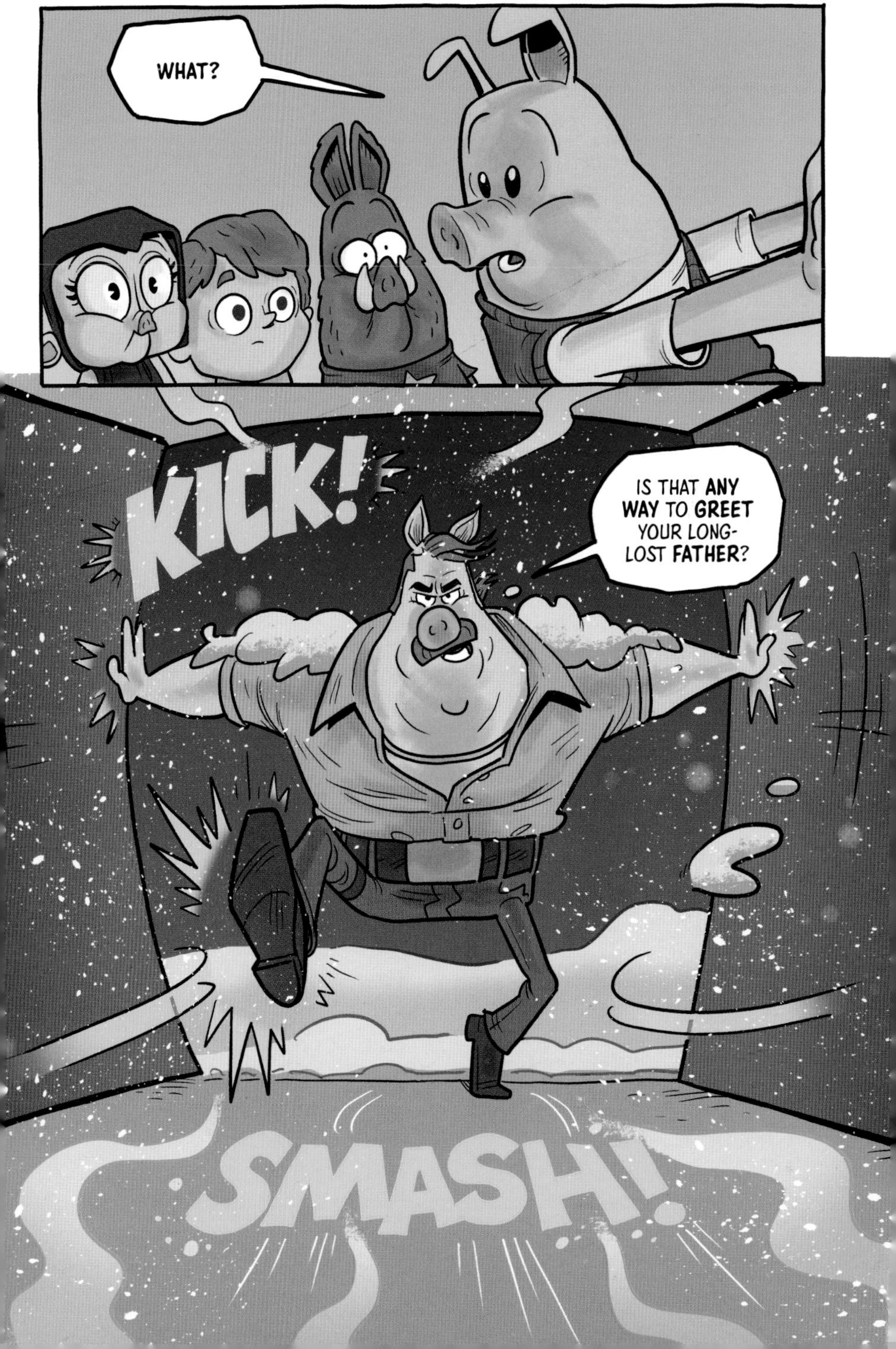
WHAT?
KICK!
IS THAT ANY WAY TO GREET YOUR LONG-LOST FATHER?
SMASH!

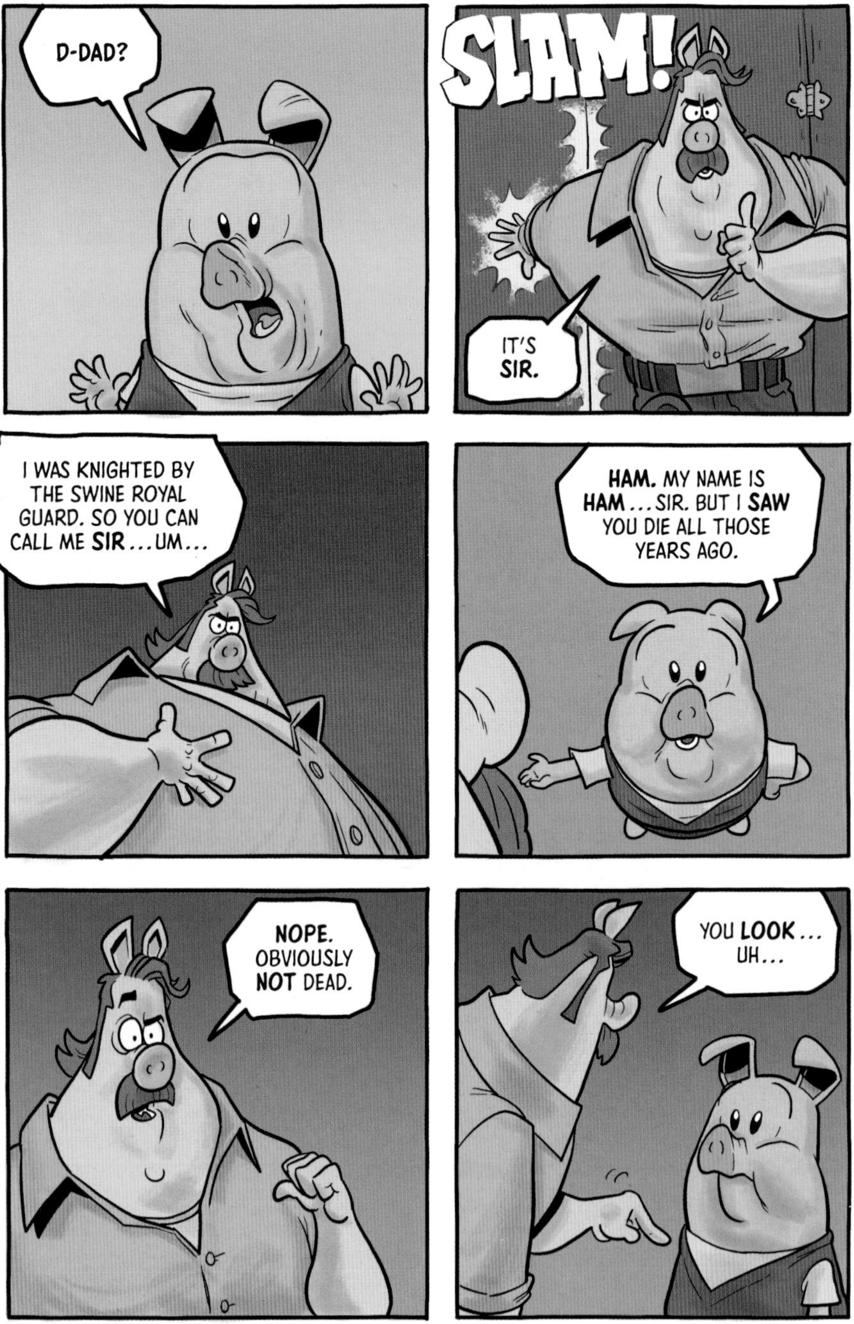
D-DAD?
SLAM!
IT'S SIR.
I WAS KNIGHTED BY THE SWINE ROYAL GUARD. SO YOU CAN CALL ME SIR...UM...
HAM. MY NAME IS HAM...SIR. BUT I SAW YOU DIE ALL THOSE YEARS AGO.
NOPE. OBVIOUSLY NOT DEAD.
YOU LOOK... UH...

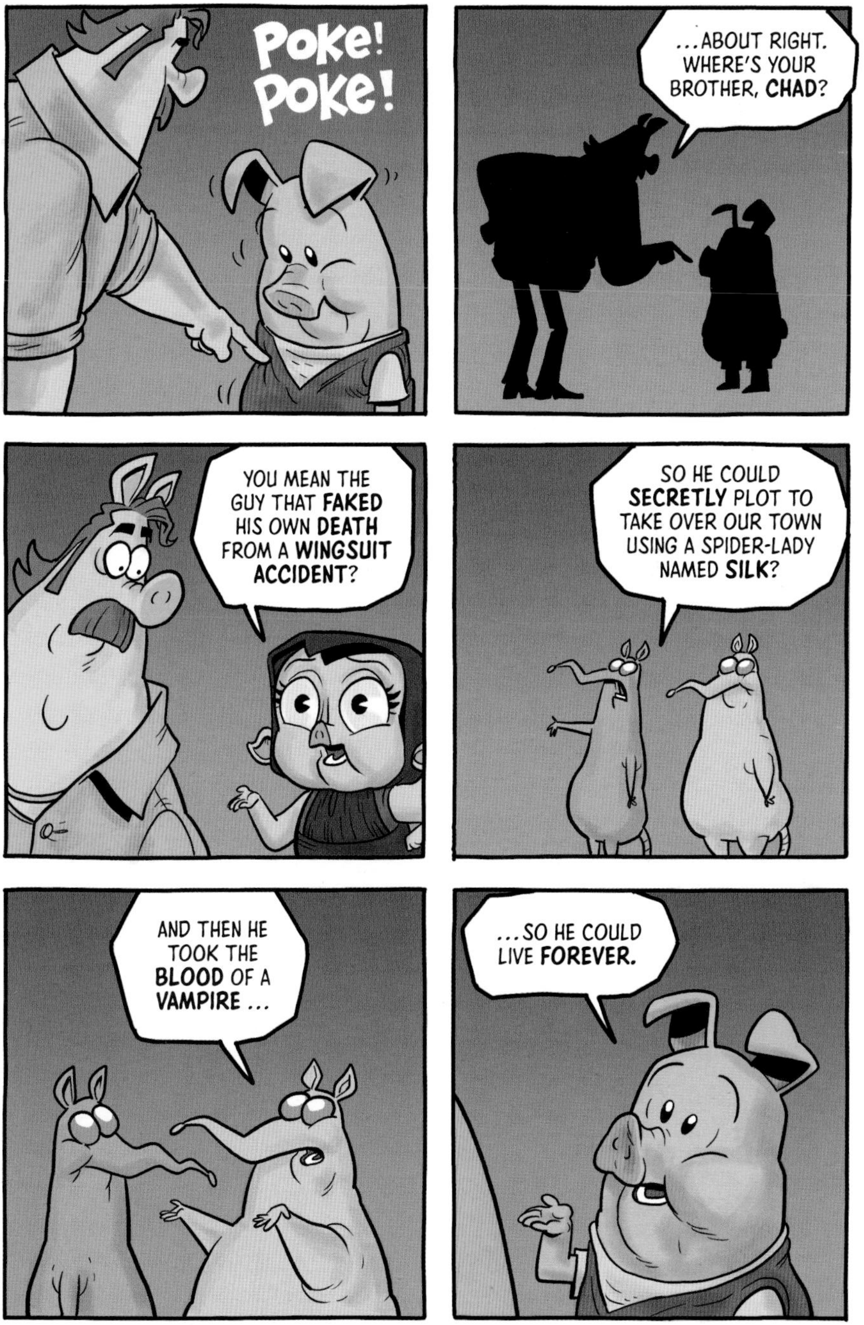
POKE!
POKE!
...ABOUT RIGHT. WHERE'S YOUR BROTHER, CHAD?
YOU MEAN THE GUY THAT FAKED HIS OWN DEATH FROM A WINGSUIT ACCIDENT?
SO HE COULD SECRETLY PLOT TO TAKE OVER OUR TOWN USING A SPIDER-LADY NAMED SILK?
AND THEN HE TOOK THE BLOOD OF A VAMPIRE ...
...SO HE COULD LIVE FOREVER.

ONLY TO DIE **AGAIN** BY, **YOU GUESSED IT**, A **WINGSUIT** ACCIDENT.

THEN HE WAS FOUND BY A MAD SCIENTIST...

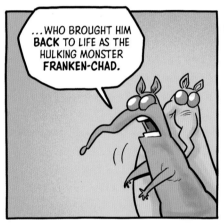

...WHO BROUGHT HIM **BACK** TO LIFE AS THE HULKING MONSTER **FRANKEN-CHAD.**

THEN HE PARTNERED WITH AN **EVIL CHICKEN** NAMED **HEN** WHO **ULTIMATELY** BETRAYED HIM...

...BY PUSHING HIM OFF A CLIFF FOR HIS **FINAL GOODBYE.** AND **GOOD RIDDANCE,** BY THE WAY.

WHEW. PANT, PANT.

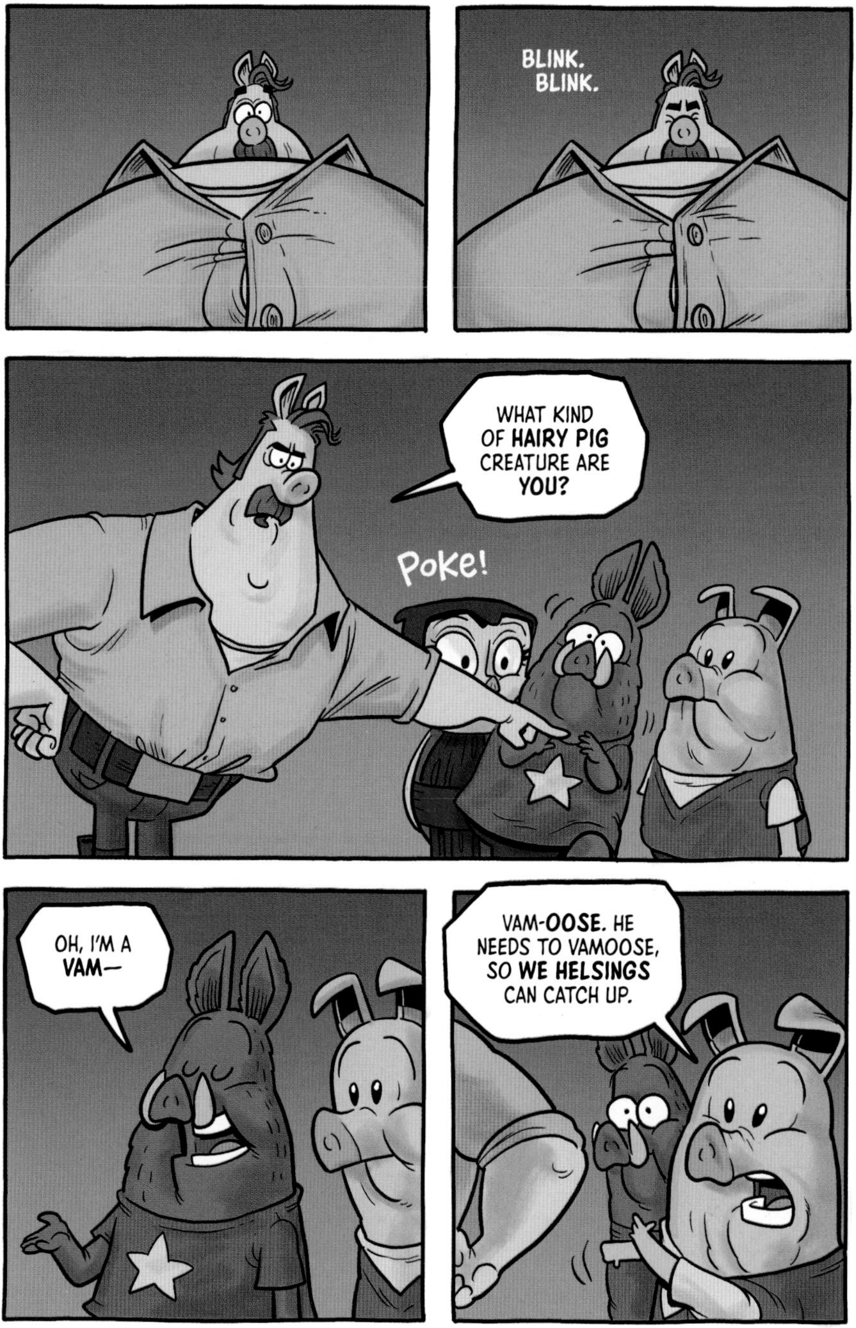
BLINK.
BLINK.
WHAT KIND OF HAIRY PIG CREATURE ARE YOU?
POKE!
OH, I'M A VAM—
VAM-OOSE. HE NEEDS TO VAMOOSE, SO WE HELSINGS CAN CATCH UP.

SO THAT'S IT? MY **OLDEST** BOY DIES FROM...

...**TOXIC** MASCULINITY.

...**AGGRESSIVE STUPIDITY.**

...OUT-OF-CONTROL **EGO.**

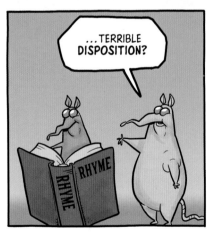

...**TERRIBLE DISPOSITION?**

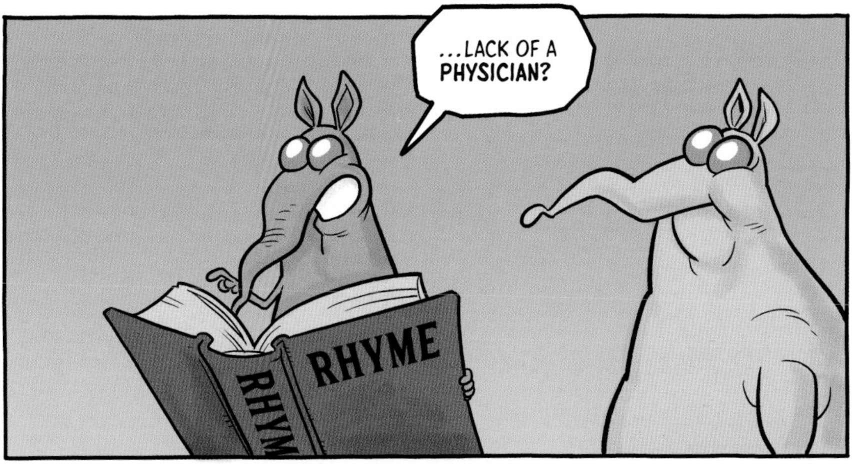
...LACK OF A PHYSICIAN?
RHYME
RHYME

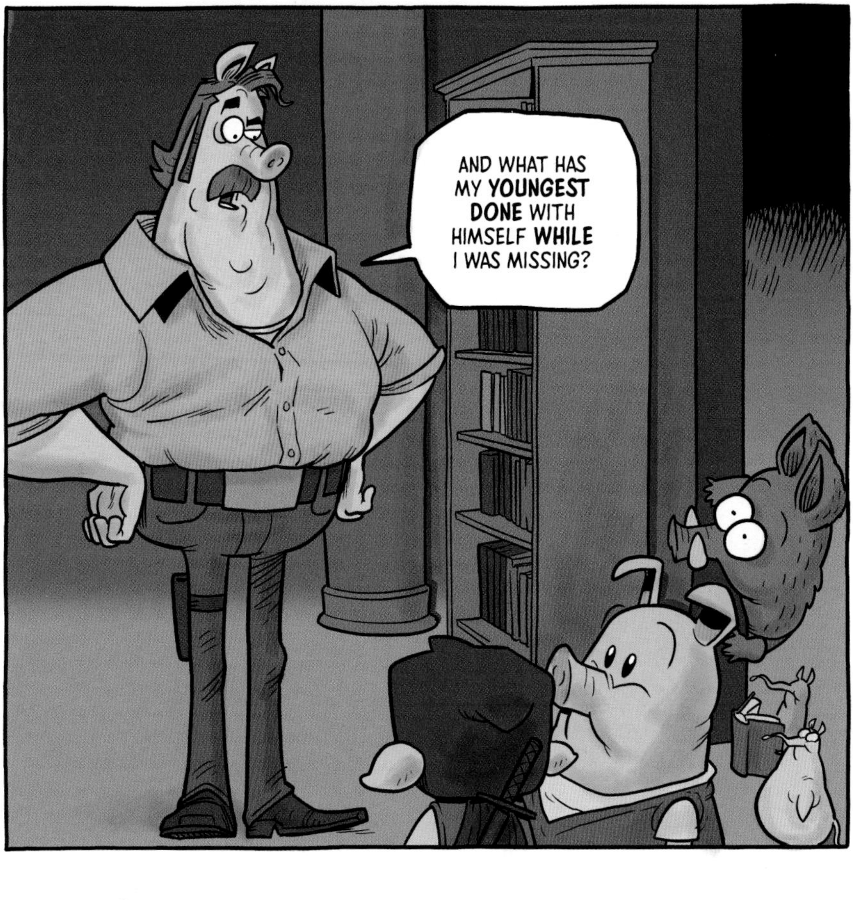
AND WHAT HAS MY YOUNGEST DONE WITH HIMSELF WHILE I WAS MISSING?

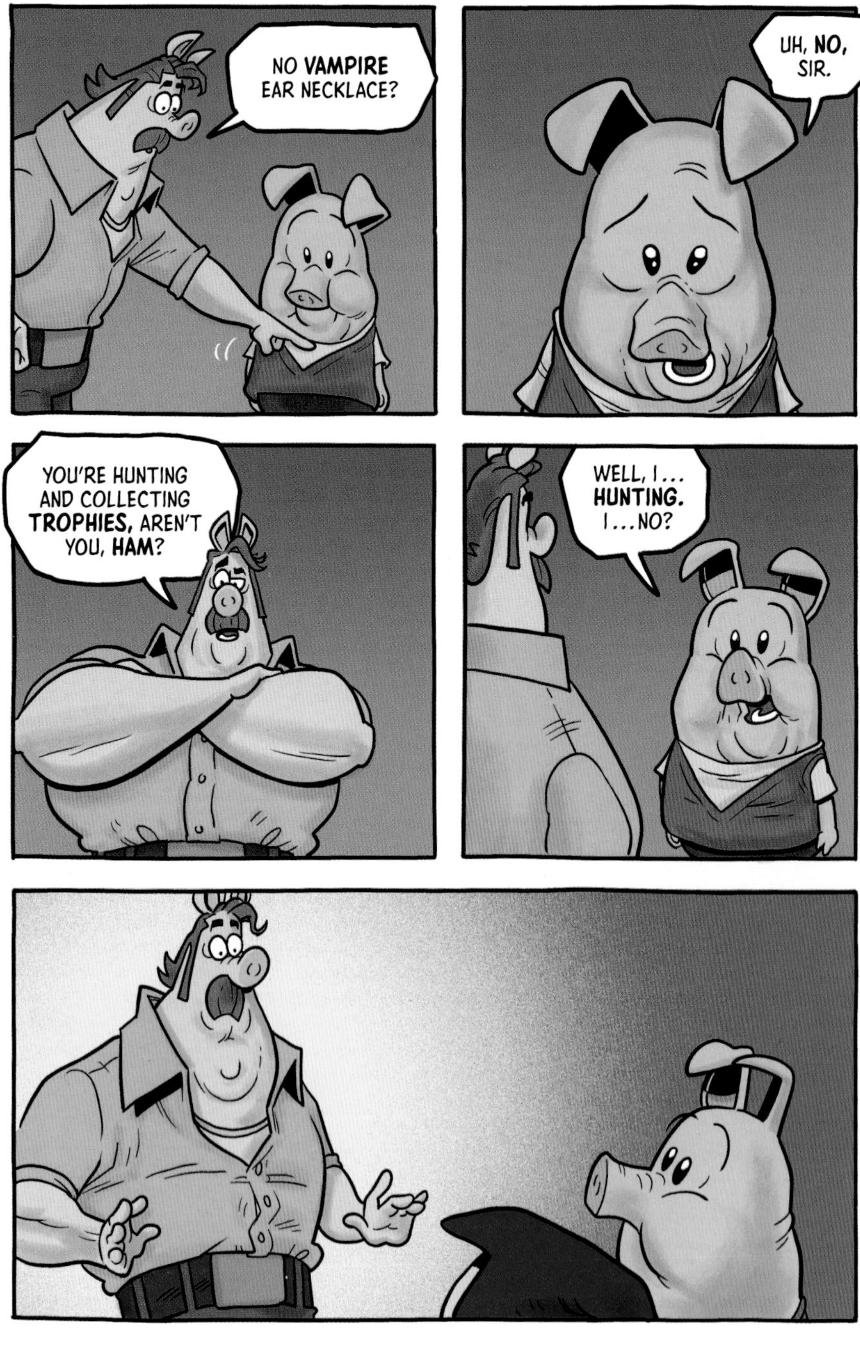
NO **VAMPIRE** EAR NECKLACE?
UH, **NO,** SIR.
YOU'RE HUNTING AND COLLECTING **TROPHIES,** AREN'T YOU, **HAM**?
WELL, I... **HUNTING.** I...NO?

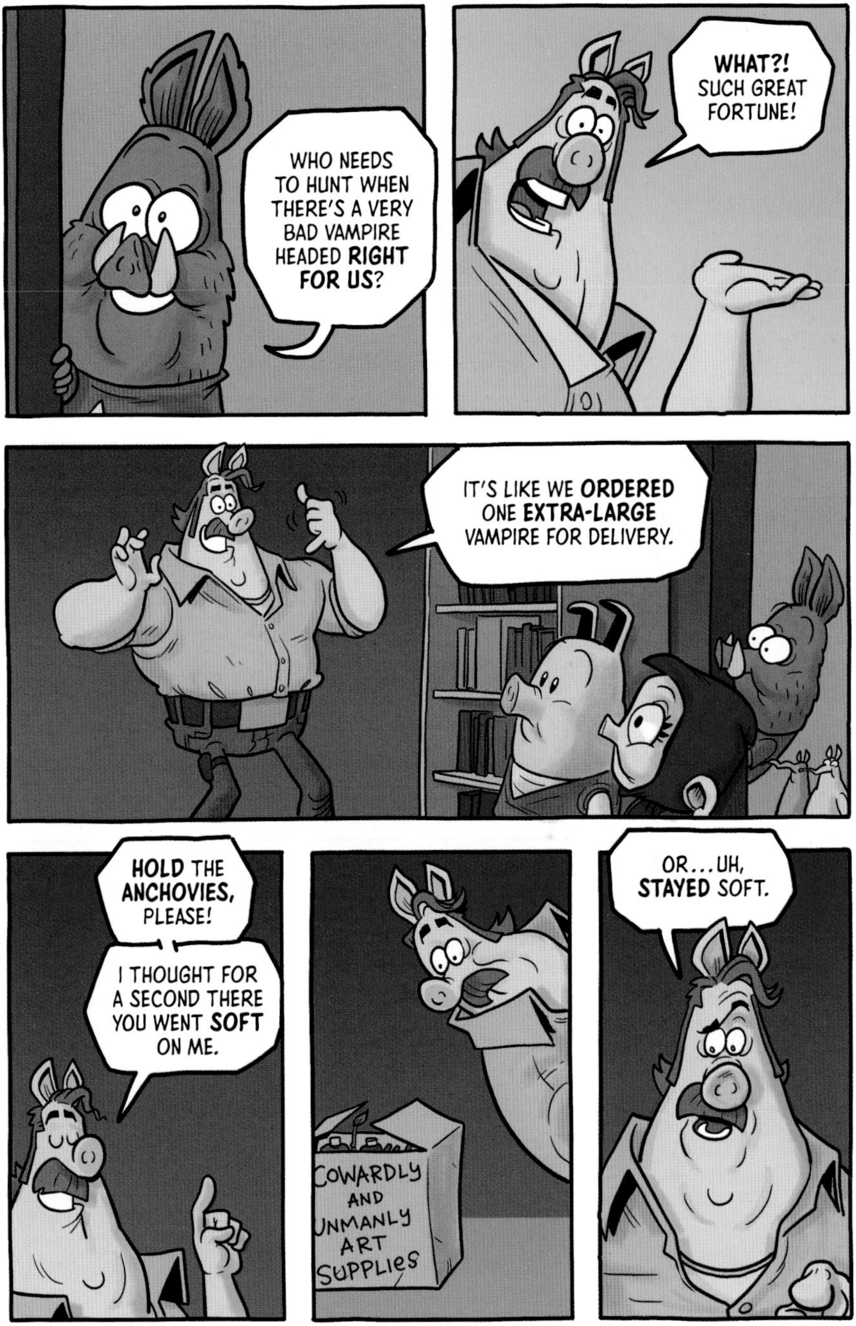
WHO NEEDS TO HUNT WHEN THERE'S A VERY BAD VAMPIRE HEADED RIGHT FOR US?
WHAT?! SUCH GREAT FORTUNE!
IT'S LIKE WE ORDERED ONE EXTRA-LARGE VAMPIRE FOR DELIVERY.
HOLD THE ANCHOVIES, PLEASE!
I THOUGHT FOR A SECOND THERE YOU WENT SOFT ON ME.
COWARDLY AND UNMANLY ART SUPPLIES
OR...UH, STAYED SOFT.

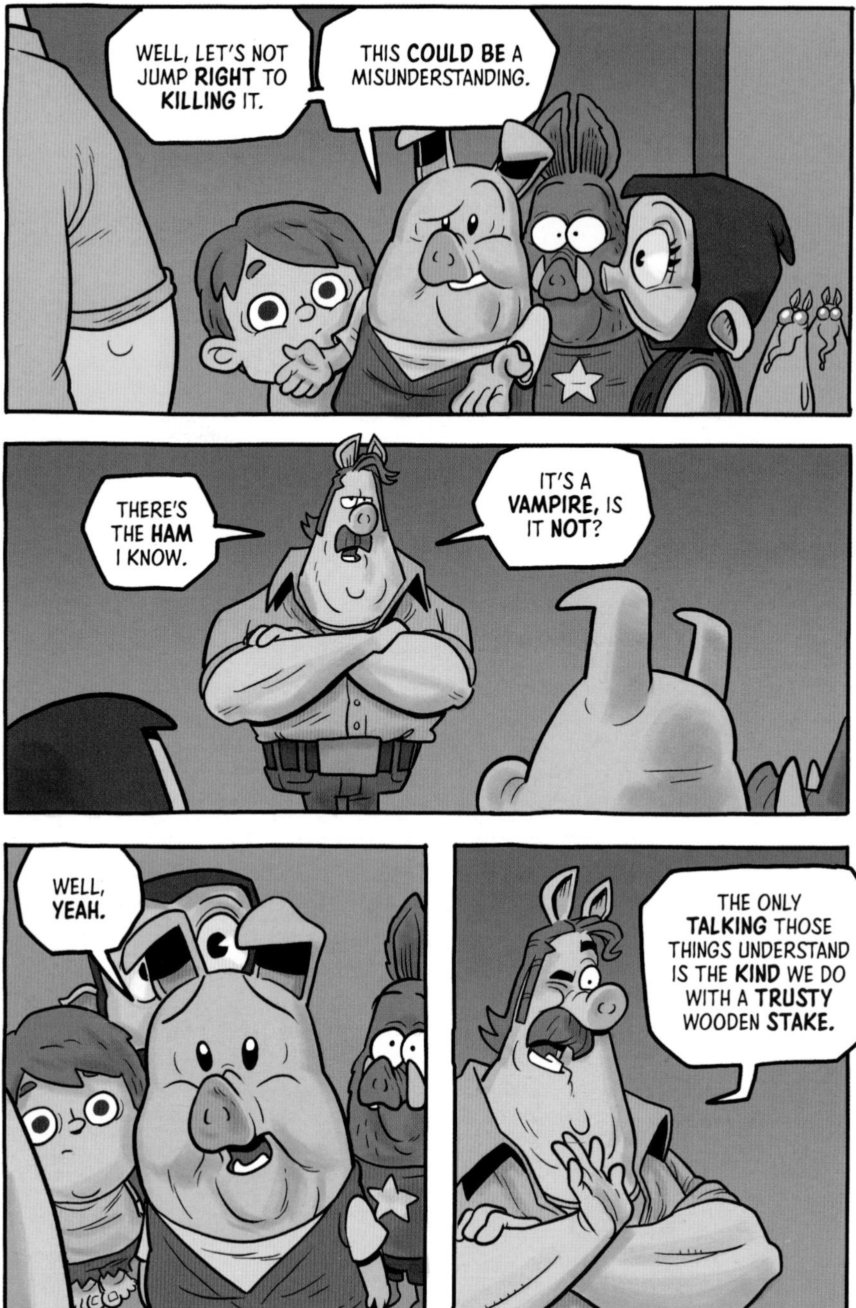
WELL, LET'S NOT JUMP RIGHT TO KILLING IT.
THIS COULD BE A MISUNDERSTANDING.
THERE'S THE HAM I KNOW.
IT'S A VAMPIRE, IS IT NOT?
WELL, YEAH.
THE ONLY TALKING THOSE THINGS UNDERSTAND IS THE KIND WE DO WITH A TRUSTY WOODEN STAKE.

CHAPTER ELEVEN

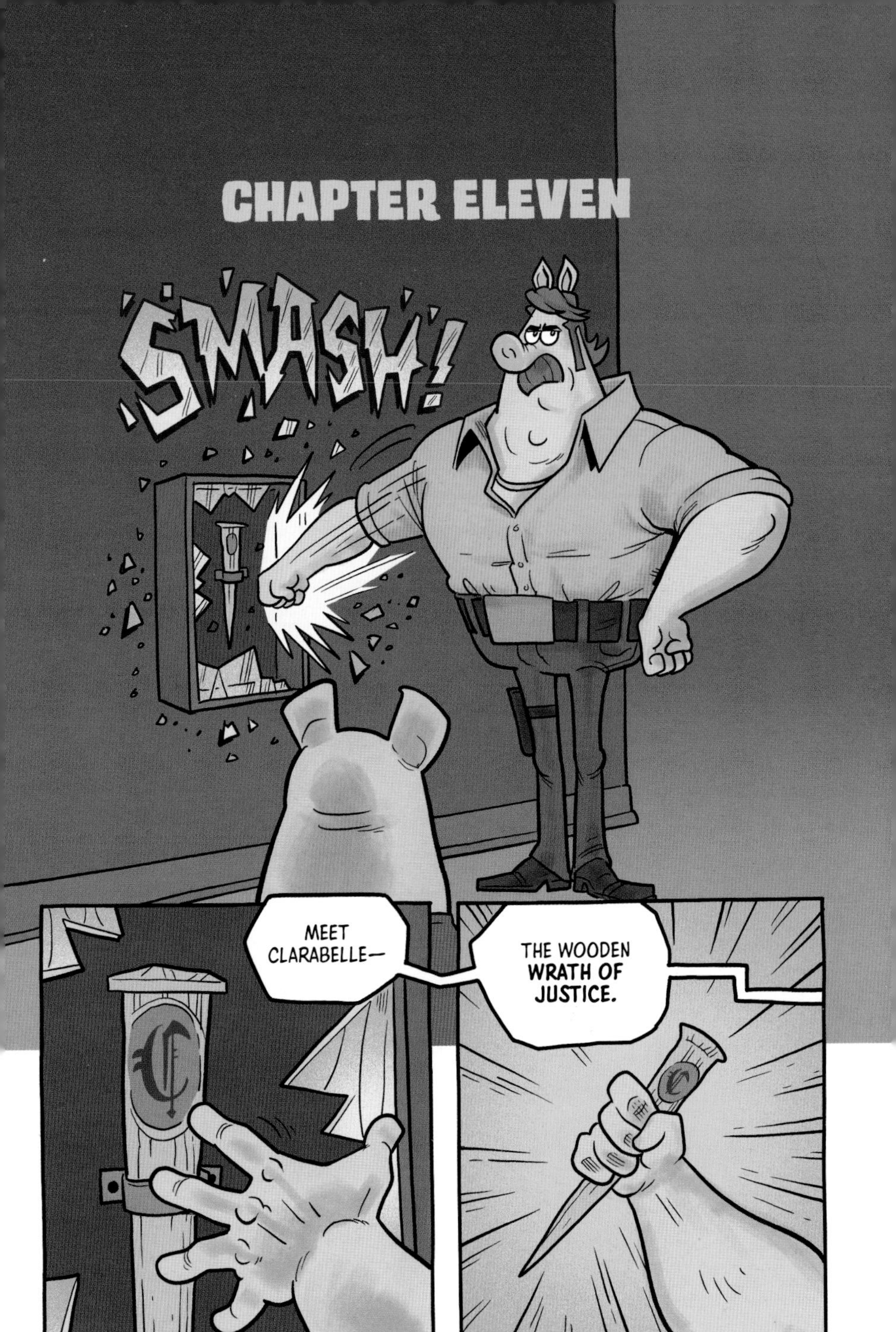
SMASH!
MEET CLARABELLE—
THE WOODEN WRATH OF JUSTICE.

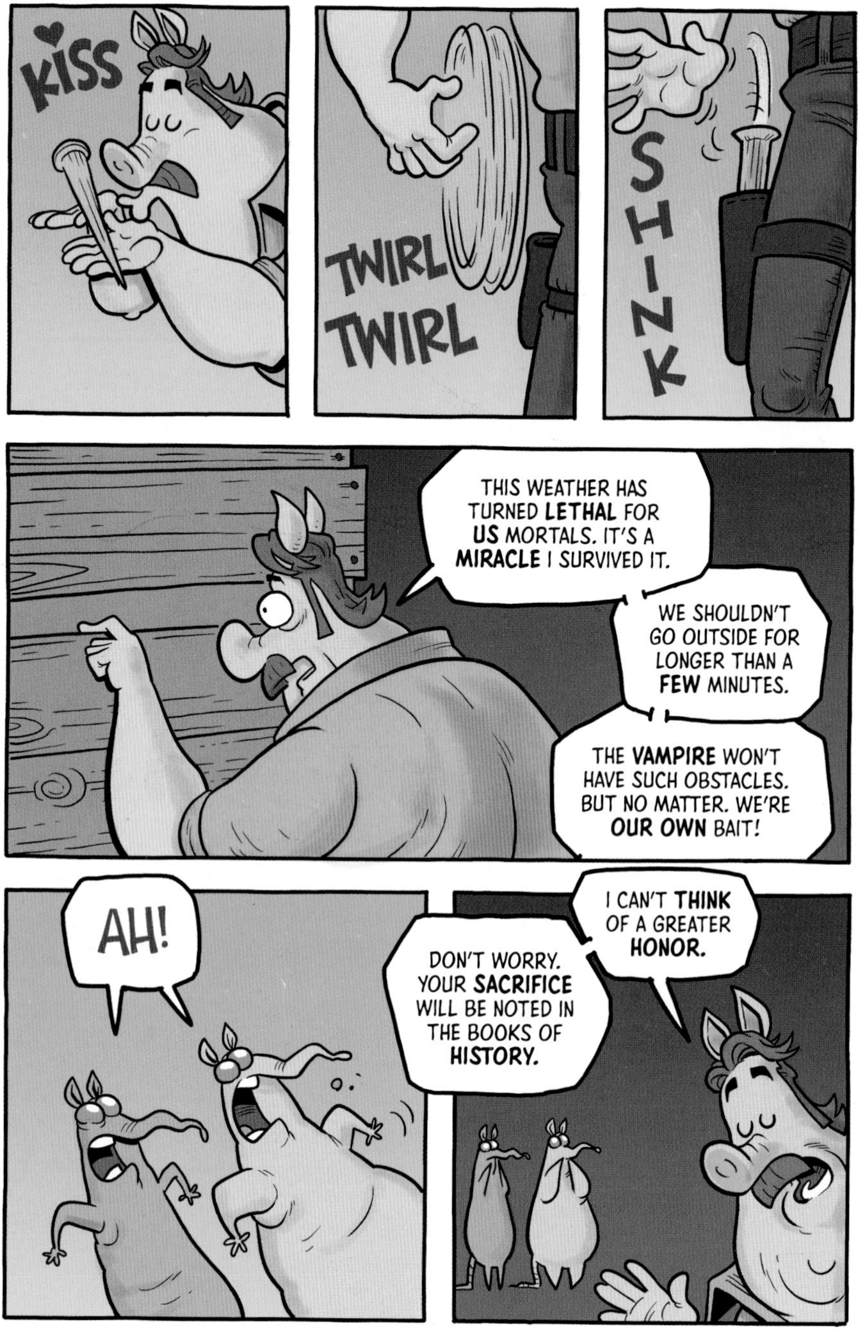
KISS
TWIRL TWIRL
SHINK
THIS WEATHER HAS TURNED LETHAL FOR US MORTALS. IT'S A MIRACLE I SURVIVED IT.
WE SHOULDN'T GO OUTSIDE FOR LONGER THAN A FEW MINUTES.
THE VAMPIRE WON'T HAVE SUCH OBSTACLES. BUT NO MATTER. WE'RE OUR OWN BAIT!
AH!
I CAN'T THINK OF A GREATER HONOR.
DON'T WORRY. YOUR SACRIFICE WILL BE NOTED IN THE BOOKS OF HISTORY.

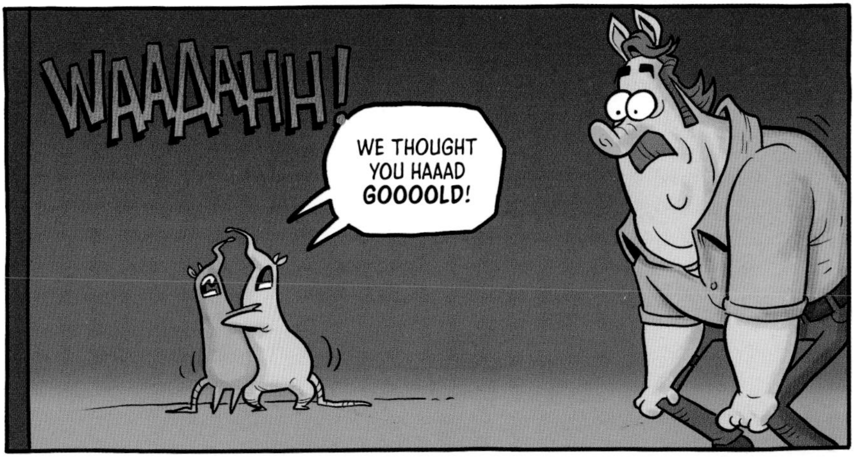
WAAAAHH!
WE THOUGHT YOU HAAAD GOOOOLD!

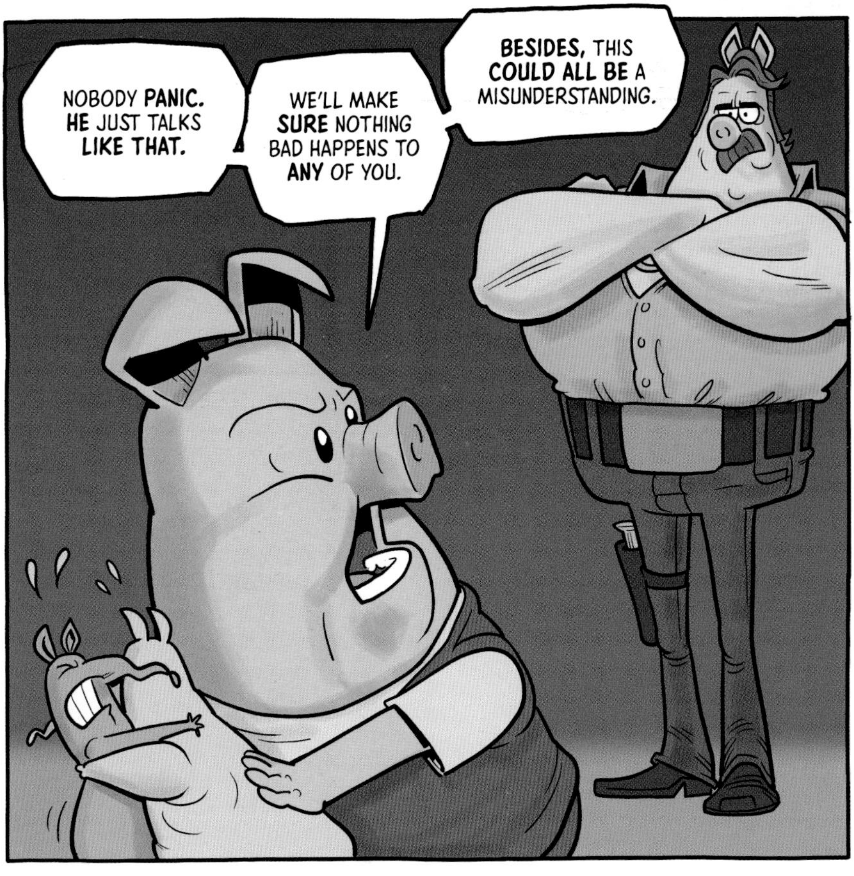
NOBODY PANIC. HE JUST TALKS LIKE THAT.
WE'LL MAKE SURE NOTHING BAD HAPPENS TO ANY OF YOU.
BESIDES, THIS COULD ALL BE A MISUNDERSTANDING.

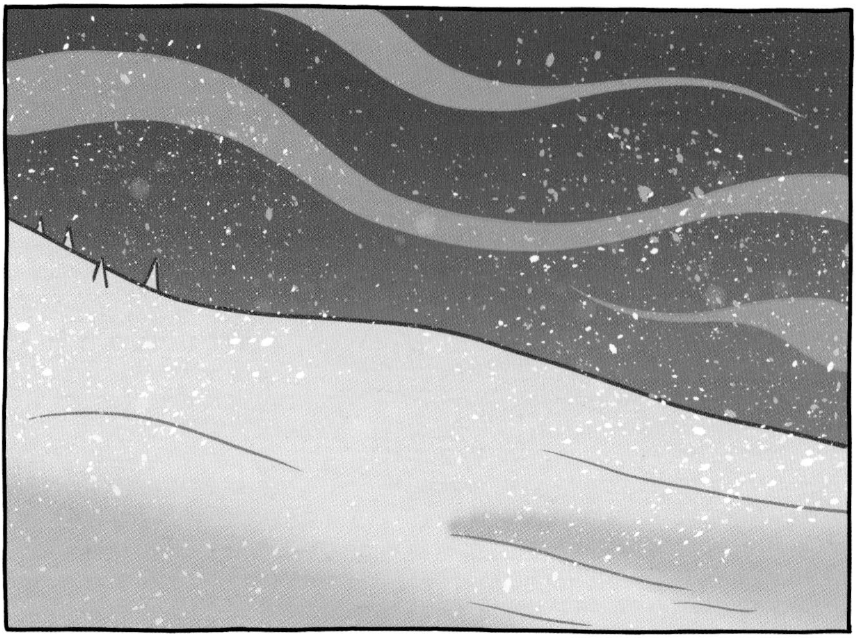

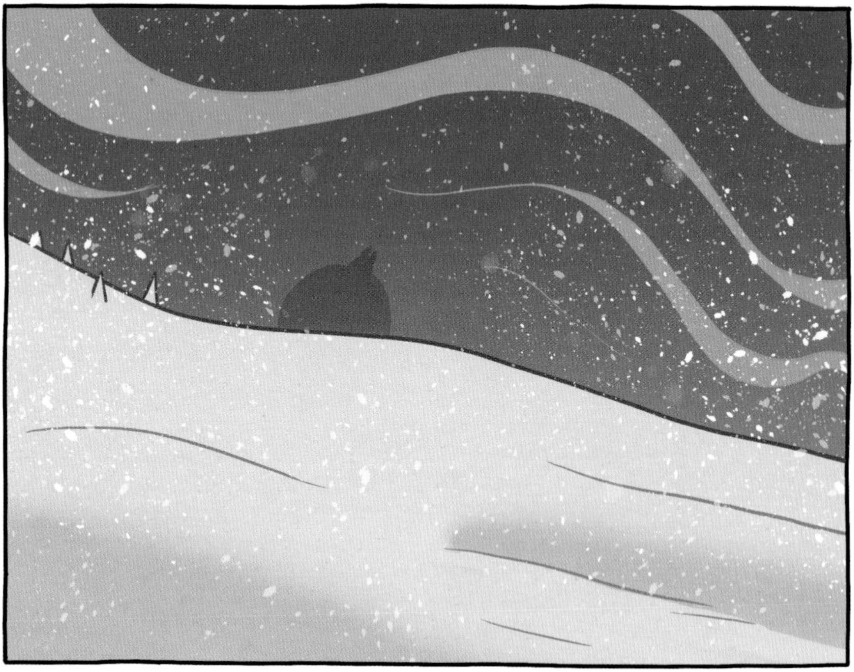

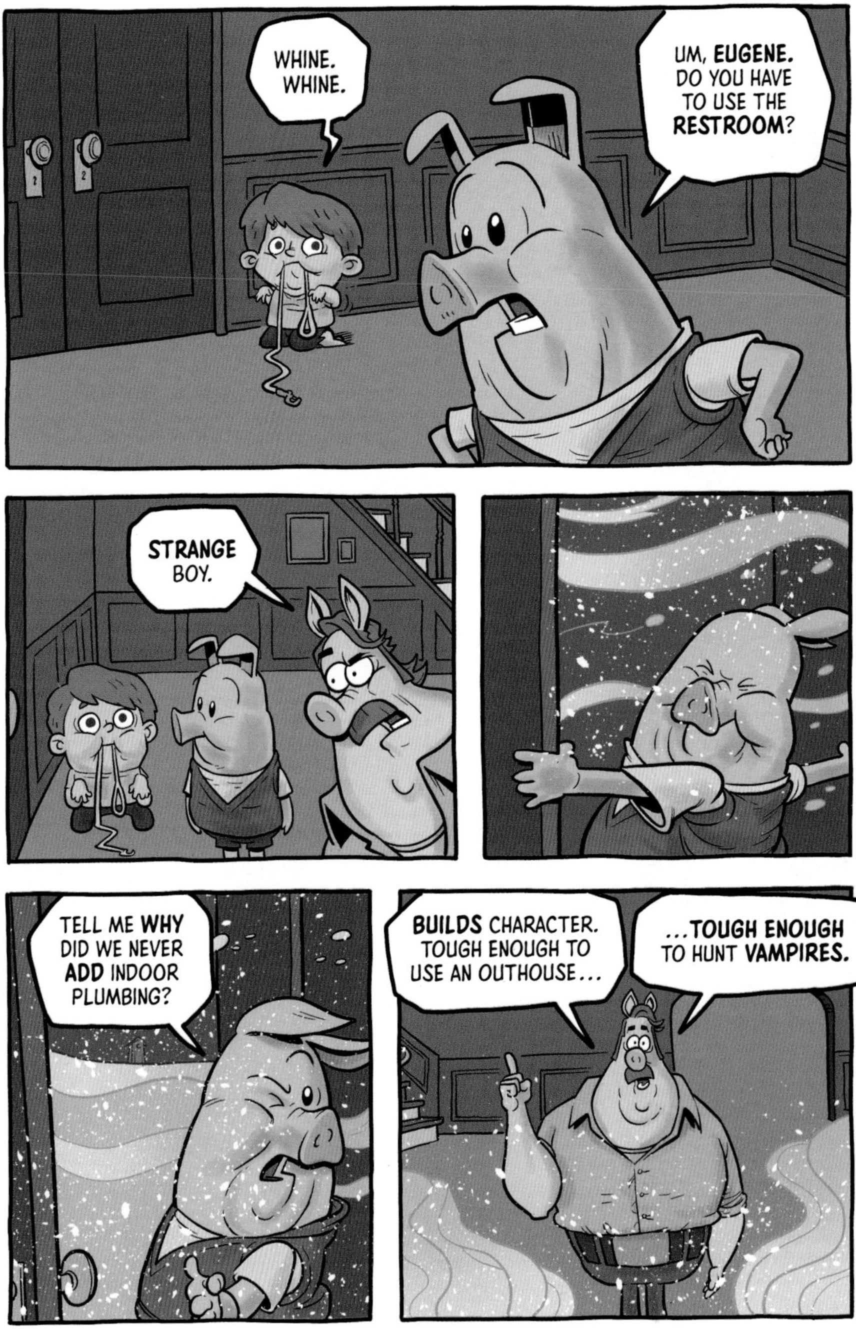
WHINE. WHINE.
UM, EUGENE. DO YOU HAVE TO USE THE RESTROOM?
STRANGE BOY.
TELL ME WHY DID WE NEVER ADD INDOOR PLUMBING?
BUILDS CHARACTER. TOUGH ENOUGH TO USE AN OUTHOUSE...
...TOUGH ENOUGH TO HUNT VAMPIRES.

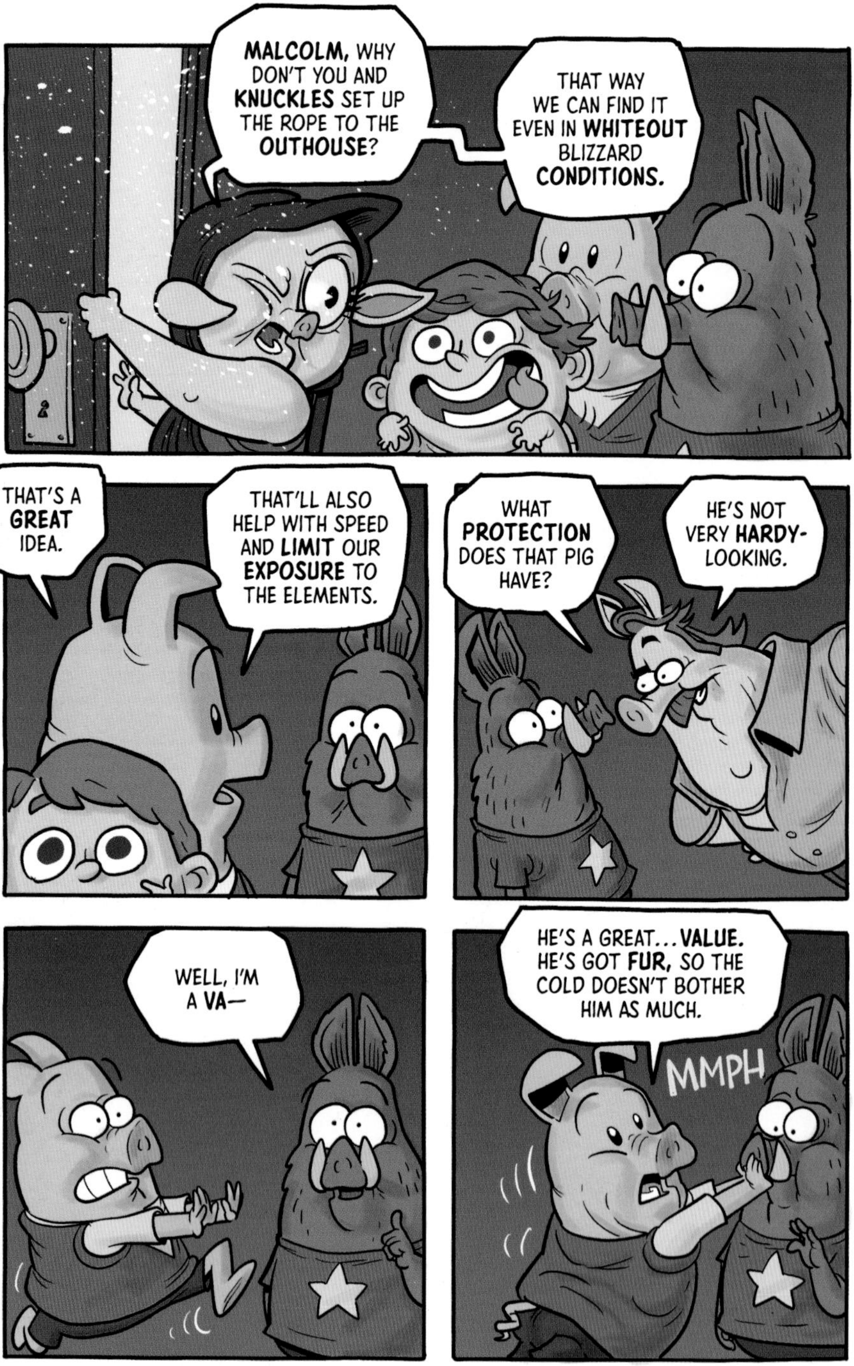

MALCOLM, WHY DON'T YOU AND KNUCKLES SET UP THE ROPE TO THE OUTHOUSE?
THAT WAY WE CAN FIND IT EVEN IN WHITEOUT BLIZZARD CONDITIONS.
THAT'S A GREAT IDEA.
THAT'LL ALSO HELP WITH SPEED AND LIMIT OUR EXPOSURE TO THE ELEMENTS.
WHAT PROTECTION DOES THAT PIG HAVE?
HE'S NOT VERY HARDY-LOOKING.
WELL, I'M A VA—
HE'S A GREAT... VALUE. HE'S GOT FUR, SO THE COLD DOESN'T BOTHER HIM AS MUCH.
MMPH

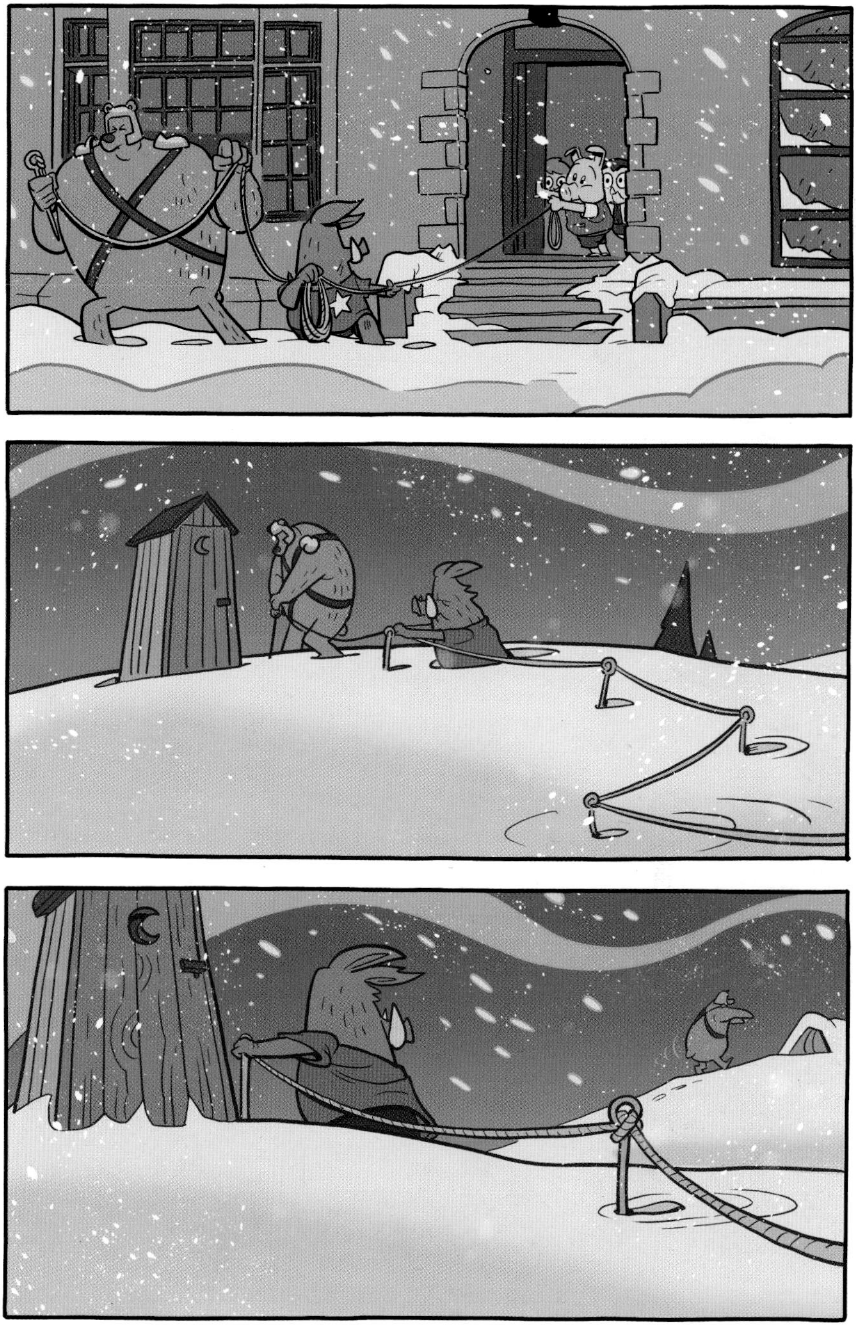

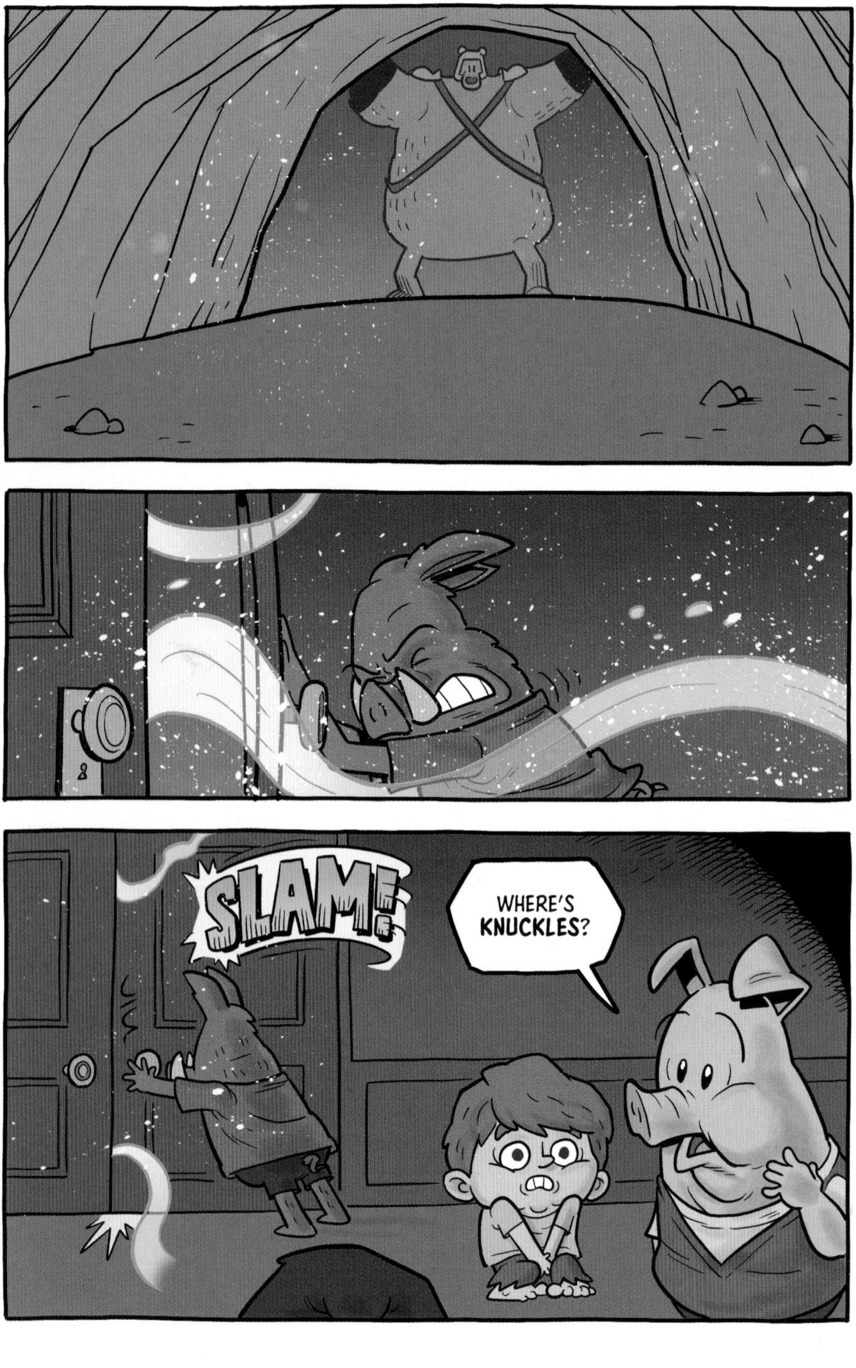
SLAM!
WHERE'S **KNUCKLES**?

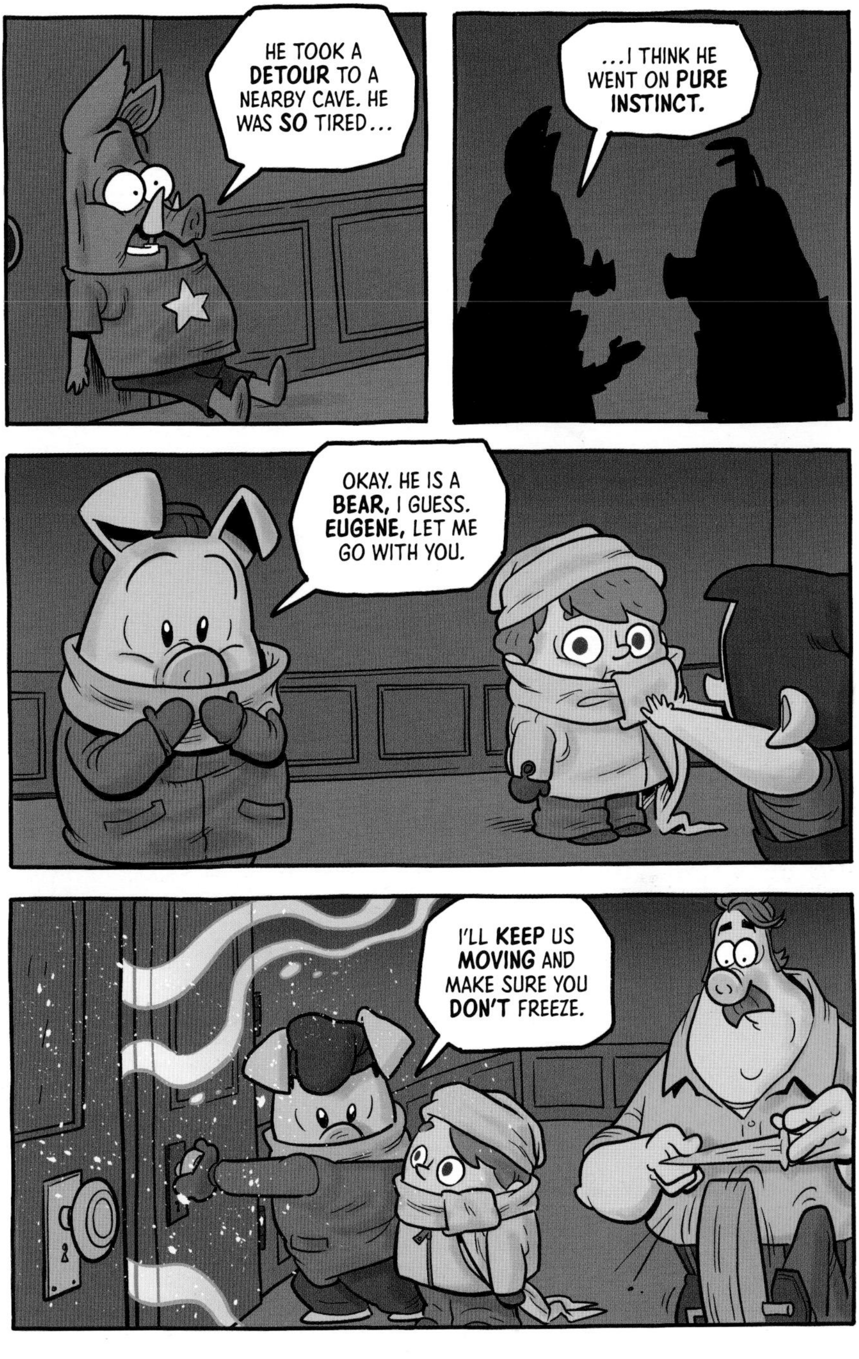
HE TOOK A DETOUR TO A NEARBY CAVE. HE WAS SO TIRED...
...I THINK HE WENT ON PURE INSTINCT.
OKAY. HE IS A BEAR, I GUESS. EUGENE, LET ME GO WITH YOU.
I'LL KEEP US MOVING AND MAKE SURE YOU DON'T FREEZE.

CHAPTER TWELVE

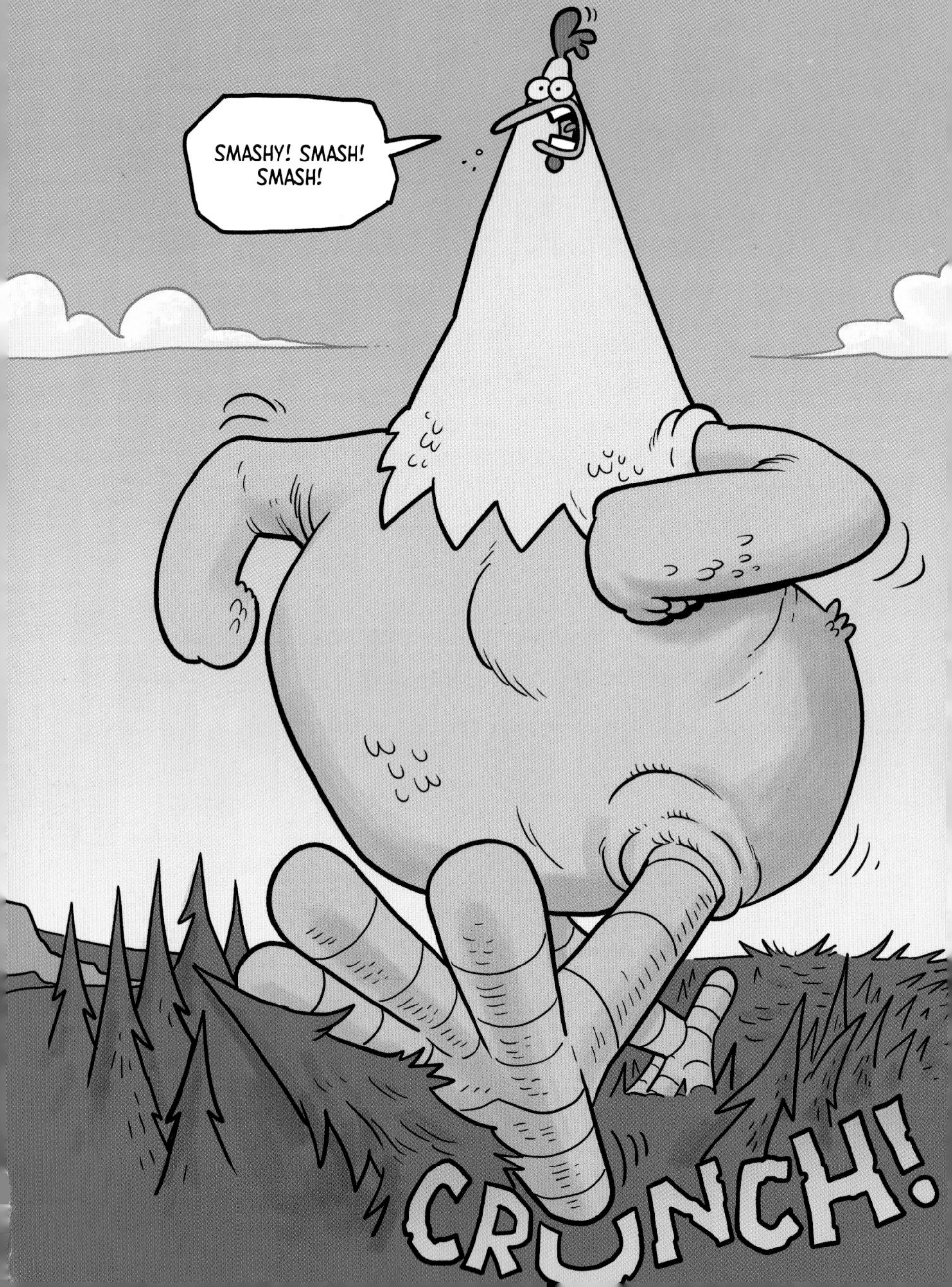
SMASHY! SMASH! SMASH!
CRUNCH!

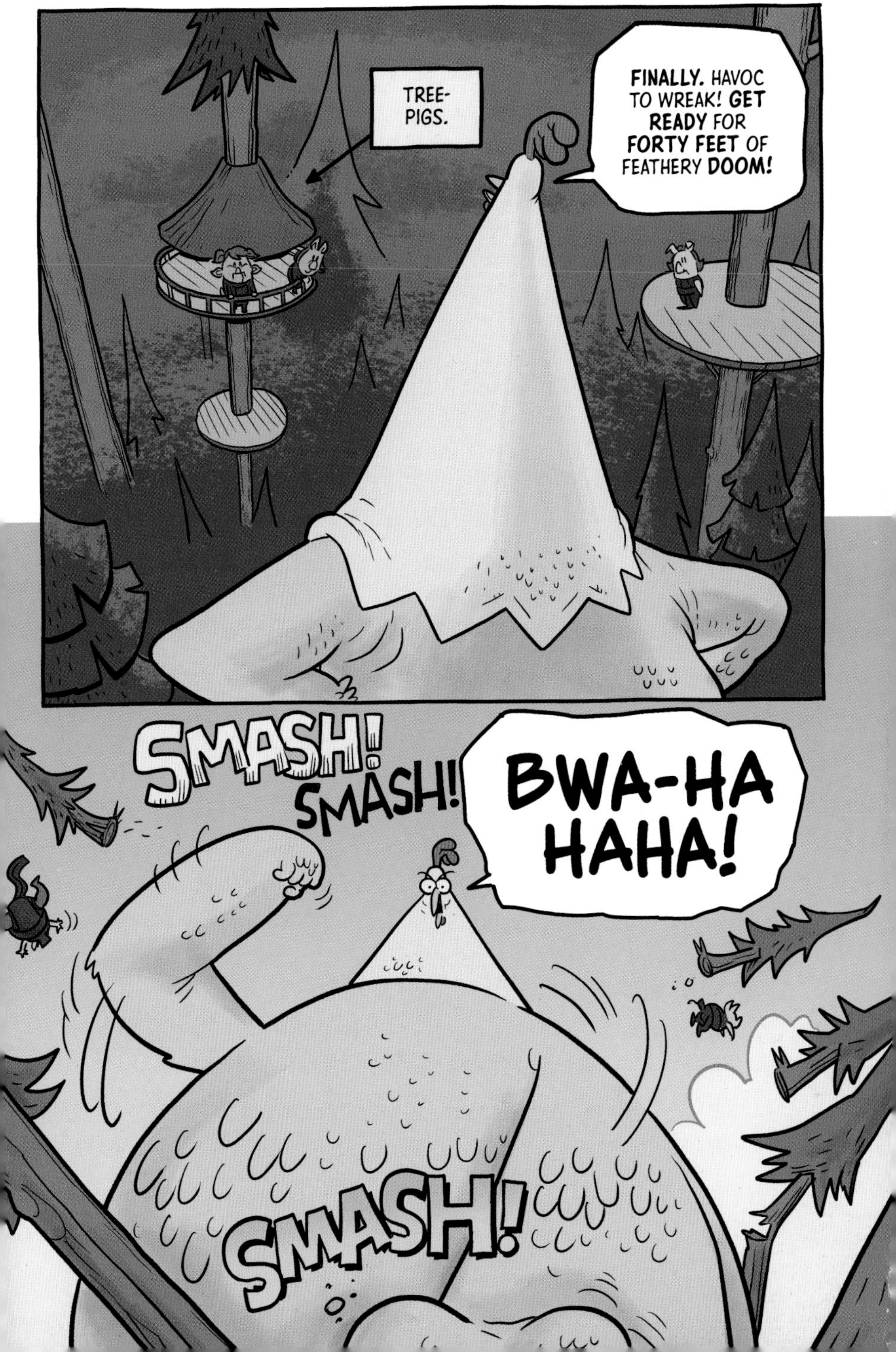
TREE-PIGS.
FINALLY. HAVOC TO WREAK! GET READY FOR FORTY FEET OF FEATHERY DOOM!
SMASH!
SMASH!
BWA-HA HAHA!
SMASH!

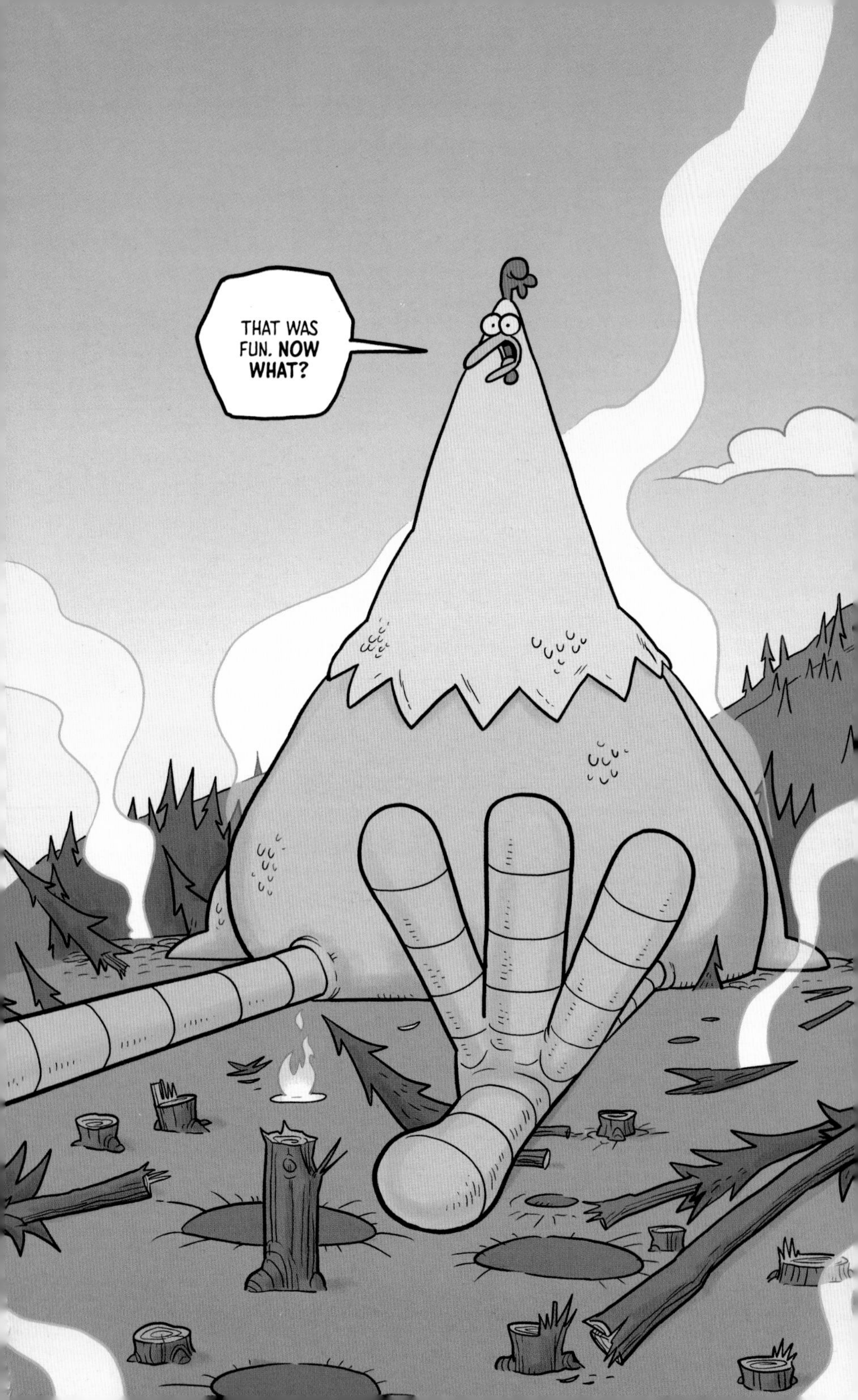
THAT WAS FUN. NOW WHAT?

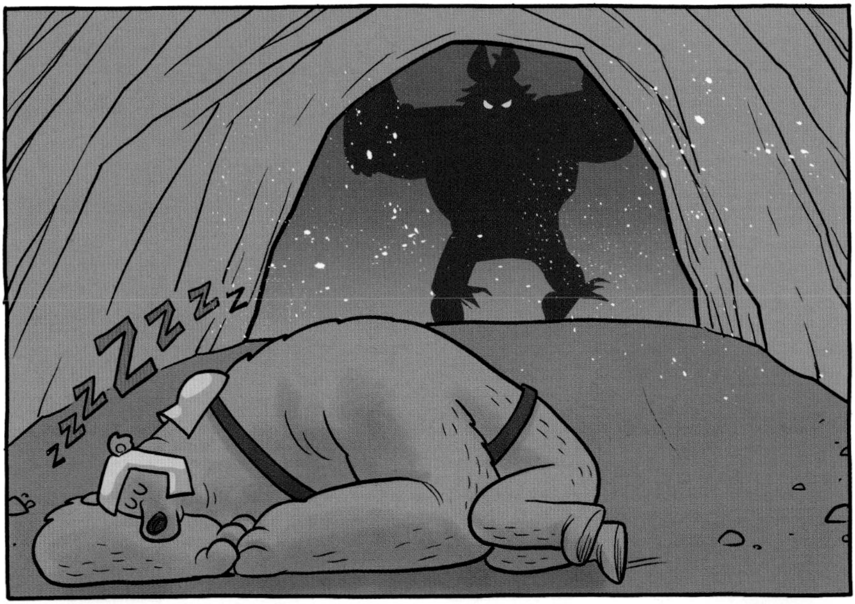
ZZZZZZZZ

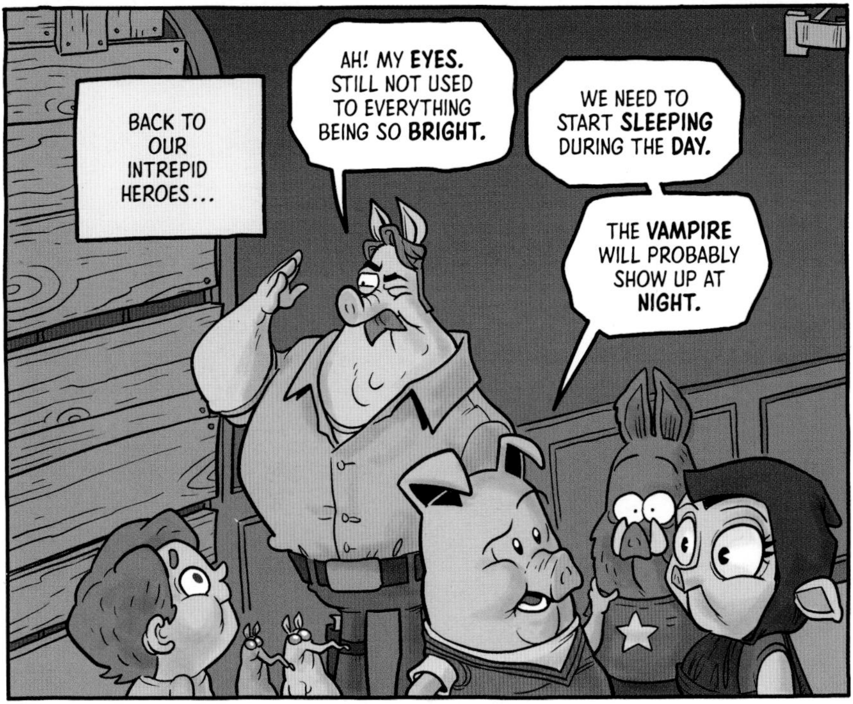
BACK TO OUR INTREPID HEROES...
AH! MY **EYES.** STILL NOT USED TO EVERYTHING BEING SO **BRIGHT.**
WE NEED TO START **SLEEPING** DURING THE **DAY.**
THE **VAMPIRE** WILL PROBABLY SHOW UP AT **NIGHT.**

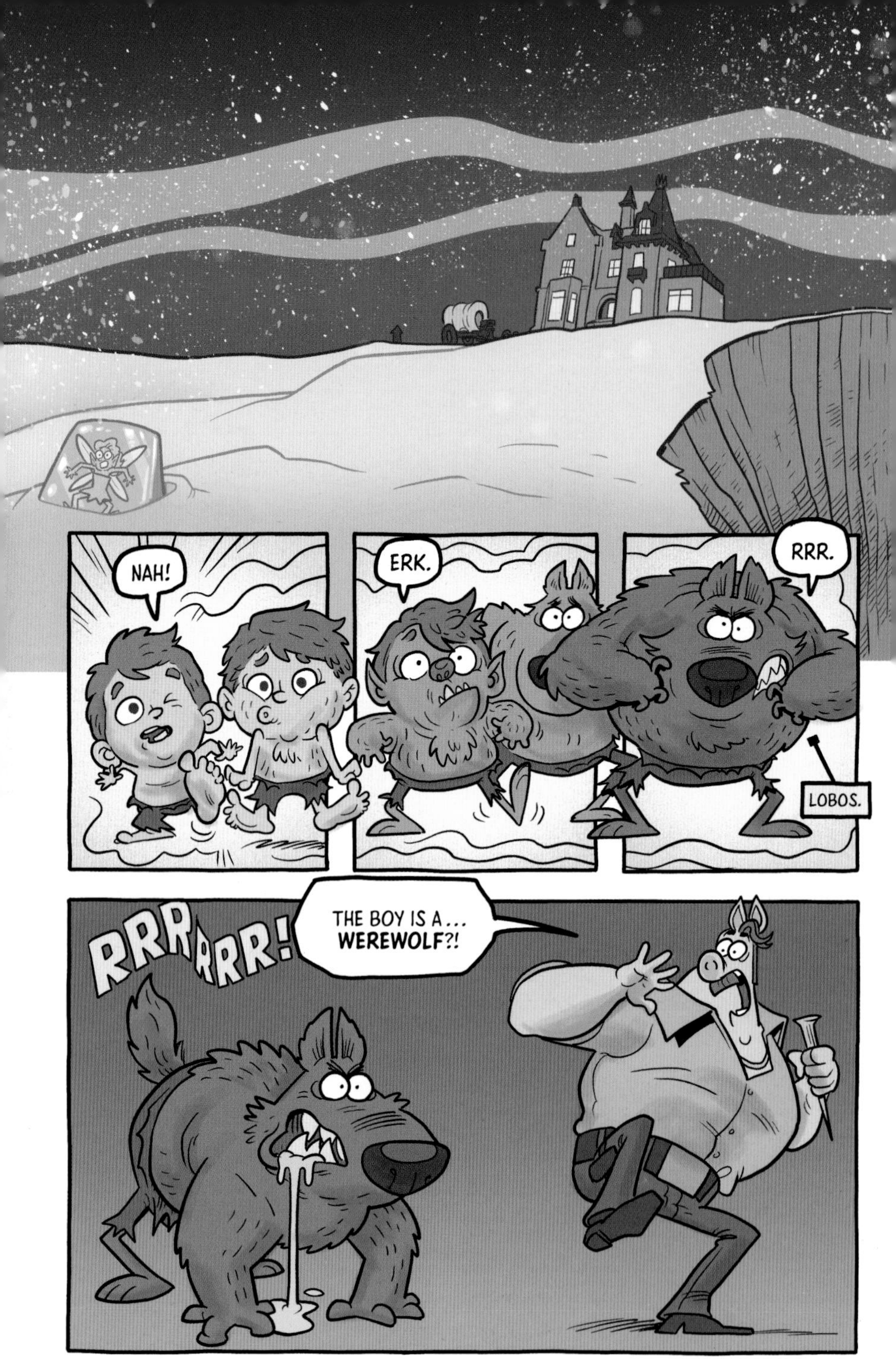
NAH!
ERK.
RRR.
LOBOS.
RRRRRR!
THE BOY IS A...
WEREWOLF?!

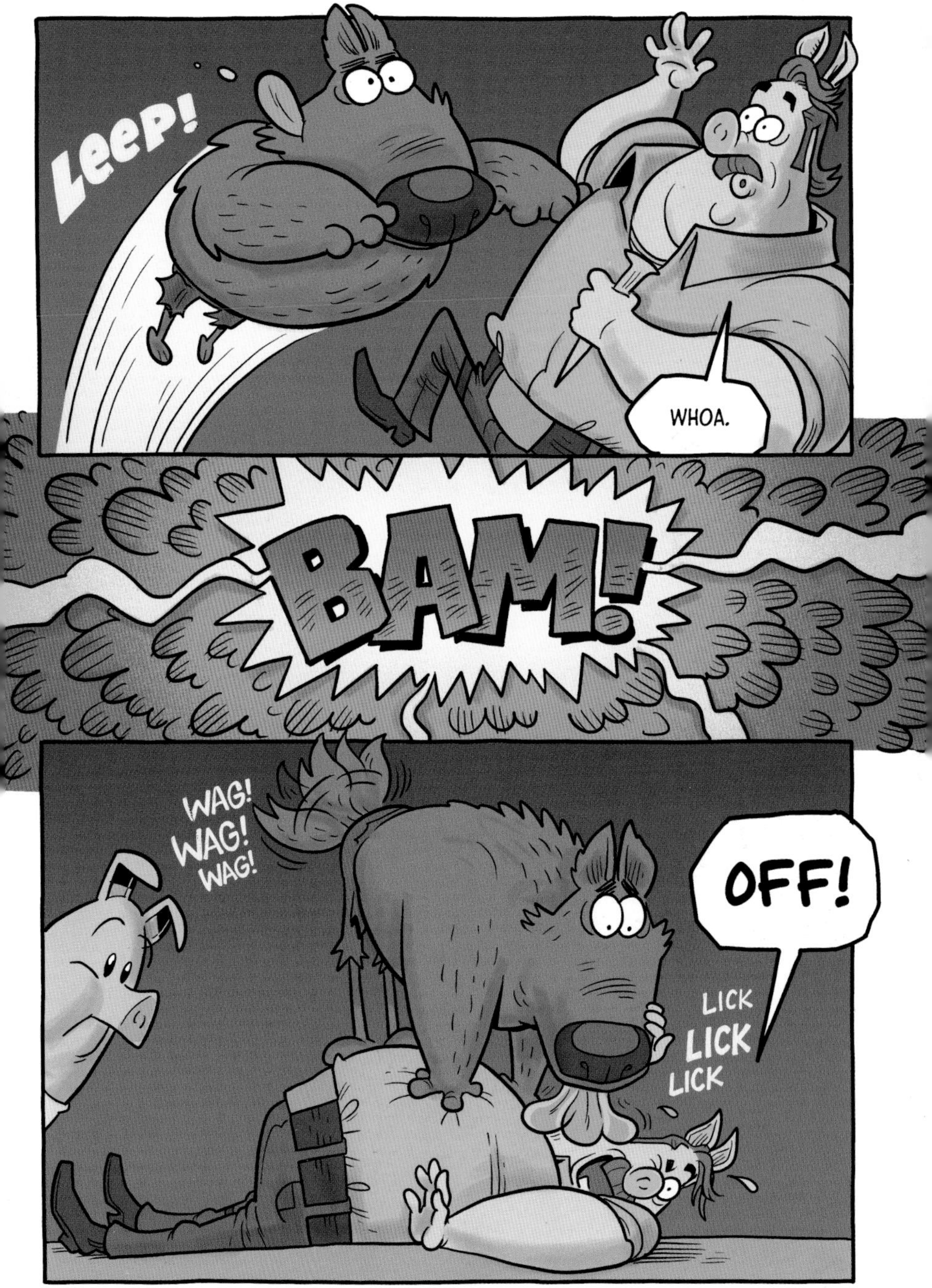
LEEP!
WHOA.
BAM!
WAG!
WAG!
WAG!
OFF!
LICK
LICK
LICK

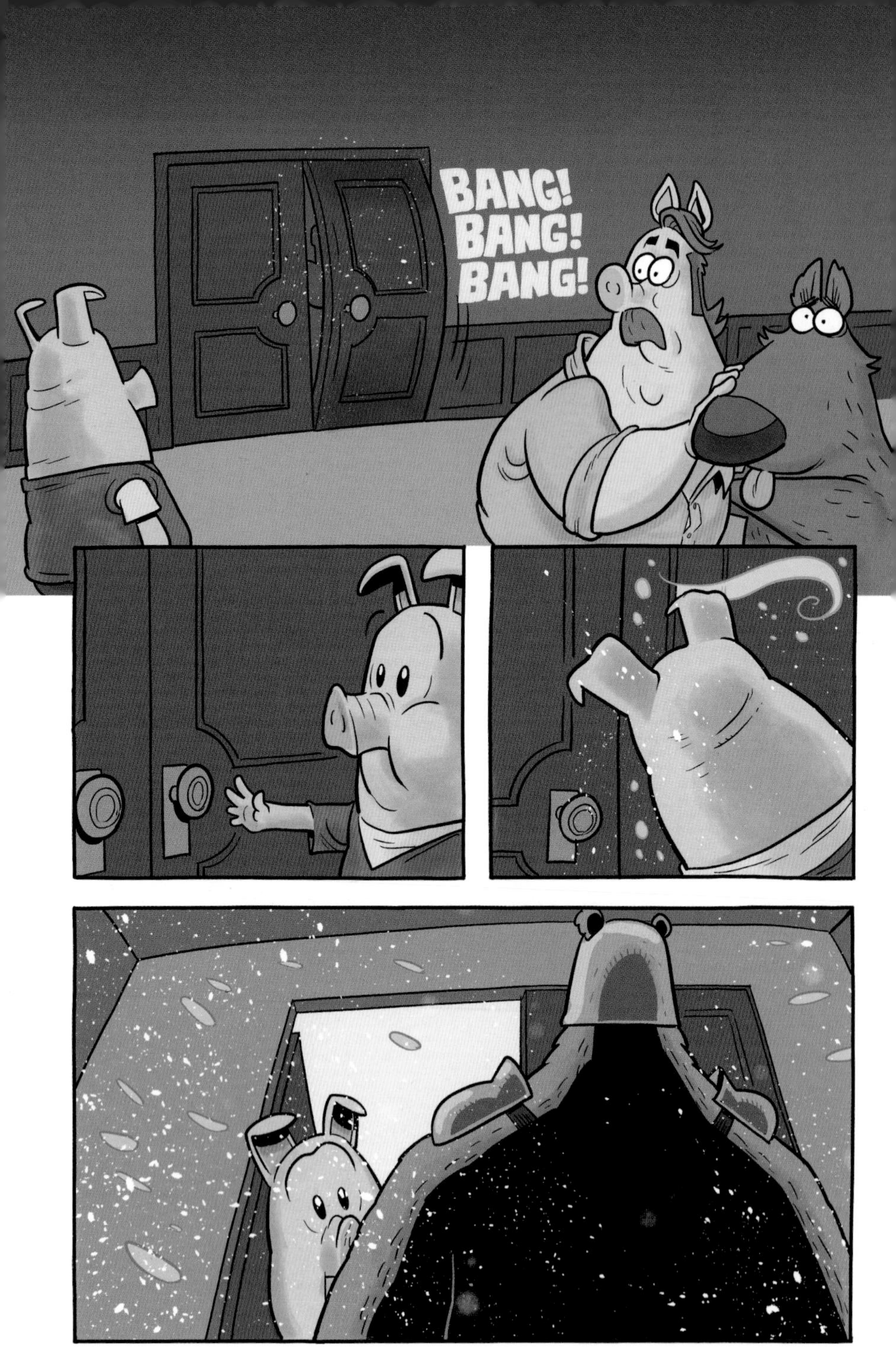
BANG!
BANG!
BANG!

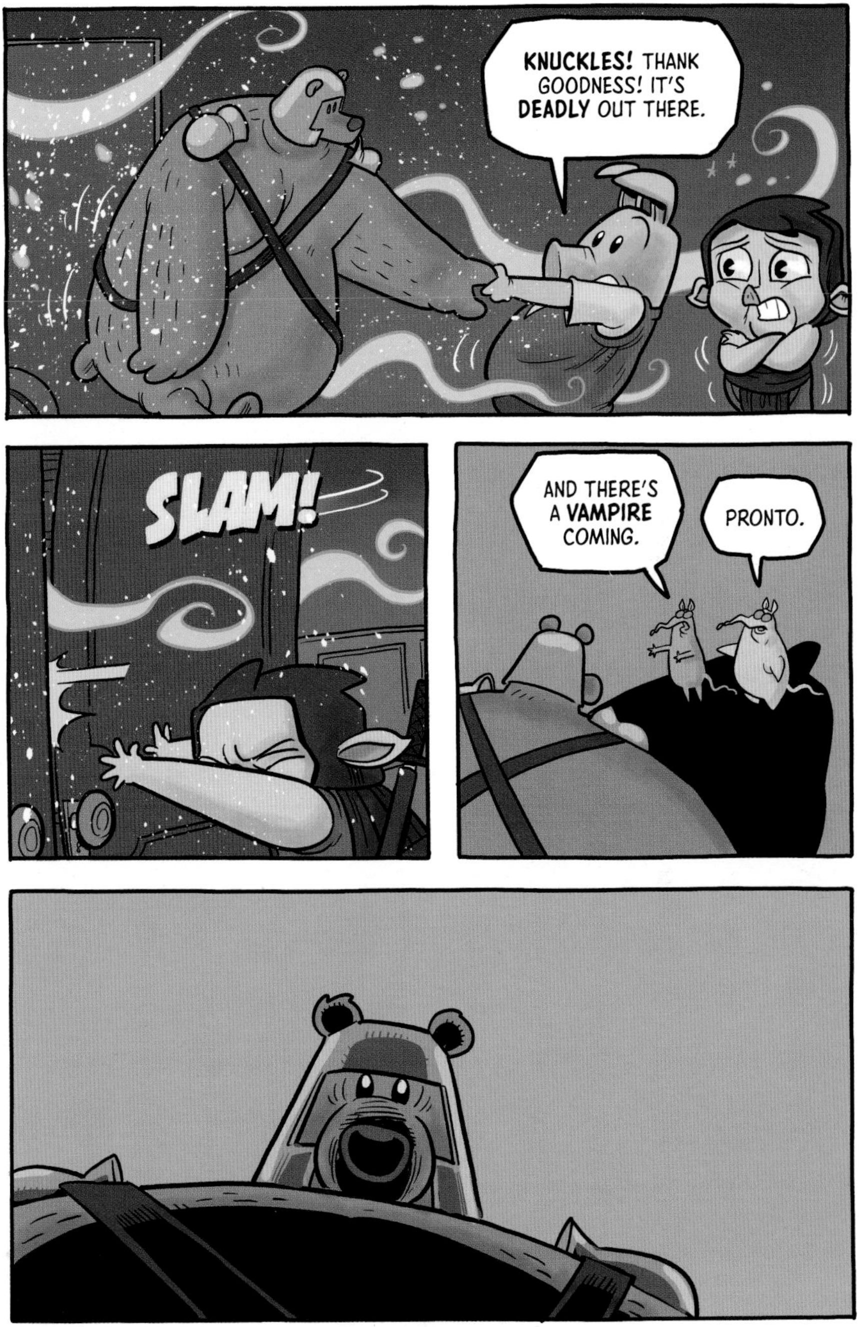
KNUCKLES! THANK GOODNESS! IT'S **DEADLY** OUT THERE.
SLAM!
AND THERE'S A **VAMPIRE** COMING.
PRONTO.

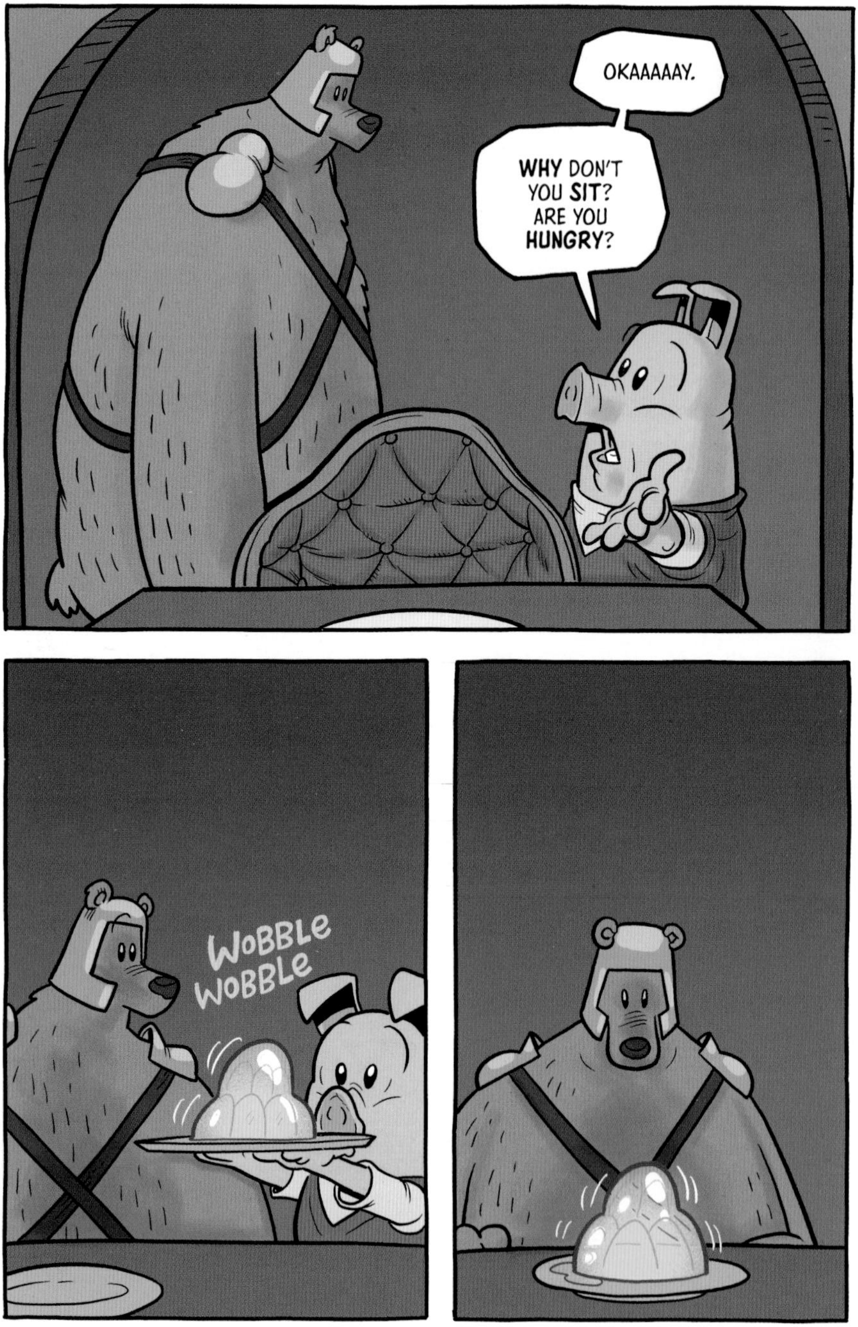
OKAAAAAY.
WHY DON'T YOU SIT? ARE YOU HUNGRY?
WOBBLE WOBBLE

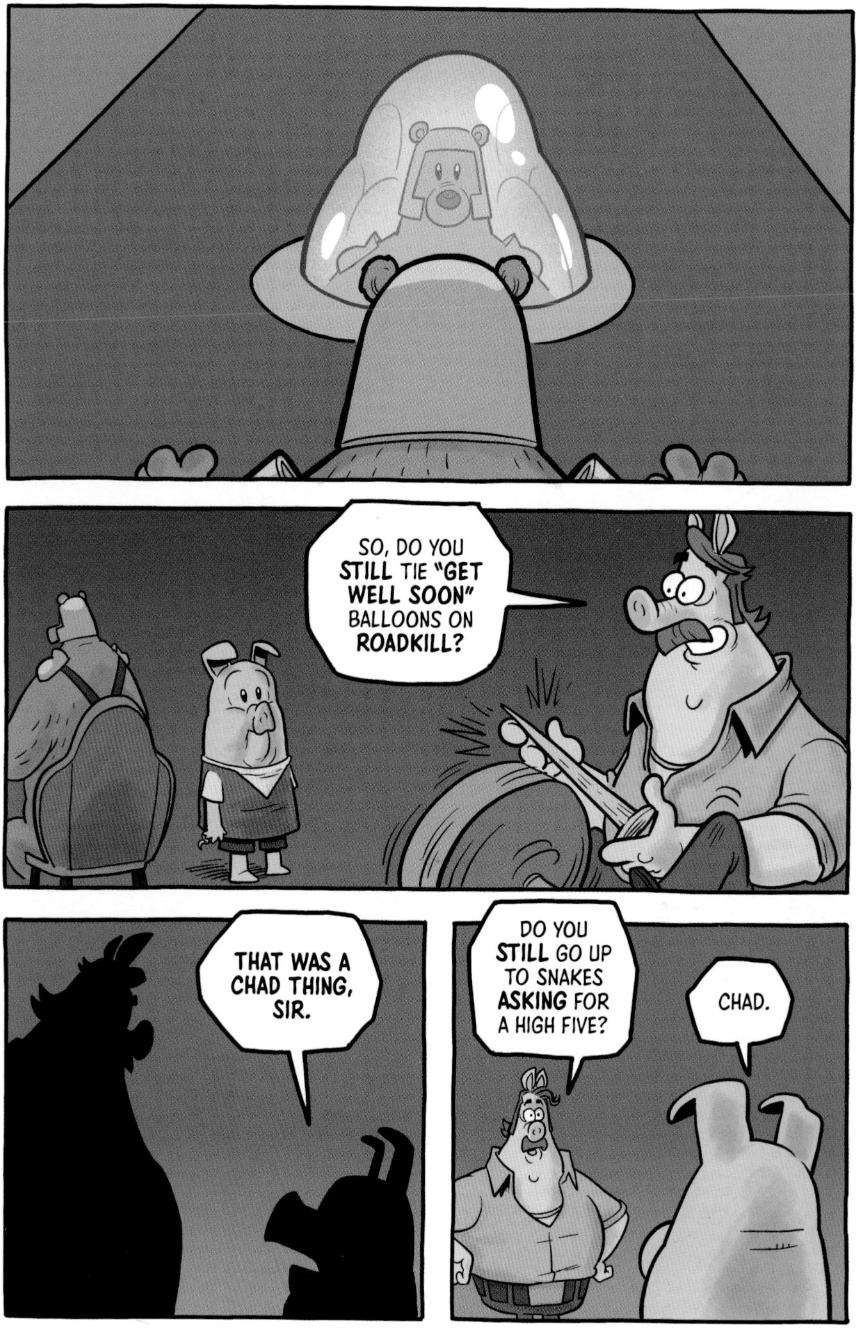
SO, DO YOU STILL TIE "GET WELL SOON" BALLOONS ON ROADKILL?
THAT WAS A CHAD THING, SIR.
DO YOU STILL GO UP TO SNAKES ASKING FOR A HIGH FIVE?
CHAD.

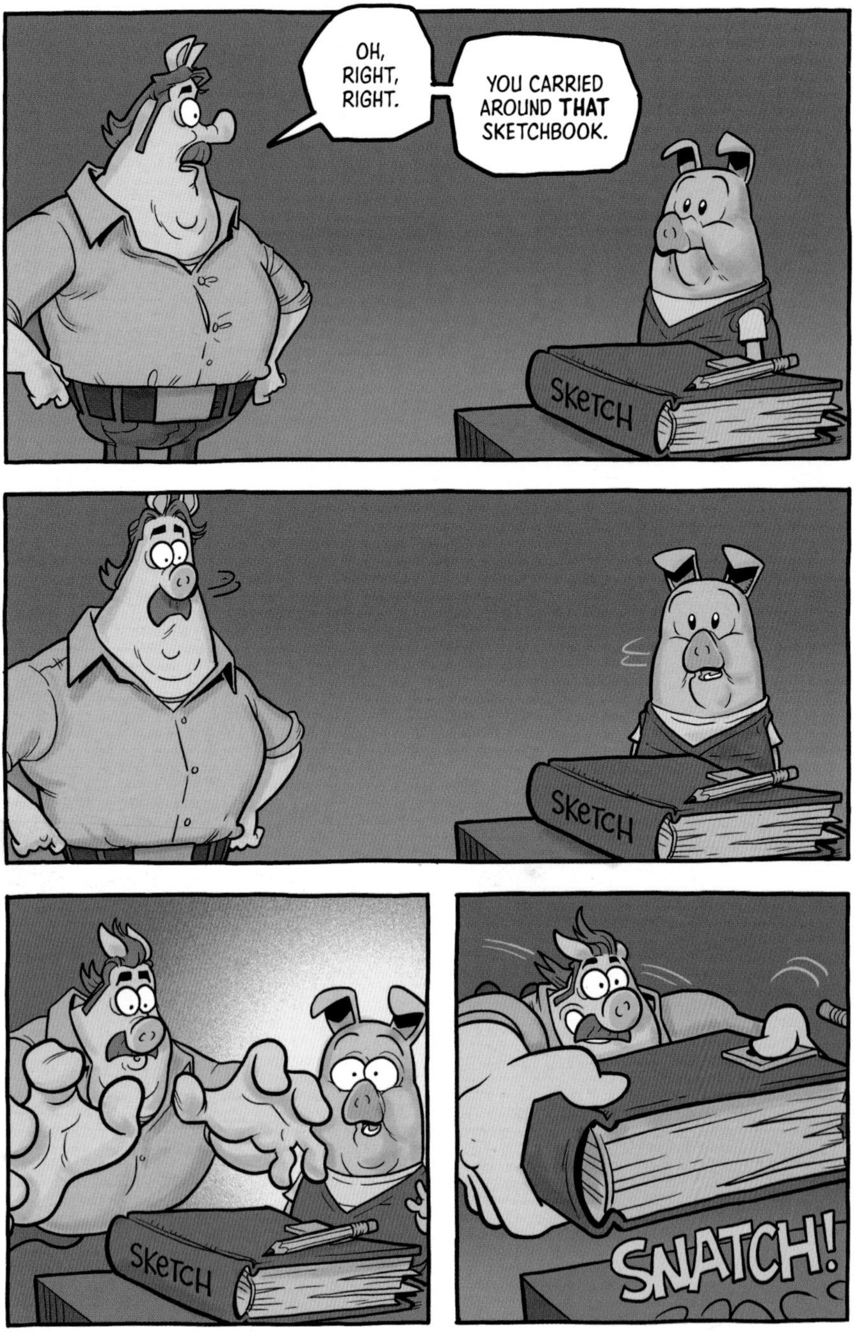
OH, RIGHT, RIGHT.
YOU CARRIED AROUND **THAT** SKETCHBOOK.
SKETCH
SKETCH
SKETCH
SNATCH!

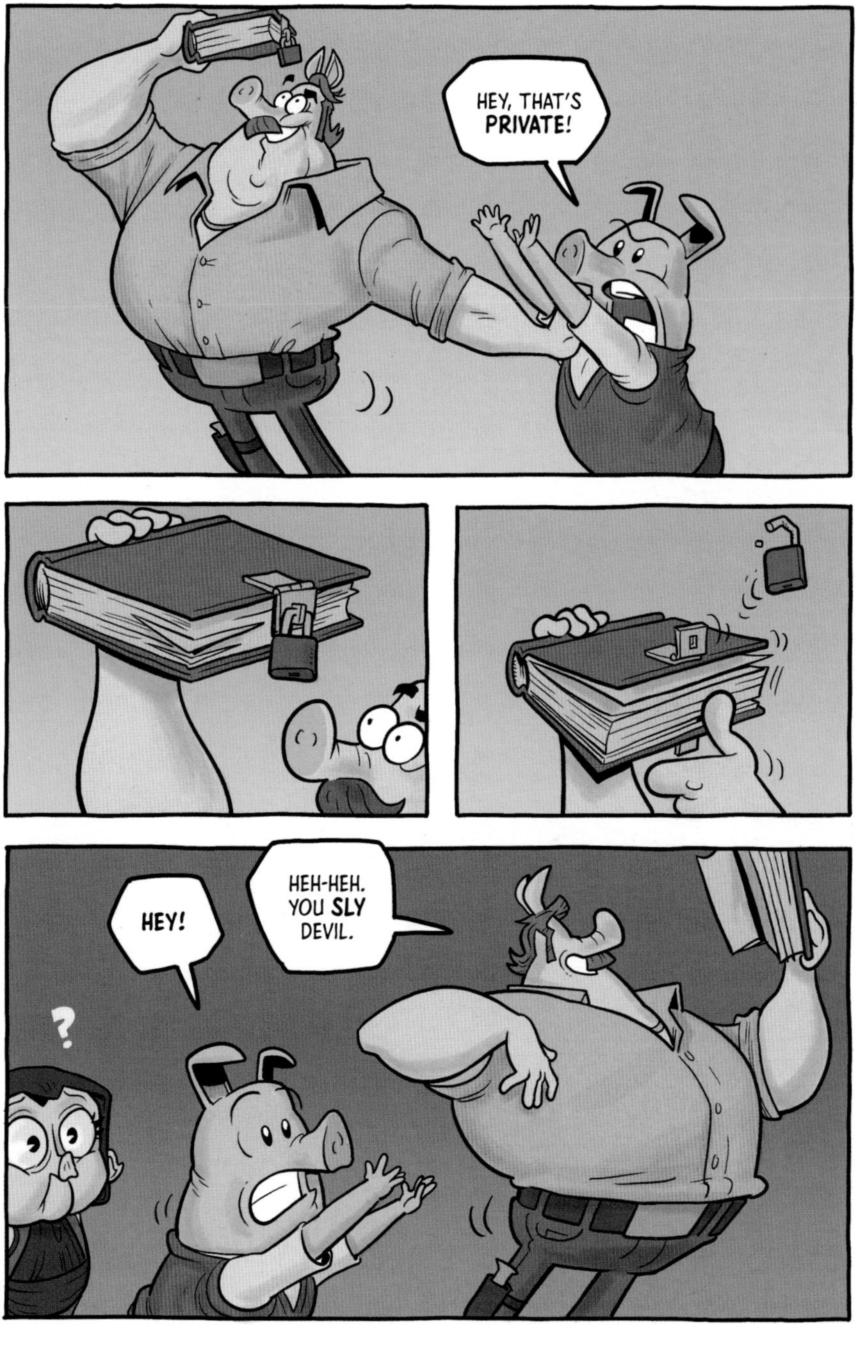
HEY, THAT'S PRIVATE!
HEY!
HEH-HEH. YOU SLY DEVIL.
?

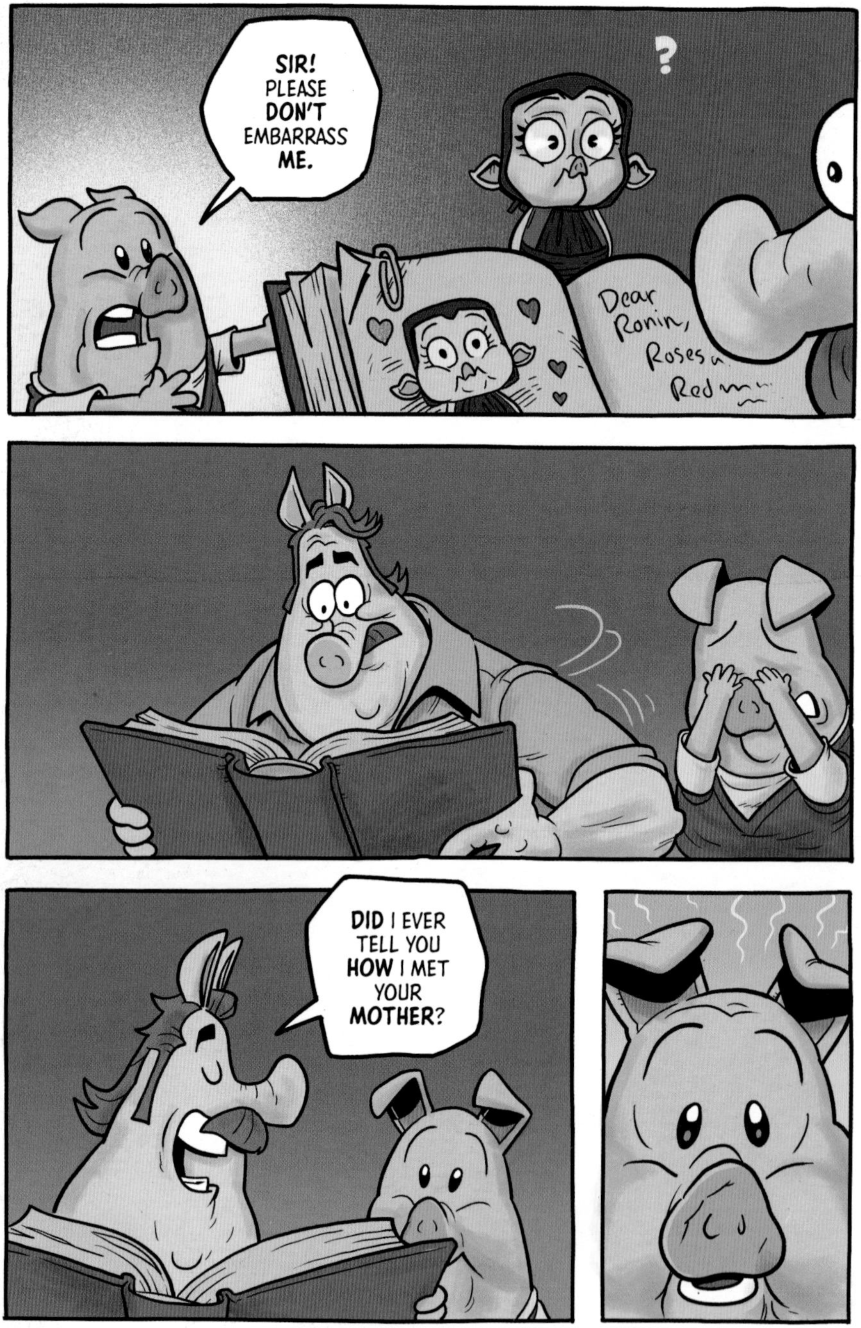
SIR! PLEASE DON'T EMBARRASS ME.
?
Dear Ronin, Roses a Red
DID I EVER TELL YOU HOW I MET YOUR MOTHER?

CHAPTER THIRTEEN

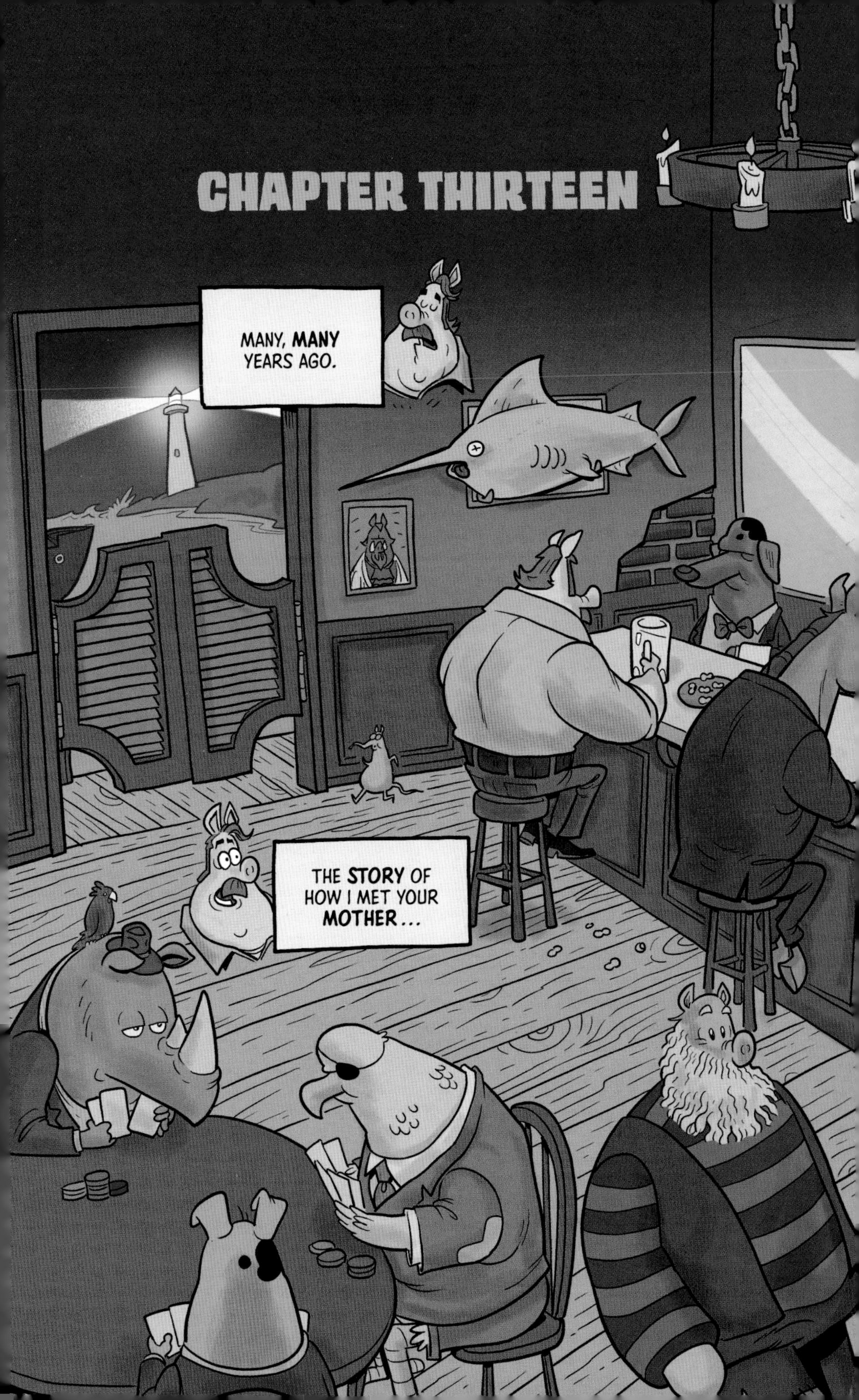
MANY, MANY YEARS AGO.
THE STORY OF HOW I MET YOUR MOTHER...

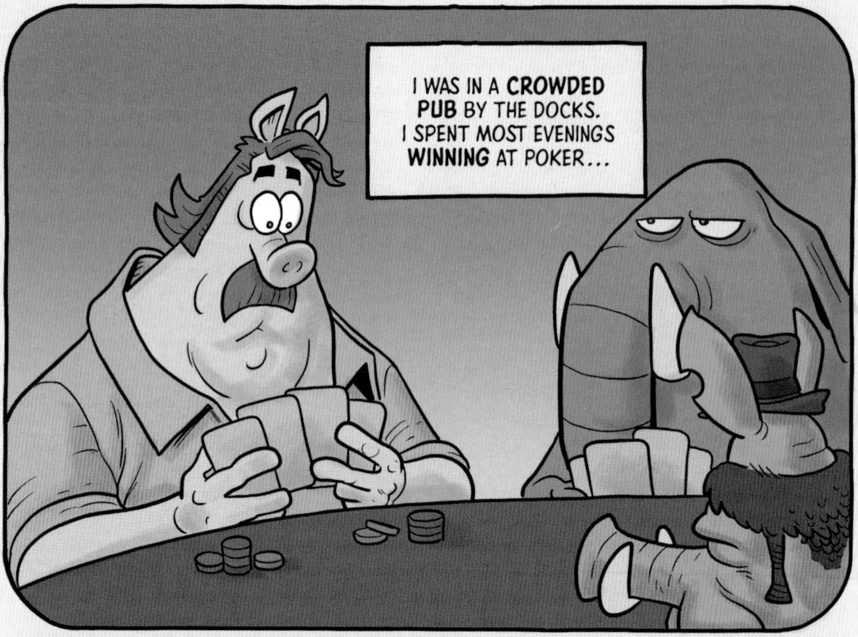
I WAS IN A **CROWDED PUB** BY THE DOCKS. I SPENT MOST EVENINGS **WINNING** AT POKER...

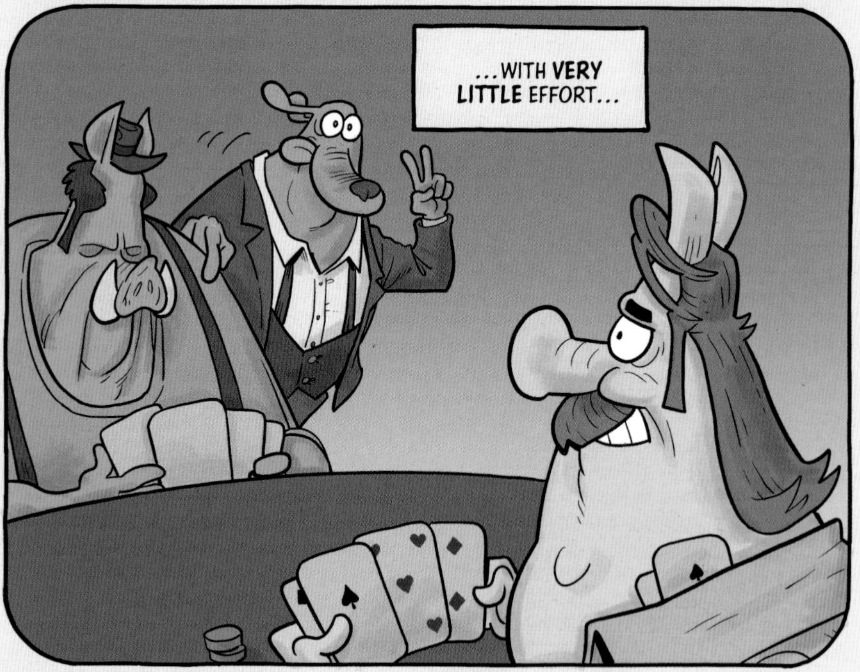
...WITH **VERY LITTLE** EFFORT...

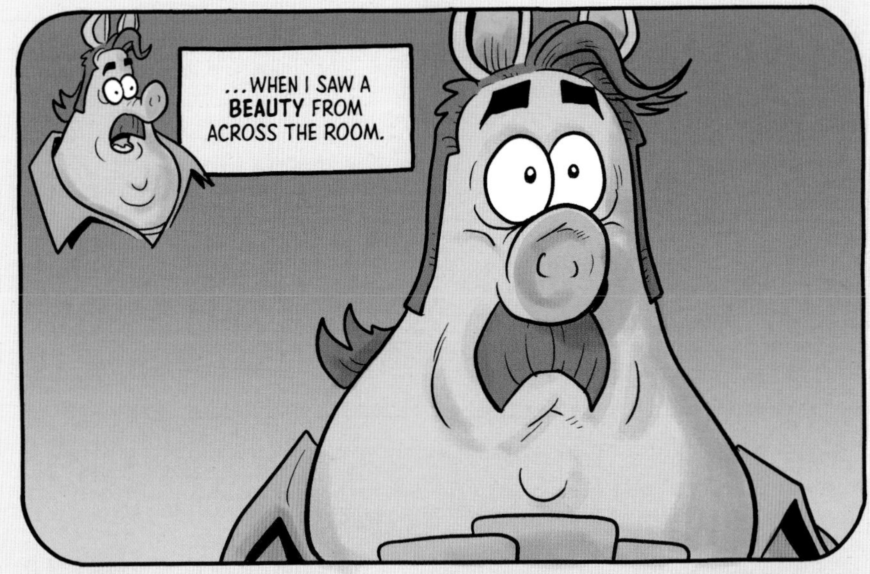
...WHEN I SAW A BEAUTY FROM ACROSS THE ROOM.

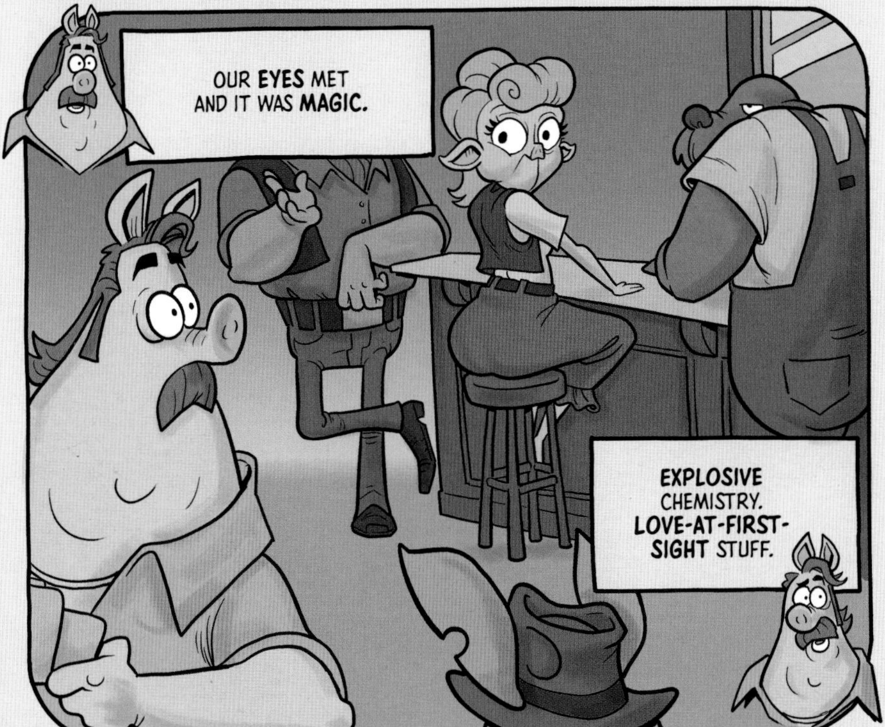
OUR EYES MET AND IT WAS MAGIC.
EXPLOSIVE CHEMISTRY. LOVE-AT-FIRST-SIGHT STUFF.

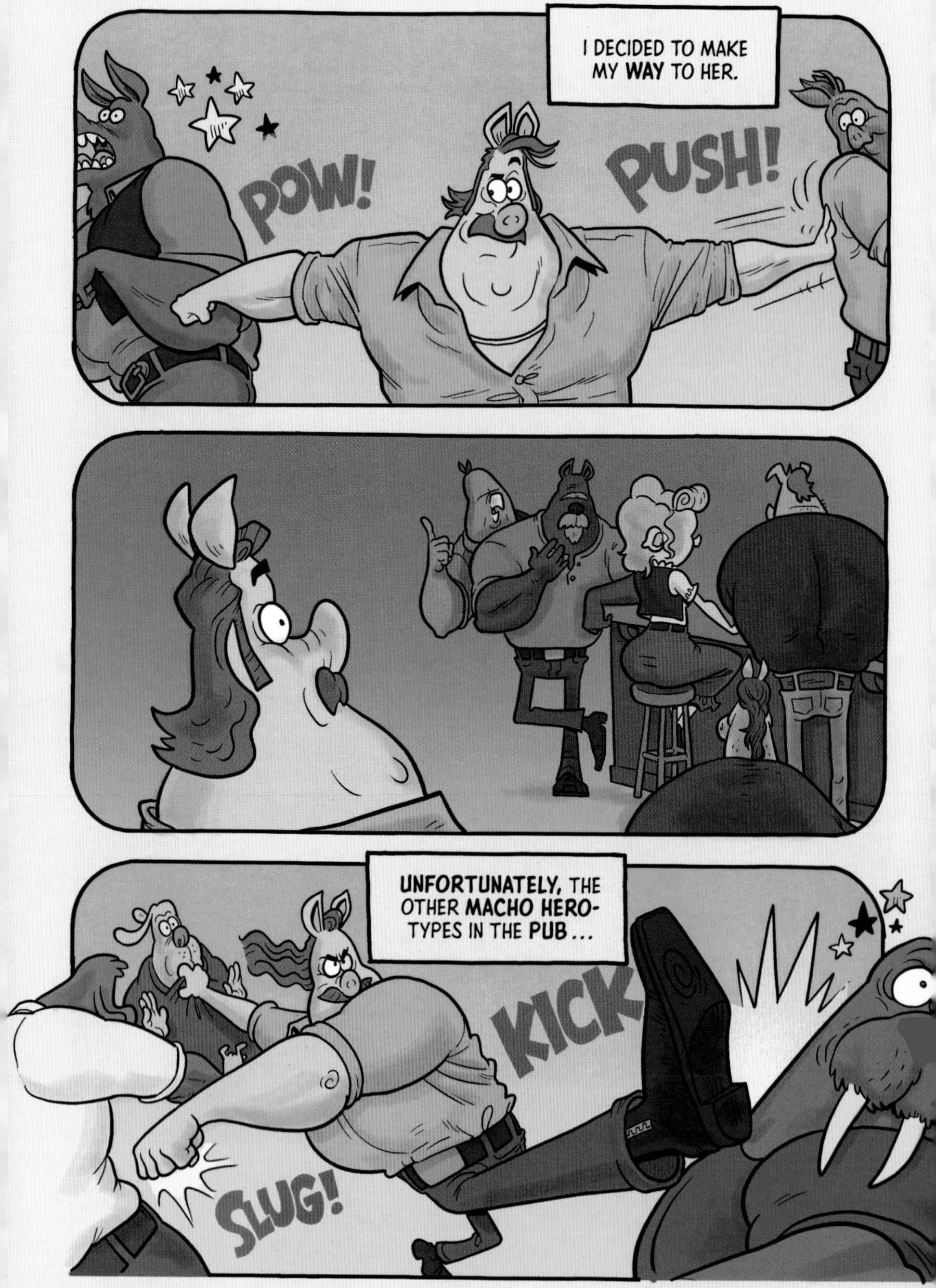
I DECIDED TO MAKE MY **WAY** TO HER.
POW!
PUSH!
UNFORTUNATELY, THE OTHER **MACHO HERO-TYPES** IN THE **PUB**...
KICK
SLUG!

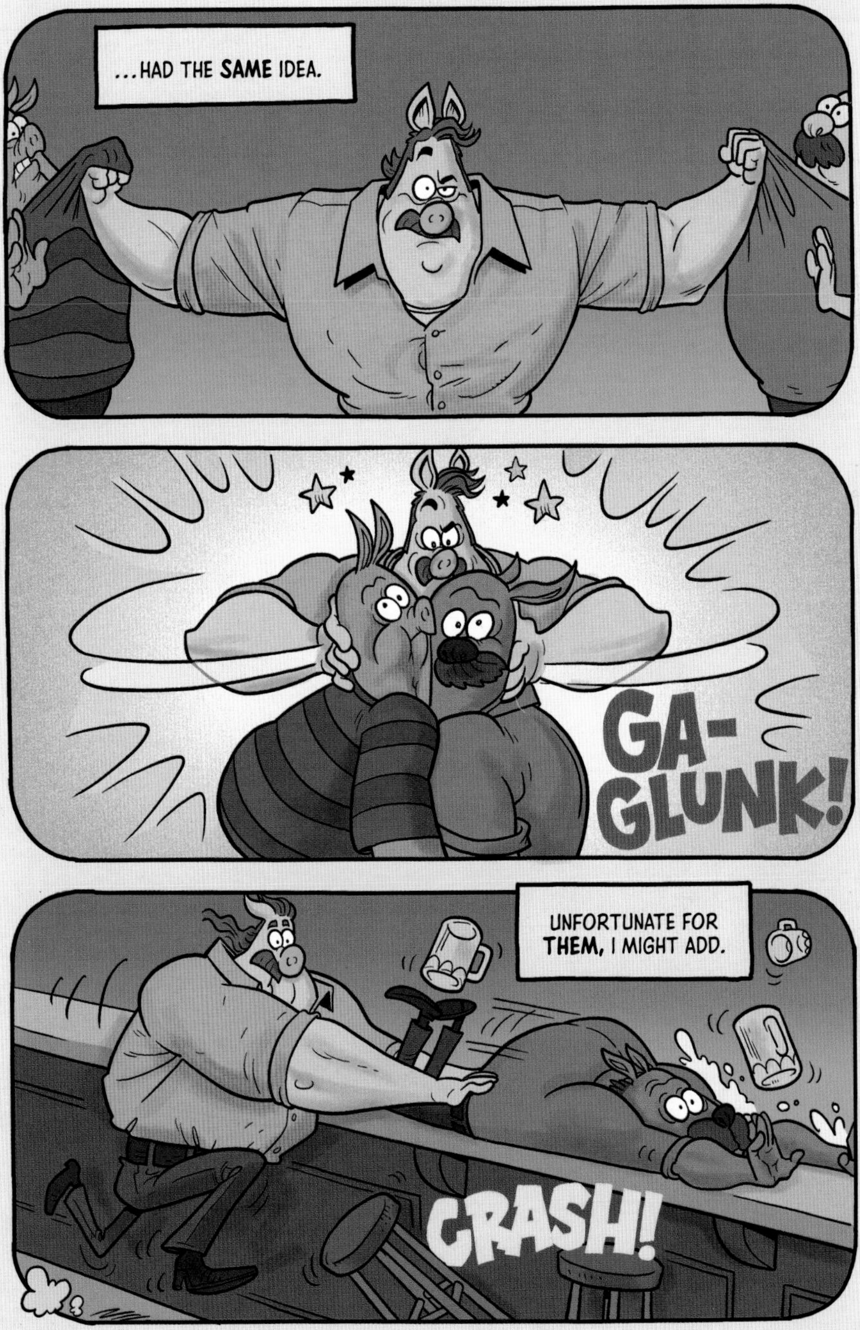
...HAD THE **SAME** IDEA.
GA-GLUNK!
UNFORTUNATE FOR **THEM,** I MIGHT ADD.
CRASH!

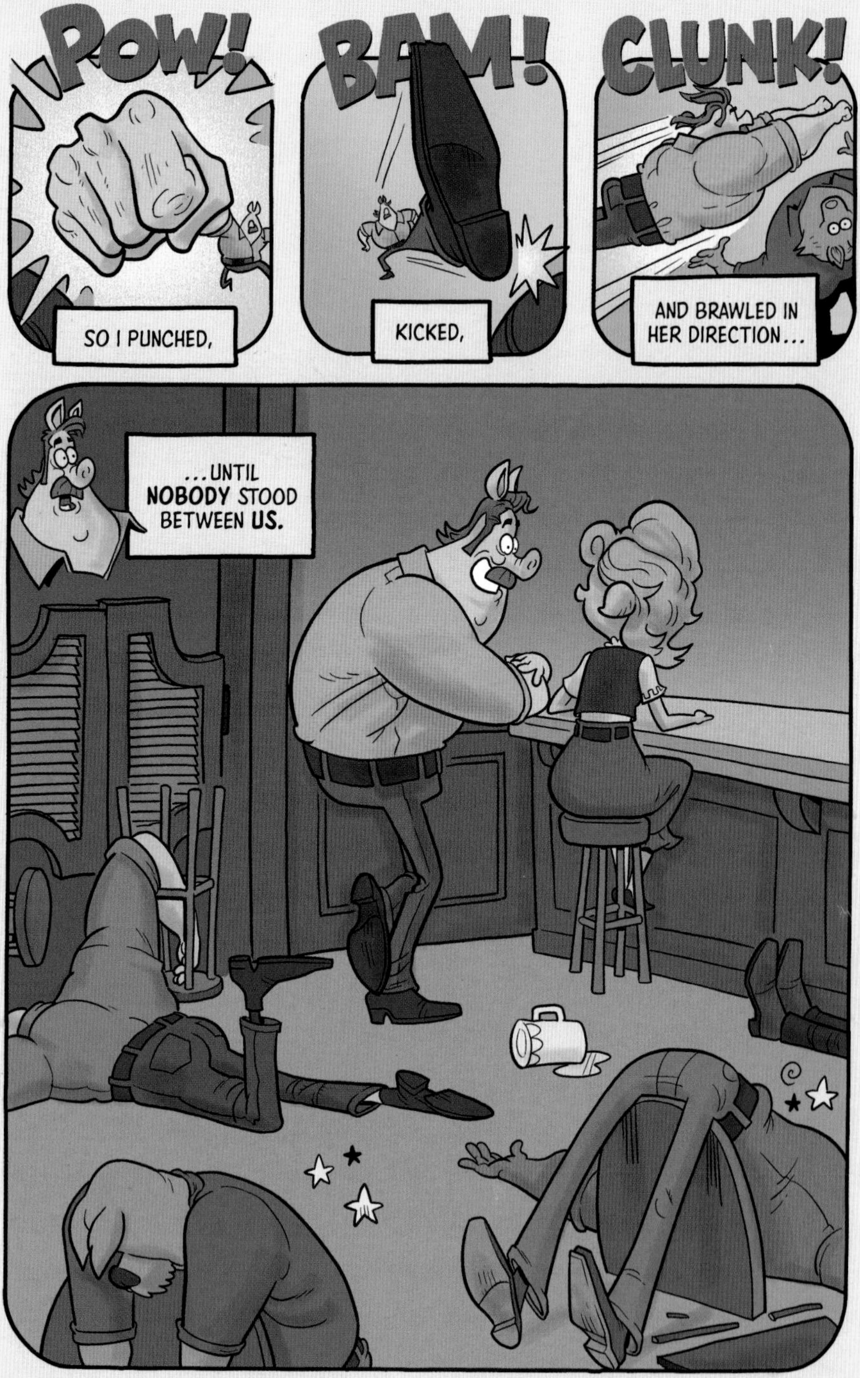
POW!
SO I PUNCHED,
BAM!
KICKED,
CLUNK!
AND BRAWLED IN HER DIRECTION...
...UNTIL NOBODY STOOD BETWEEN US.

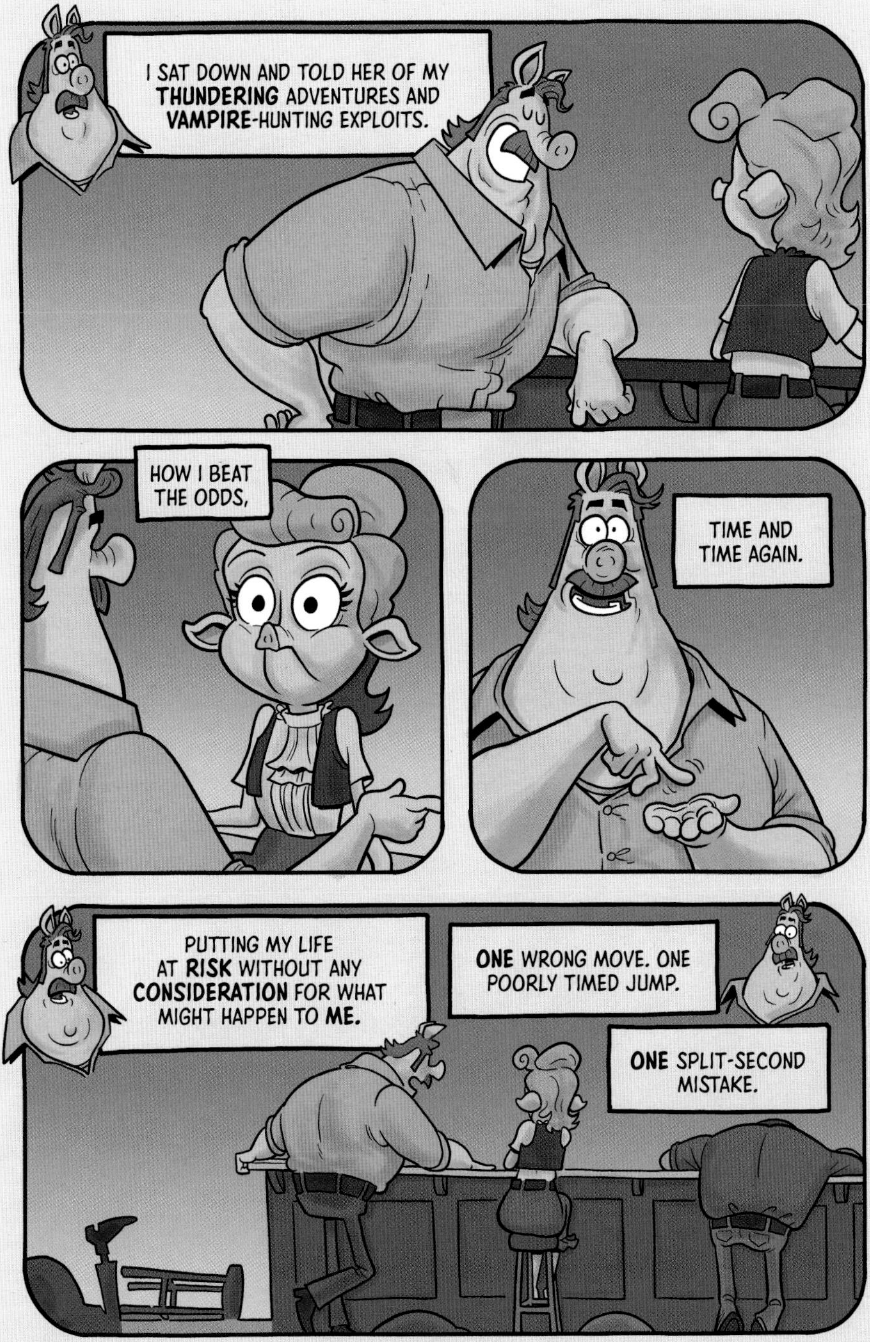
I SAT DOWN AND TOLD HER OF MY **THUNDERING** ADVENTURES AND **VAMPIRE**-HUNTING EXPLOITS.
HOW I BEAT THE ODDS,
TIME AND TIME AGAIN.
PUTTING MY LIFE AT **RISK** WITHOUT ANY **CONSIDERATION** FOR WHAT MIGHT HAPPEN TO **ME.**
ONE WRONG MOVE. ONE POORLY TIMED JUMP.
ONE SPLIT-SECOND MISTAKE.

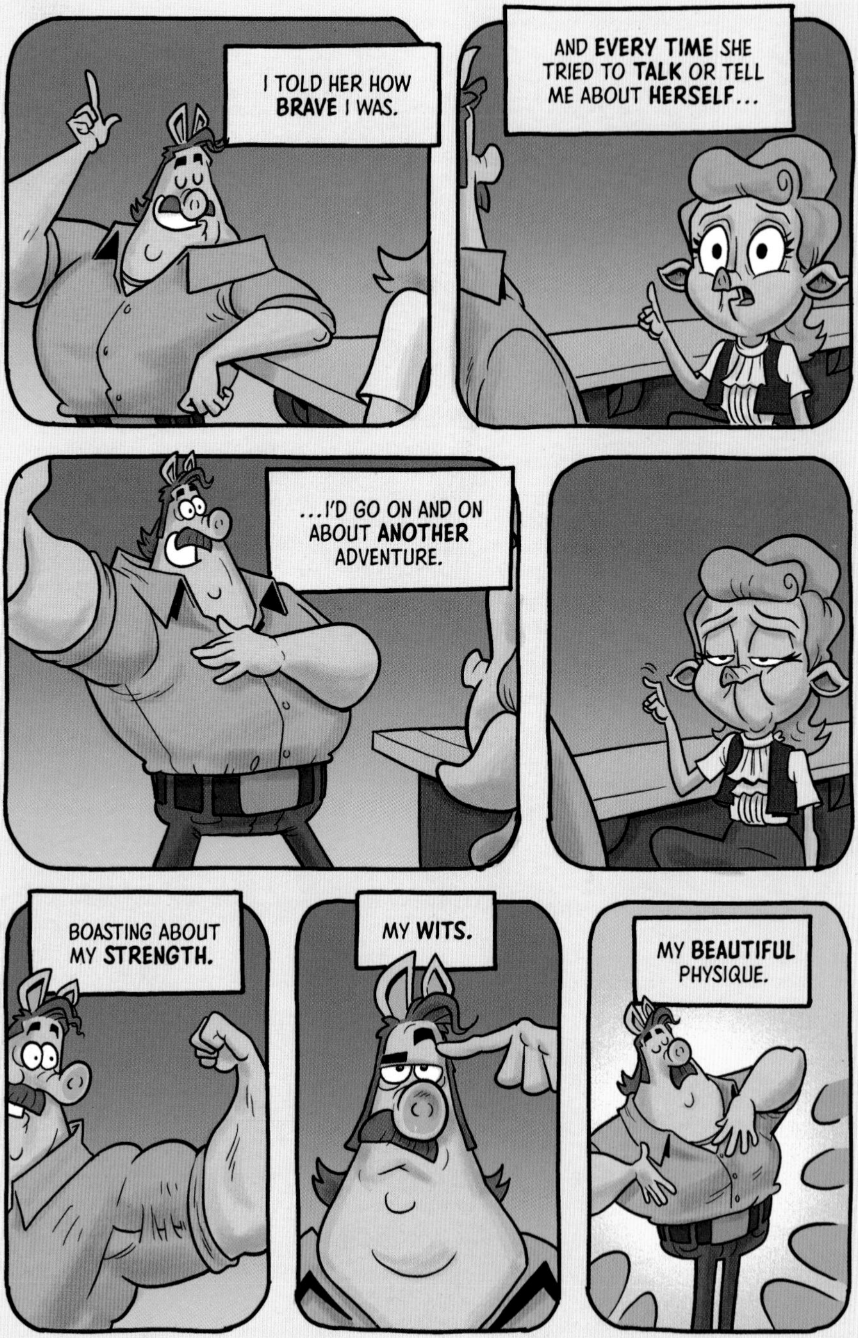
I TOLD HER HOW **BRAVE** I WAS.
AND **EVERY TIME** SHE TRIED TO **TALK** OR TELL ME ABOUT **HERSELF**...
...I'D GO ON AND ON ABOUT **ANOTHER** ADVENTURE.
BOASTING ABOUT MY **STRENGTH.**
MY **WITS.**
MY **BEAUTIFUL** PHYSIQUE.

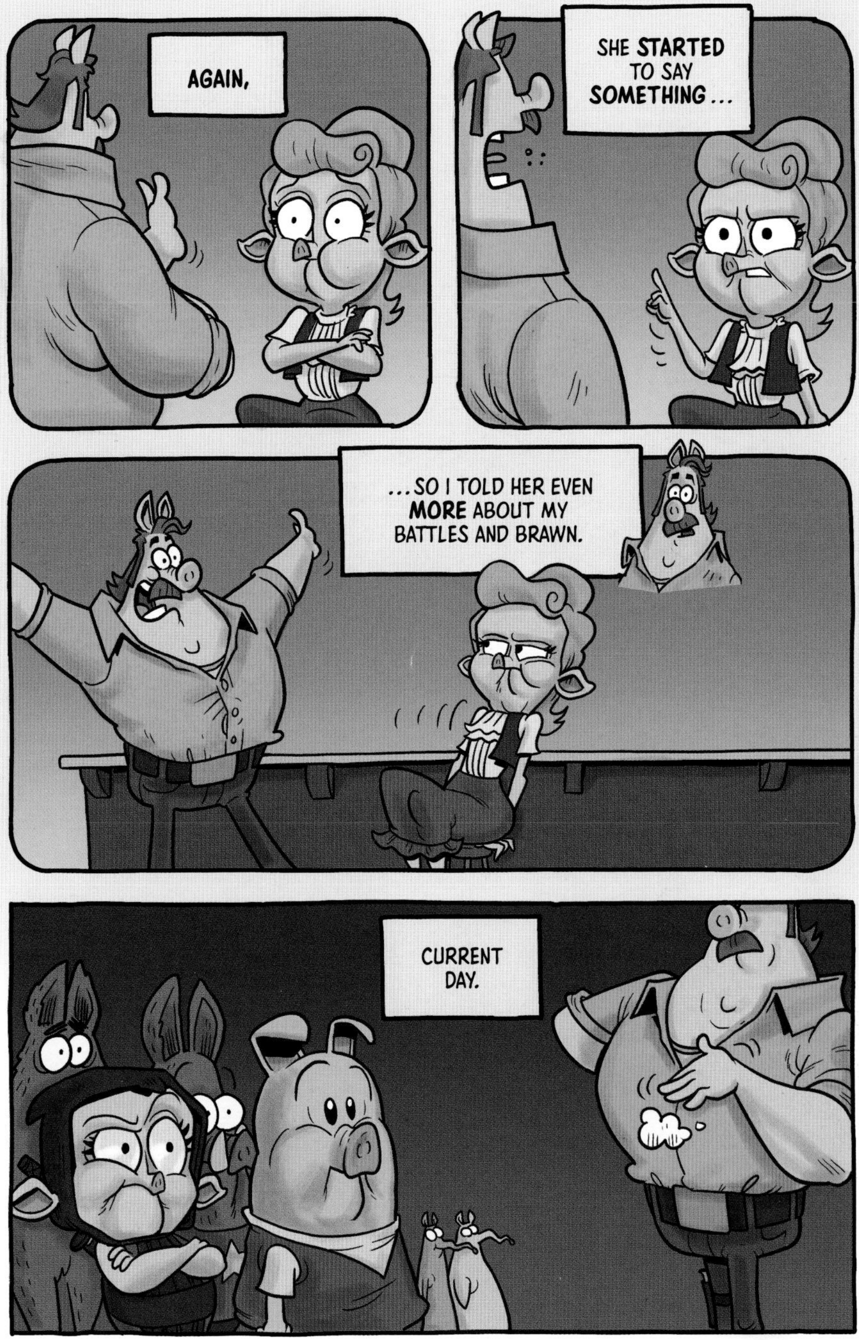
AGAIN,
SHE STARTED TO SAY SOMETHING...
...SO I TOLD HER EVEN MORE ABOUT MY BATTLES AND BRAWN.
CURRENT DAY.

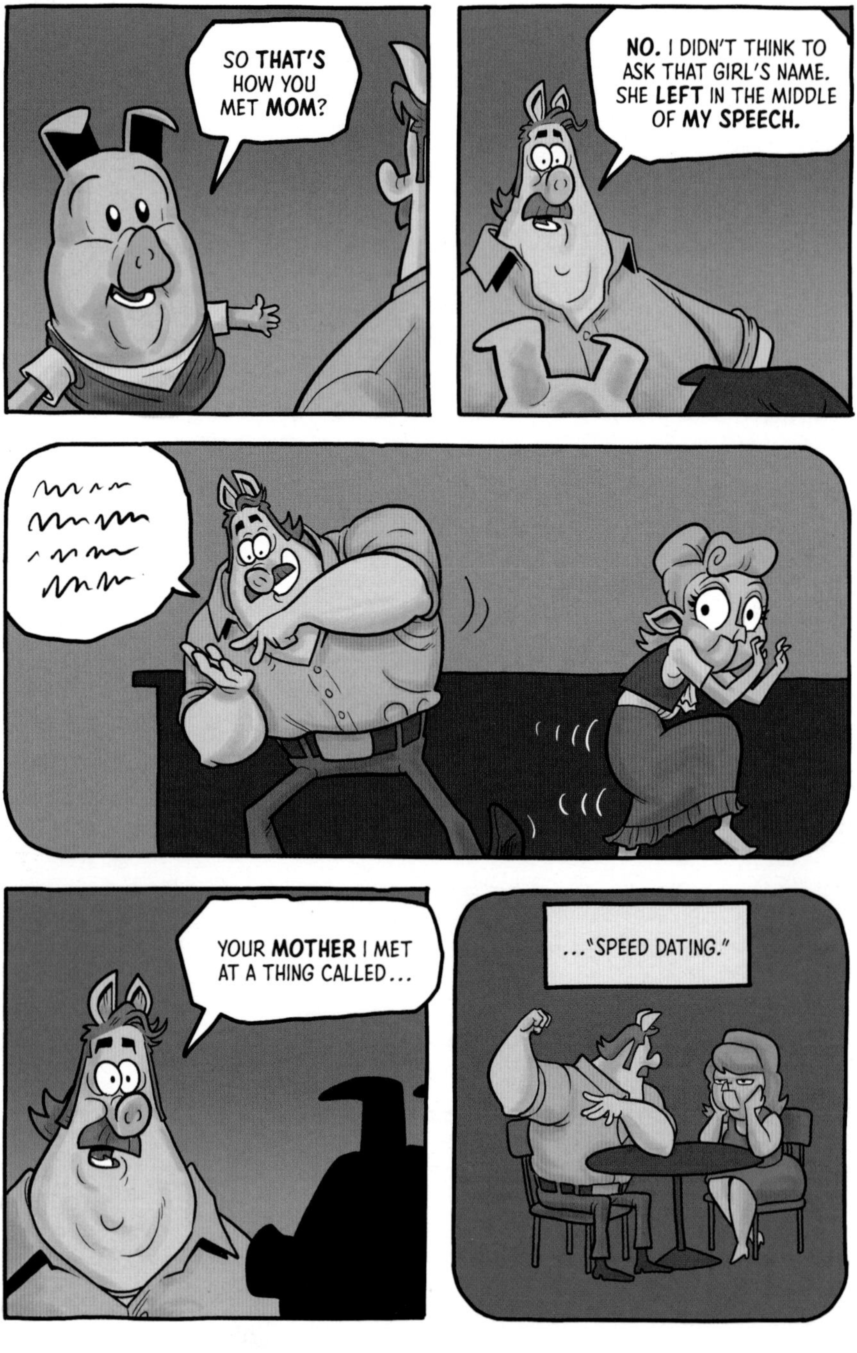
SO THAT'S HOW YOU MET MOM?
NO. I DIDN'T THINK TO ASK THAT GIRL'S NAME. SHE LEFT IN THE MIDDLE OF MY SPEECH.
YOUR MOTHER I MET AT A THING CALLED...
..."SPEED DATING."

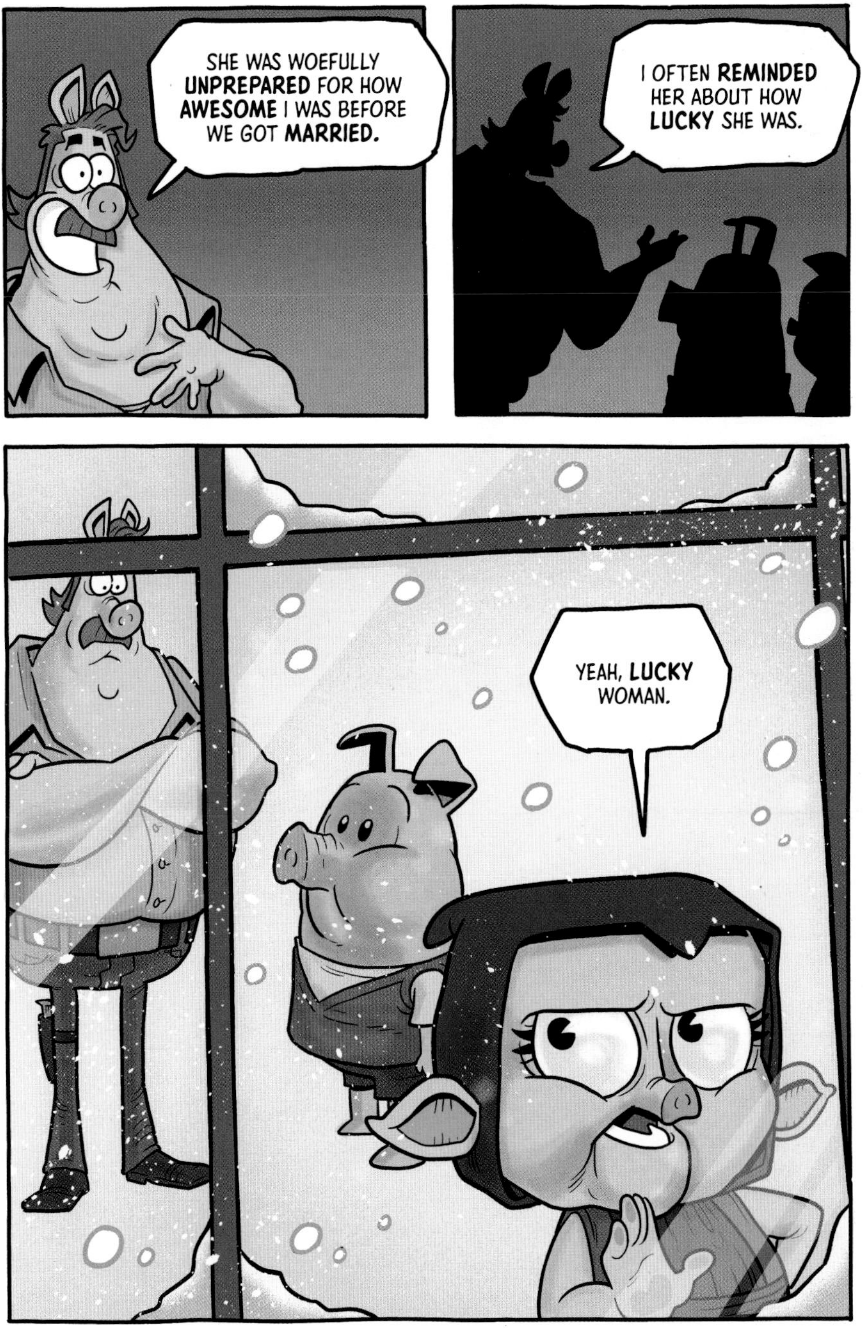
SHE WAS WOEFULLY **UNPREPARED** FOR HOW **AWESOME** I WAS BEFORE WE GOT **MARRIED.**
I OFTEN **REMINDED** HER ABOUT HOW **LUCKY** SHE WAS.
YEAH, **LUCKY** WOMAN.

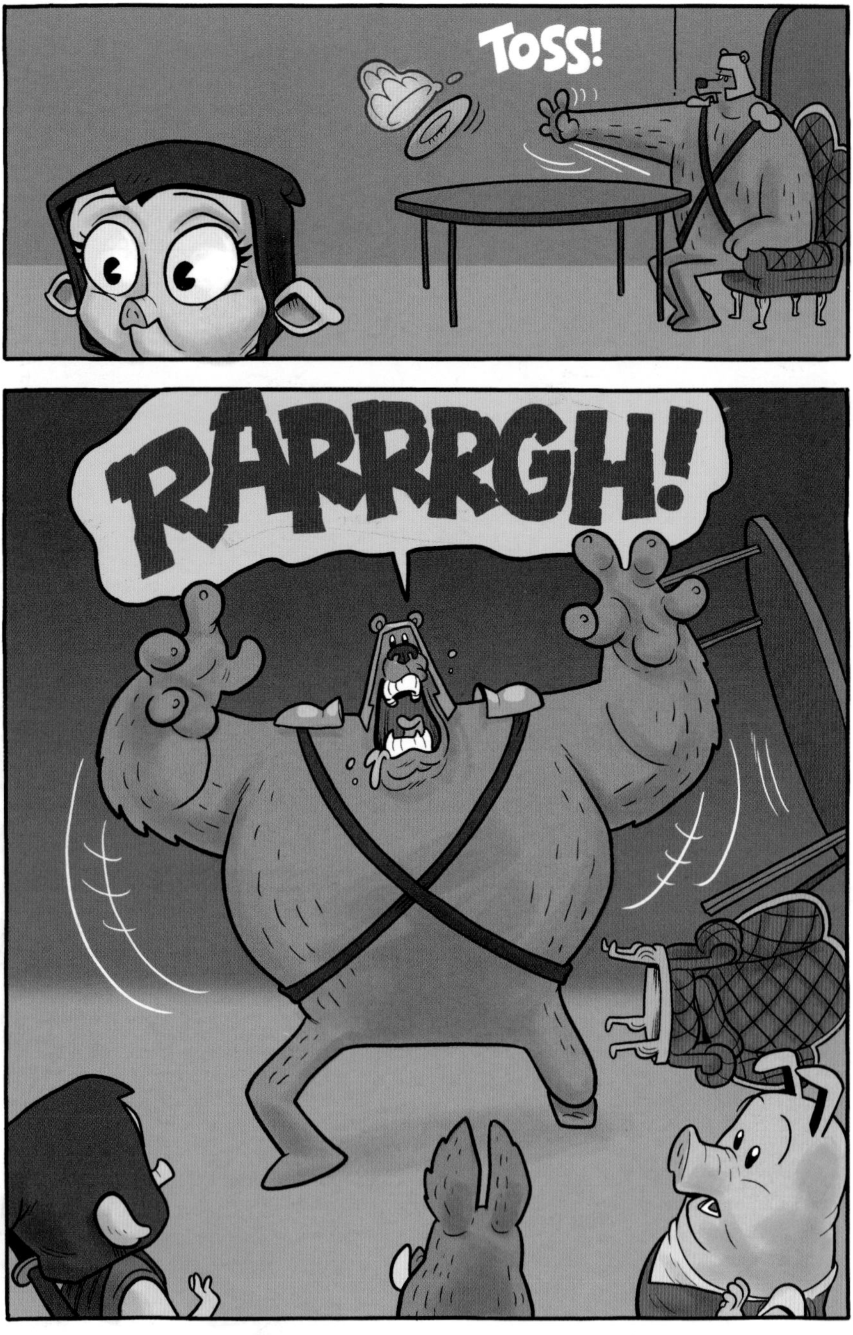
TOSS!
RARRRGH!

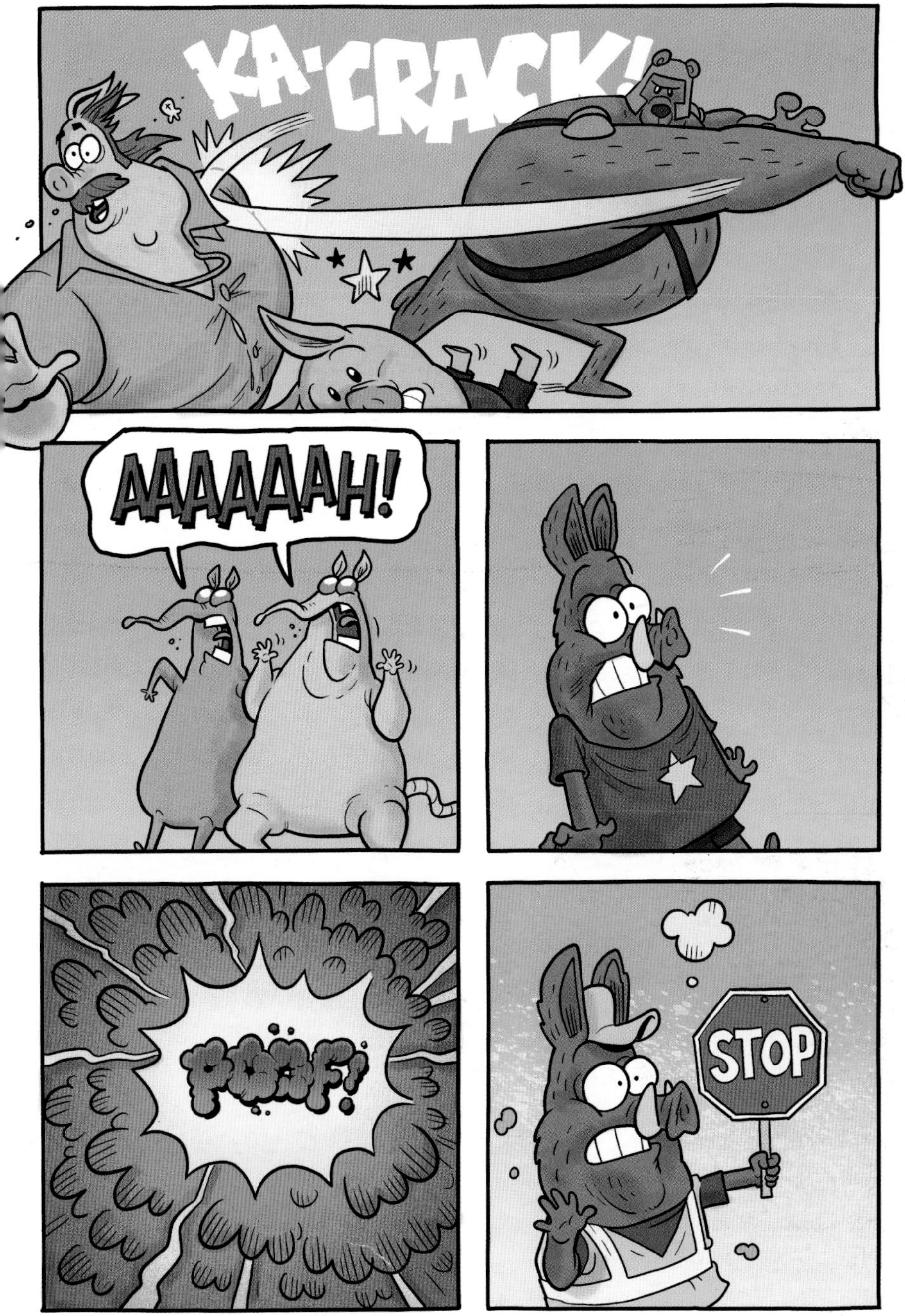
KA-CRACK!
AAAAAAH!
POOF!
STOP

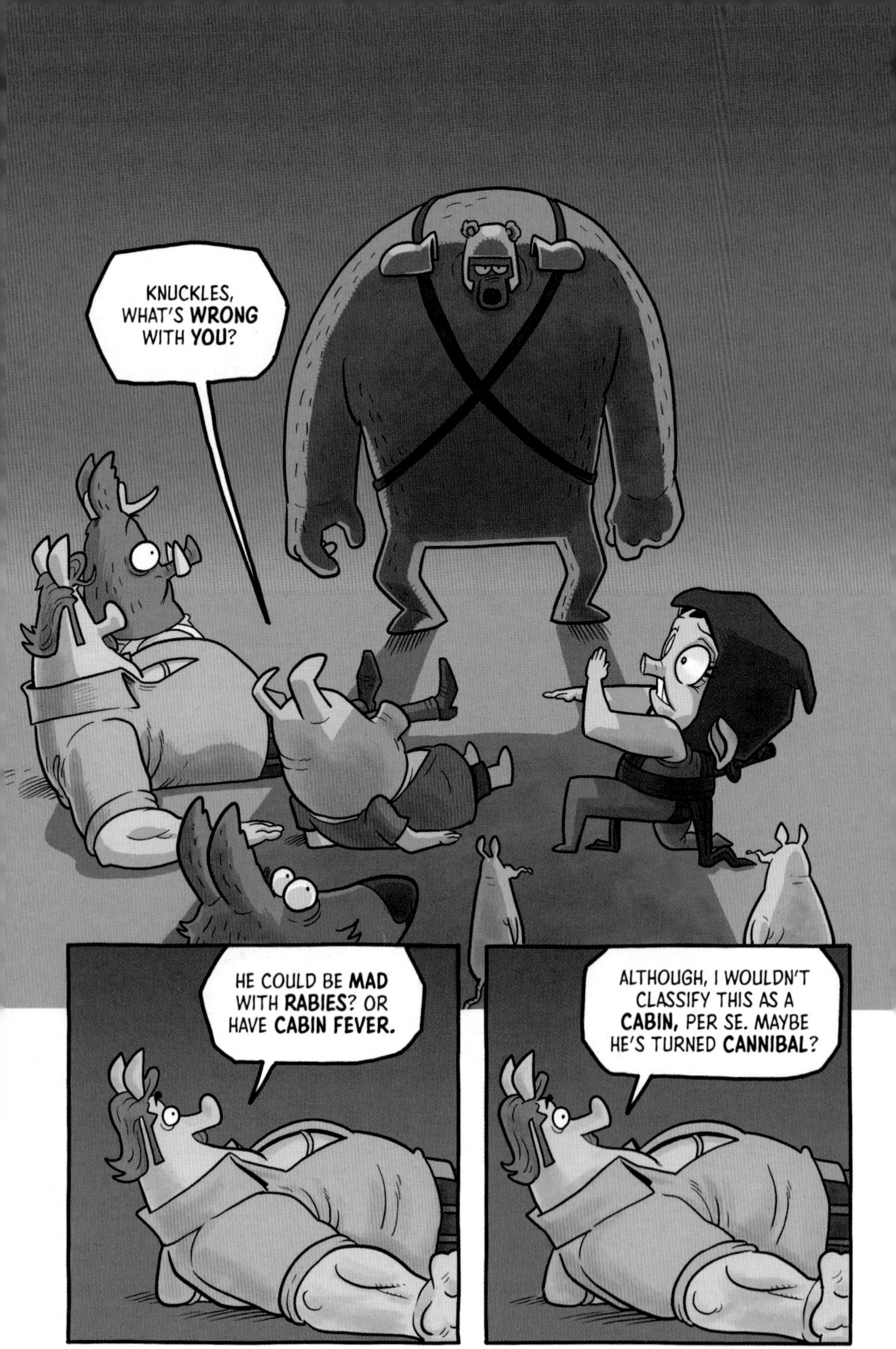
KNUCKLES, WHAT'S WRONG WITH YOU?
HE COULD BE MAD WITH RABIES? OR HAVE CABIN FEVER.
ALTHOUGH, I WOULDN'T CLASSIFY THIS AS A CABIN, PER SE. MAYBE HE'S TURNED CANNIBAL?

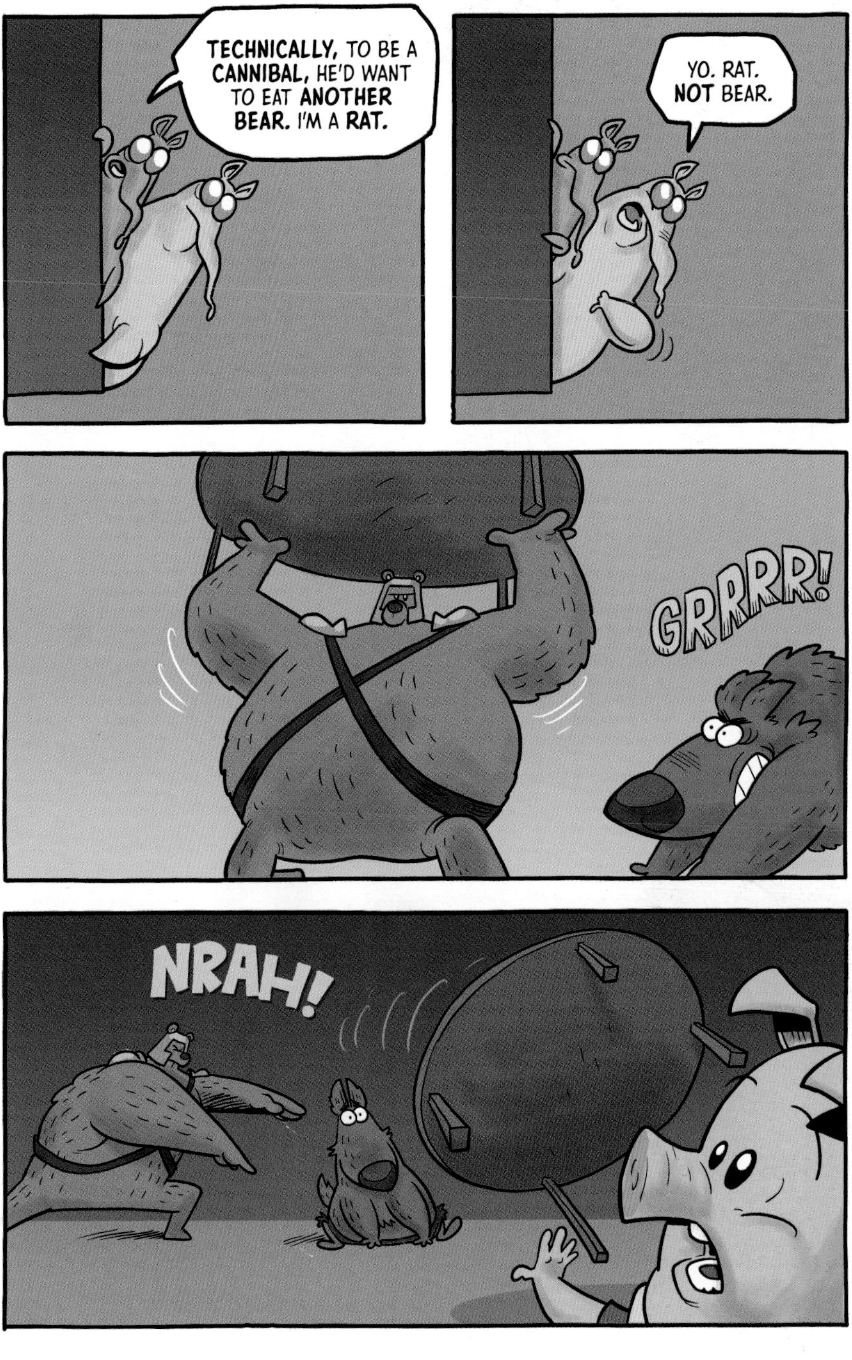
TECHNICALLY, TO BE A CANNIBAL, HE'D WANT TO EAT ANOTHER BEAR. I'M A RAT.
YO. RAT. NOT BEAR.
GRRRR!
NRAH!

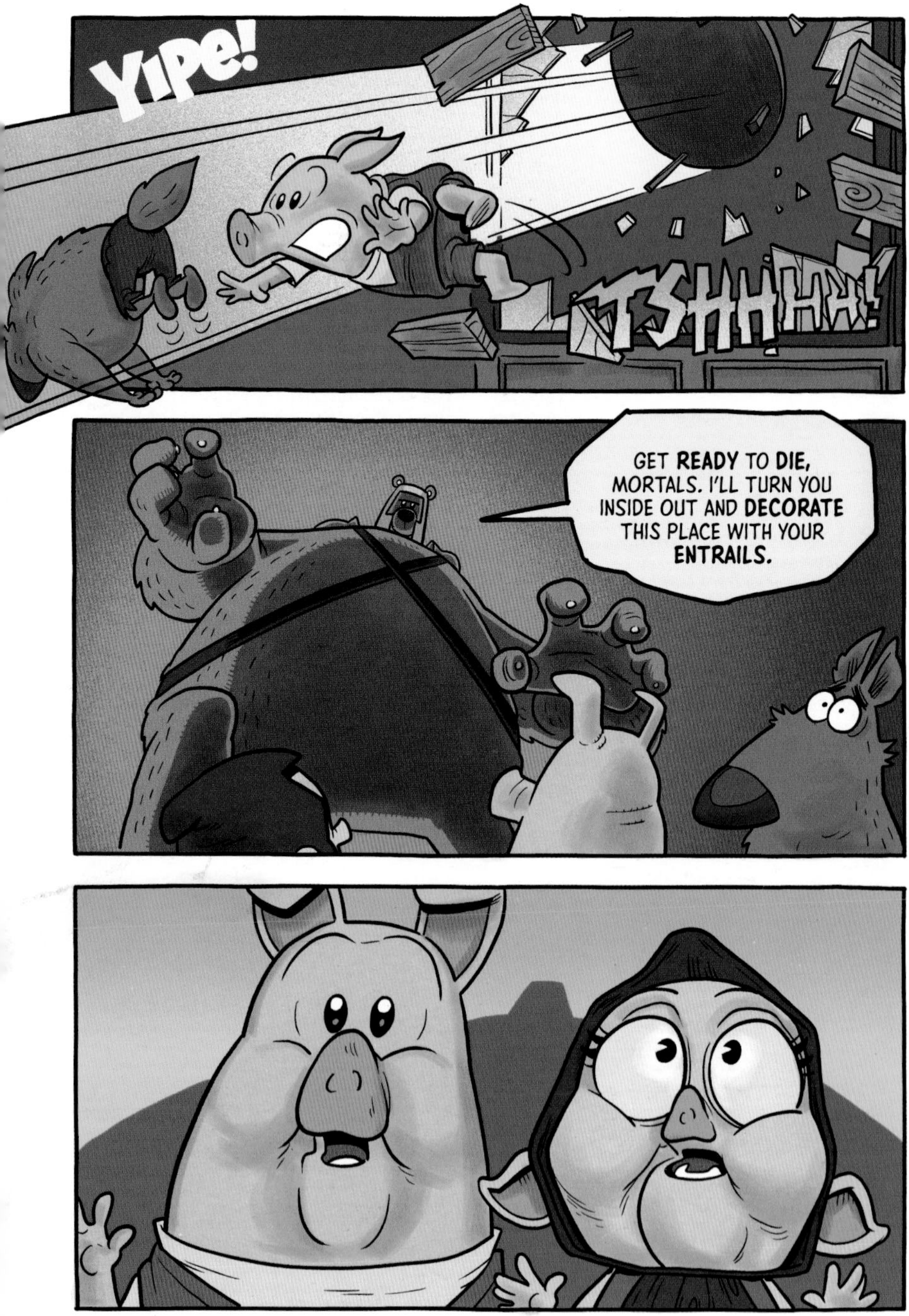
YIPE!
TSHHHH!
GET READY TO DIE, MORTALS. I'LL TURN YOU INSIDE OUT AND DECORATE THIS PLACE WITH YOUR ENTRAILS.

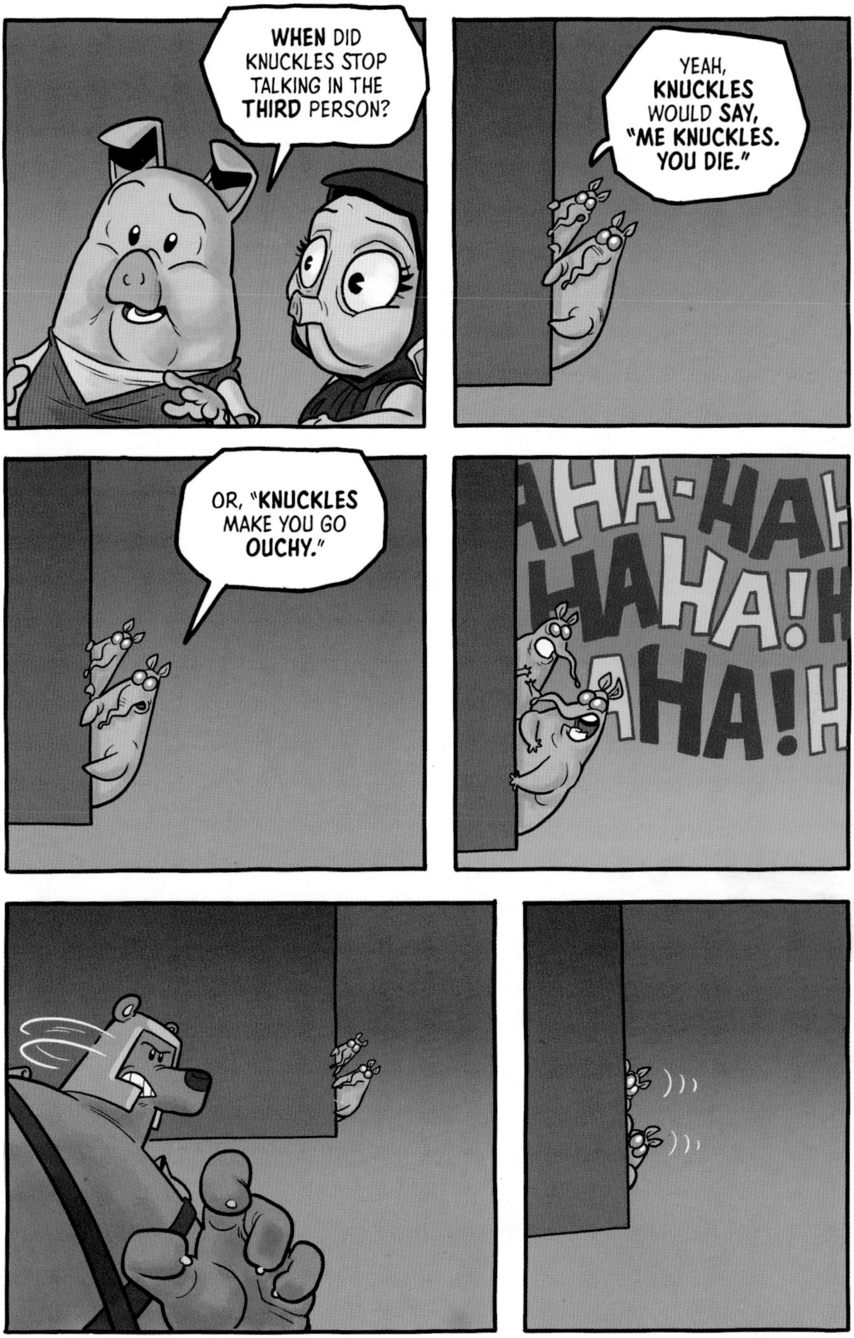
WHEN DID KNUCKLES STOP TALKING IN THE THIRD PERSON?
YEAH, KNUCKLES WOULD SAY, "ME KNUCKLES. YOU DIE."
OR, "KNUCKLES MAKE YOU GO OUCHY."
HA-HA HAHA! AHA!

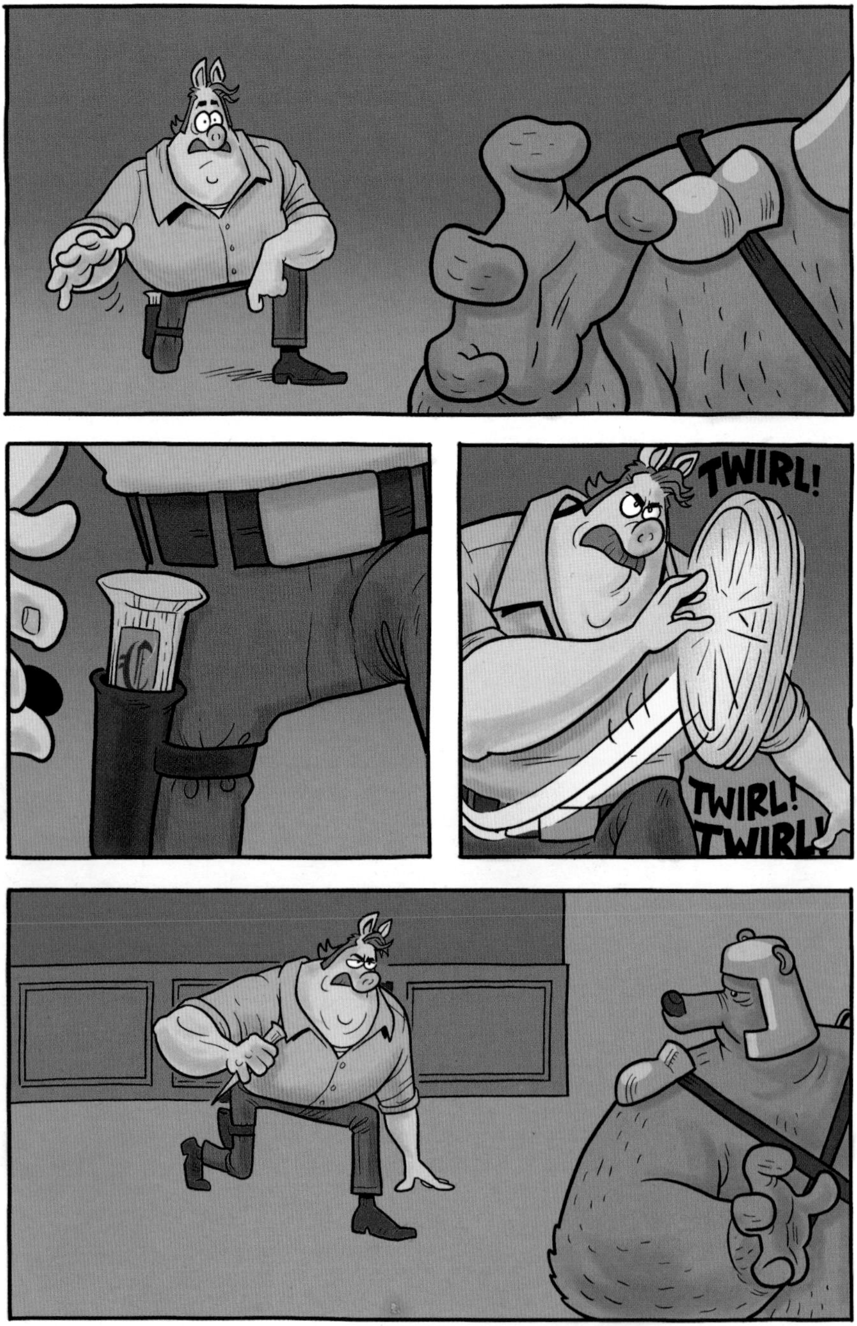
TWIRL!
TWIRL!
TWIRL!

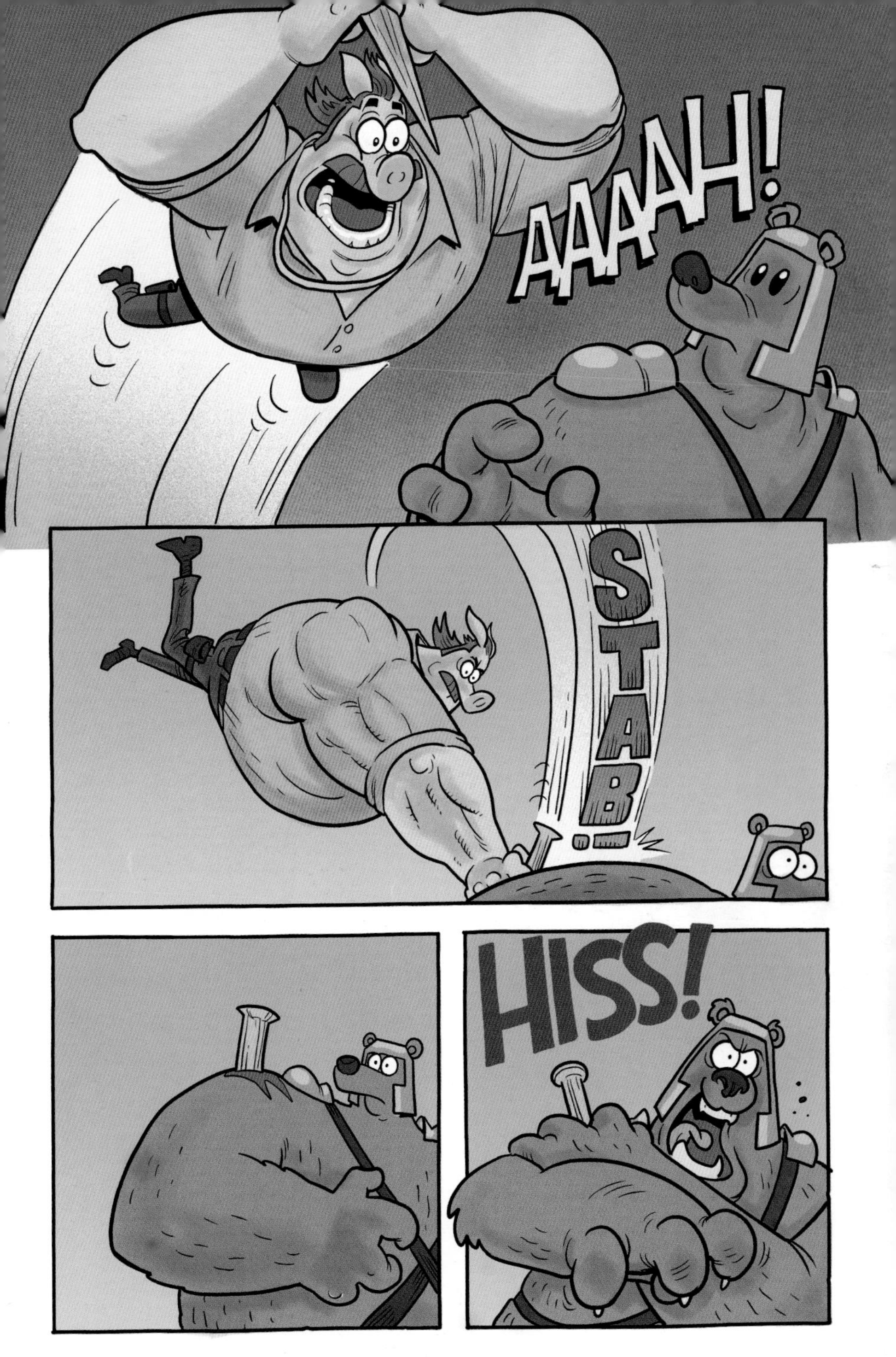
AAAAH!
STAB!!
HISS!

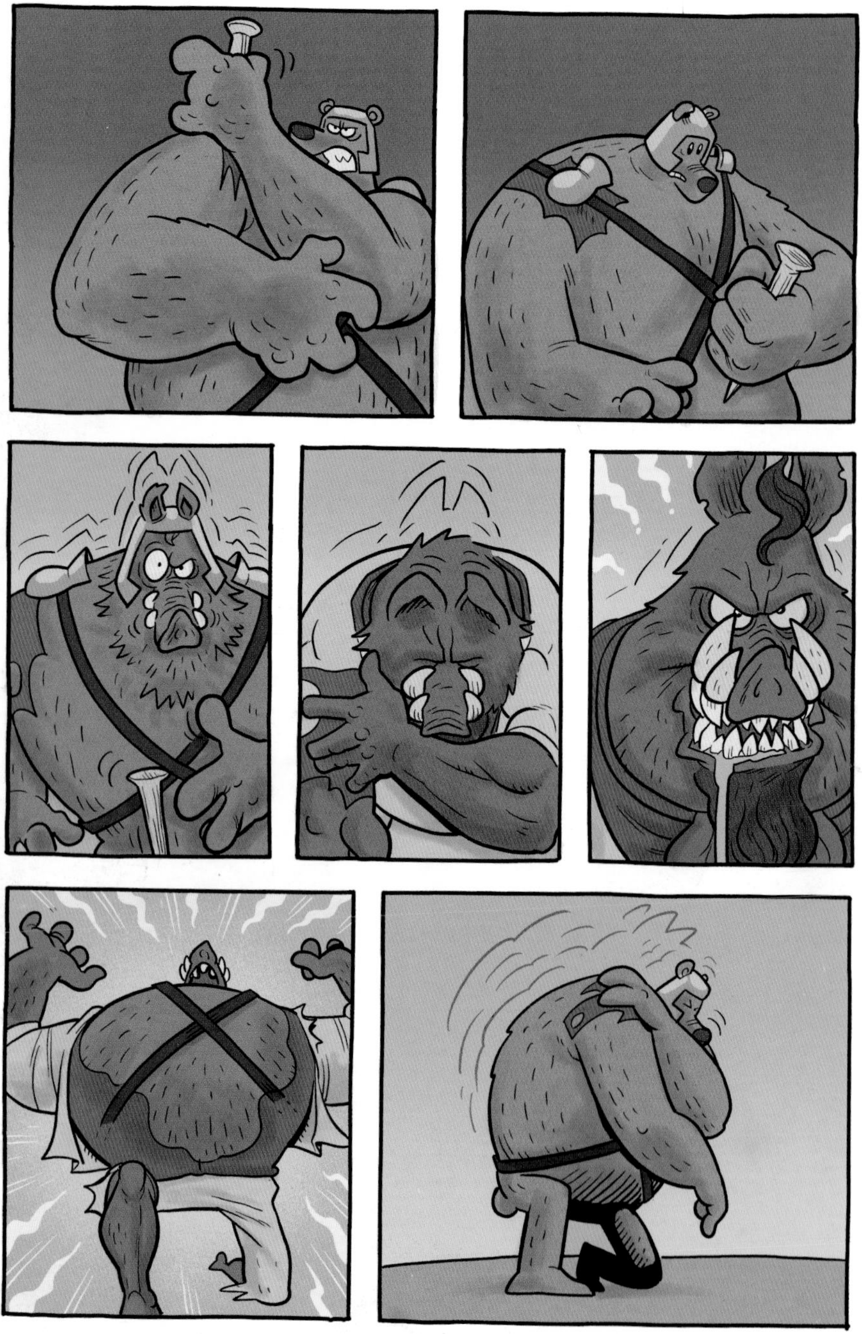

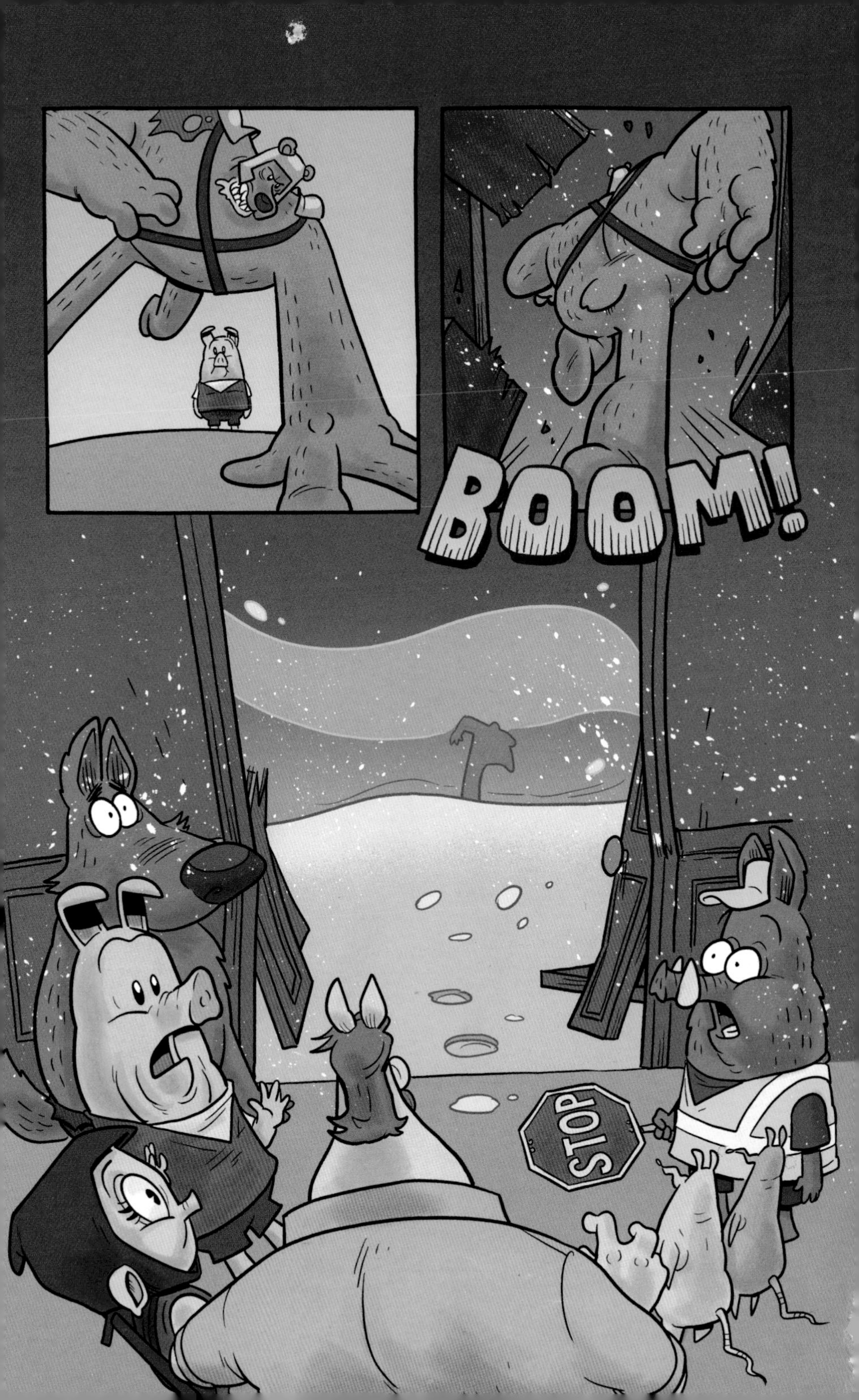
BOOM!
STOP

CHAPTER FOURTEEN

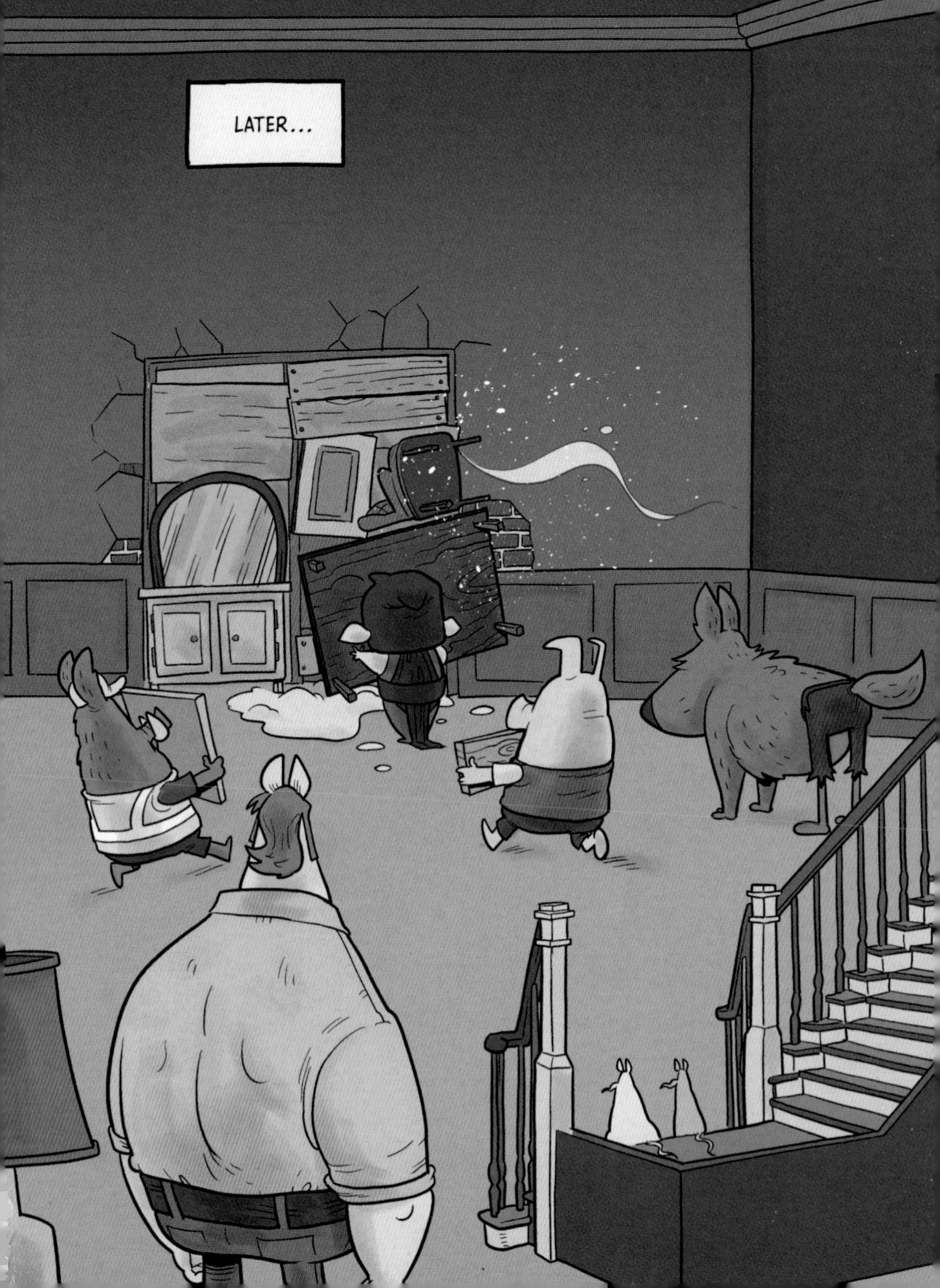
LATER...

THE VAMPIRE CHANGED FORM AND MADE THE **FIRST MOVE.**

IT HAD THE **ELEMENT** OF SURPRISE. **NOT** ANYMORE.

I **DIDN'T** REALIZE HE COULD CHANGE INTO... **ONE OF US.**

YEAH, HE'S AN **ANCIENT** VAMPIRE.

HE CAN CHANGE **MORE** THAN JUST HIS **CLOTHES.**

POOF!

HE CAN CHANGE INTO ANYTHING OF FLESH AND BLOOD.

AND HE CAN KEEP HIS **VAMPIRE STRENGTH** IN ANY FORM HE CHOOSES.

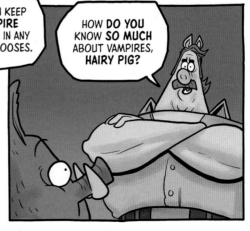

HOW **DO YOU** KNOW **SO MUCH** ABOUT VAMPIRES, **HAIRY PIG?**

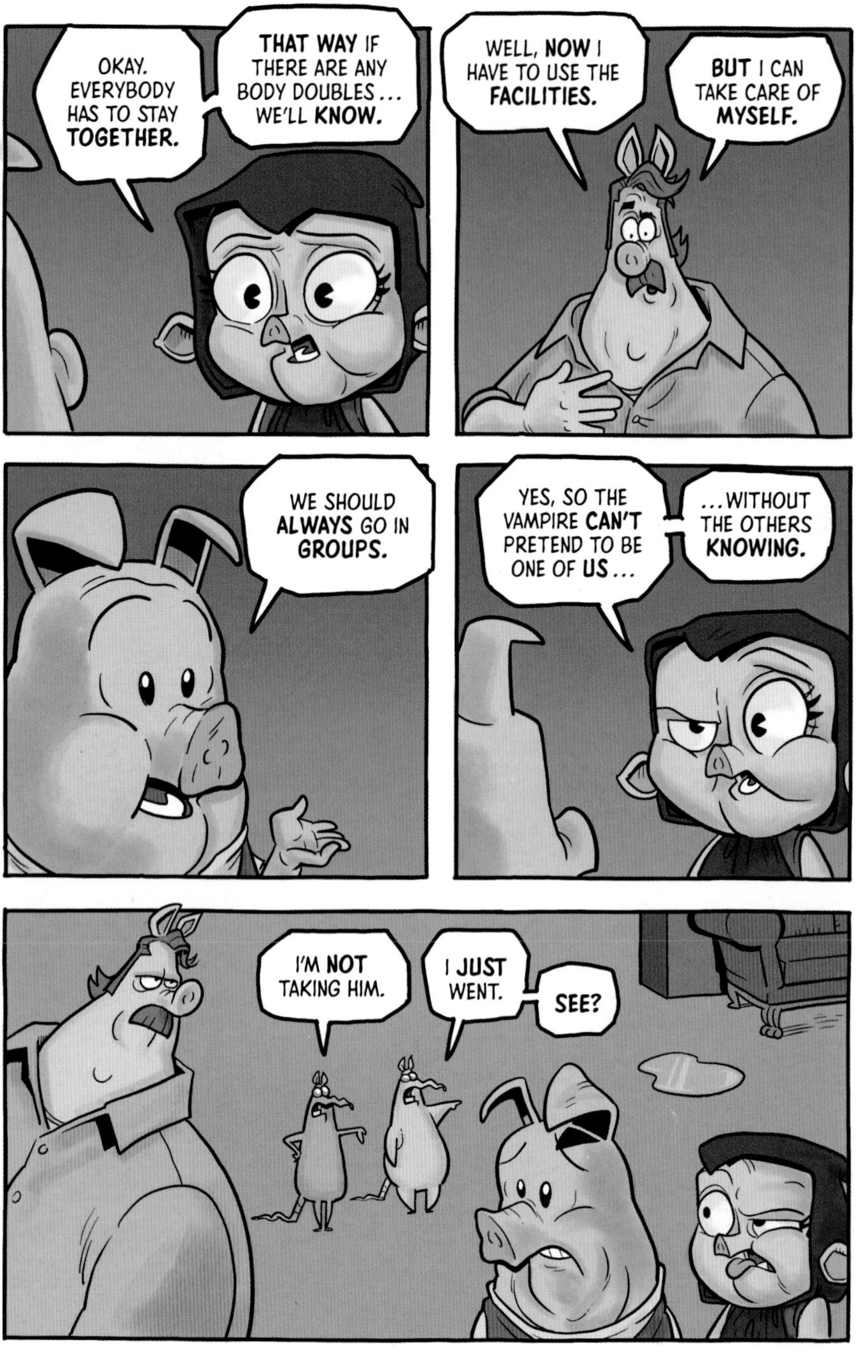
OKAY. EVERYBODY HAS TO STAY TOGETHER.
THAT WAY IF THERE ARE ANY BODY DOUBLES... WE'LL KNOW.
WELL, NOW I HAVE TO USE THE FACILITIES.
BUT I CAN TAKE CARE OF MYSELF.
WE SHOULD ALWAYS GO IN GROUPS.
YES, SO THE VAMPIRE CAN'T PRETEND TO BE ONE OF US...
...WITHOUT THE OTHERS KNOWING.
I'M NOT TAKING HIM.
I JUST WENT.
SEE?

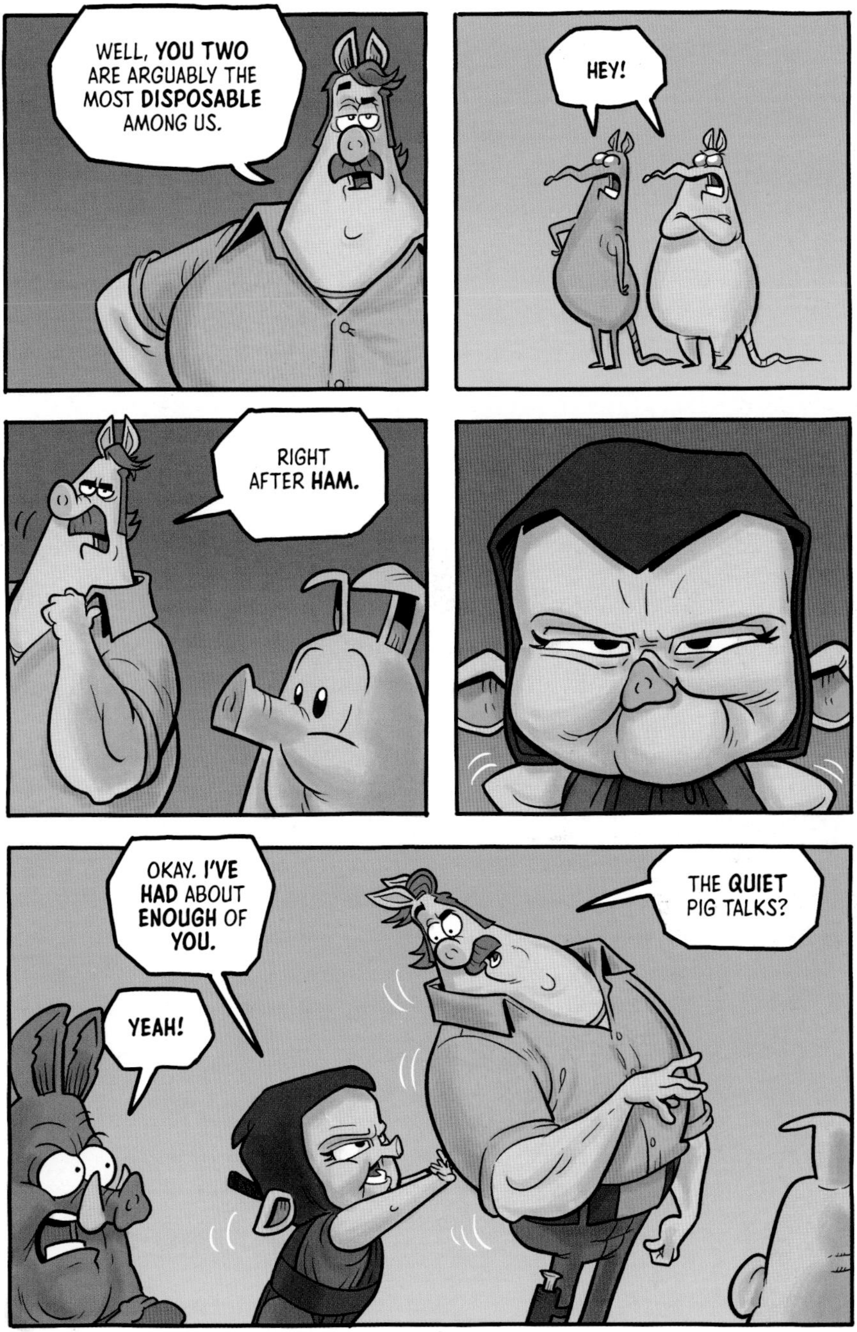
WELL, YOU TWO ARE ARGUABLY THE MOST DISPOSABLE AMONG US.
HEY!
RIGHT AFTER HAM.
OKAY. I'VE HAD ABOUT ENOUGH OF YOU.
YEAH!
THE QUIET PIG TALKS?

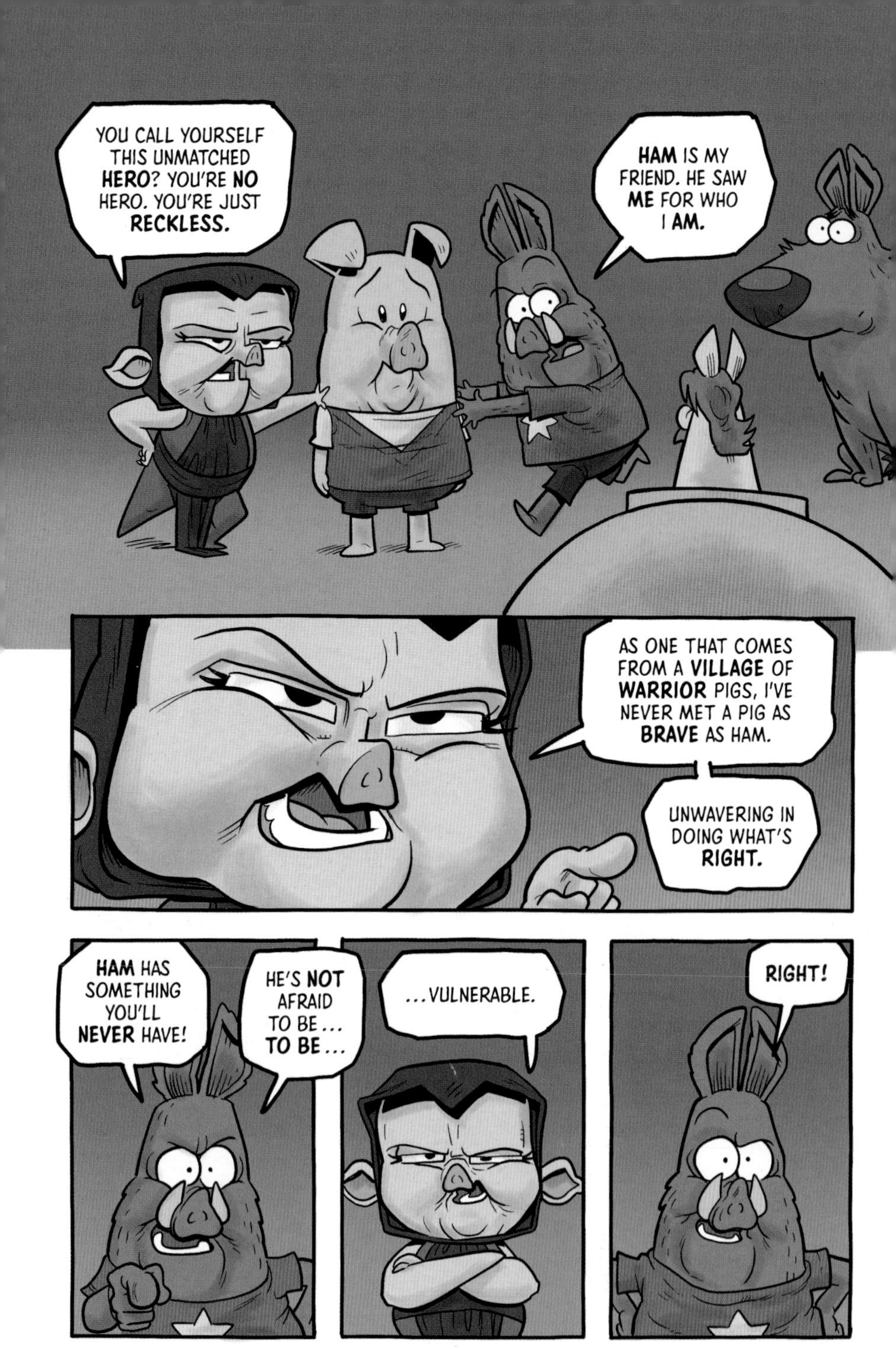
YOU CALL YOURSELF THIS UNMATCHED HERO? YOU'RE NO HERO. YOU'RE JUST RECKLESS.
HAM IS MY FRIEND. HE SAW ME FOR WHO I AM.
AS ONE THAT COMES FROM A VILLAGE OF WARRIOR PIGS, I'VE NEVER MET A PIG AS BRAVE AS HAM.
UNWAVERING IN DOING WHAT'S RIGHT.
HAM HAS SOMETHING YOU'LL NEVER HAVE!
HE'S NOT AFRAID TO BE... TO BE...
...VULNERABLE.
RIGHT!

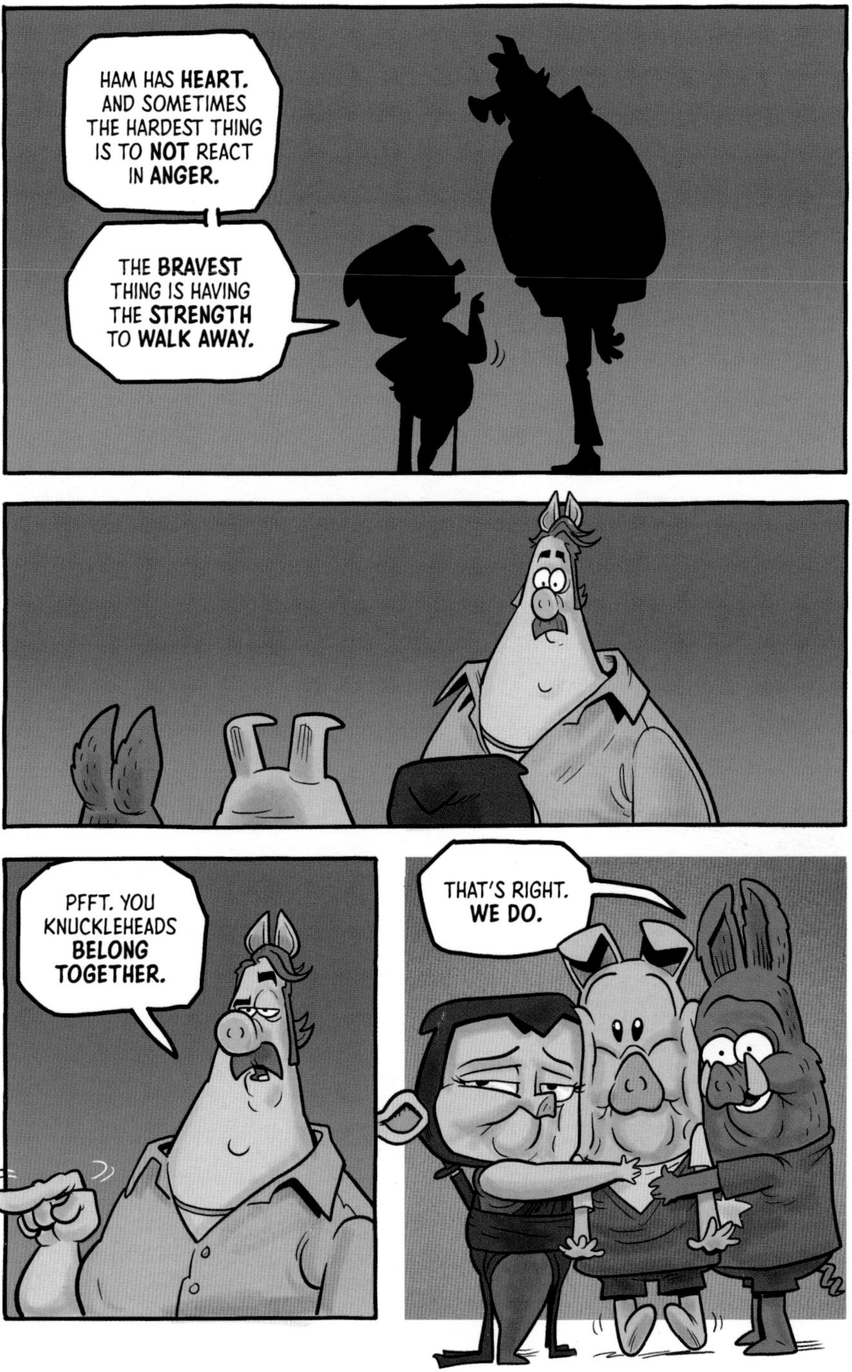

HAM HAS **HEART.** AND SOMETIMES THE HARDEST THING IS TO **NOT** REACT IN **ANGER.**
THE **BRAVEST** THING IS HAVING THE **STRENGTH** TO **WALK AWAY.**
PFFT. YOU KNUCKLEHEADS **BELONG TOGETHER.**
THAT'S RIGHT. **WE DO.**

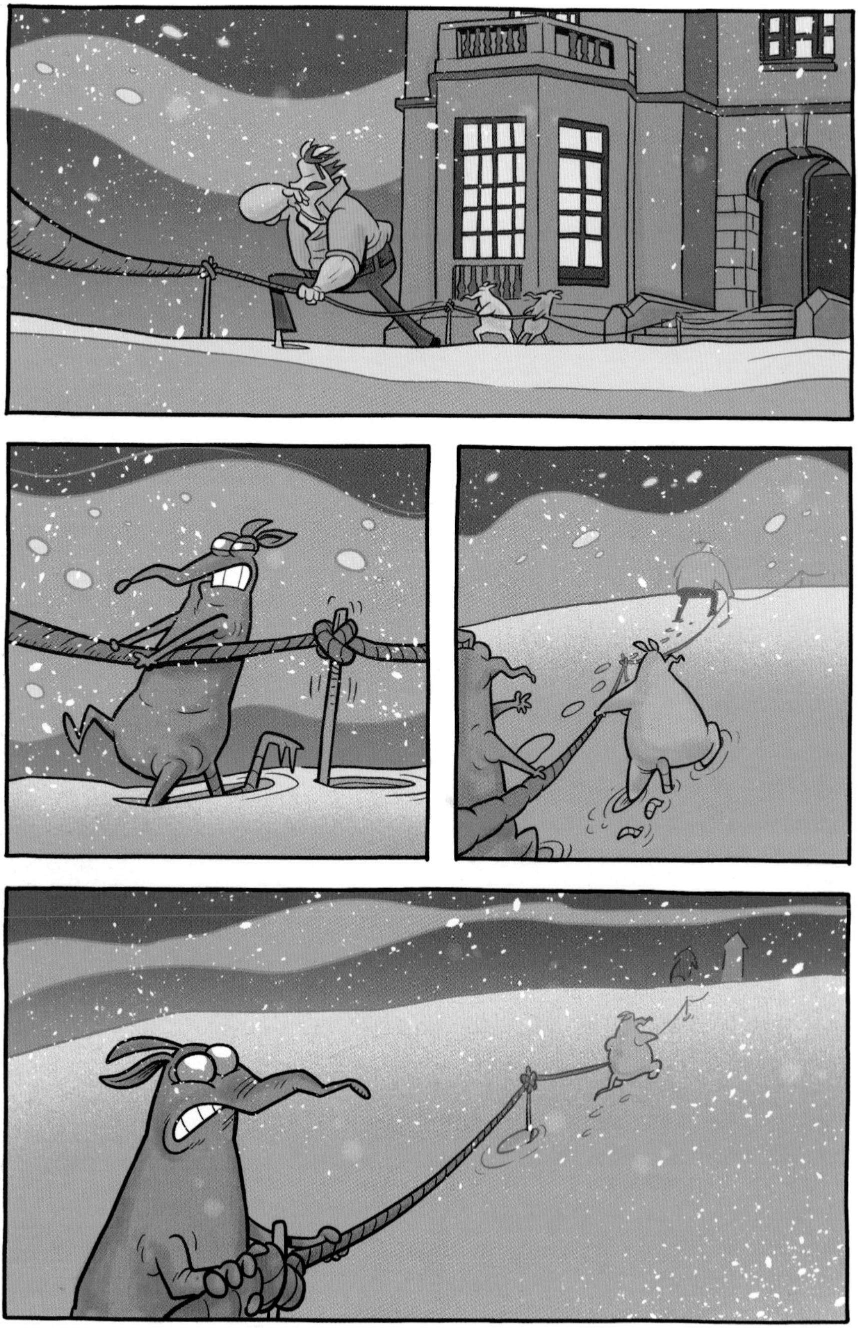

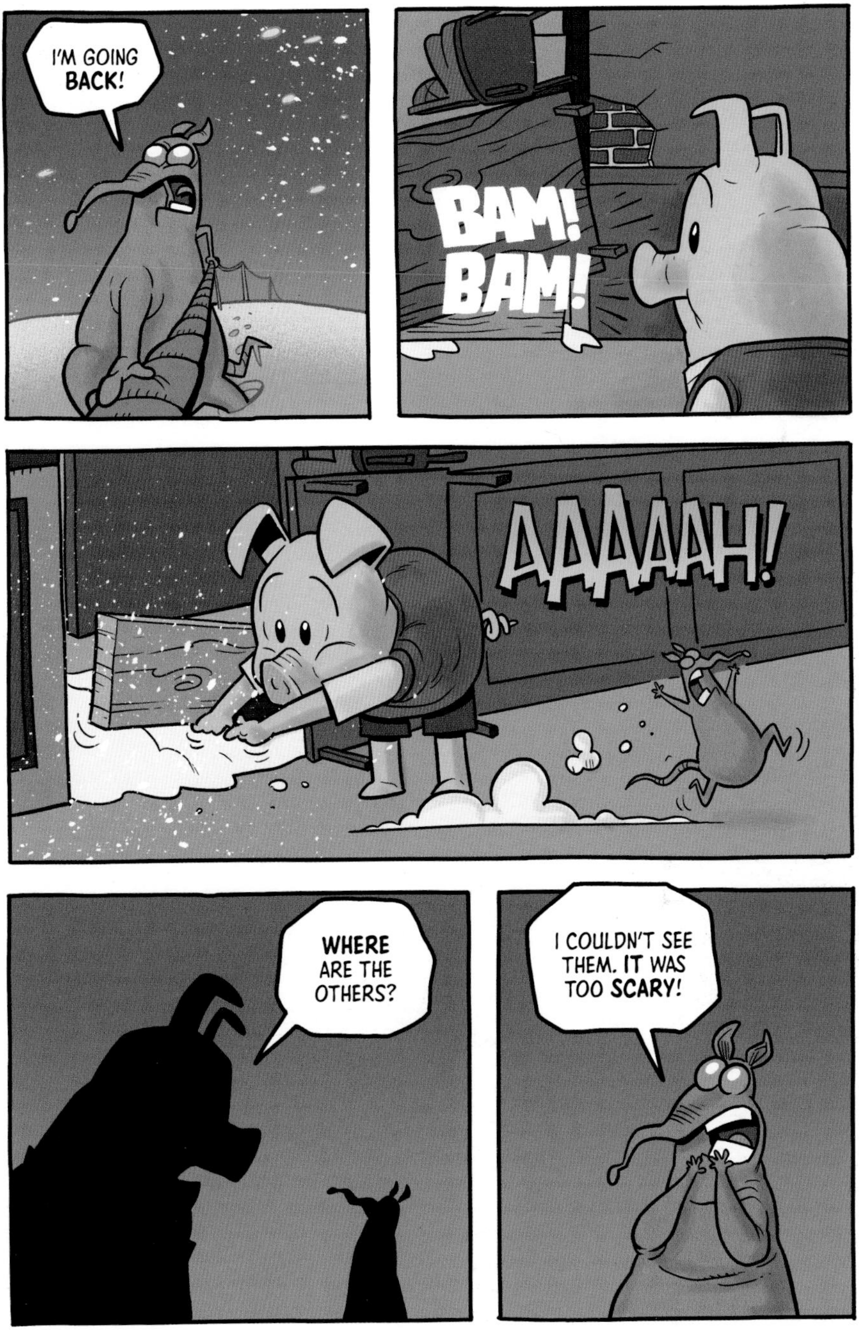
I'M GOING BACK!
BAM! BAM!
AAAAAH!
WHERE ARE THE OTHERS?
I COULDN'T SEE THEM. IT WAS TOO SCARY!

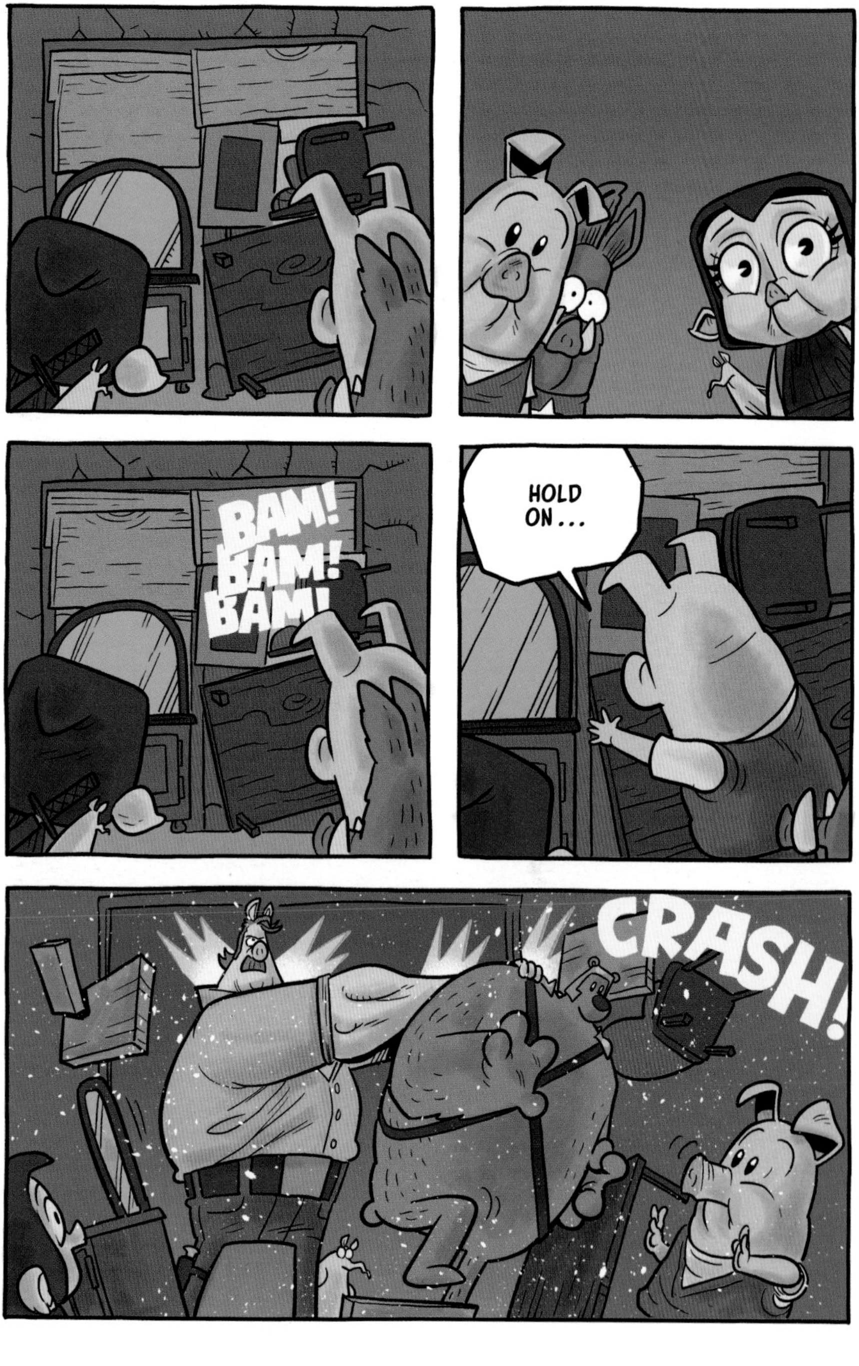
BAM!
BAM!
BAM!
HOLD ON . . .
CRASH!

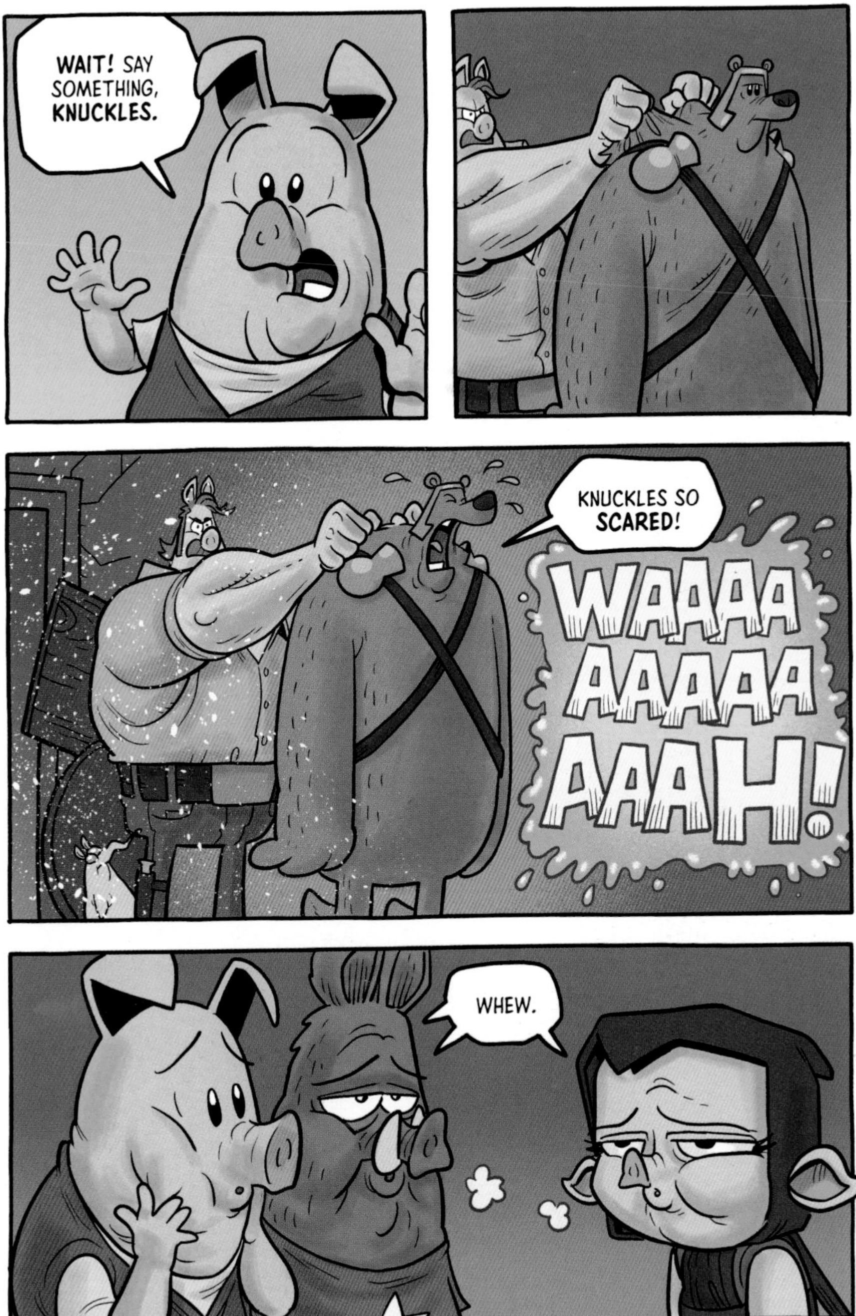
WAIT! SAY SOMETHING, KNUCKLES.
KNUCKLES SO SCARED!
WAAAAAAAAAAAAH!
WHEW.

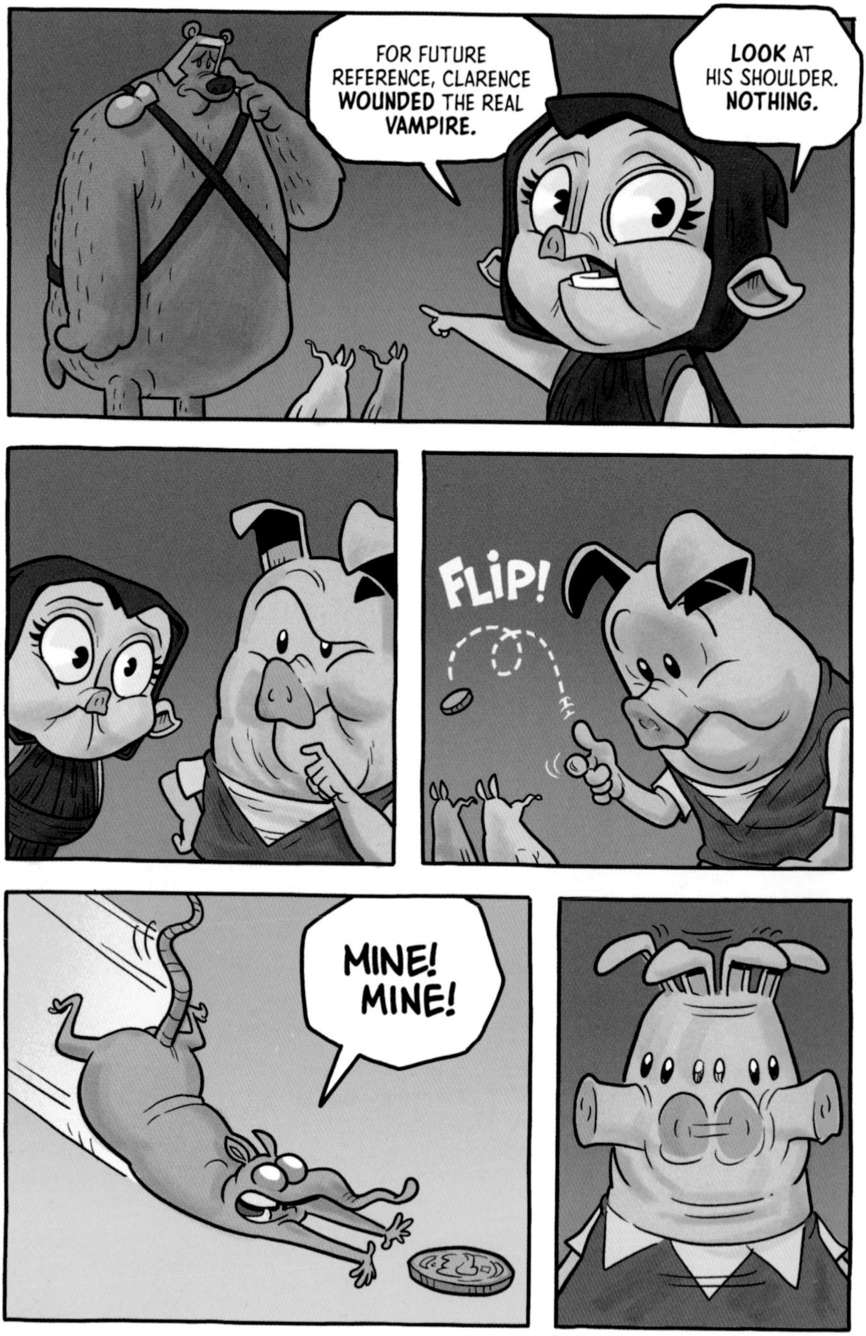
FOR FUTURE REFERENCE, CLARENCE WOUNDED THE REAL VAMPIRE.
LOOK AT HIS SHOULDER. NOTHING.
FLIP!
MINE! MINE!

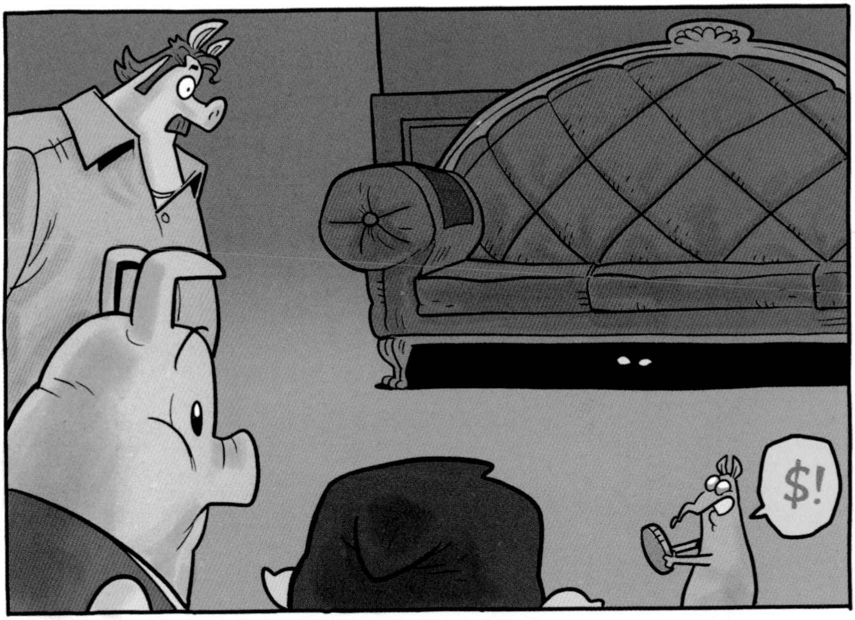
$!

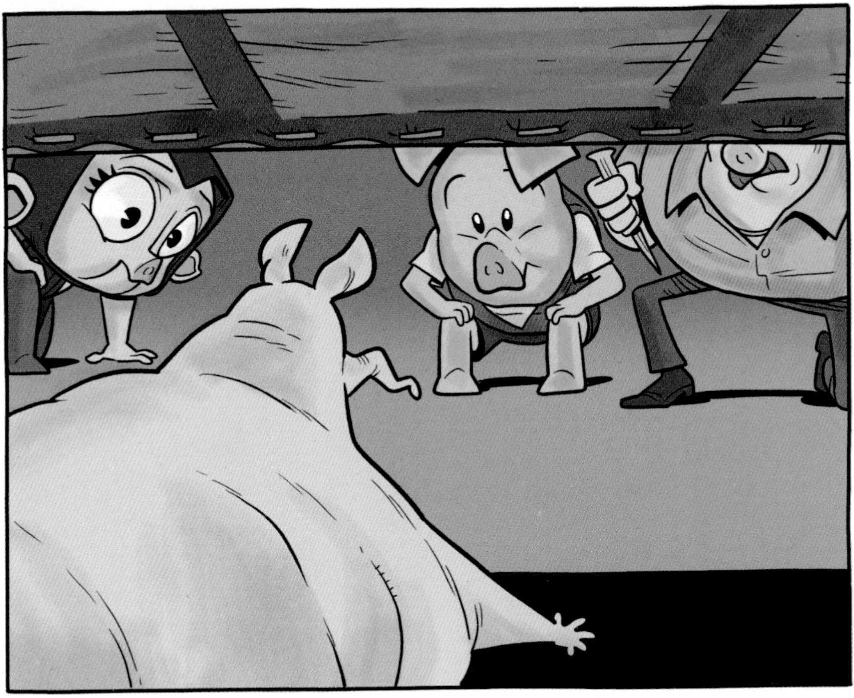

CHAPTER FIFTEEN

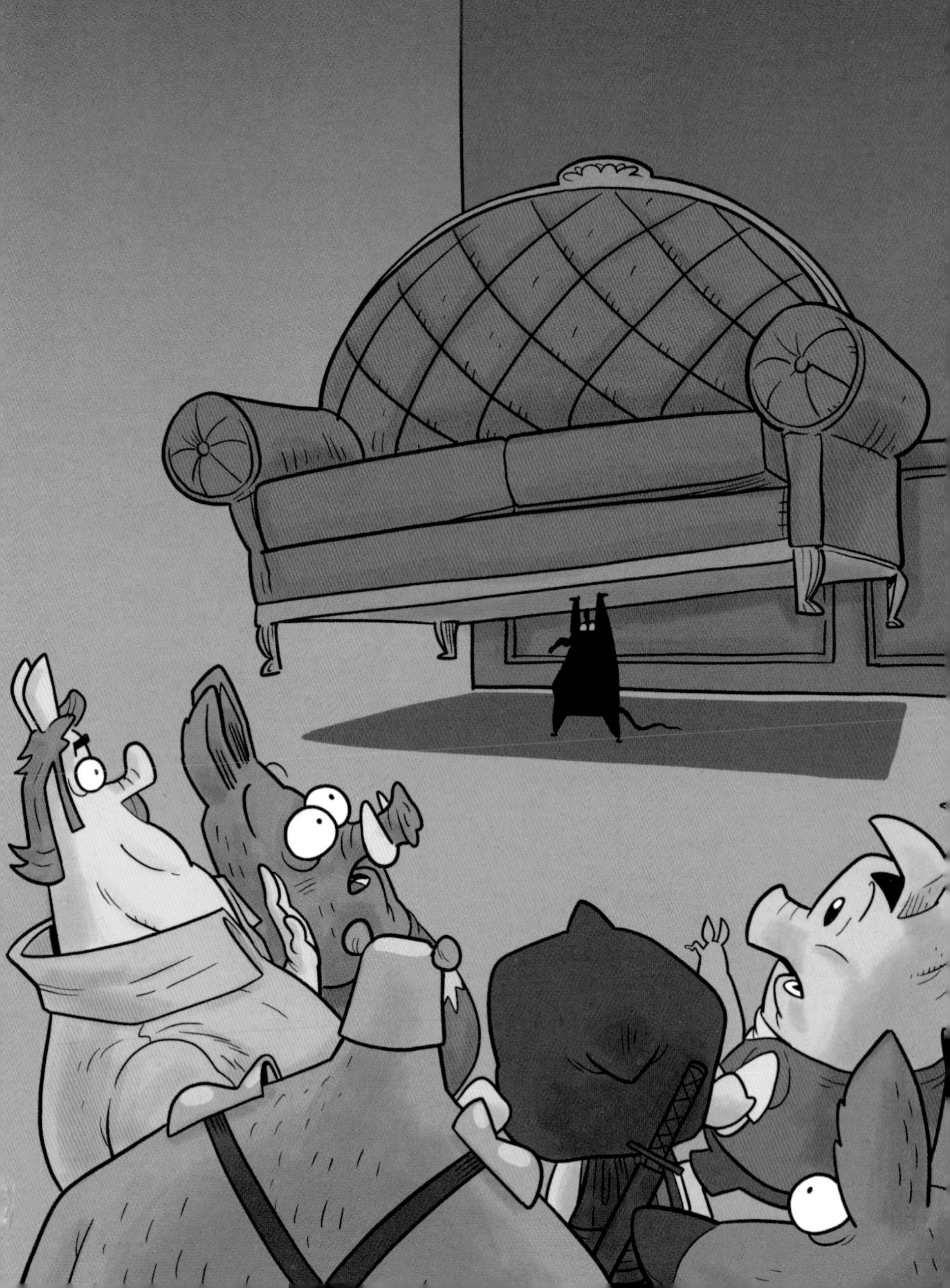

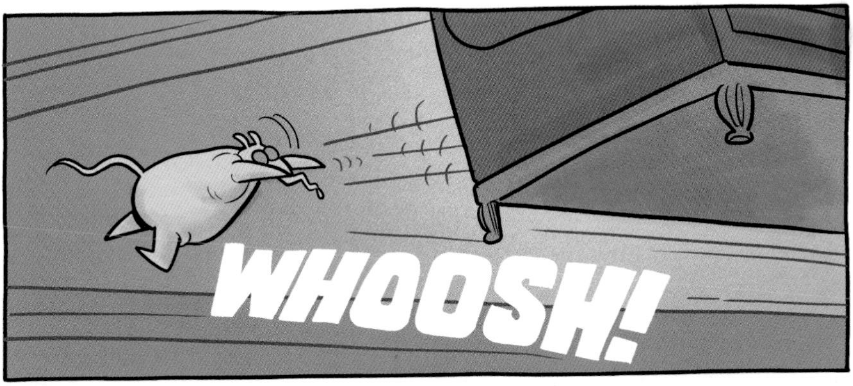
WHOOSH!

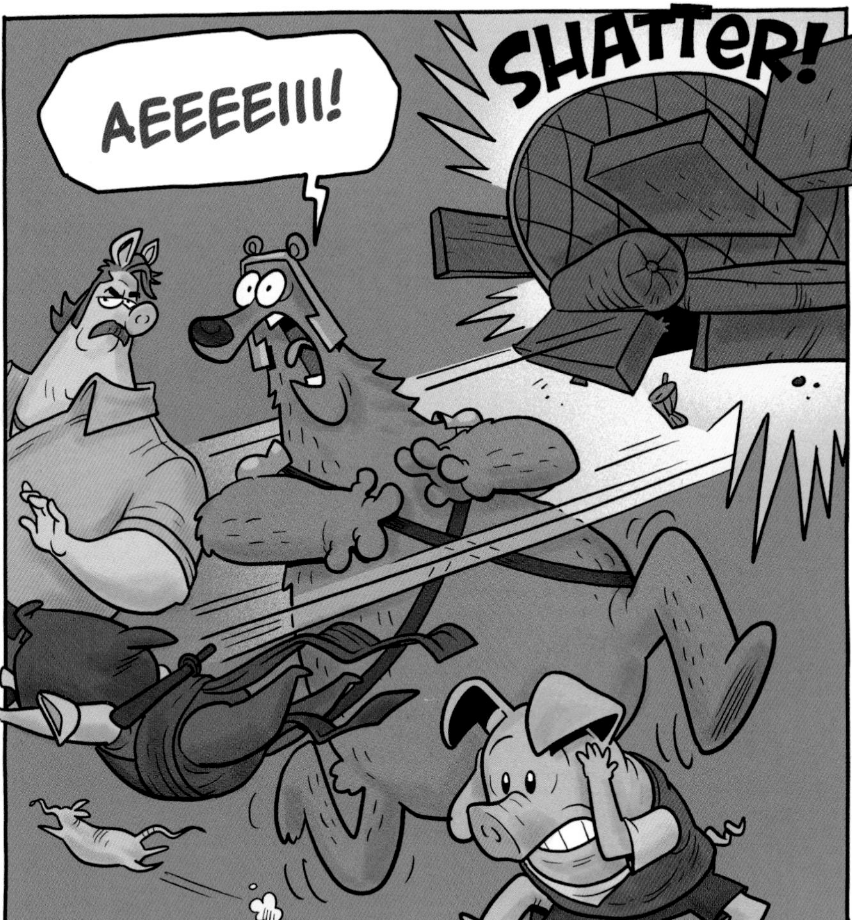
AEEEEIII!
SHATTER!

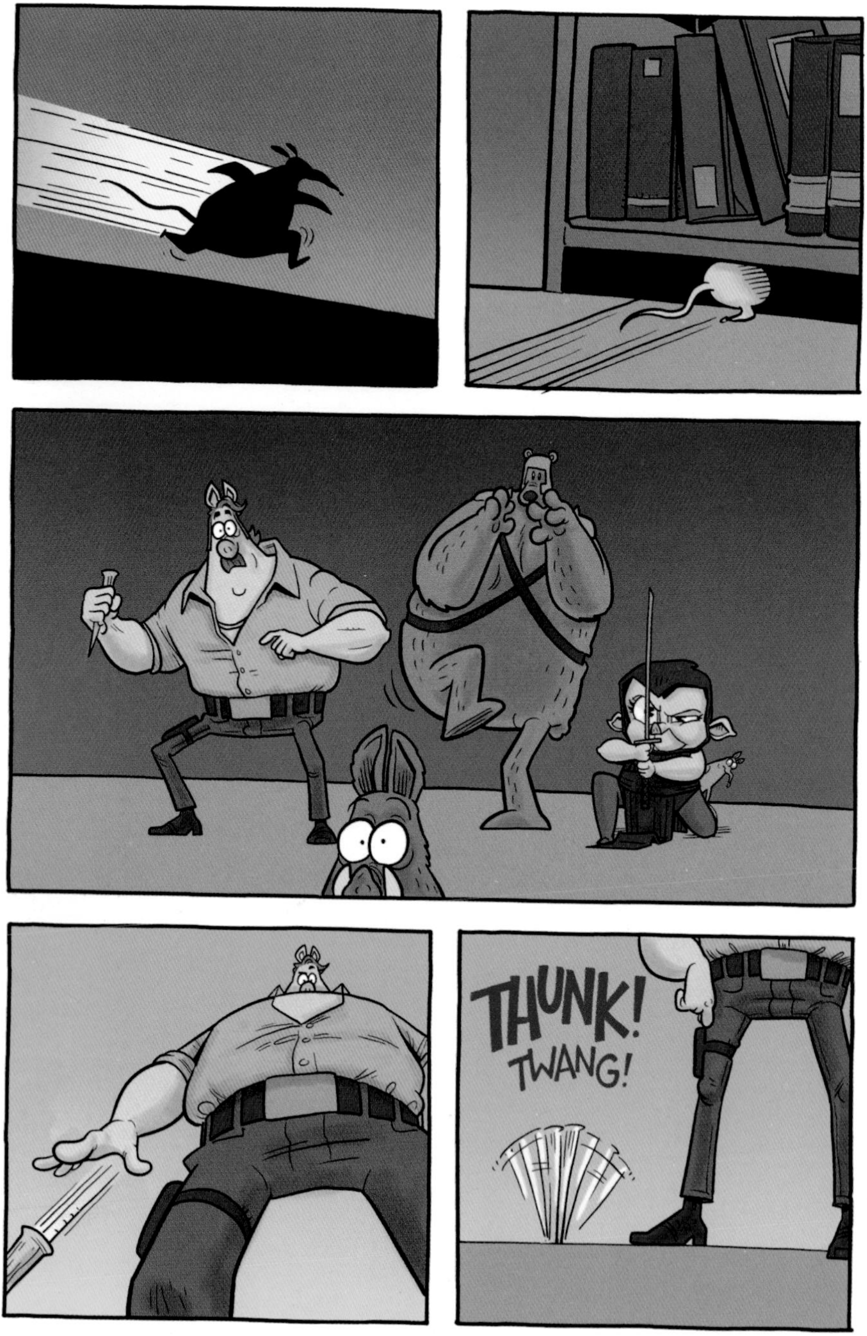
THUNK!
TWANG!

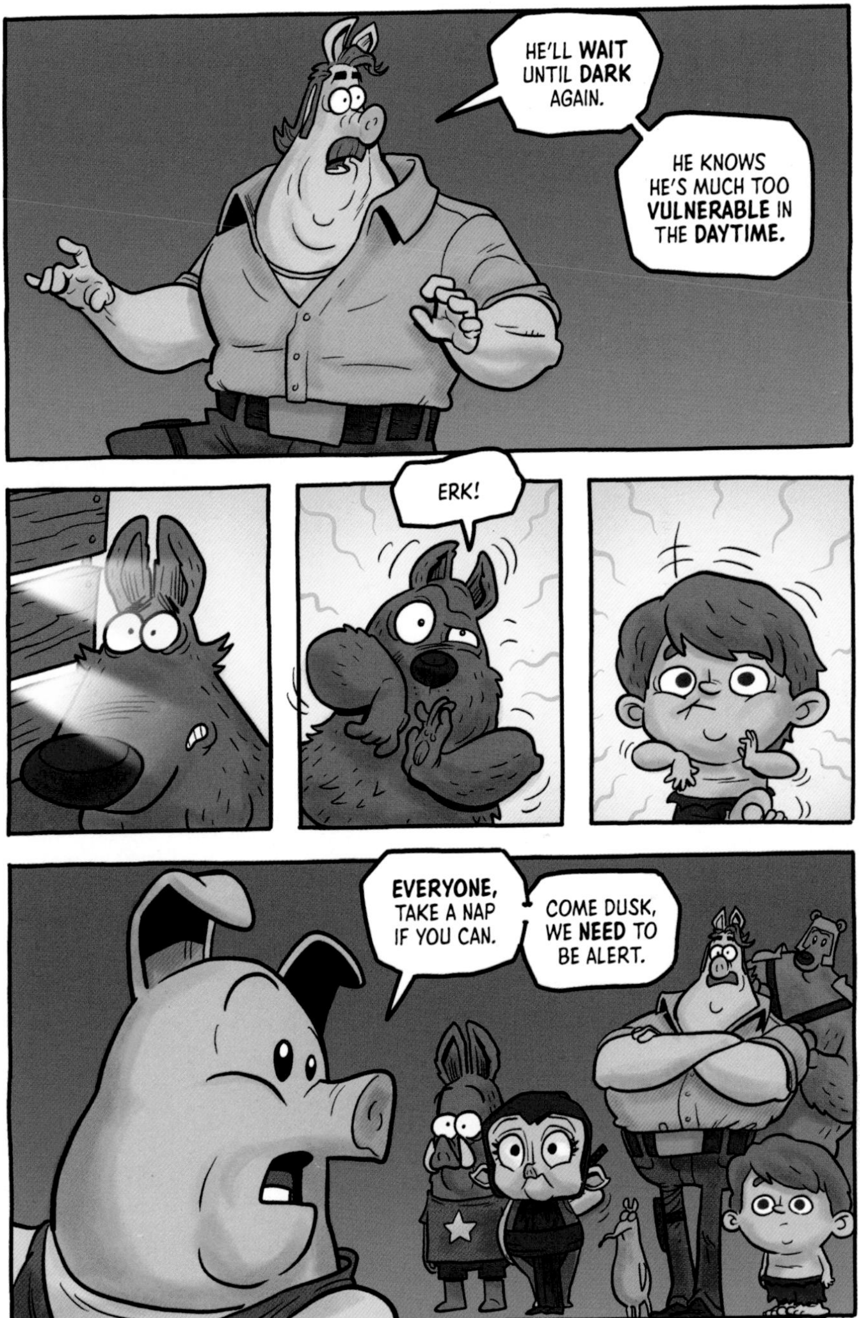
HE'LL WAIT UNTIL DARK AGAIN.
HE KNOWS HE'S MUCH TOO VULNERABLE IN THE DAYTIME.
ERK!
EVERYONE, TAKE A NAP IF YOU CAN.
COME DUSK, WE NEED TO BE ALERT.

zZZzzZZ
zzzz

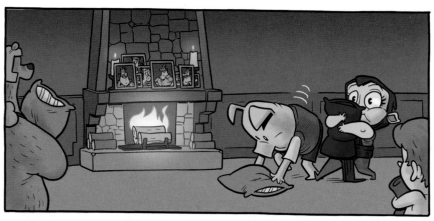

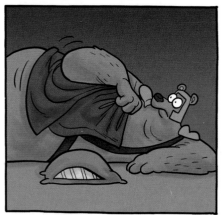

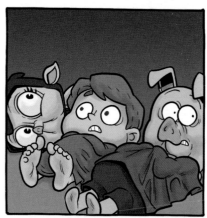

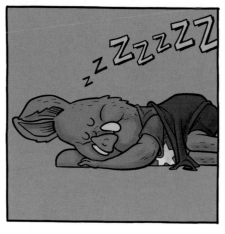

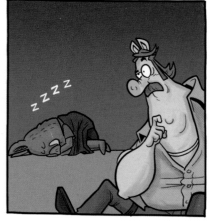

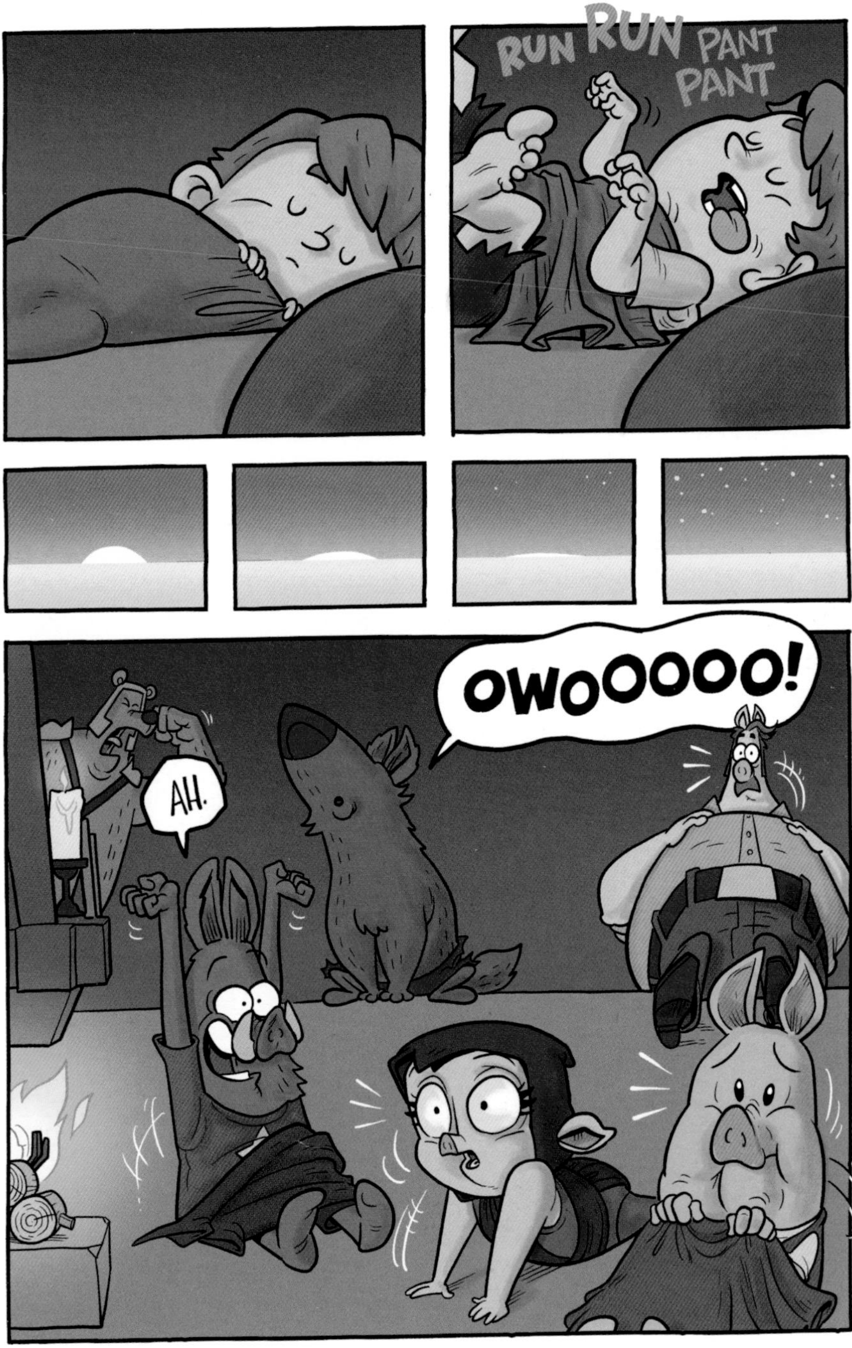
RUN RUN PANT PANT
OWOOOOO!
AH.

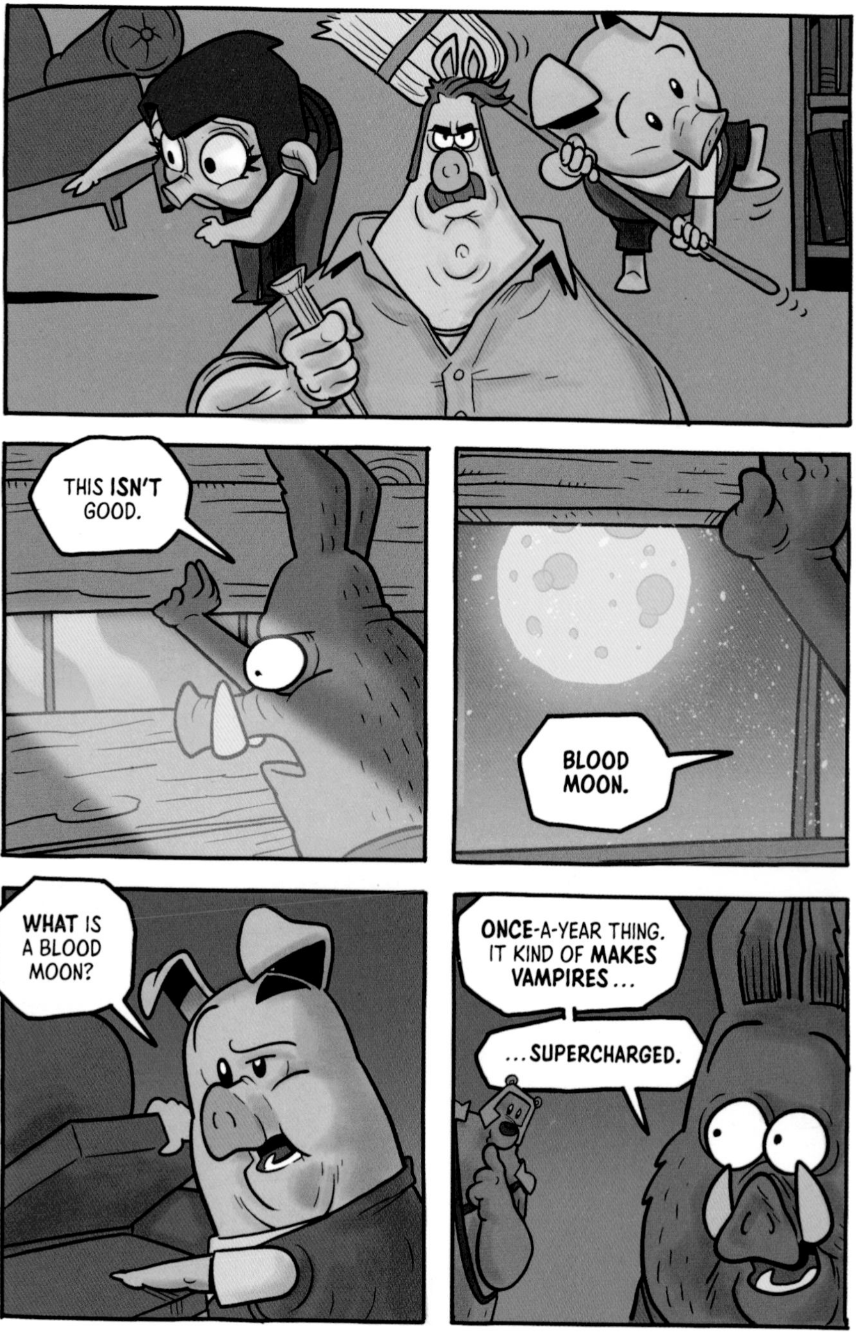
THIS ISN'T GOOD.
BLOOD MOON.
WHAT IS A BLOOD MOON?
ONCE-A-YEAR THING. IT KIND OF MAKES VAMPIRES...
...SUPERCHARGED.

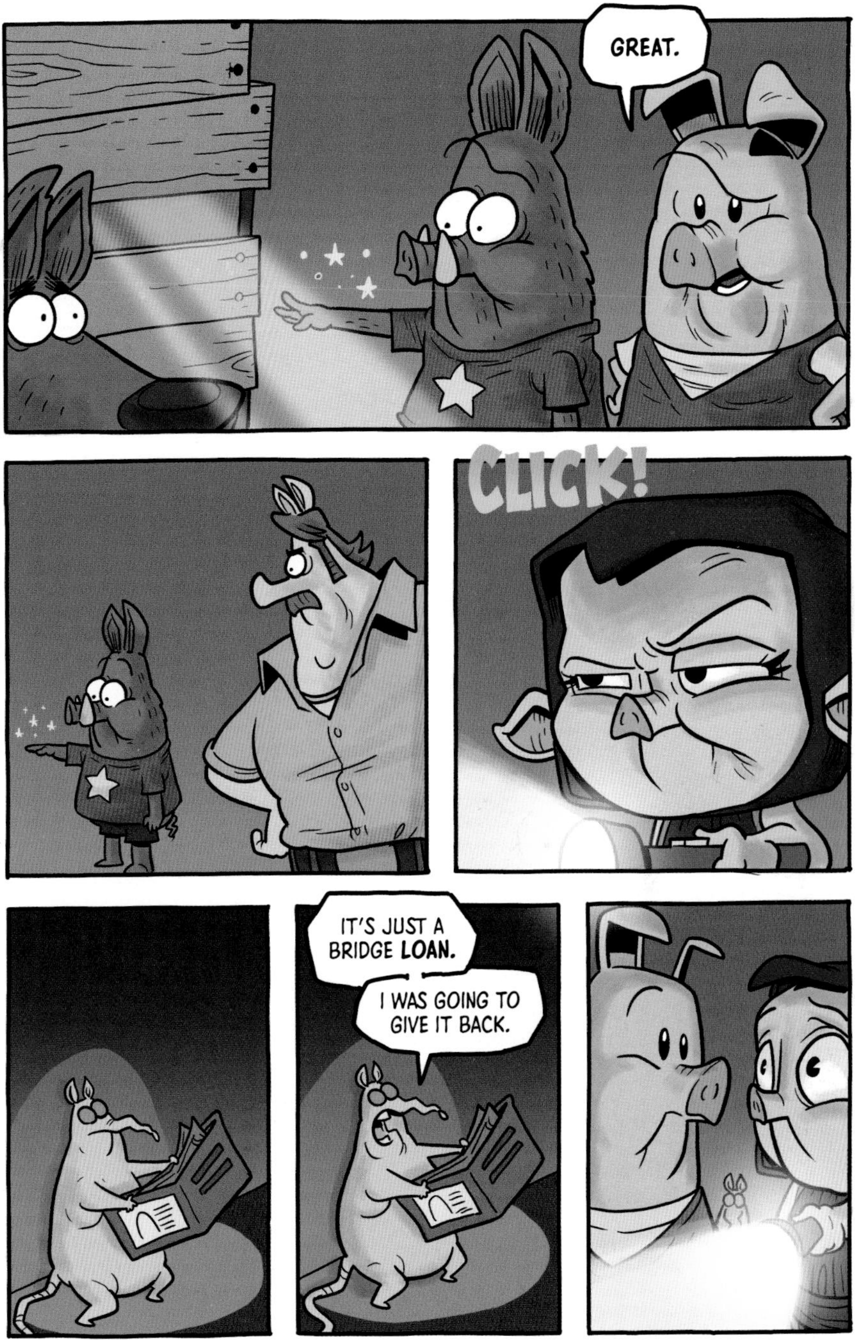
GREAT.
CLICK!
IT'S JUST A BRIDGE LOAN.
I WAS GOING TO GIVE IT BACK.

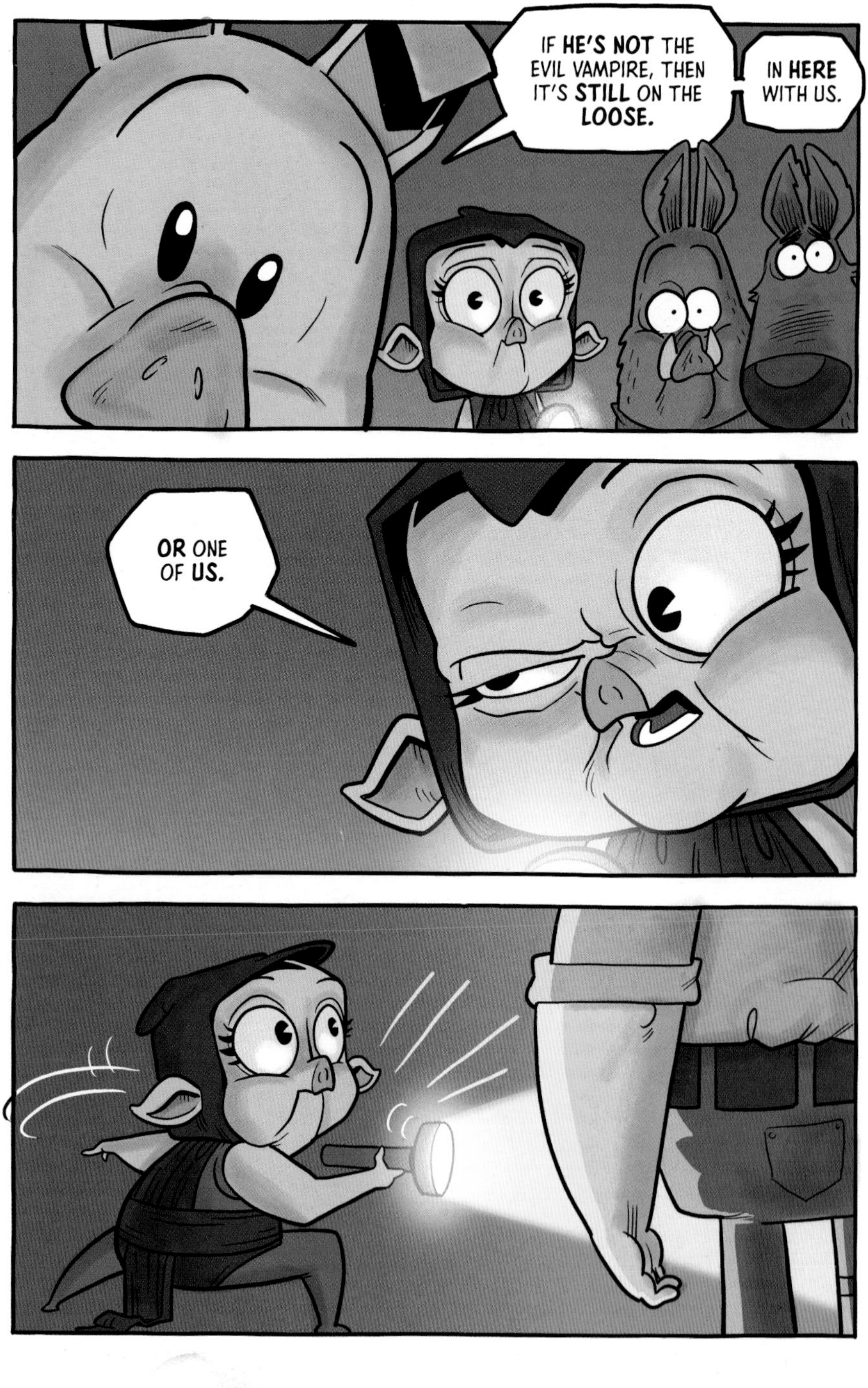
IF HE'S NOT THE EVIL VAMPIRE, THEN IT'S STILL ON THE LOOSE.
IN HERE WITH US.
OR ONE OF US.

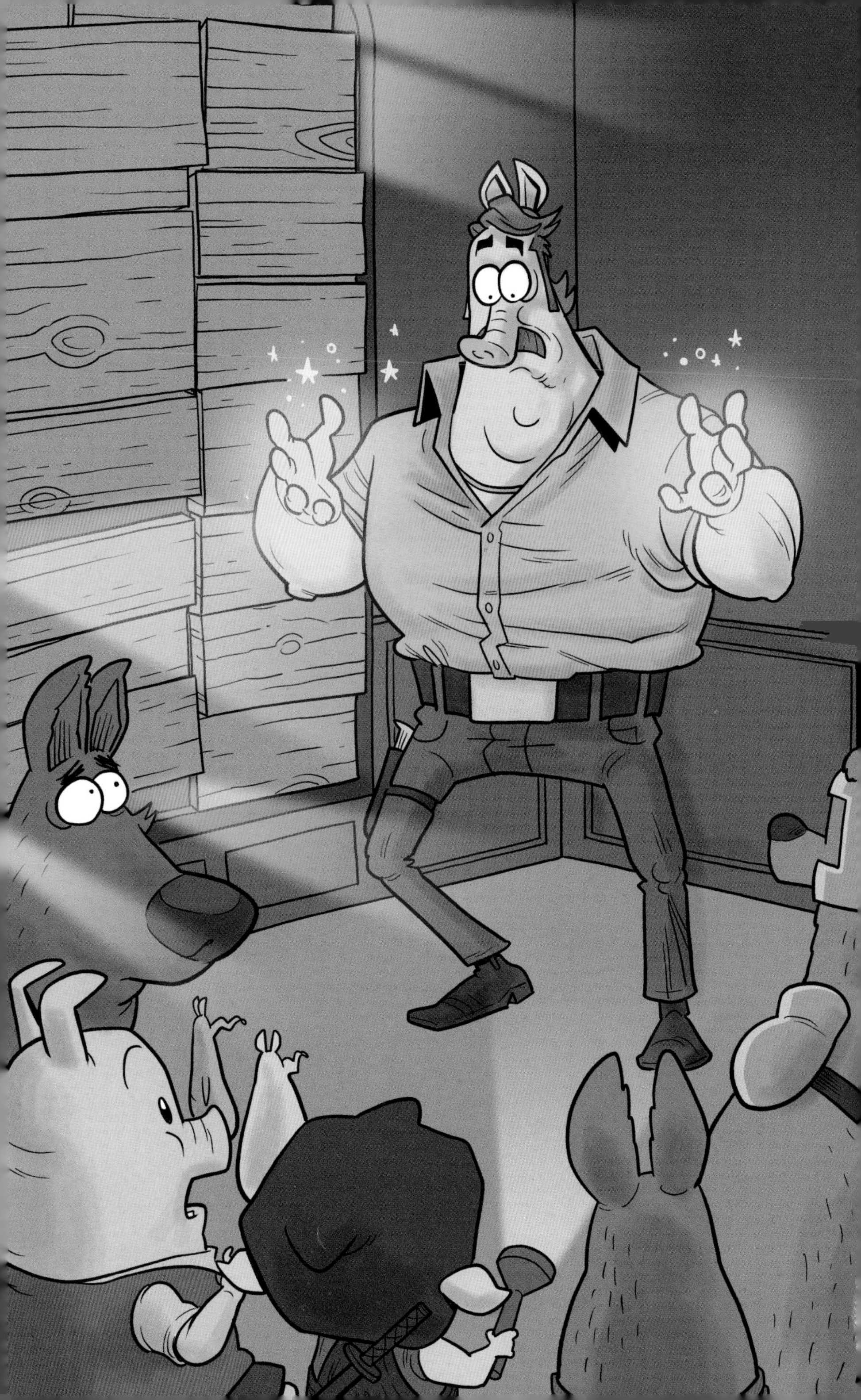

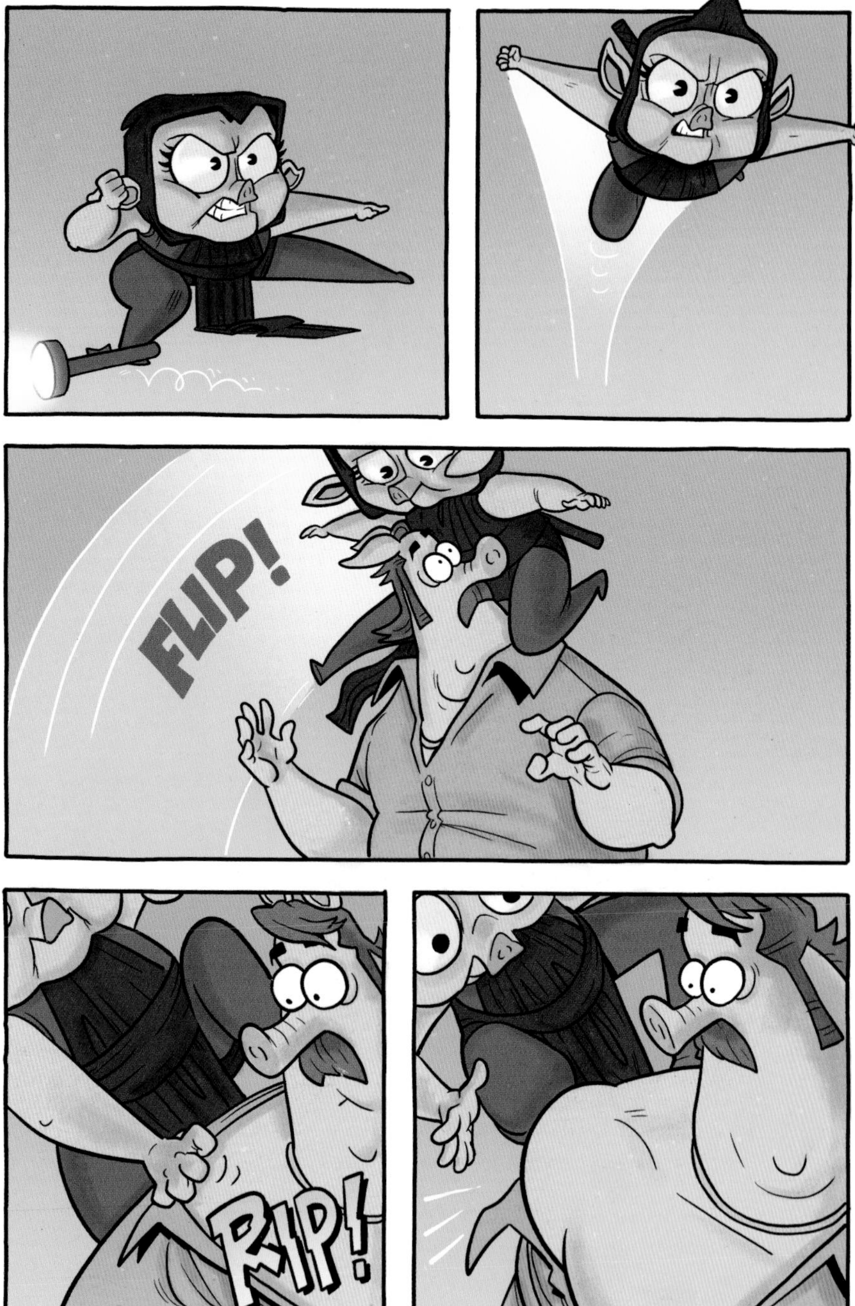
FLIP!
RIP!

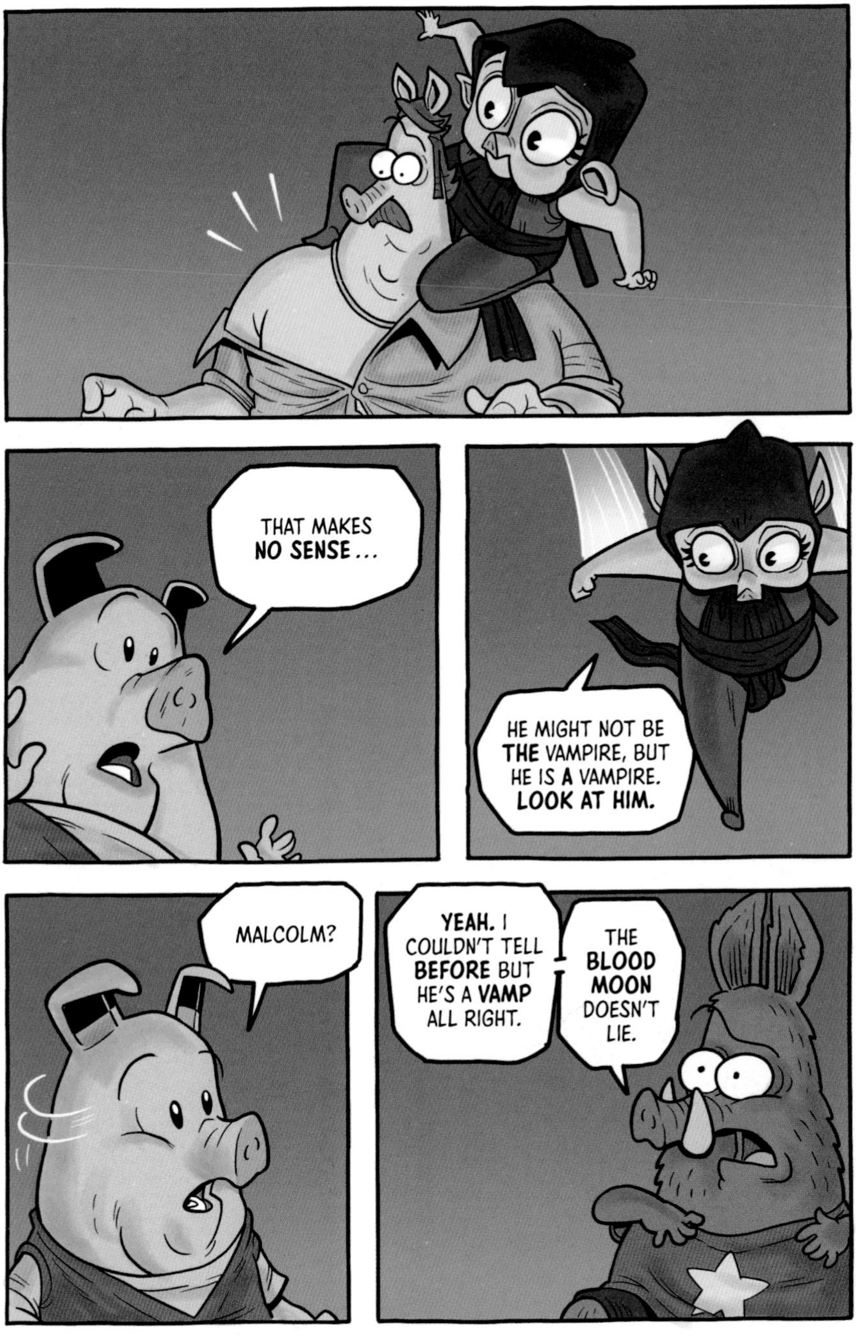
THAT MAKES NO SENSE...
HE MIGHT NOT BE THE VAMPIRE, BUT HE IS A VAMPIRE. LOOK AT HIM.
MALCOLM?
YEAH. I COULDN'T TELL BEFORE BUT HE'S A VAMP ALL RIGHT.
THE BLOOD MOON DOESN'T LIE.

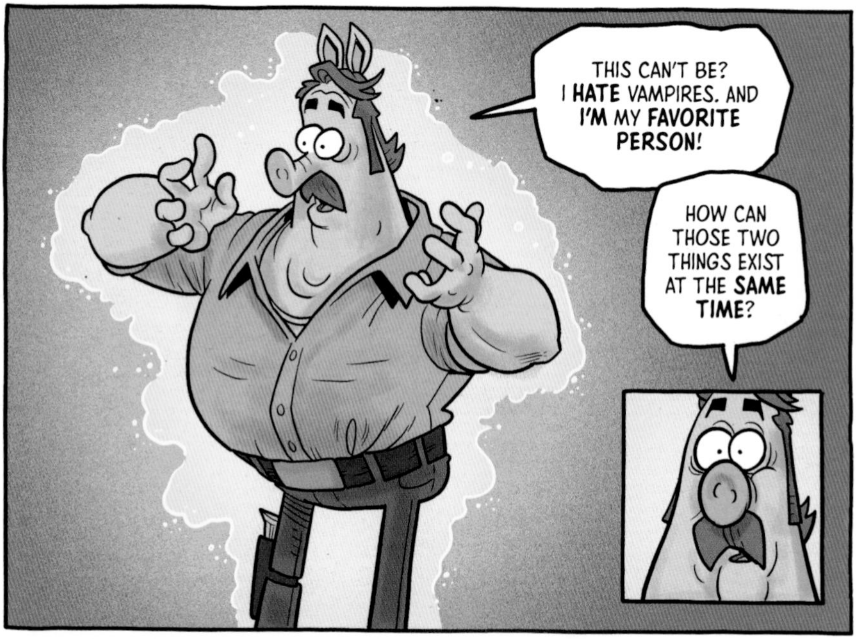
THIS CAN'T BE? I HATE VAMPIRES. AND I'M MY FAVORITE PERSON!
HOW CAN THOSE TWO THINGS EXIST AT THE SAME TIME?

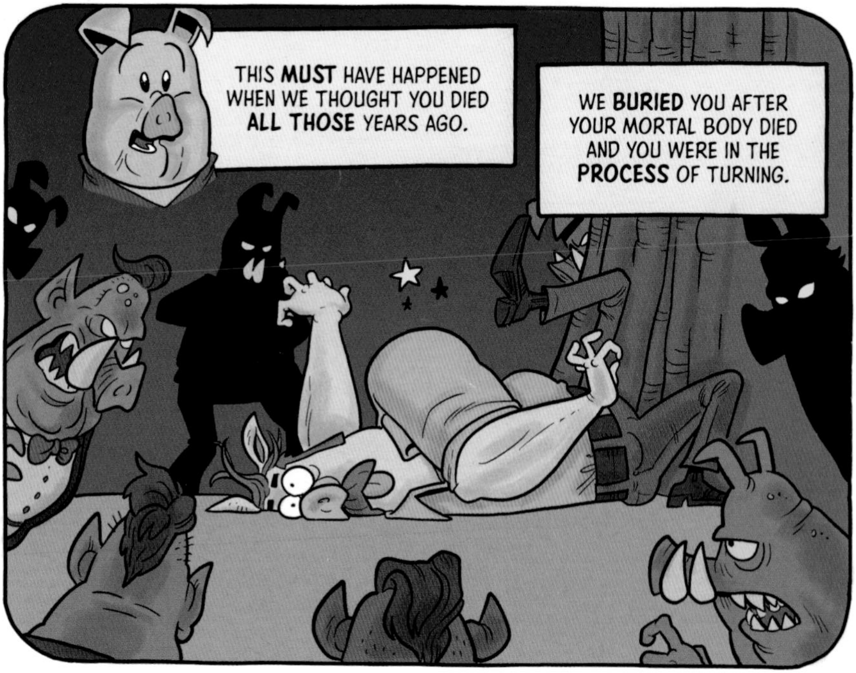
THIS MUST HAVE HAPPENED WHEN WE THOUGHT YOU DIED ALL THOSE YEARS AGO.
WE BURIED YOU AFTER YOUR MORTAL BODY DIED AND YOU WERE IN THE PROCESS OF TURNING.

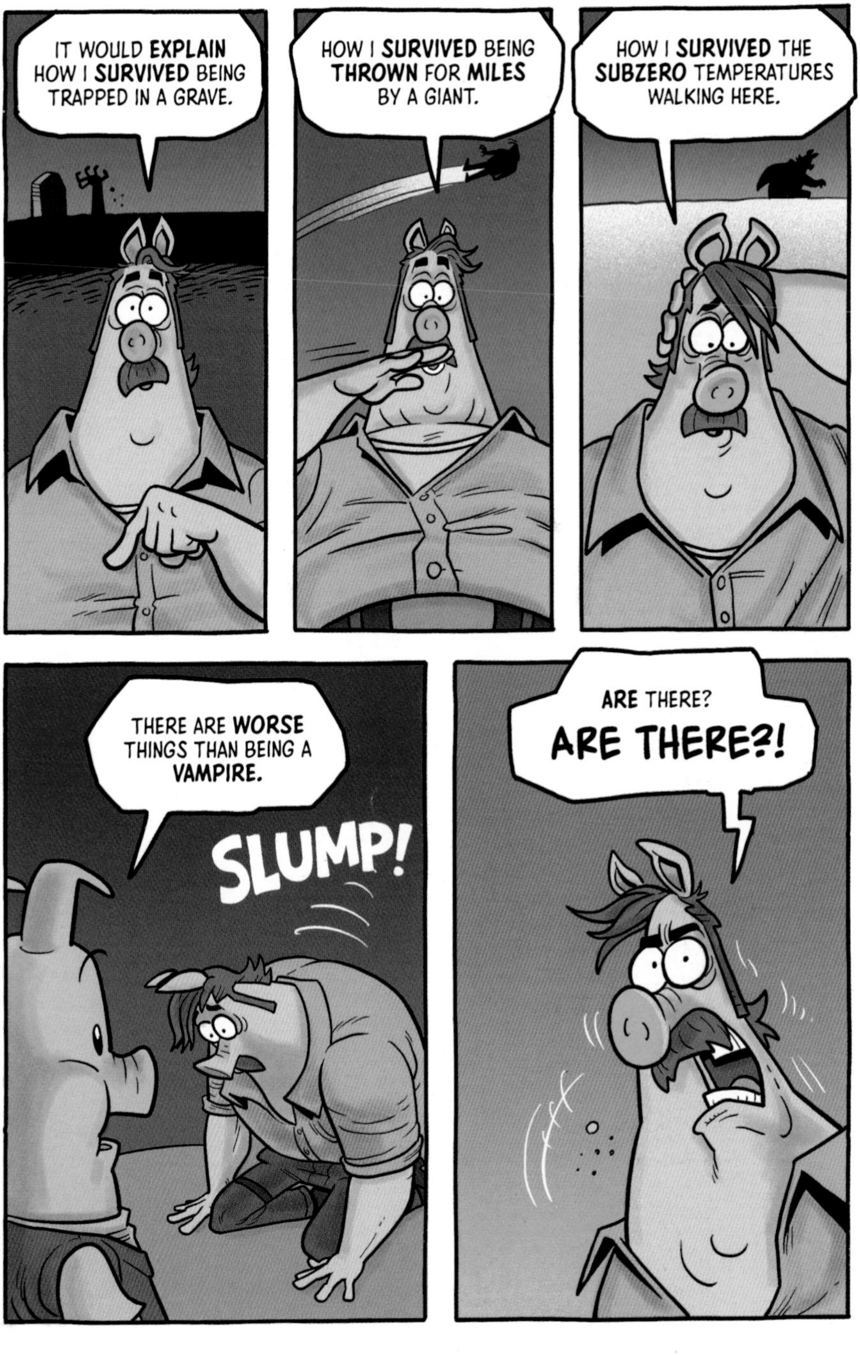
IT WOULD EXPLAIN HOW I SURVIVED BEING TRAPPED IN A GRAVE.
HOW I SURVIVED BEING THROWN FOR MILES BY A GIANT.
HOW I SURVIVED THE SUBZERO TEMPERATURES WALKING HERE.
THERE ARE WORSE THINGS THAN BEING A VAMPIRE.
SLUMP!
ARE THERE? ARE THERE?!

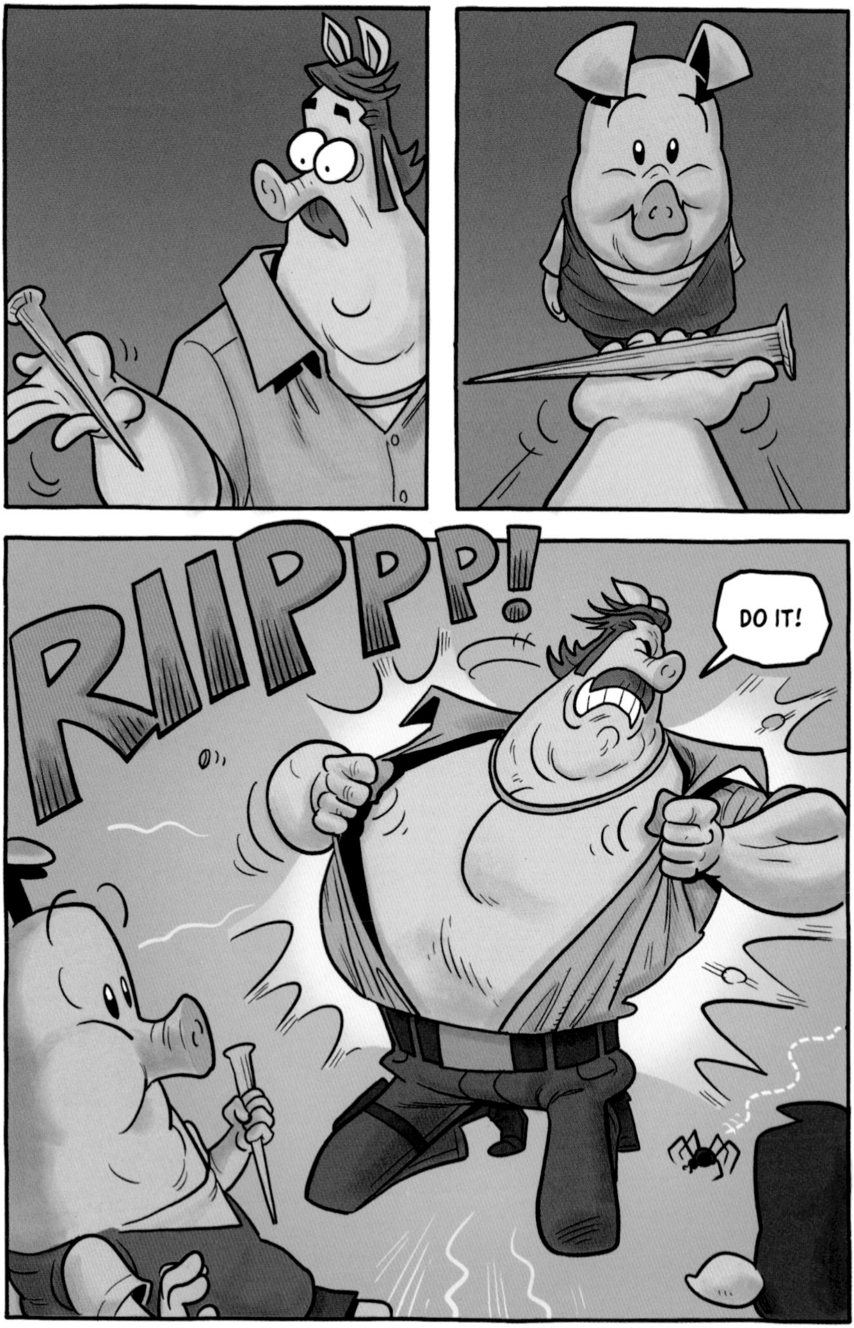
RIIPPP!
DO IT!

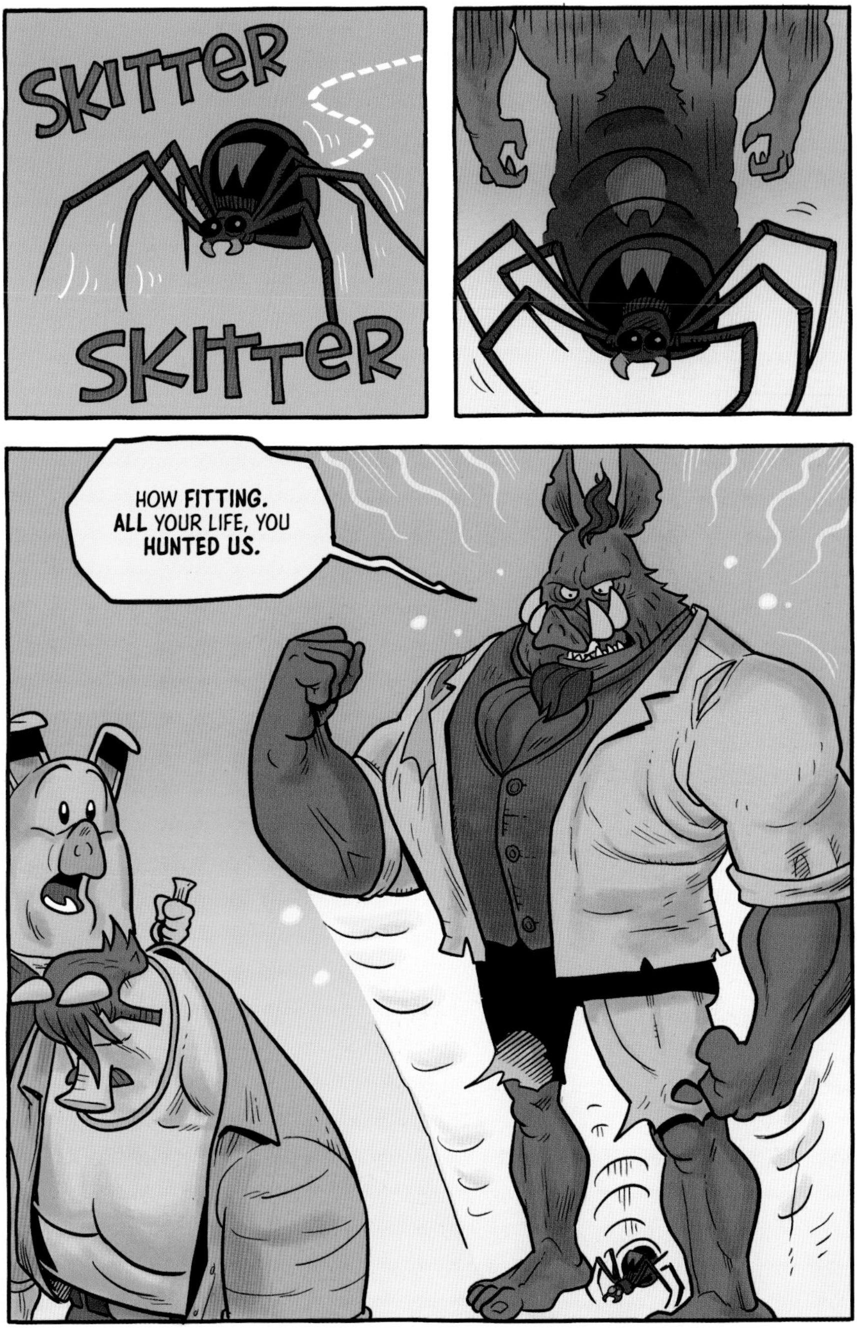
SKITTER
SKITTER
HOW FITTING. ALL YOUR LIFE, YOU HUNTED US.

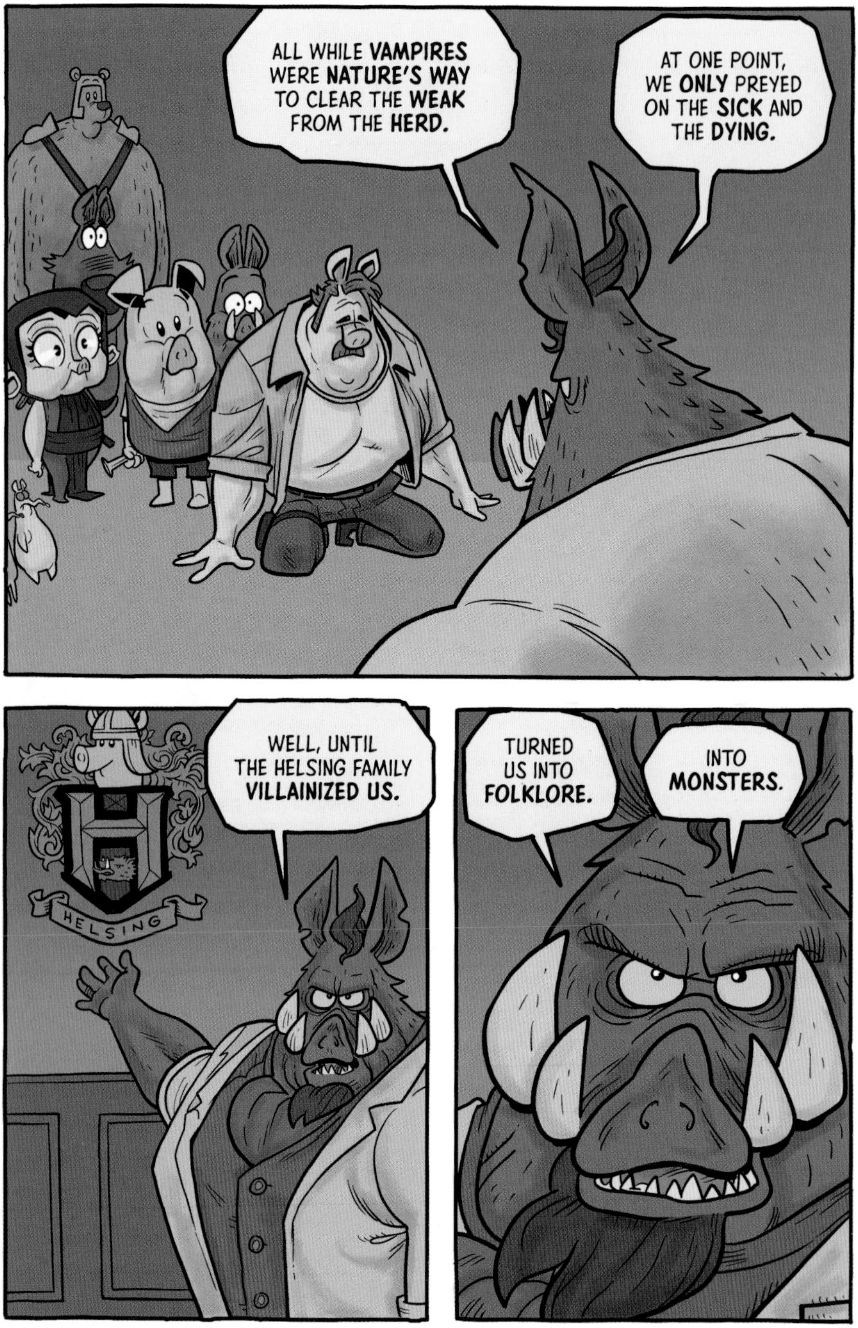
ALL WHILE VAMPIRES WERE NATURE'S WAY TO CLEAR THE WEAK FROM THE HERD.
AT ONE POINT, WE ONLY PREYED ON THE SICK AND THE DYING.
HELSING
WELL, UNTIL THE HELSING FAMILY VILLAINIZED US.
TURNED US INTO FOLKLORE.
INTO MONSTERS.

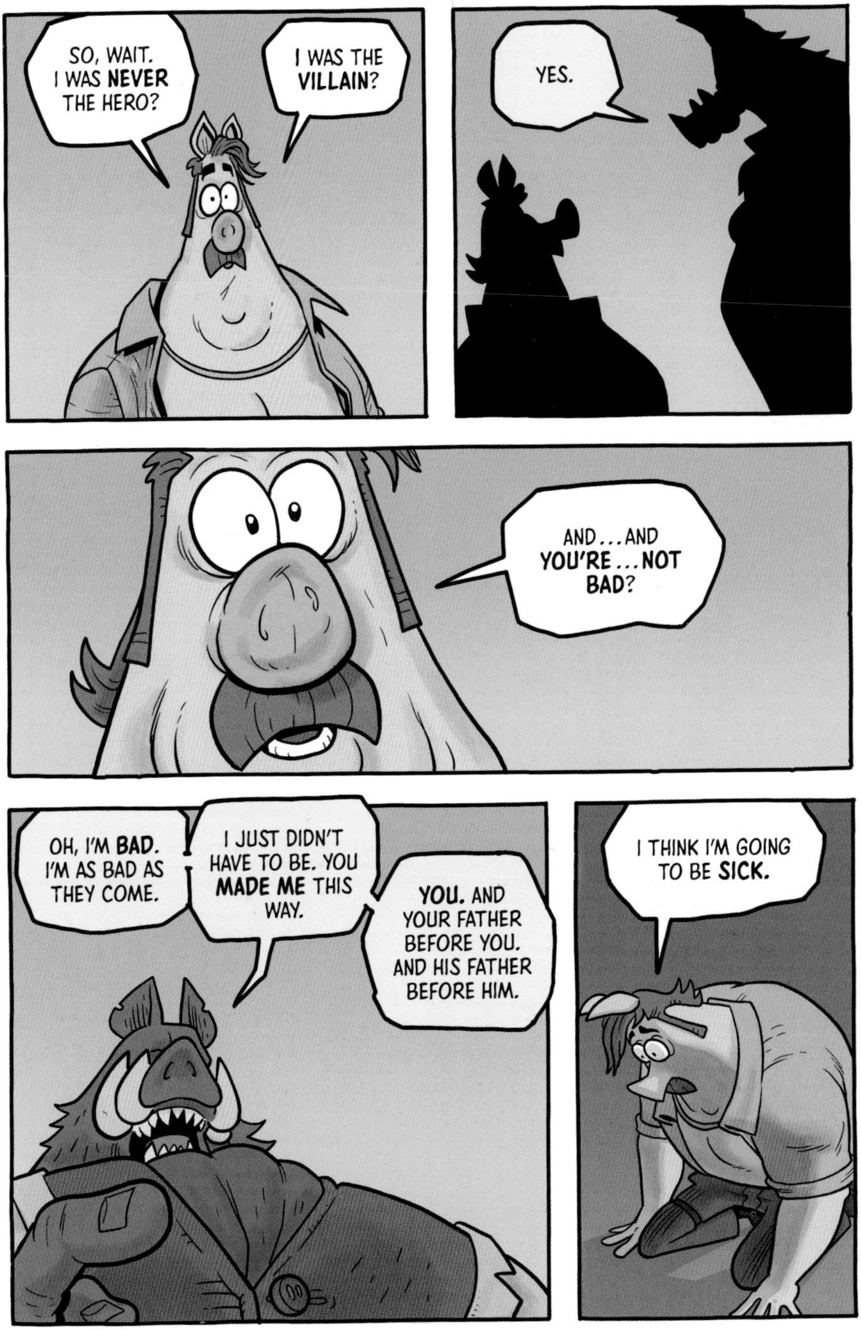
SO, WAIT. I WAS **NEVER** THE HERO?
I WAS THE **VILLAIN**?
YES.
AND... AND **YOU'RE... NOT BAD**?
OH, I'M **BAD.** I'M AS BAD AS THEY COME.
I JUST DIDN'T HAVE TO BE. YOU **MADE ME** THIS WAY.
YOU. AND YOUR FATHER BEFORE YOU. AND HIS FATHER BEFORE HIM.
I THINK I'M GOING TO BE **SICK.**

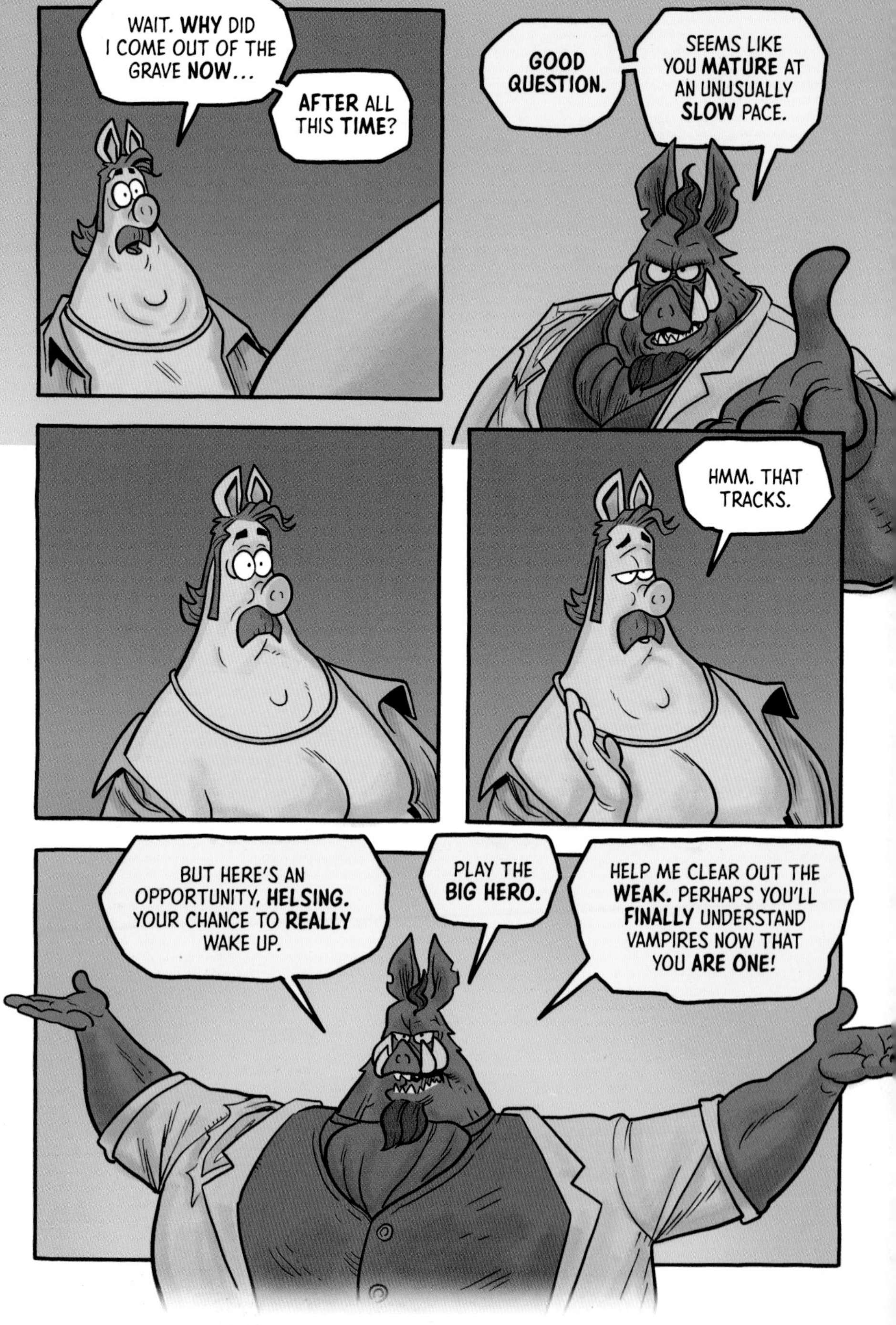
WAIT. WHY DID I COME OUT OF THE GRAVE NOW...
AFTER ALL THIS TIME?
GOOD QUESTION.
SEEMS LIKE YOU MATURE AT AN UNUSUALLY SLOW PACE.
HMM. THAT TRACKS.
BUT HERE'S AN OPPORTUNITY, HELSING. YOUR CHANCE TO REALLY WAKE UP.
PLAY THE BIG HERO.
HELP ME CLEAR OUT THE WEAK. PERHAPS YOU'LL FINALLY UNDERSTAND VAMPIRES NOW THAT YOU ARE ONE!

CHAPTER SIXTEEN

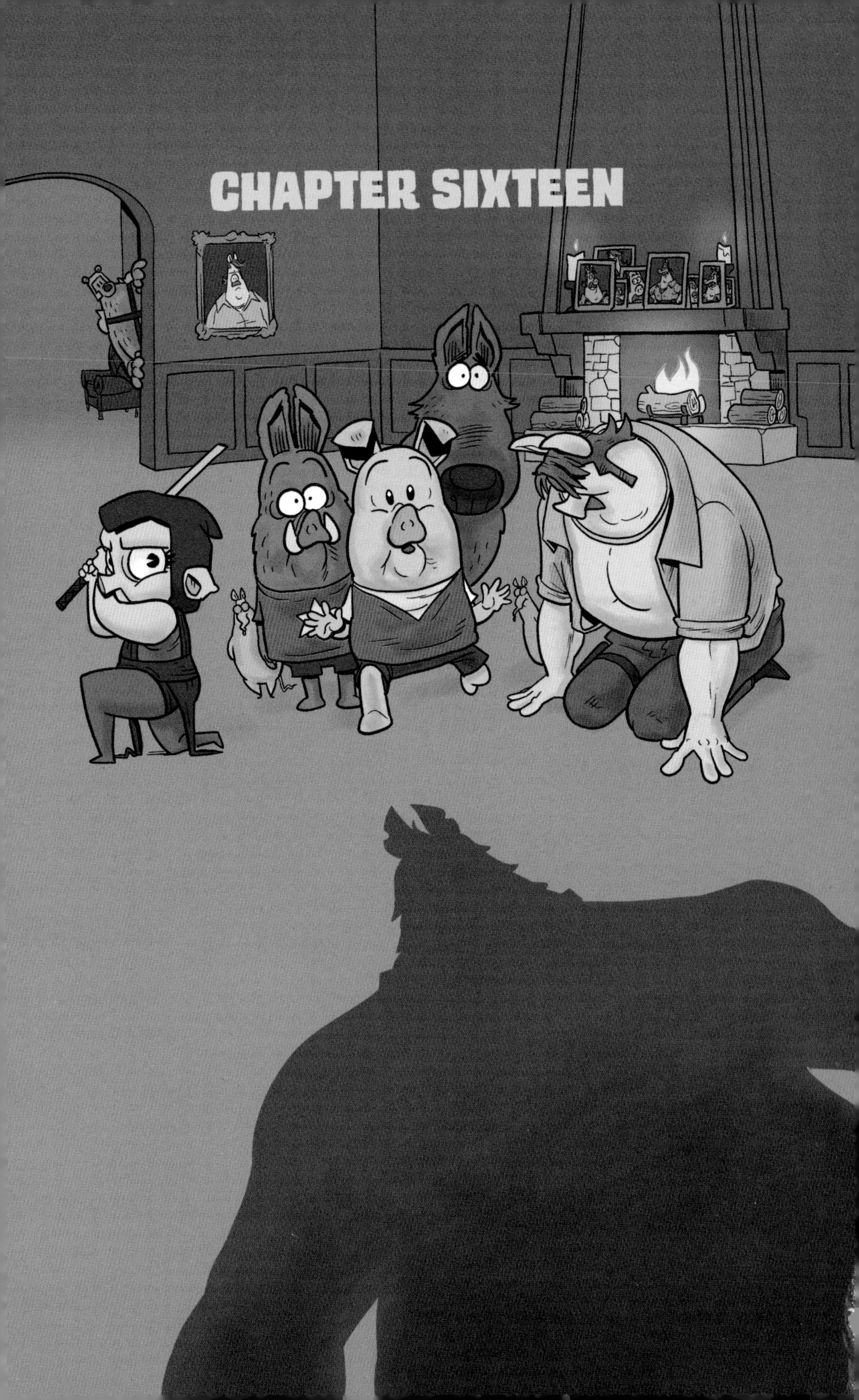

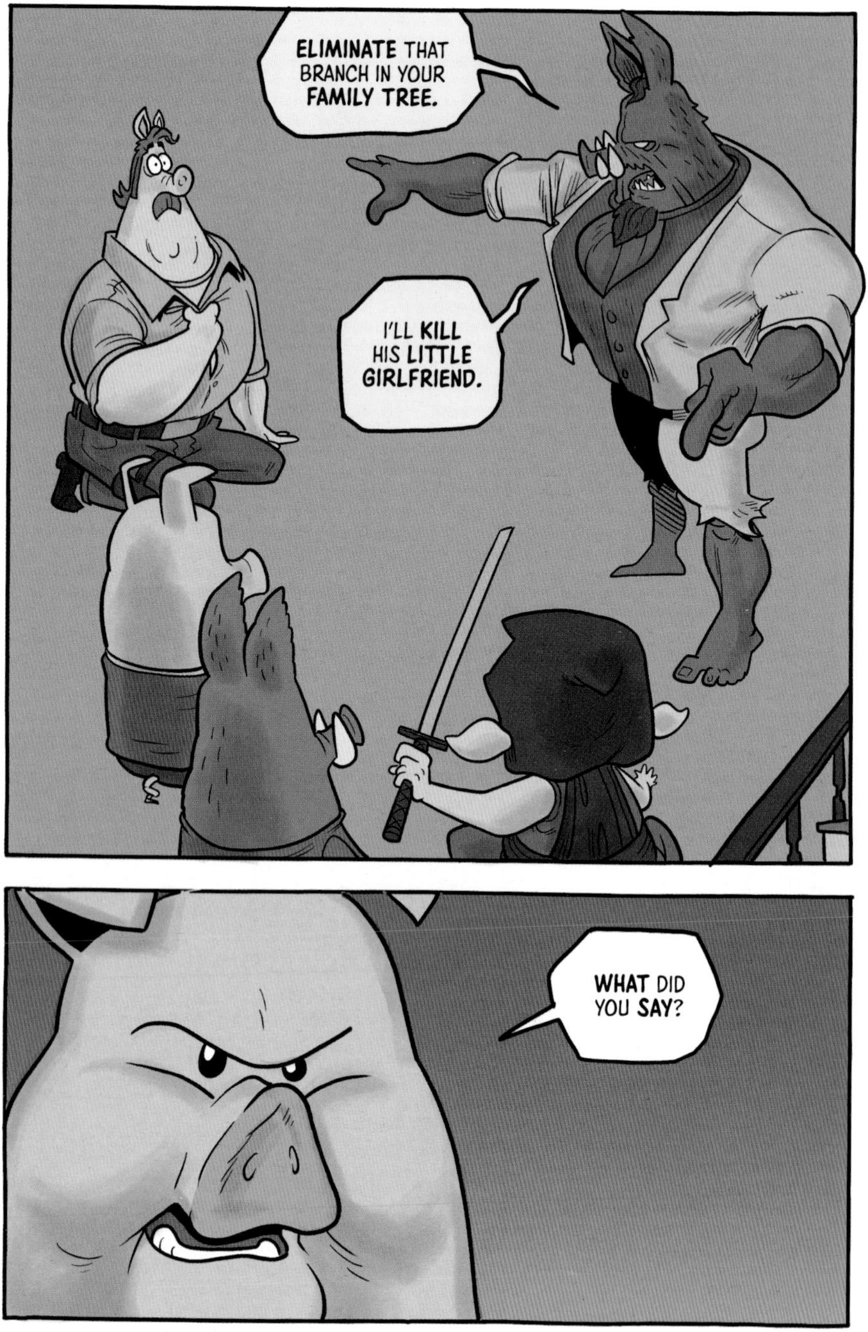
ELIMINATE THAT BRANCH IN YOUR FAMILY TREE.
I'LL KILL HIS LITTLE GIRLFRIEND.
WHAT DID YOU SAY?

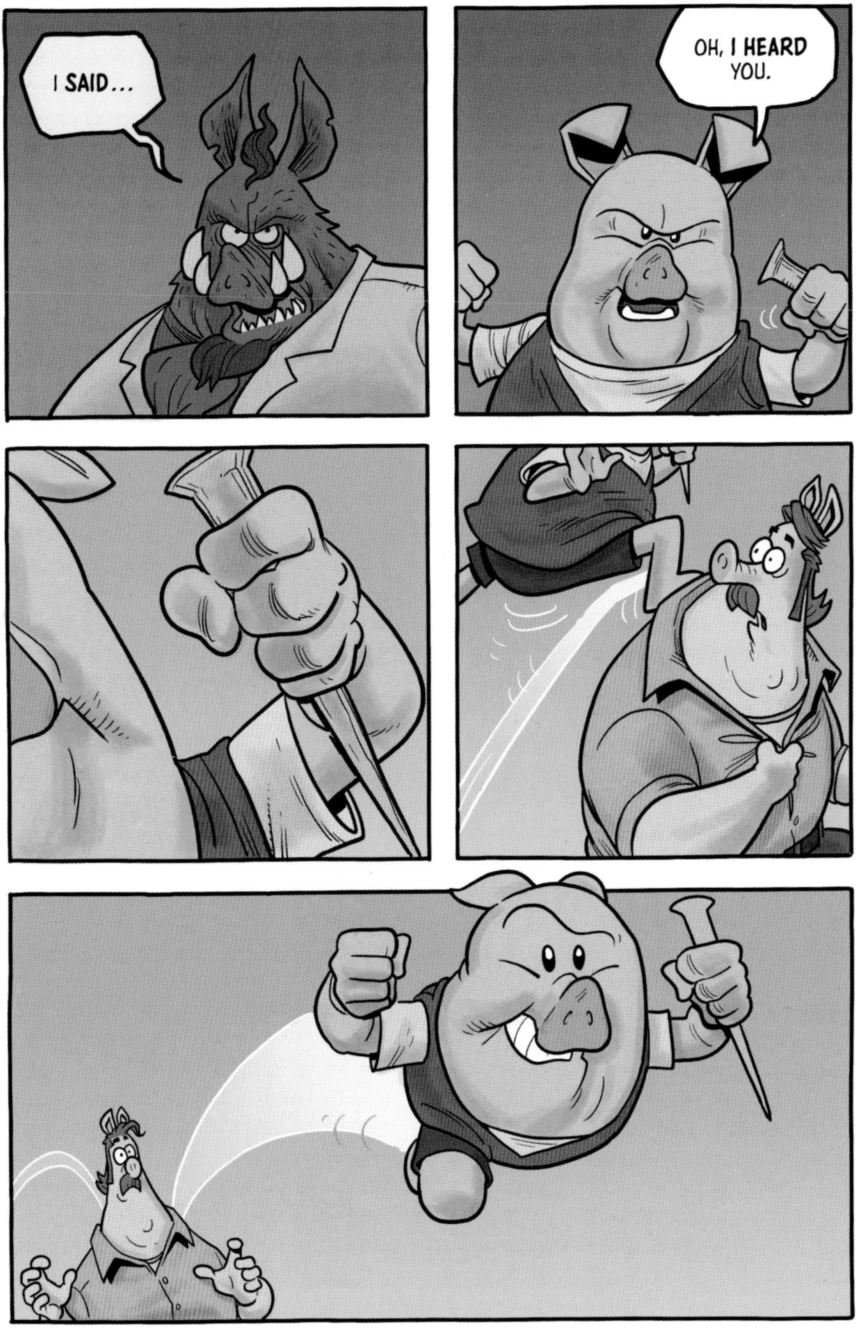
I SAID...
OH, I HEARD YOU.

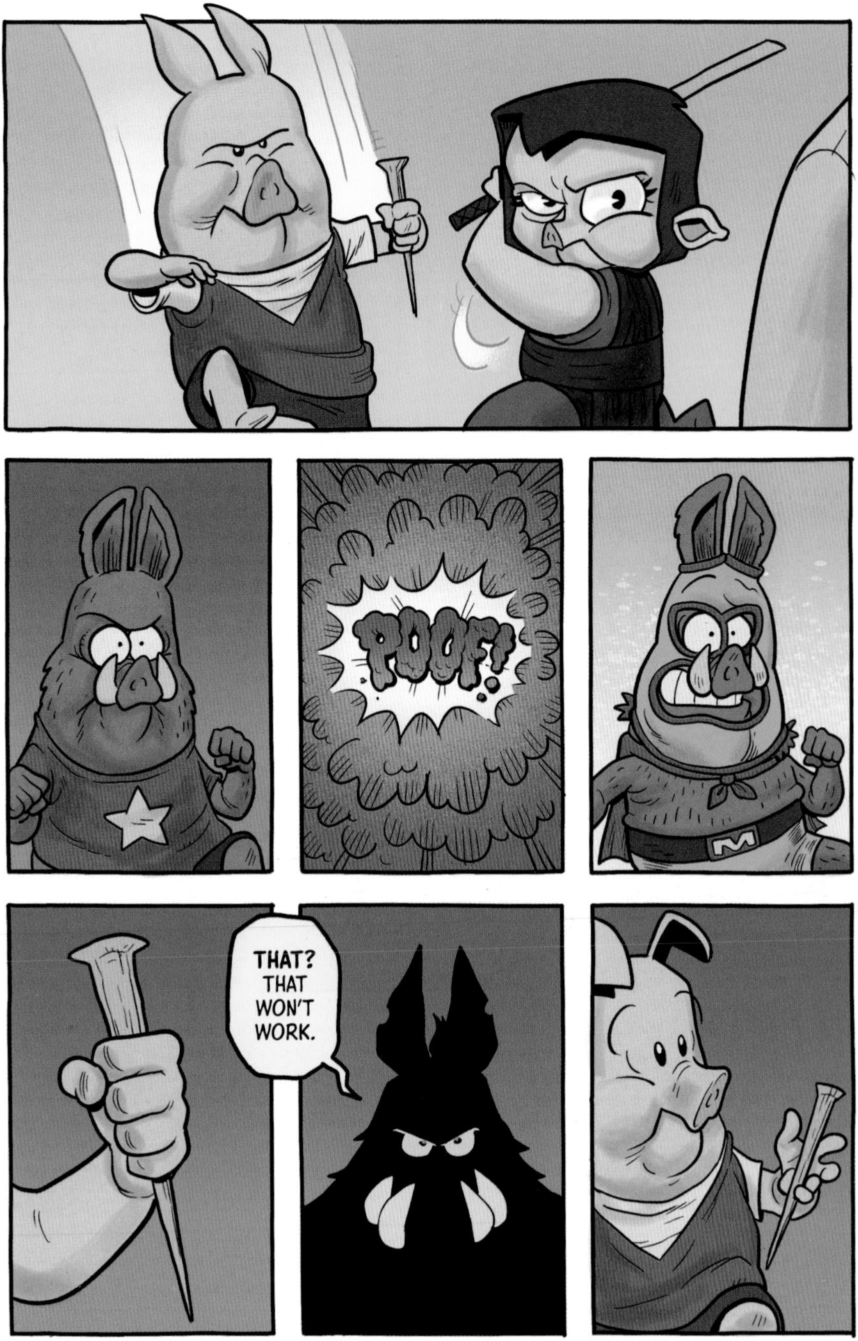
POOF!
THAT? THAT WON'T WORK.

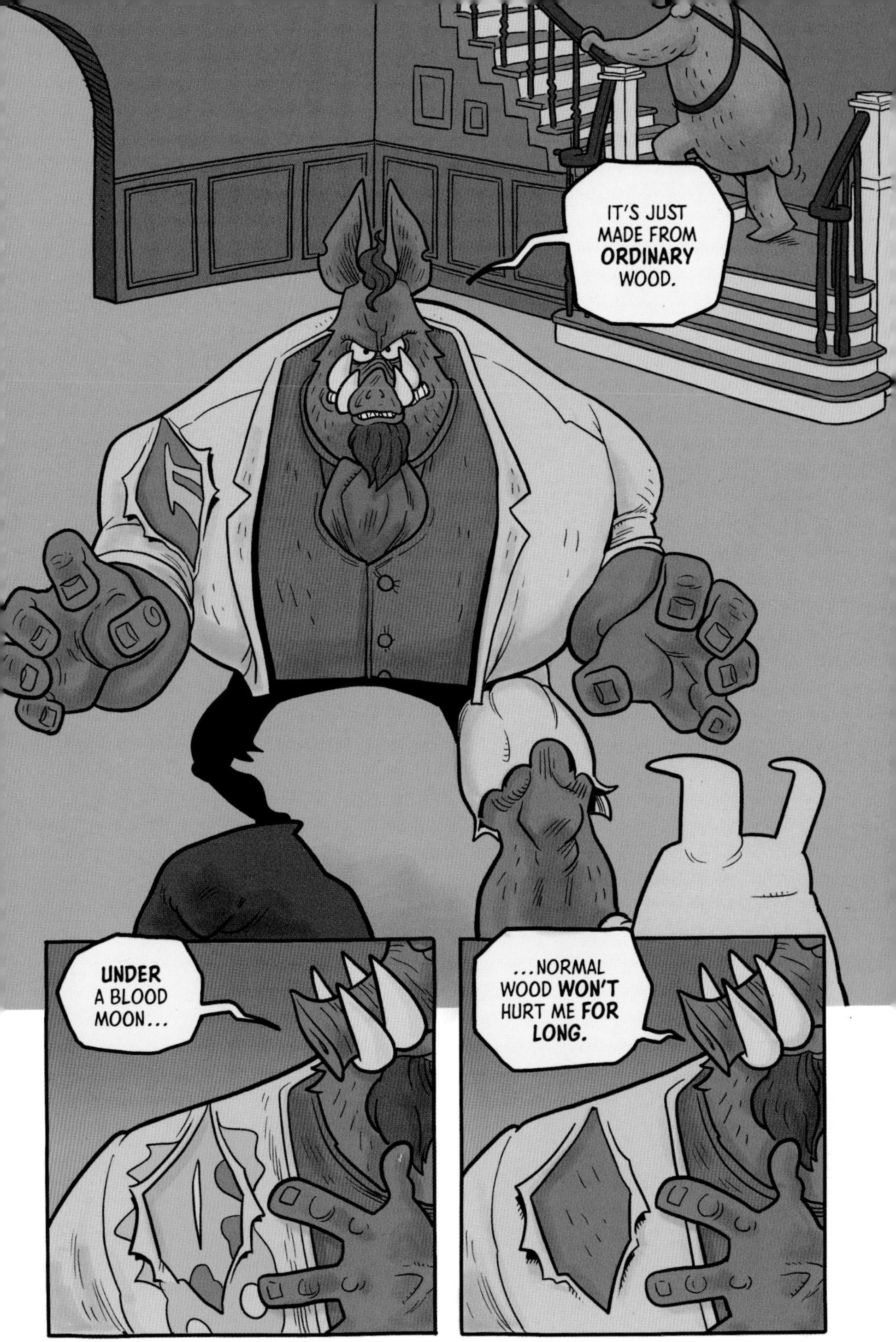
IT'S JUST MADE FROM ORDINARY WOOD.
UNDER A BLOOD MOON...
...NORMAL WOOD WON'T HURT ME FOR LONG.

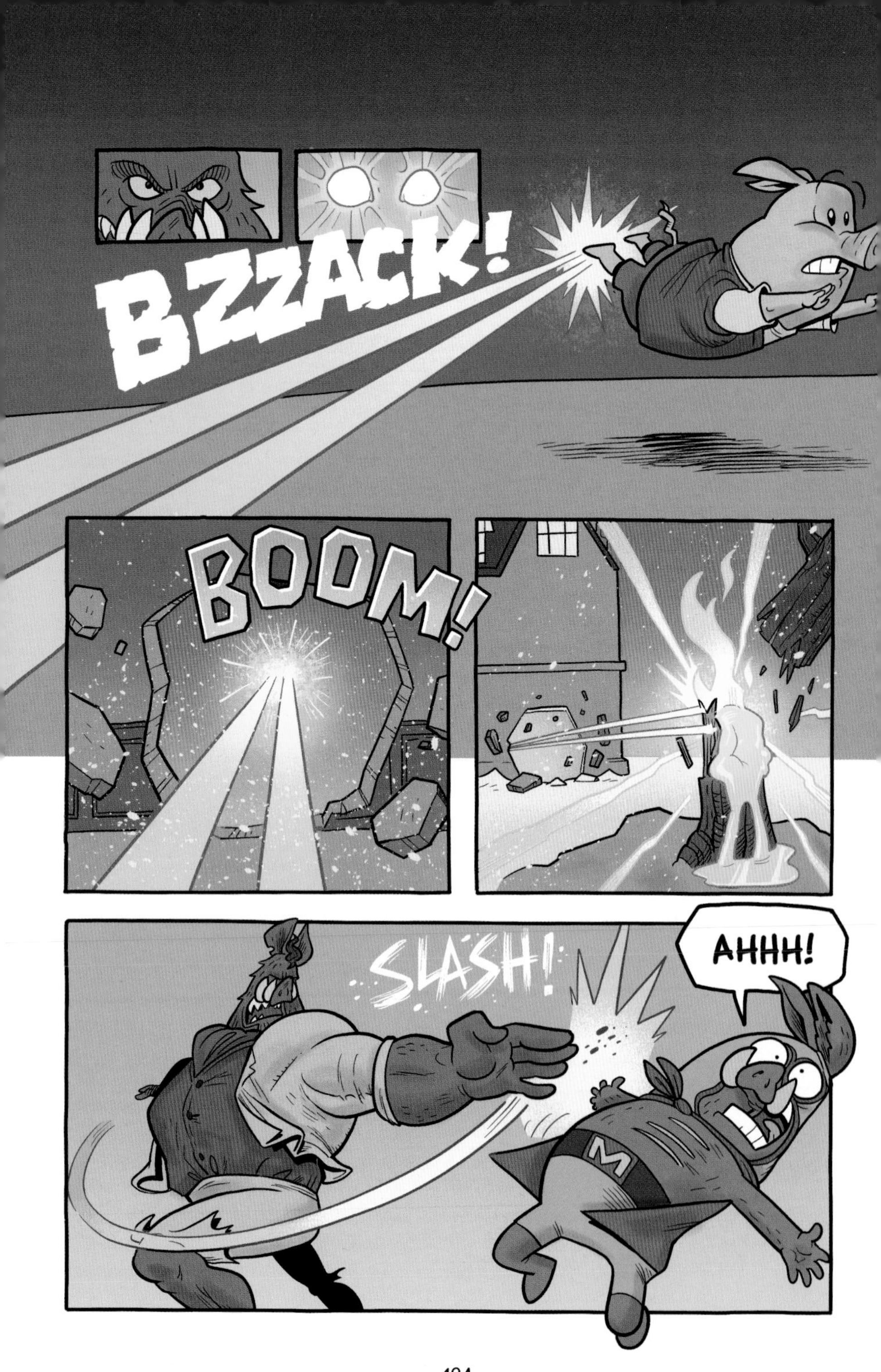
BZZACK!
BOOM!
SLASH!
AHHH!

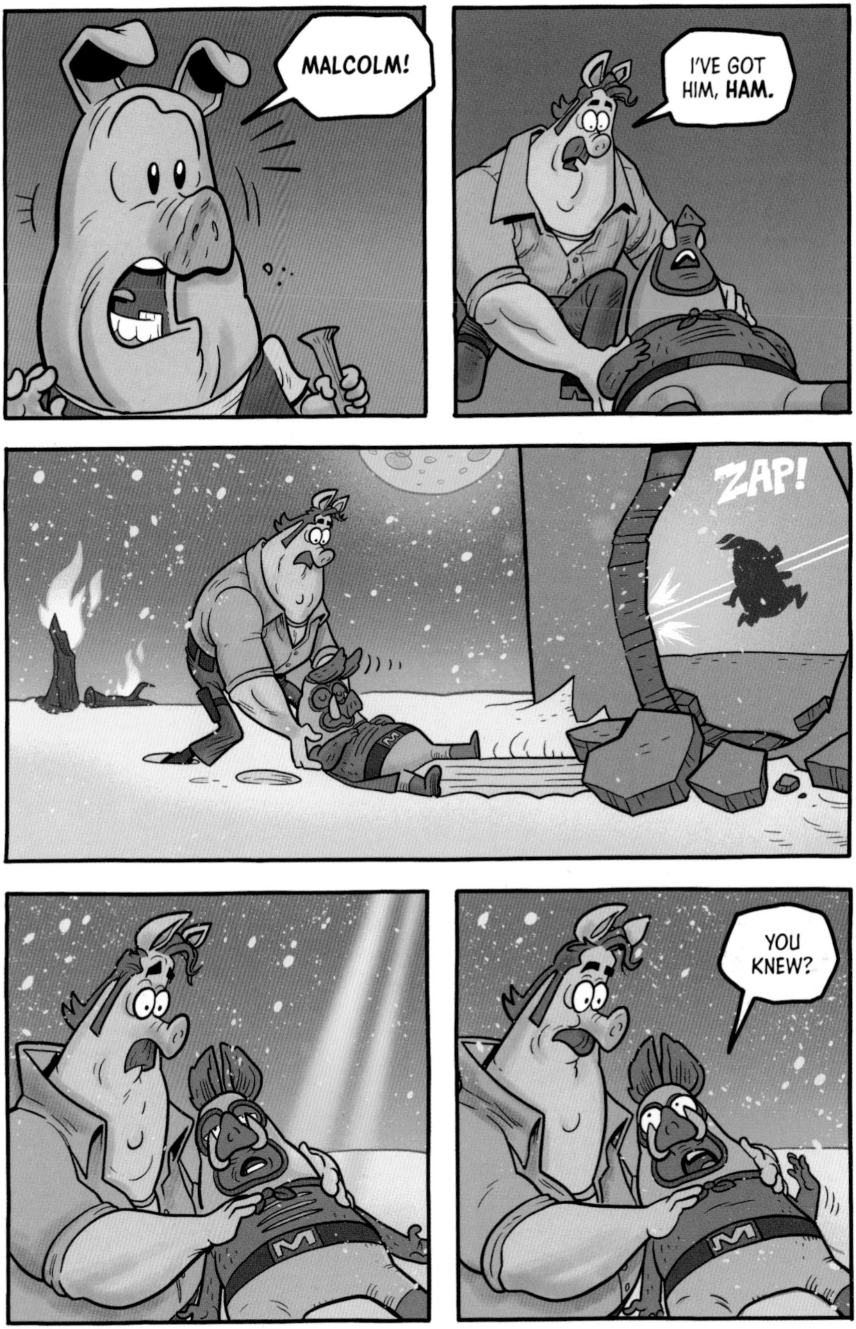
MALCOLM!
I'VE GOT HIM, **HAM.**
ZAP!
YOU KNEW?

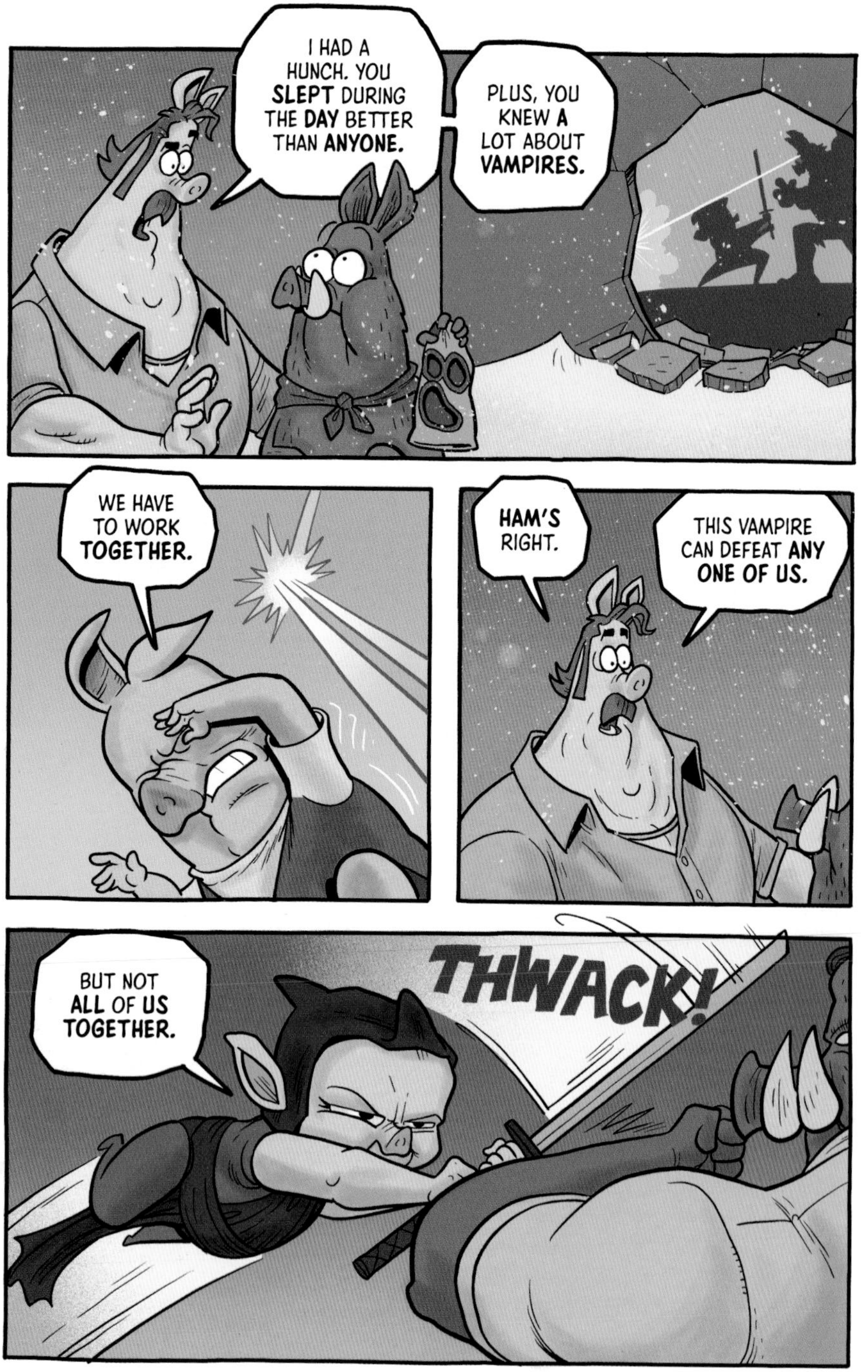
I HAD A HUNCH. YOU SLEPT DURING THE DAY BETTER THAN ANYONE.
PLUS, YOU KNEW A LOT ABOUT VAMPIRES.
WE HAVE TO WORK TOGETHER.
HAM'S RIGHT.
THIS VAMPIRE CAN DEFEAT ANY ONE OF US.
BUT NOT ALL OF US TOGETHER.
THWACK!

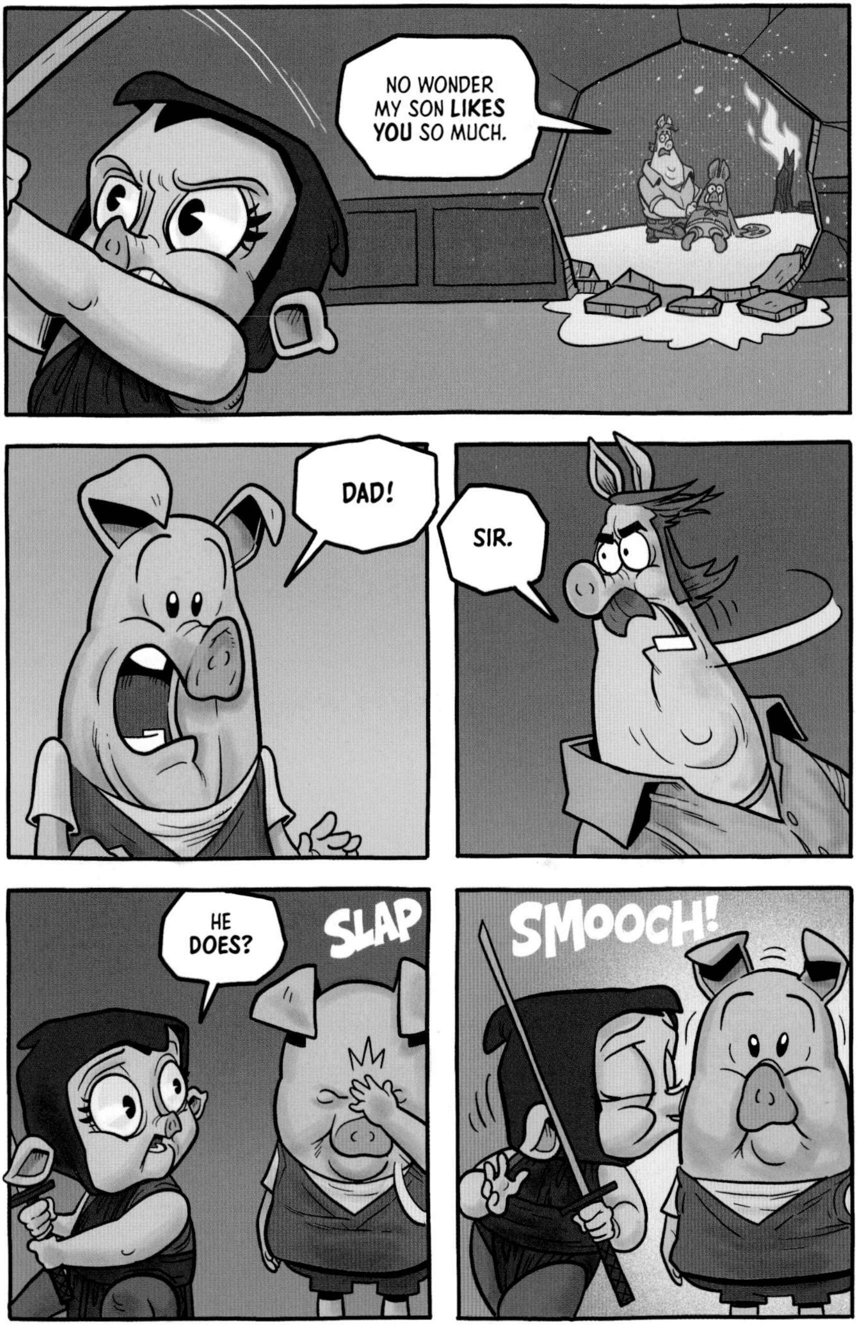
NO WONDER MY SON **LIKES** **YOU** SO MUCH.
DAD!
SIR.
HE **DOES?**
SLAP
SMOOCH!

CHAPTER SEVENTEEN

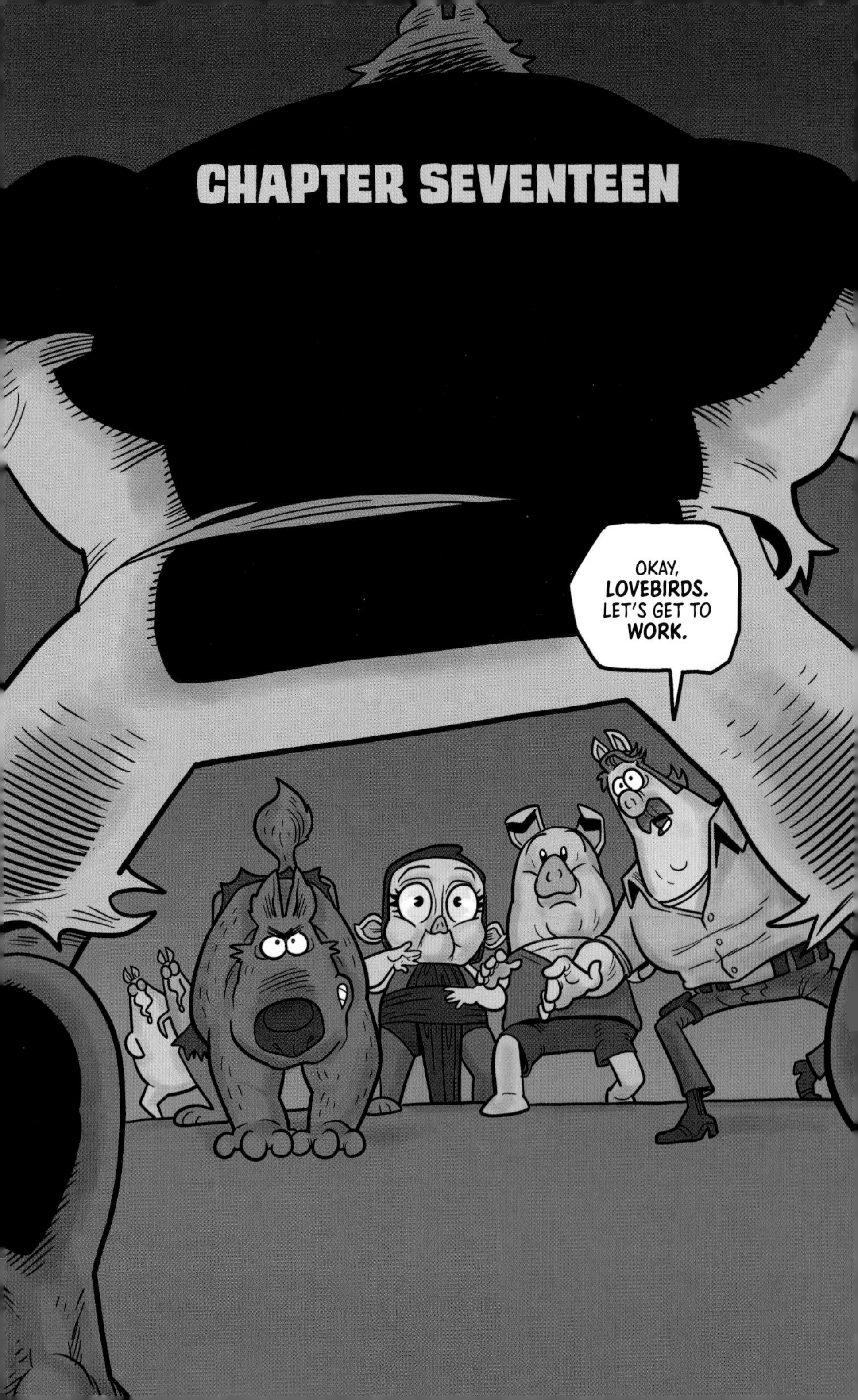
OKAY, LOVEBIRDS. LET'S GET TO WORK.

WHAT DO WE KNOW?
IT CAN BE HURT.
BZZAAP!
EVEN THOUGH IT HEALS FAST...
THUD!
FLIP!
ZZT!
...IT DOES BLEED.

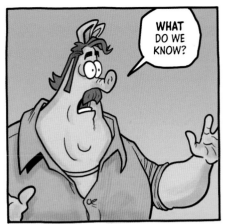

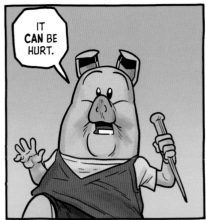

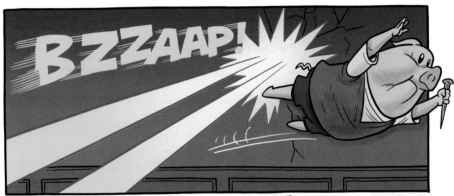

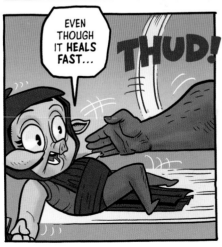

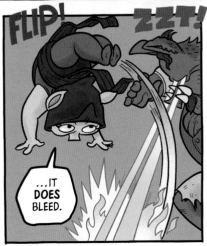

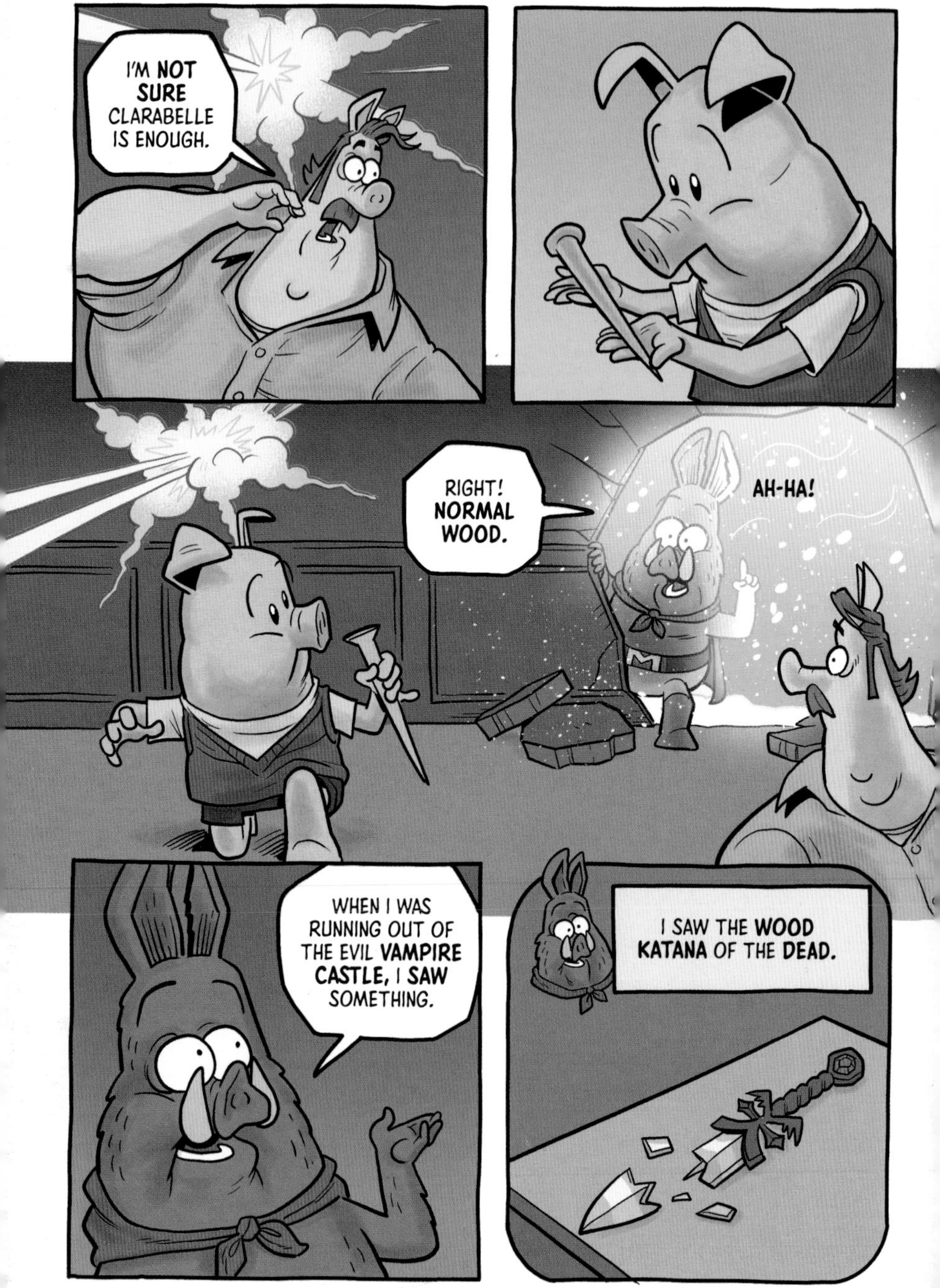
I'M NOT SURE CLARABELLE IS ENOUGH.
RIGHT! NORMAL WOOD.
AH-HA!
WHEN I WAS RUNNING OUT OF THE EVIL VAMPIRE CASTLE, I SAW SOMETHING.
I SAW THE WOOD KATANA OF THE DEAD.

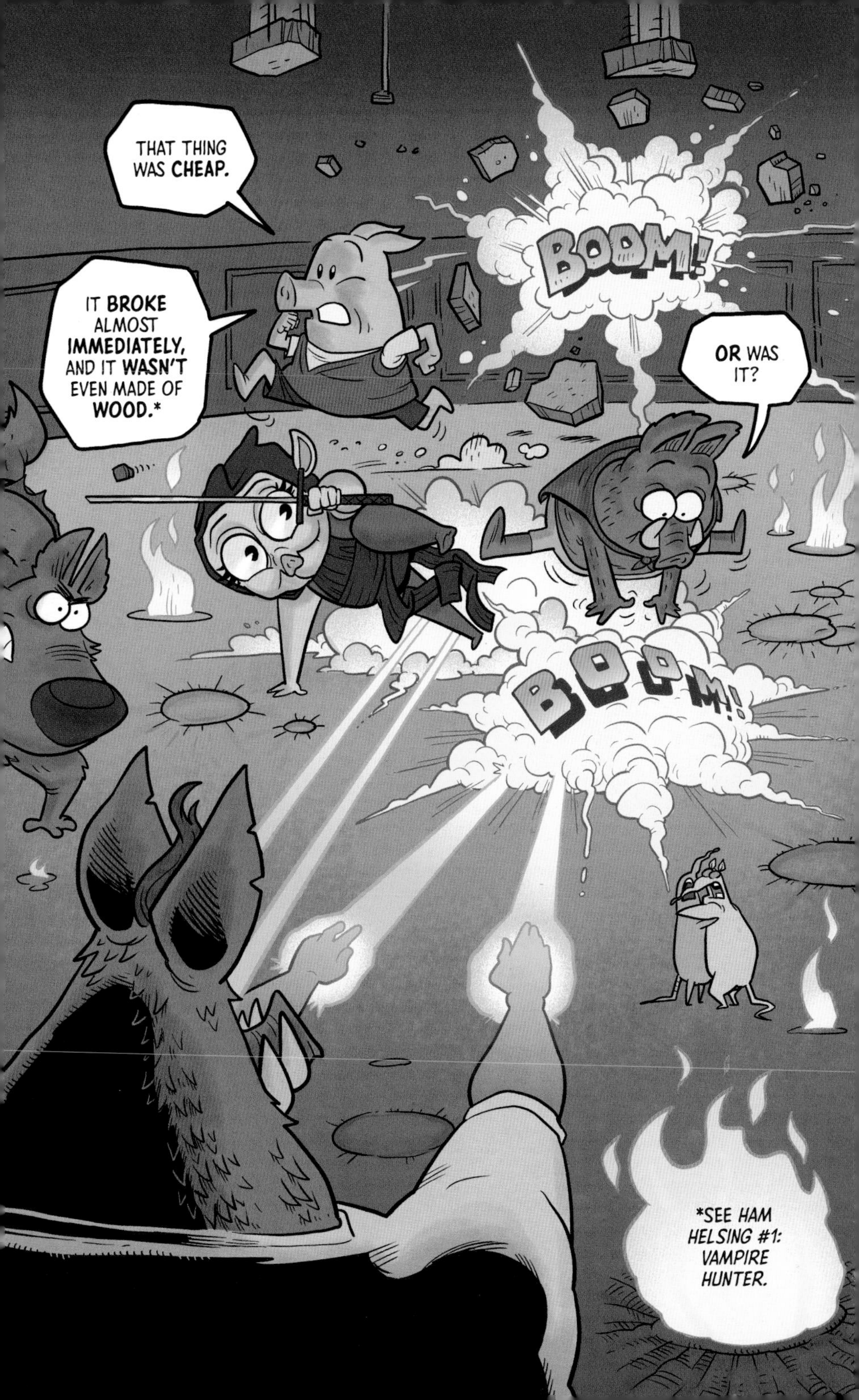
THAT THING WAS CHEAP.
IT BROKE ALMOST IMMEDIATELY, AND IT WASN'T EVEN MADE OF WOOD.*
BOOM!
OR WAS IT?
BOOM!
*SEE HAM HELSING #1: VAMPIRE HUNTER.

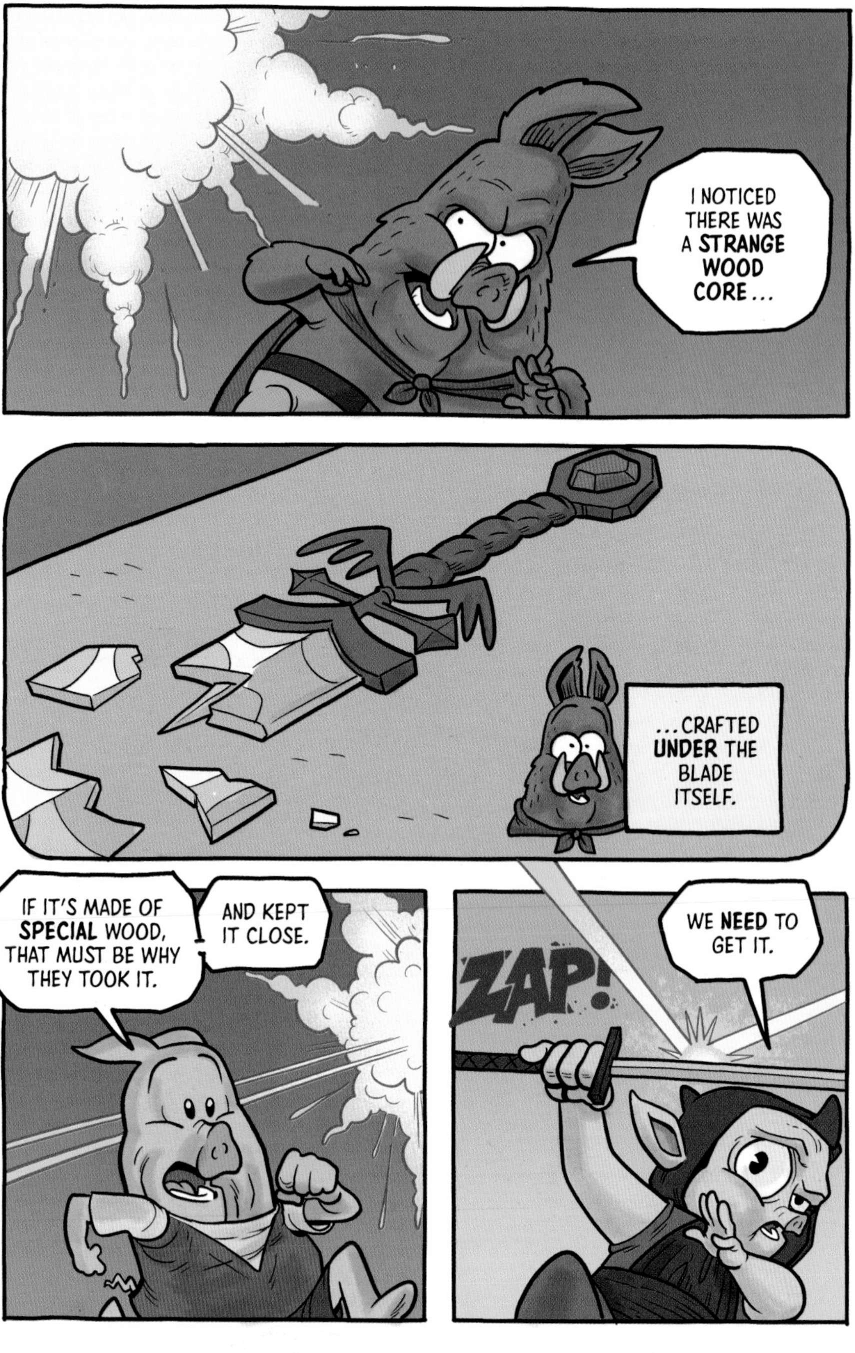
I NOTICED THERE WAS A STRANGE WOOD CORE...
...CRAFTED UNDER THE BLADE ITSELF.
IF IT'S MADE OF SPECIAL WOOD, THAT MUST BE WHY THEY TOOK IT.
AND KEPT IT CLOSE.
ZAP!
WE NEED TO GET IT.

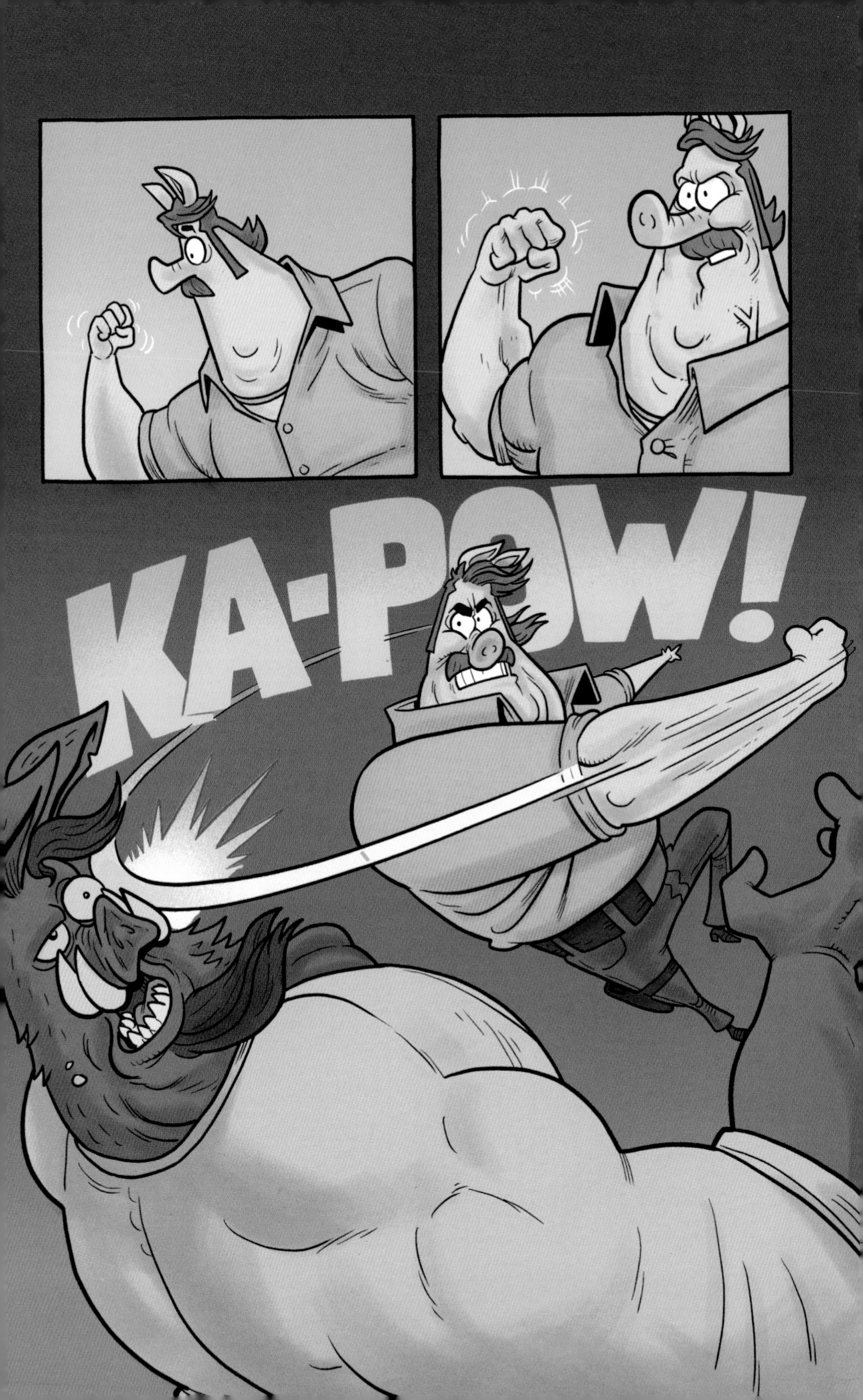
KA-POW!

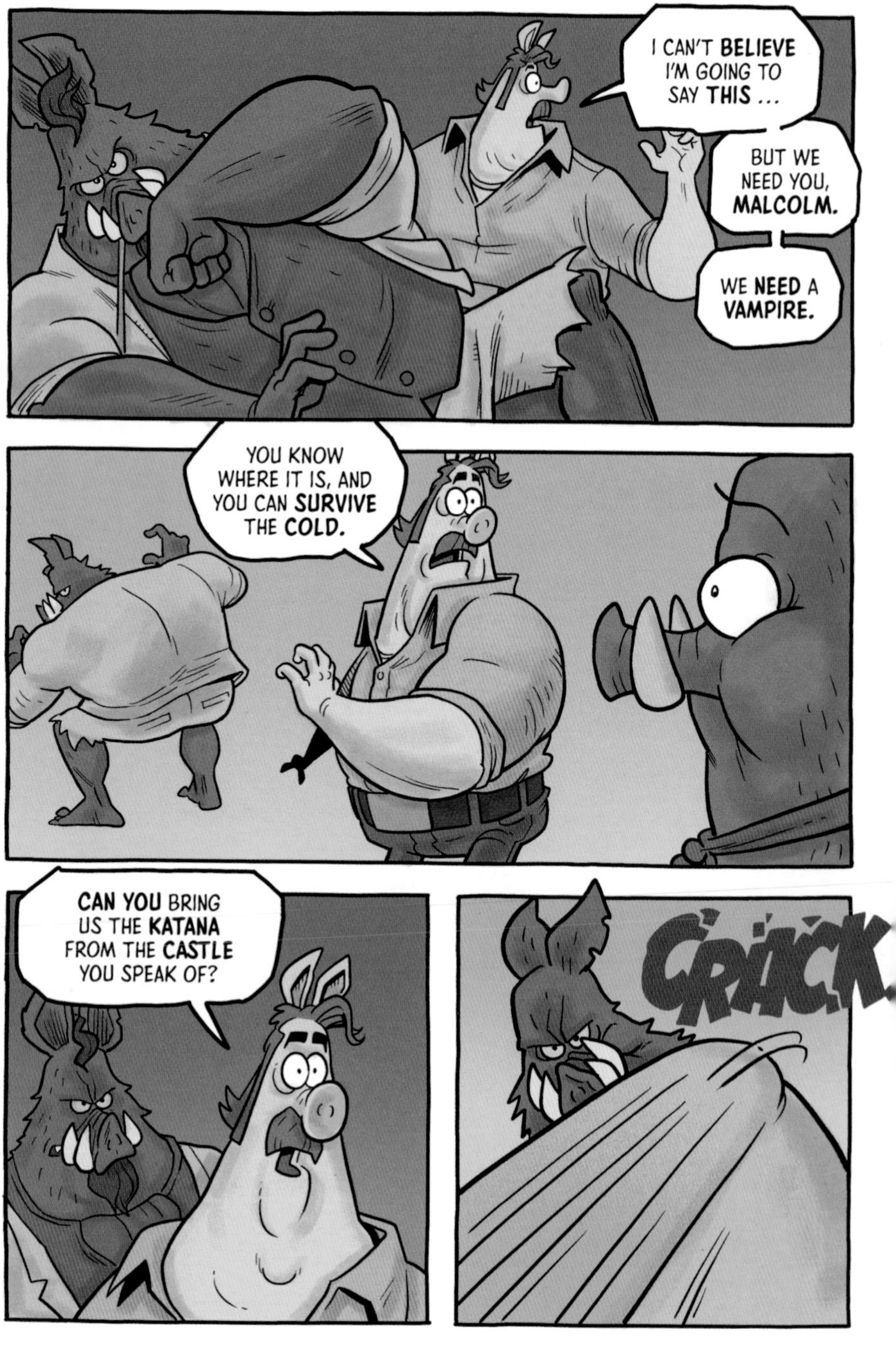
I CAN'T **BELIEVE** I'M GOING TO SAY **THIS** ...
BUT WE NEED YOU, **MALCOLM.**
WE **NEED** A **VAMPIRE.**
YOU KNOW WHERE IT IS, AND YOU CAN **SURVIVE** THE **COLD.**
CAN YOU BRING US THE **KATANA** FROM THE **CASTLE** YOU SPEAK OF?
CRACK

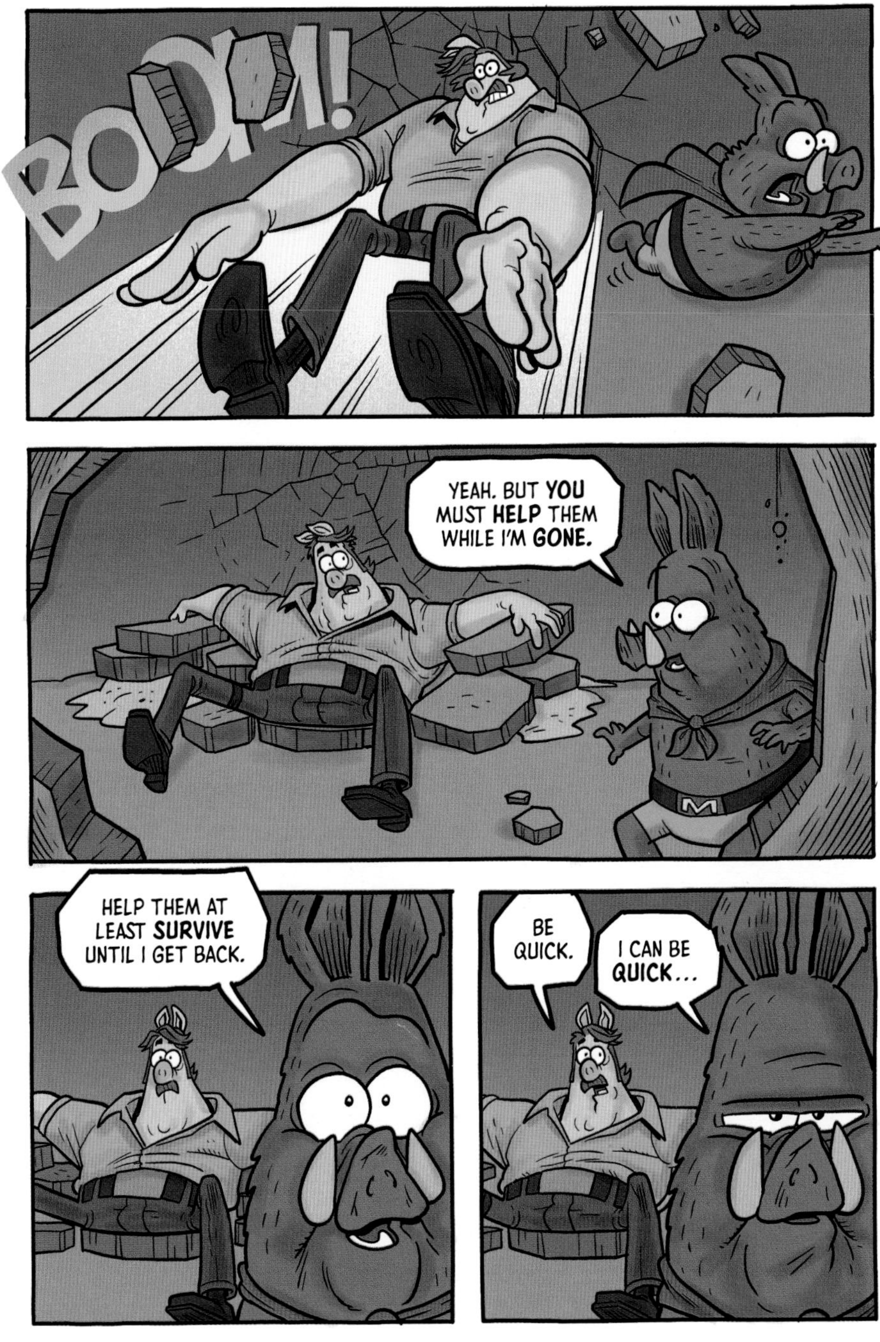
BOOM!
YEAH. BUT **YOU** MUST **HELP** THEM WHILE I'M **GONE.**
HELP THEM AT LEAST **SURVIVE** UNTIL I GET BACK.
BE QUICK.
I CAN BE **QUICK**...

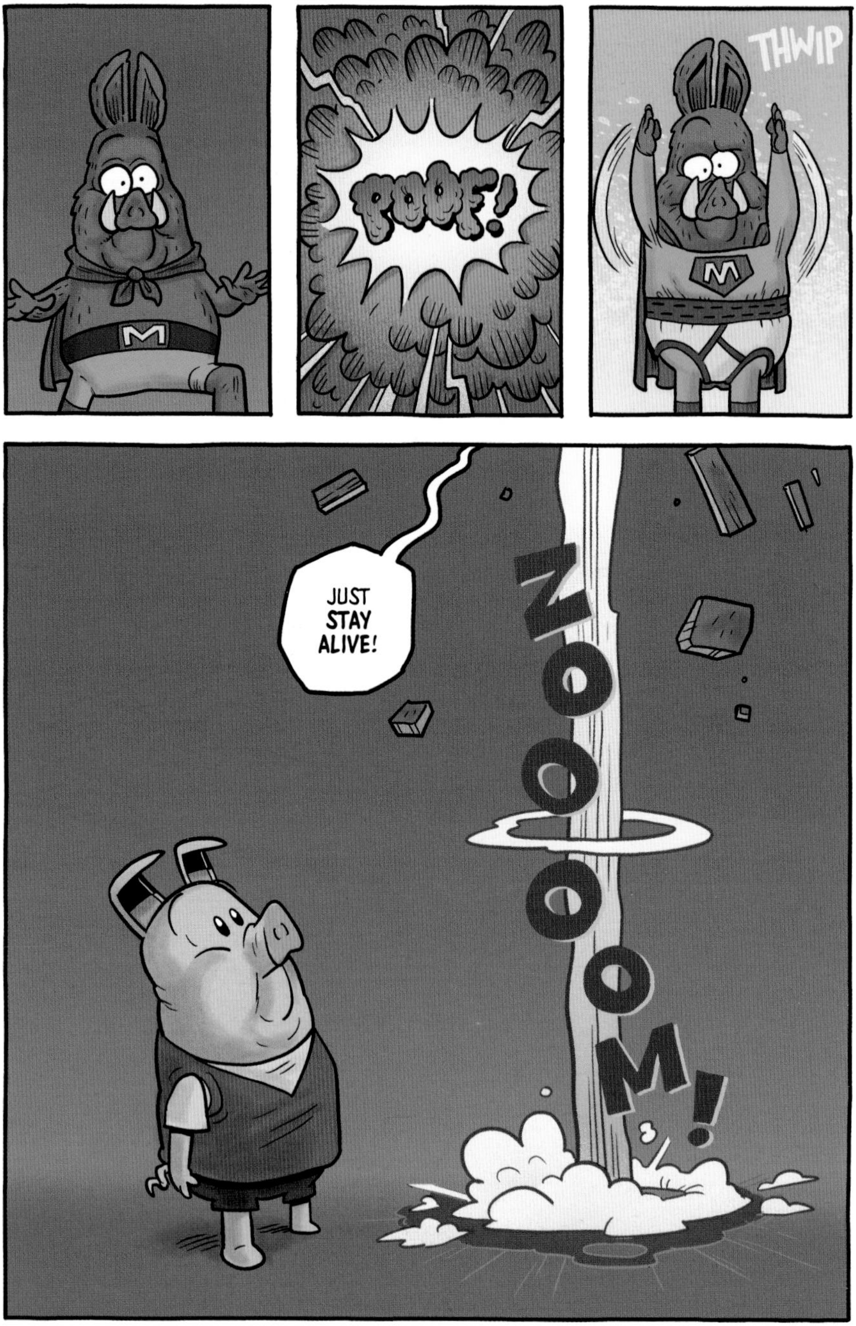
POOF!
THWIP
JUST STAY ALIVE!
ZOOOOOM!

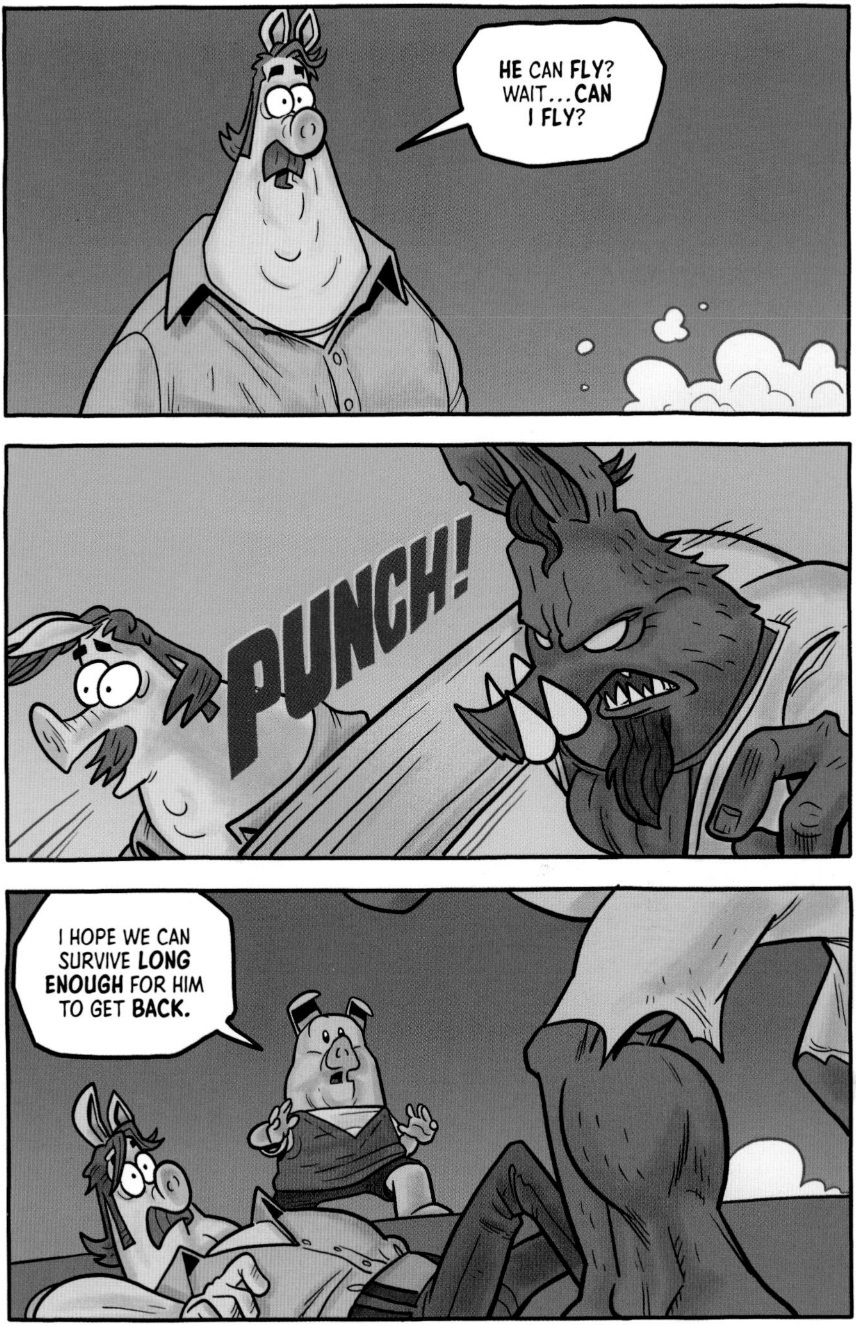
HE CAN FLY? WAIT...CAN I FLY?
PUNCH!
I HOPE WE CAN SURVIVE LONG ENOUGH FOR HIM TO GET BACK.

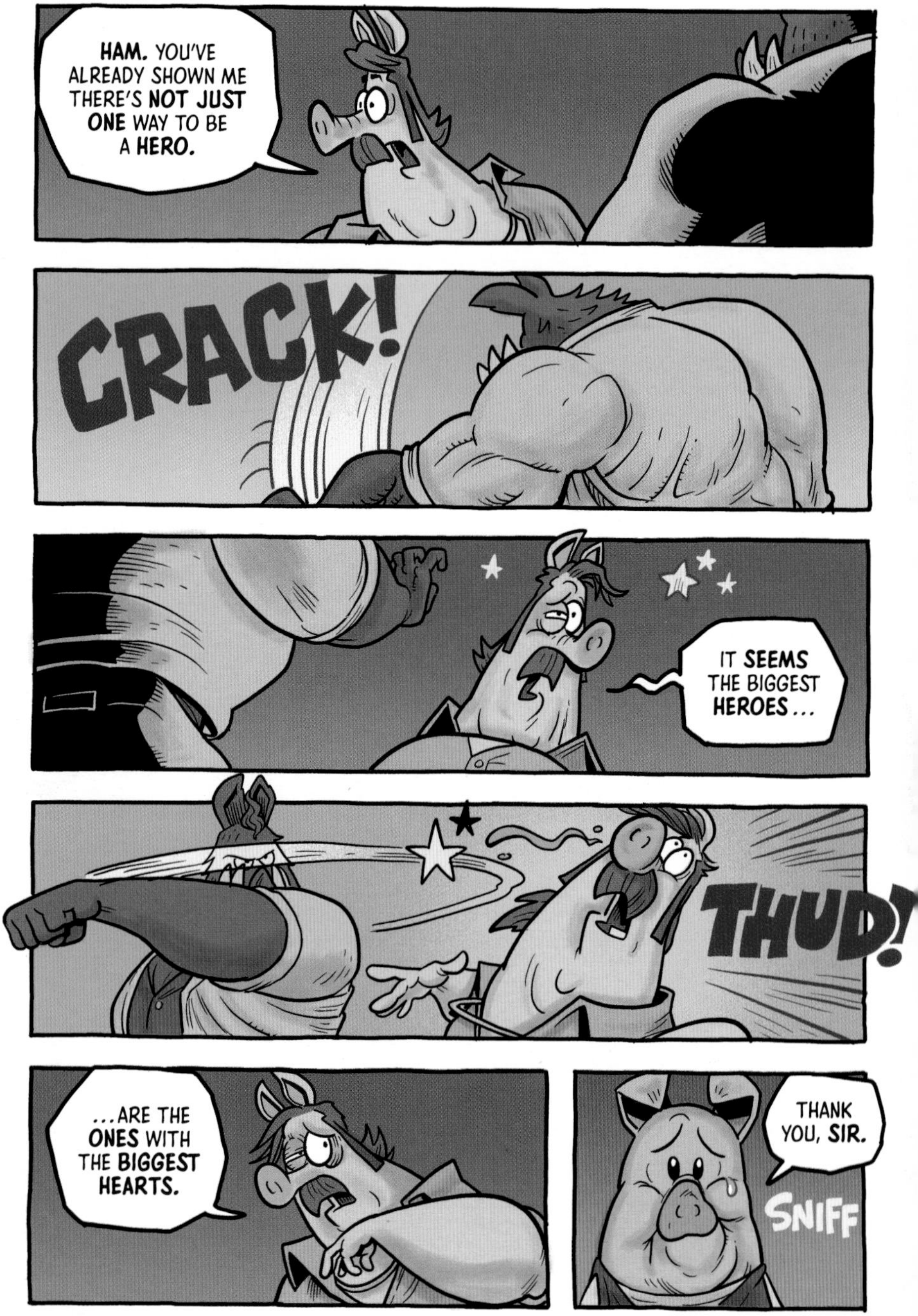
HAM. YOU'VE ALREADY SHOWN ME THERE'S NOT JUST ONE WAY TO BE A HERO.
CRACK!
IT SEEMS THE BIGGEST HEROES...
THUD!
...ARE THE ONES WITH THE BIGGEST HEARTS.
THANK YOU, SIR.
SNIFF

CHAPTER EIGHTEEN

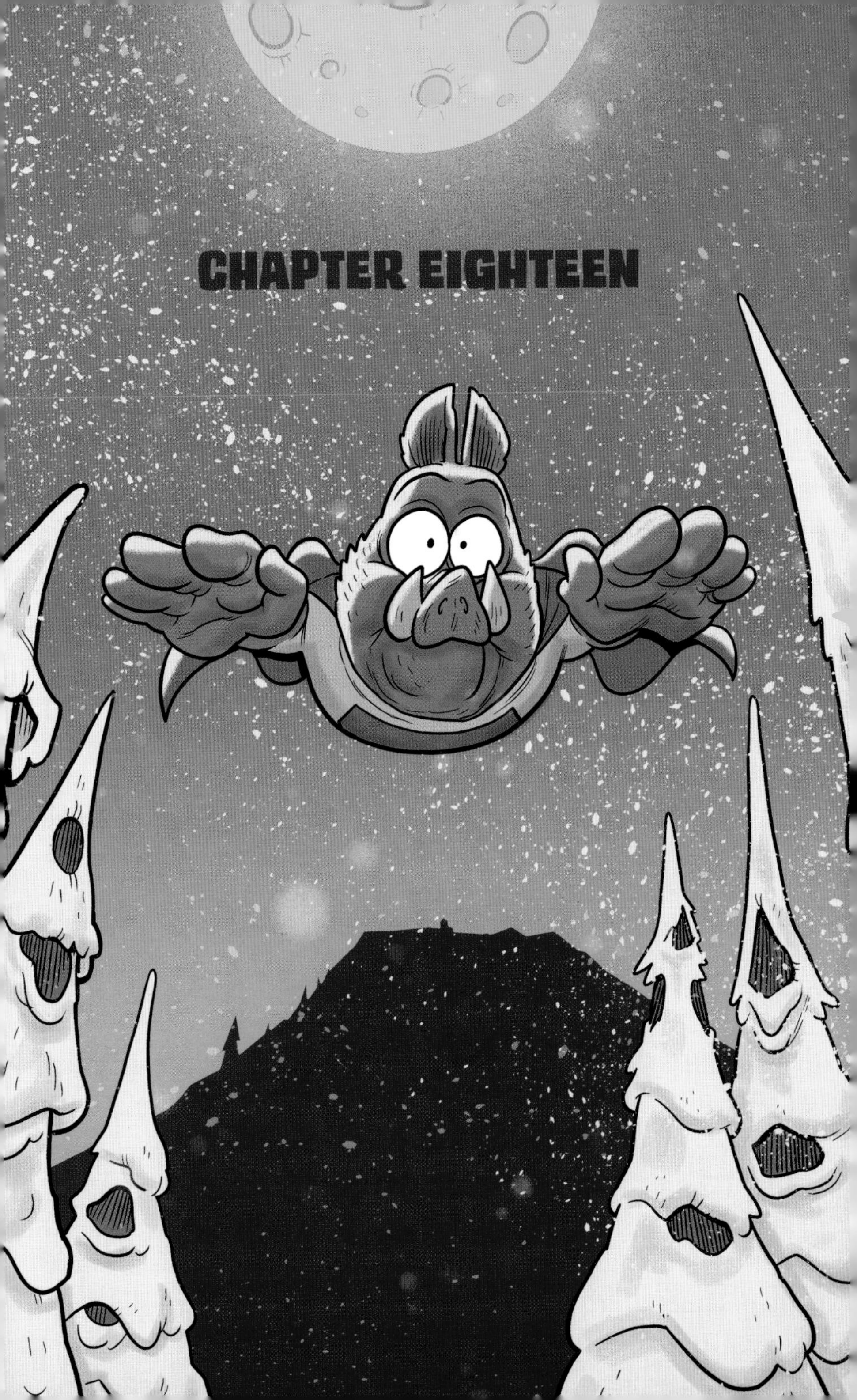

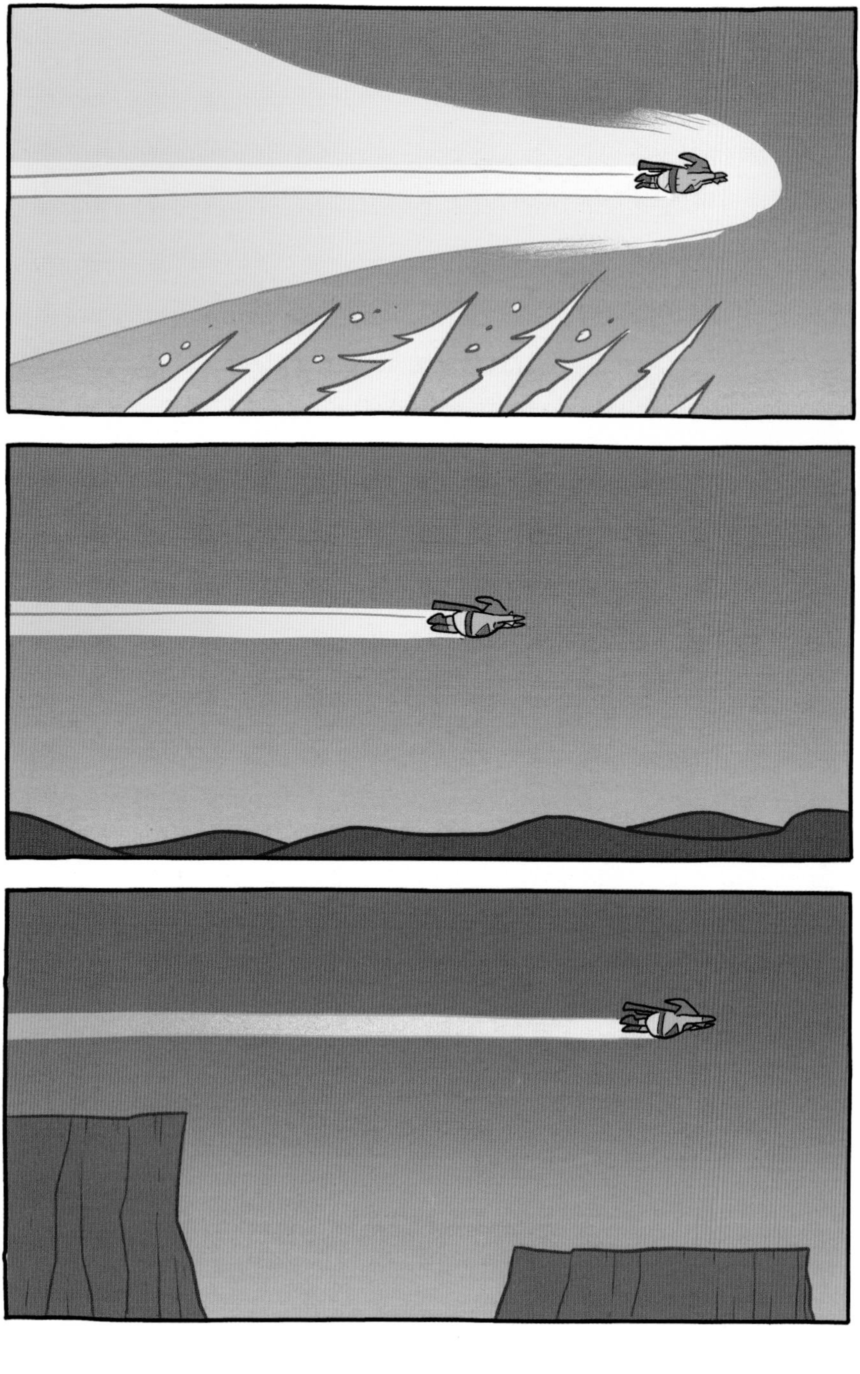

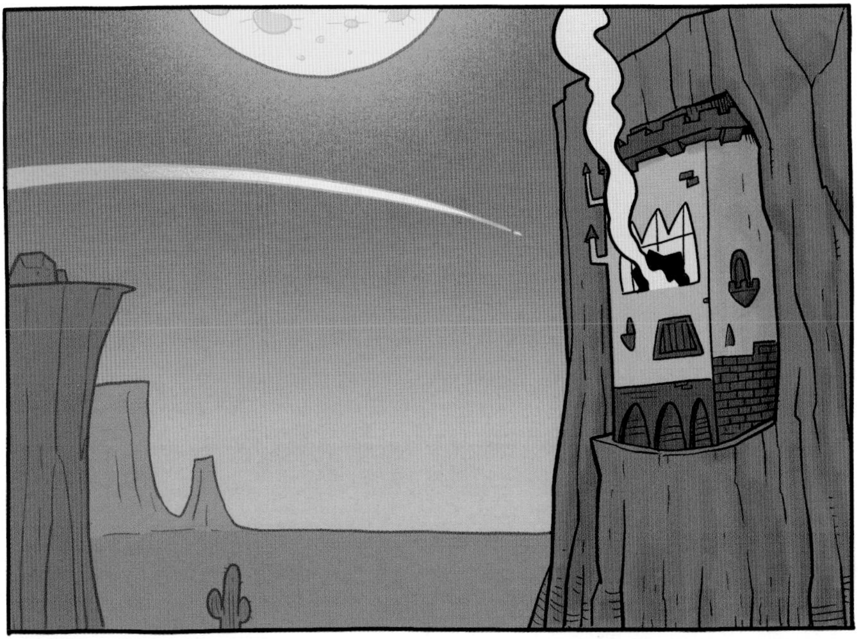

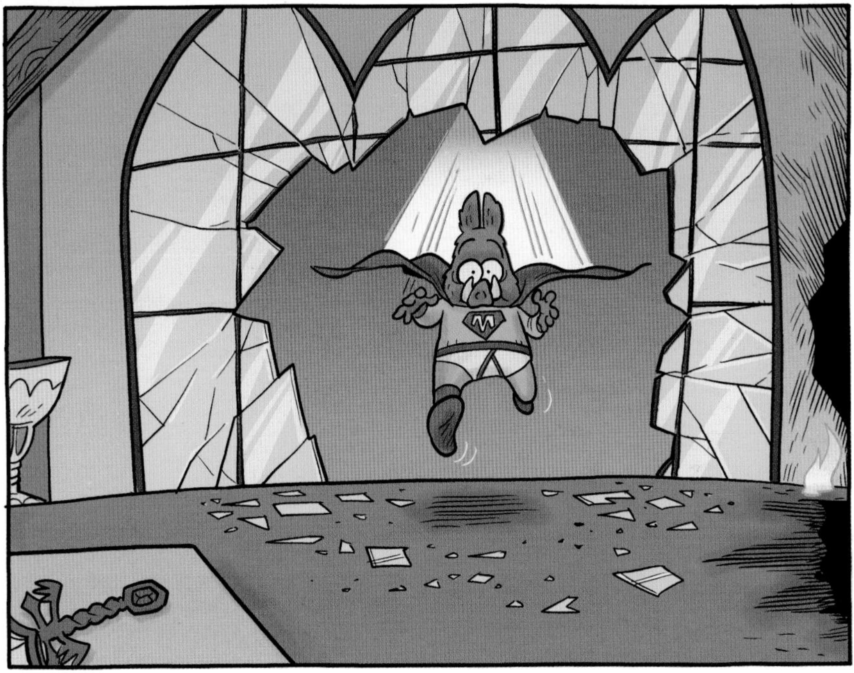

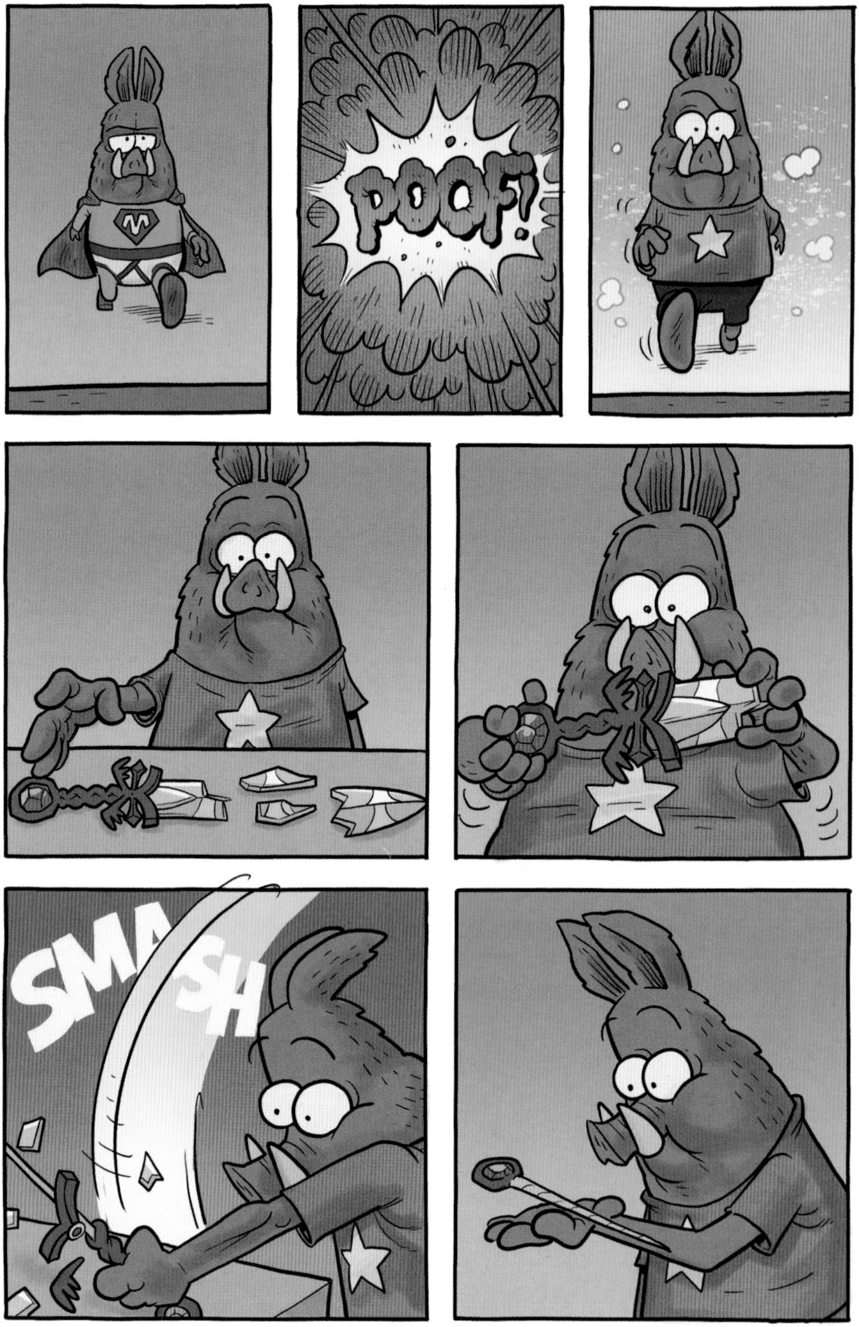
POOF!
SMASH

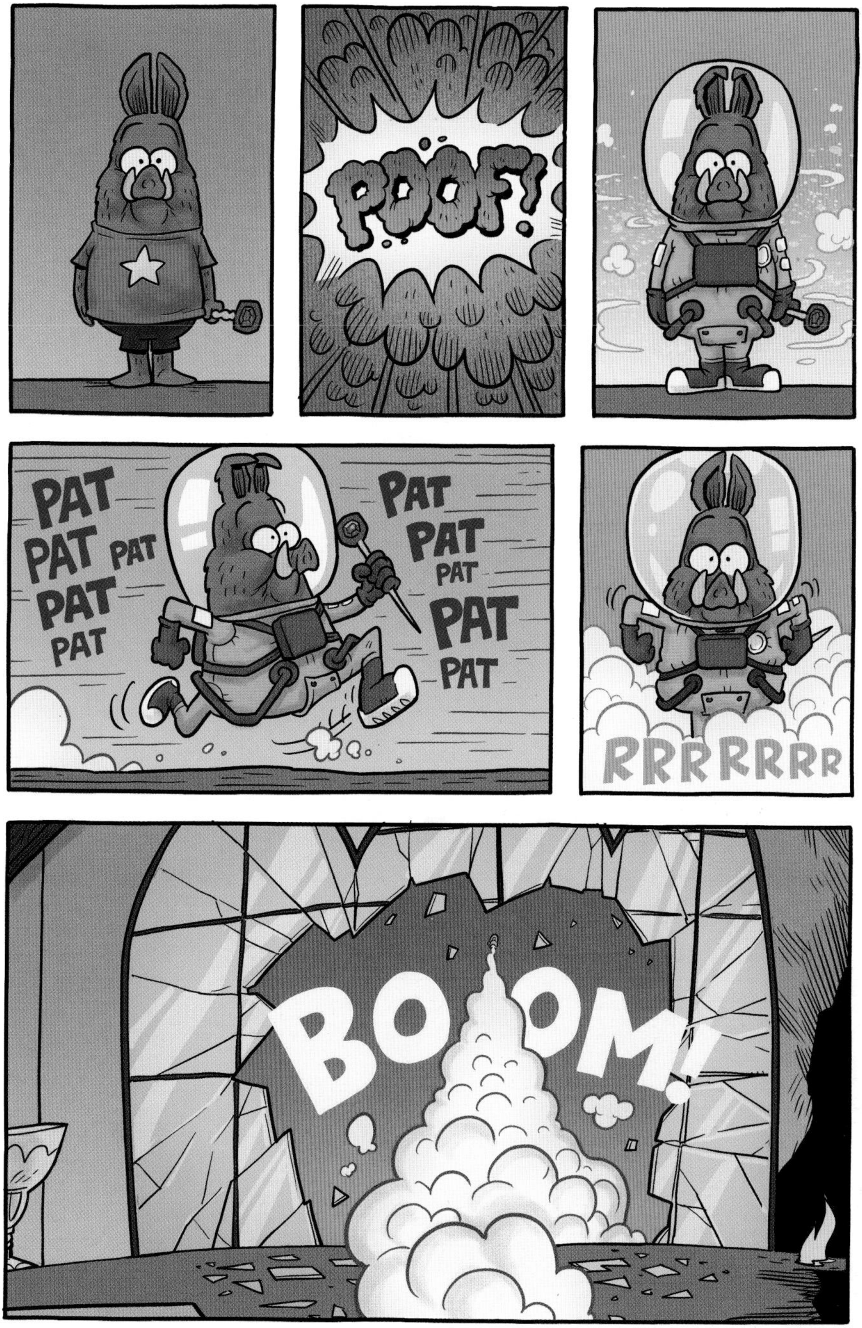
POOF!
PAT
PAT PAT
PAT
PAT
PAT
PAT
PAT
PAT
PAT
RRRRRRR
BOOM!

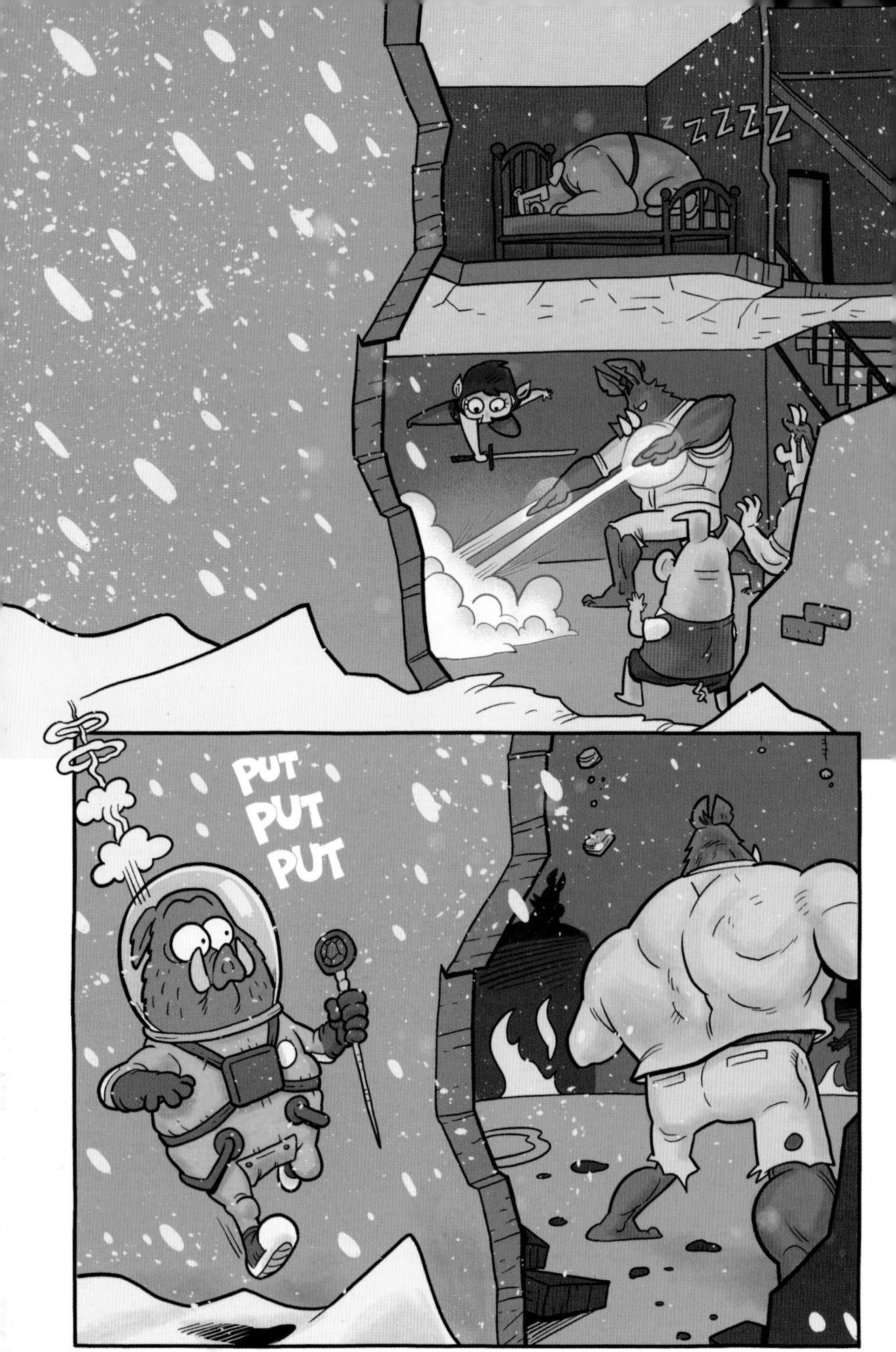
ZZZZZ
PUT
PUT
PUT

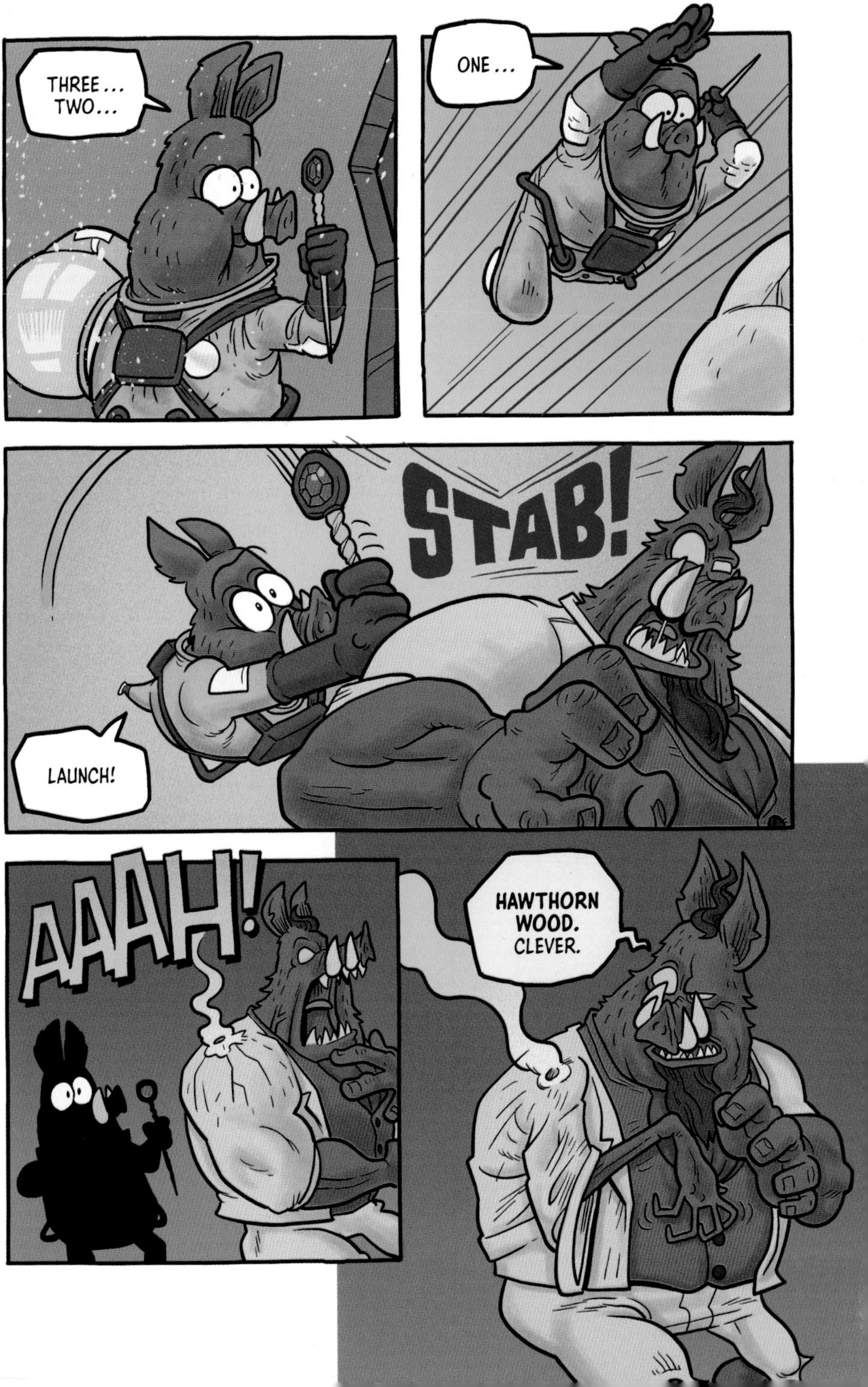
THREE... TWO...
ONE...
STAB!
LAUNCH!
AAAH!
HAWTHORN WOOD. CLEVER.

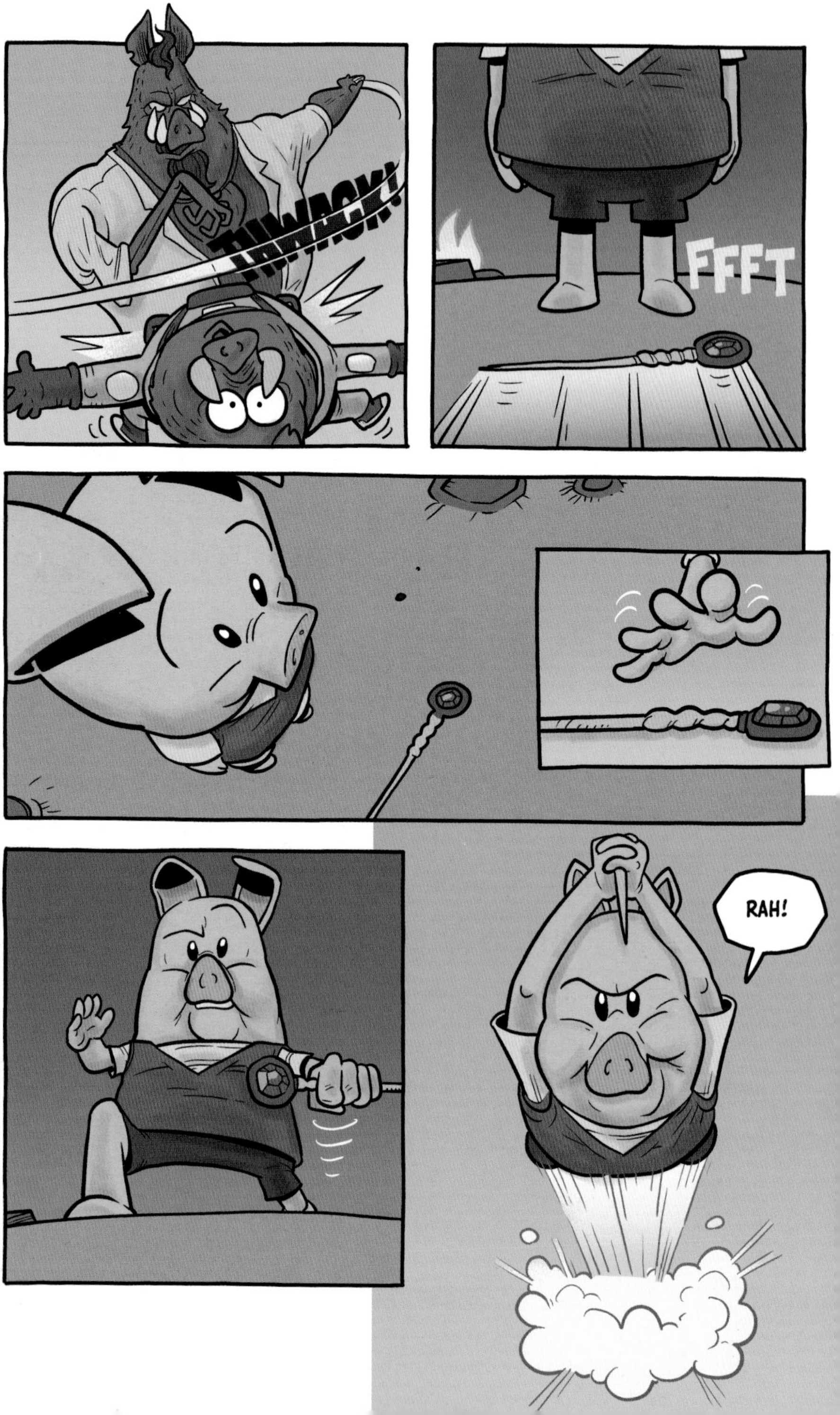
THWACK!
FFFT
RAH!

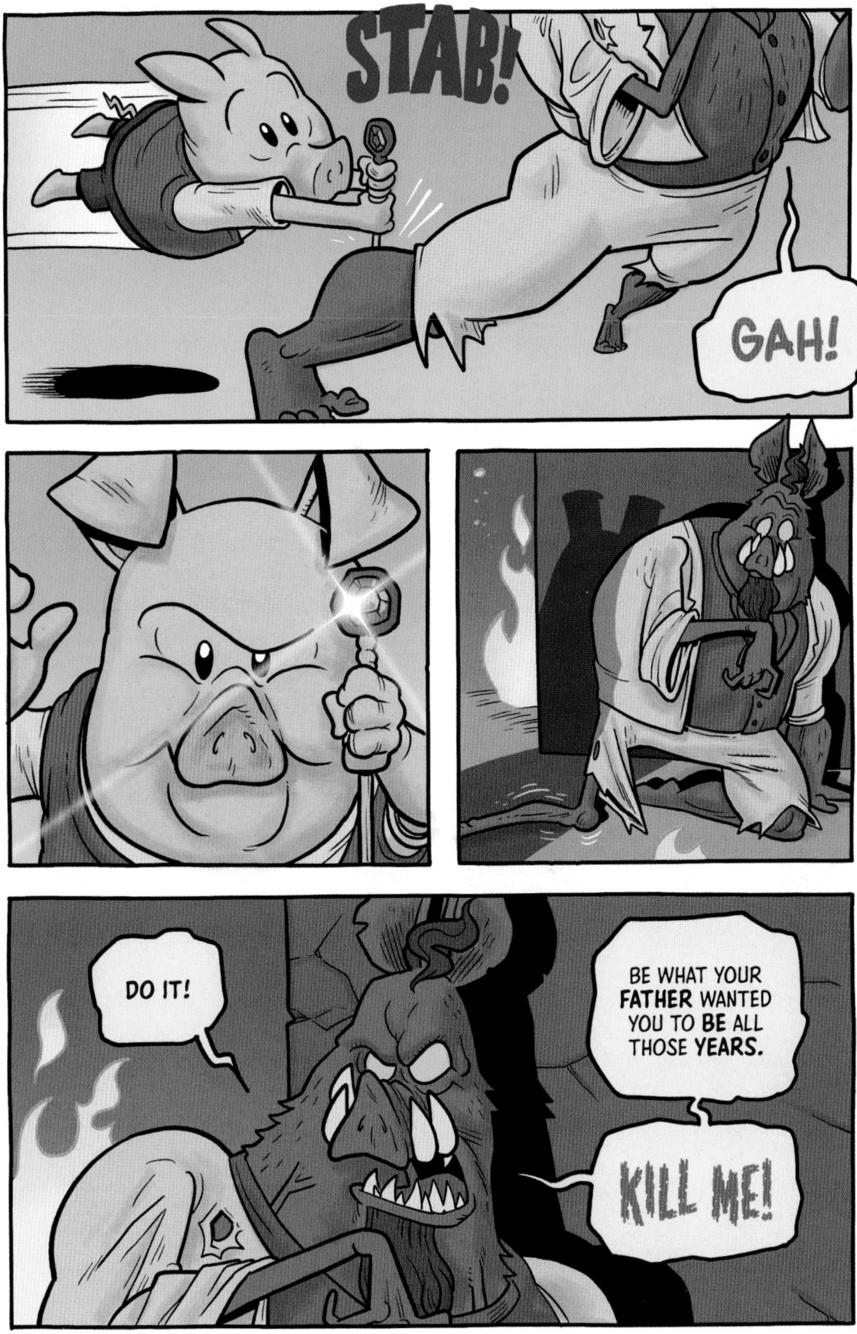
STAB!
GAH!
DO IT!
BE WHAT YOUR FATHER WANTED YOU TO BE ALL THOSE YEARS.
KILL ME!

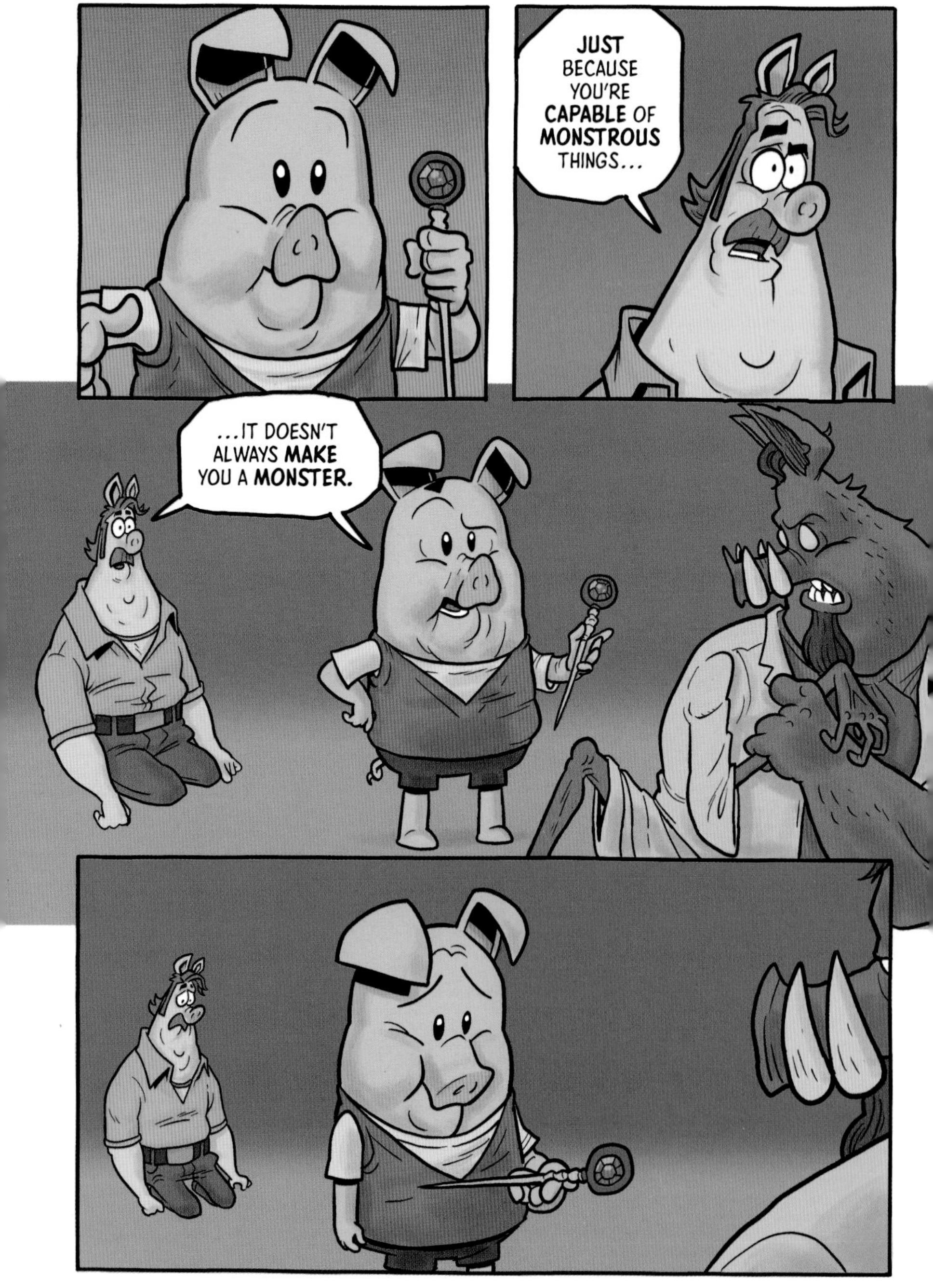
JUST BECAUSE YOU'RE CAPABLE OF MONSTROUS THINGS...
...IT DOESN'T ALWAYS MAKE YOU A MONSTER.

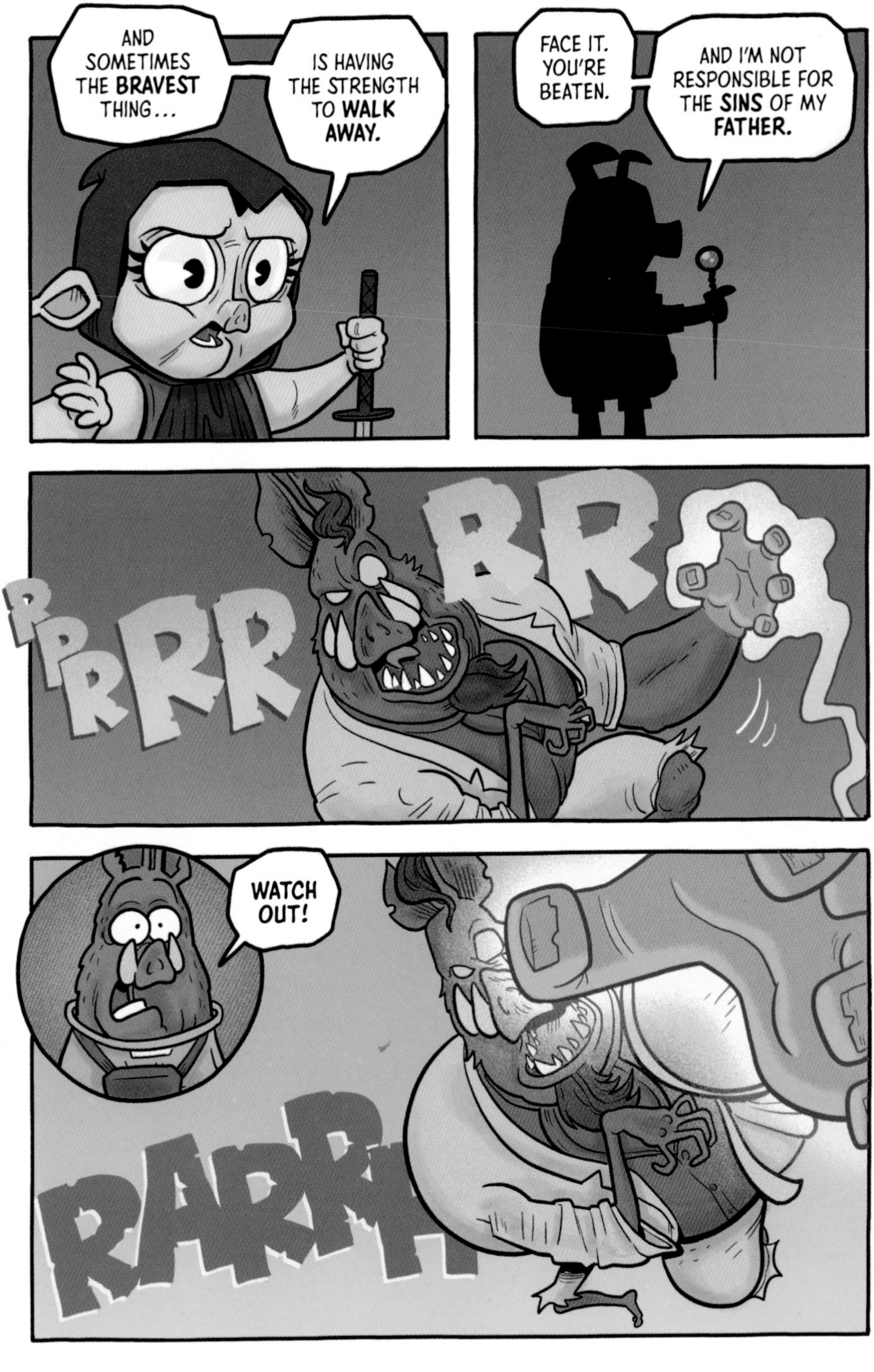
AND SOMETIMES THE **BRAVEST** THING...
IS HAVING THE STRENGTH TO **WALK AWAY.**
FACE IT. YOU'RE BEATEN.
AND I'M NOT RESPONSIBLE FOR THE **SINS** OF MY **FATHER.**
RRRRR
BR
WATCH OUT!
RARRR

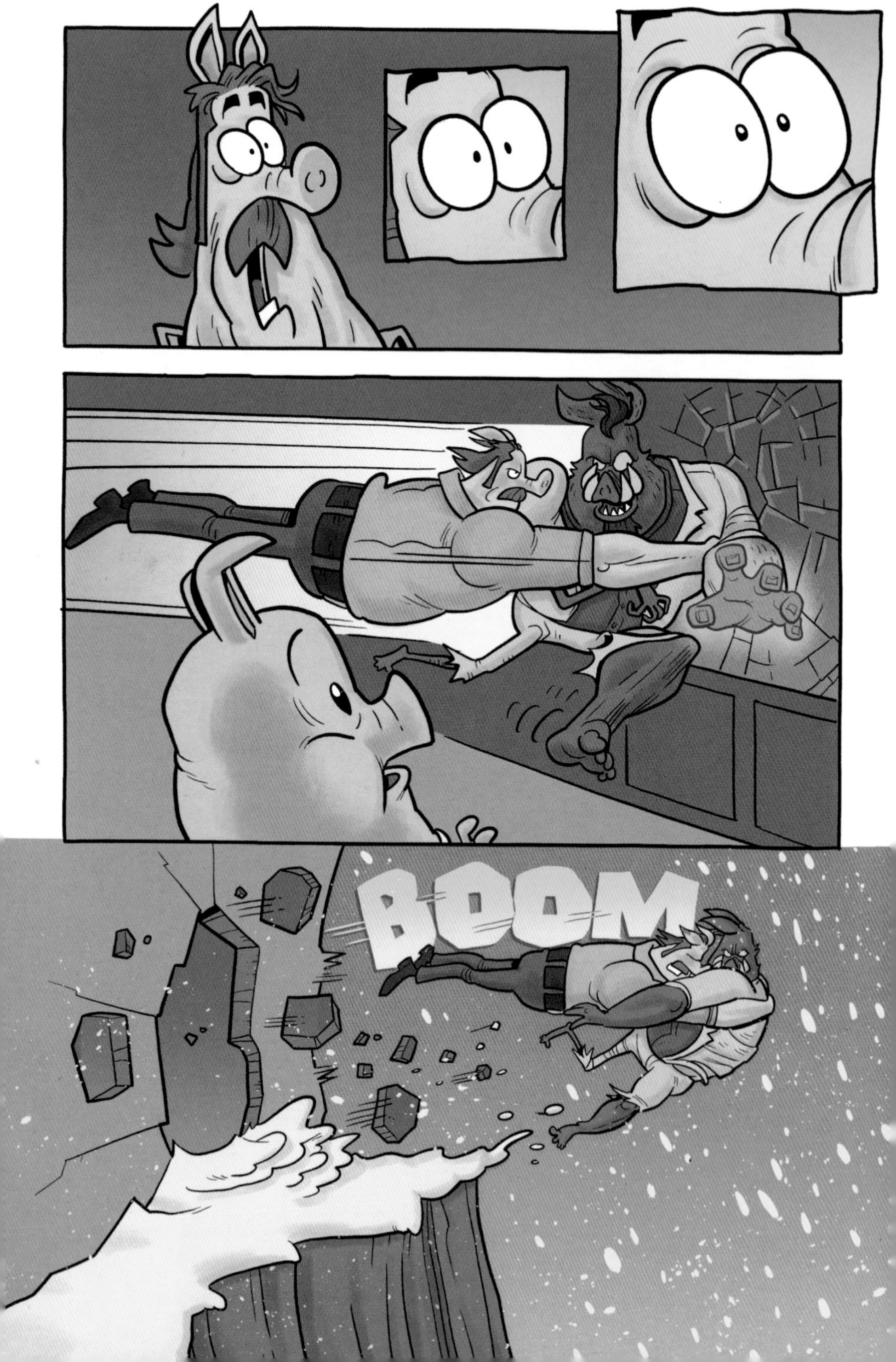
BOOM

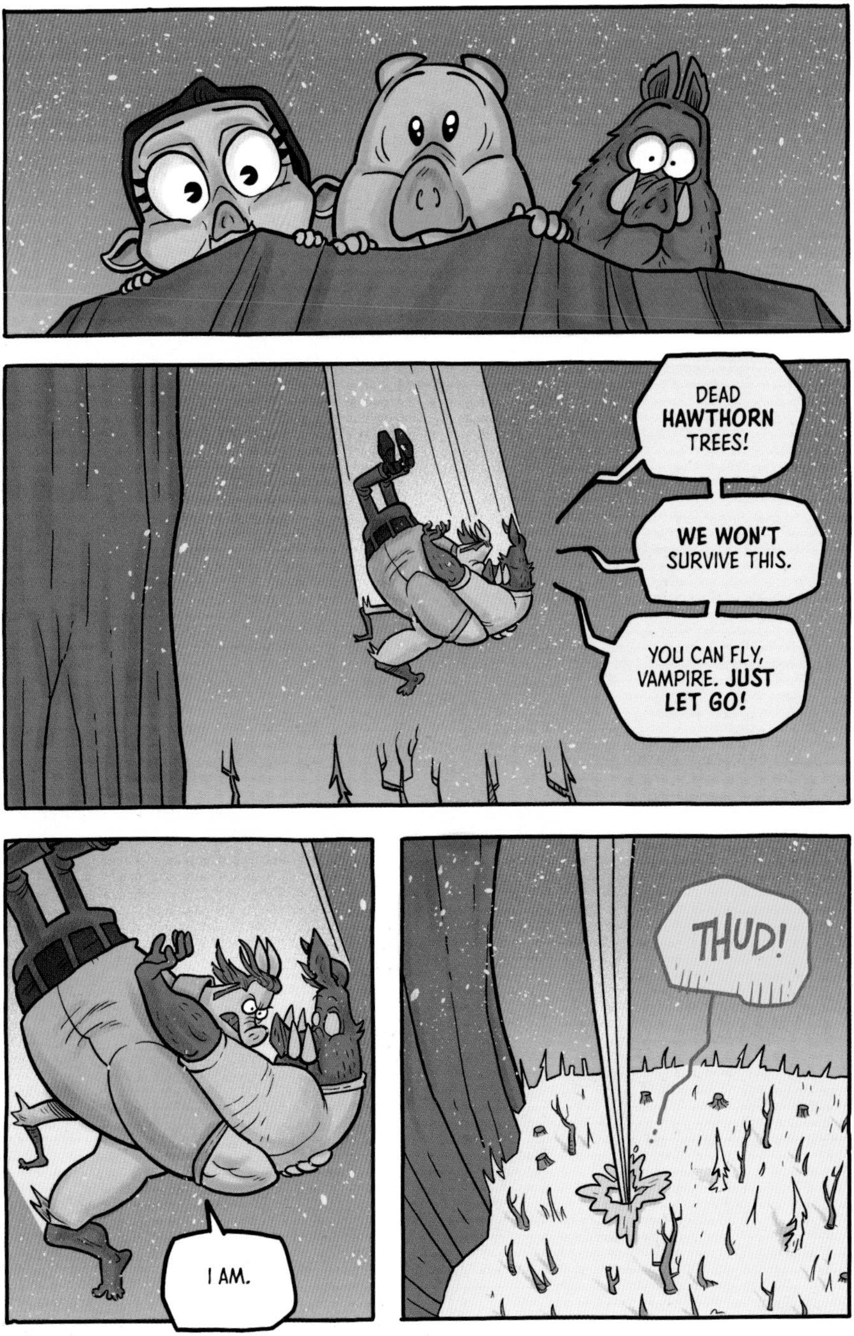
DEAD HAWTHORN TREES!
WE WON'T SURVIVE THIS.
YOU CAN FLY, VAMPIRE. JUST LET GO!
I AM.
THUD!

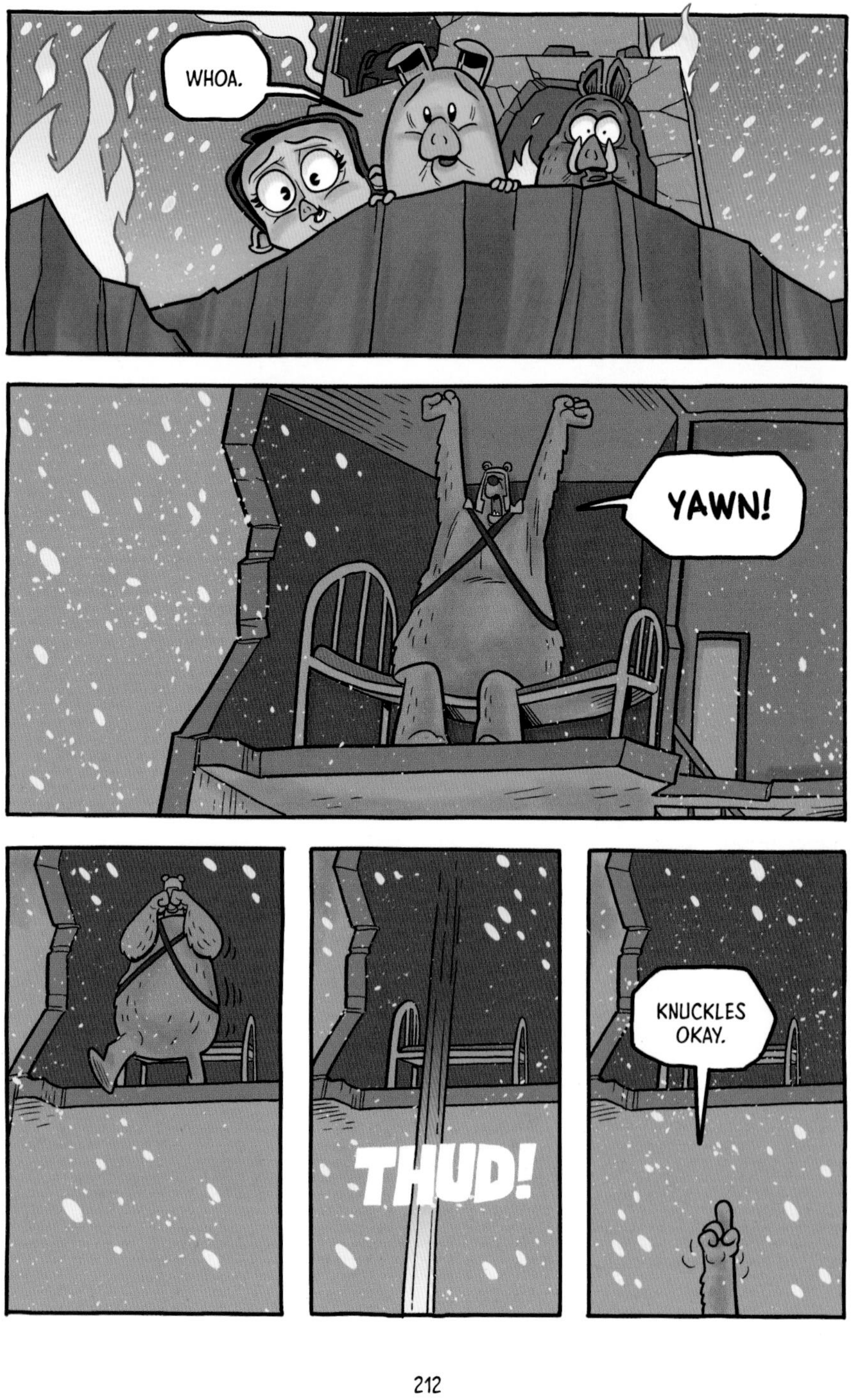
WHOA.
YAWN!
THUD!
KNUCKLES OKAY.

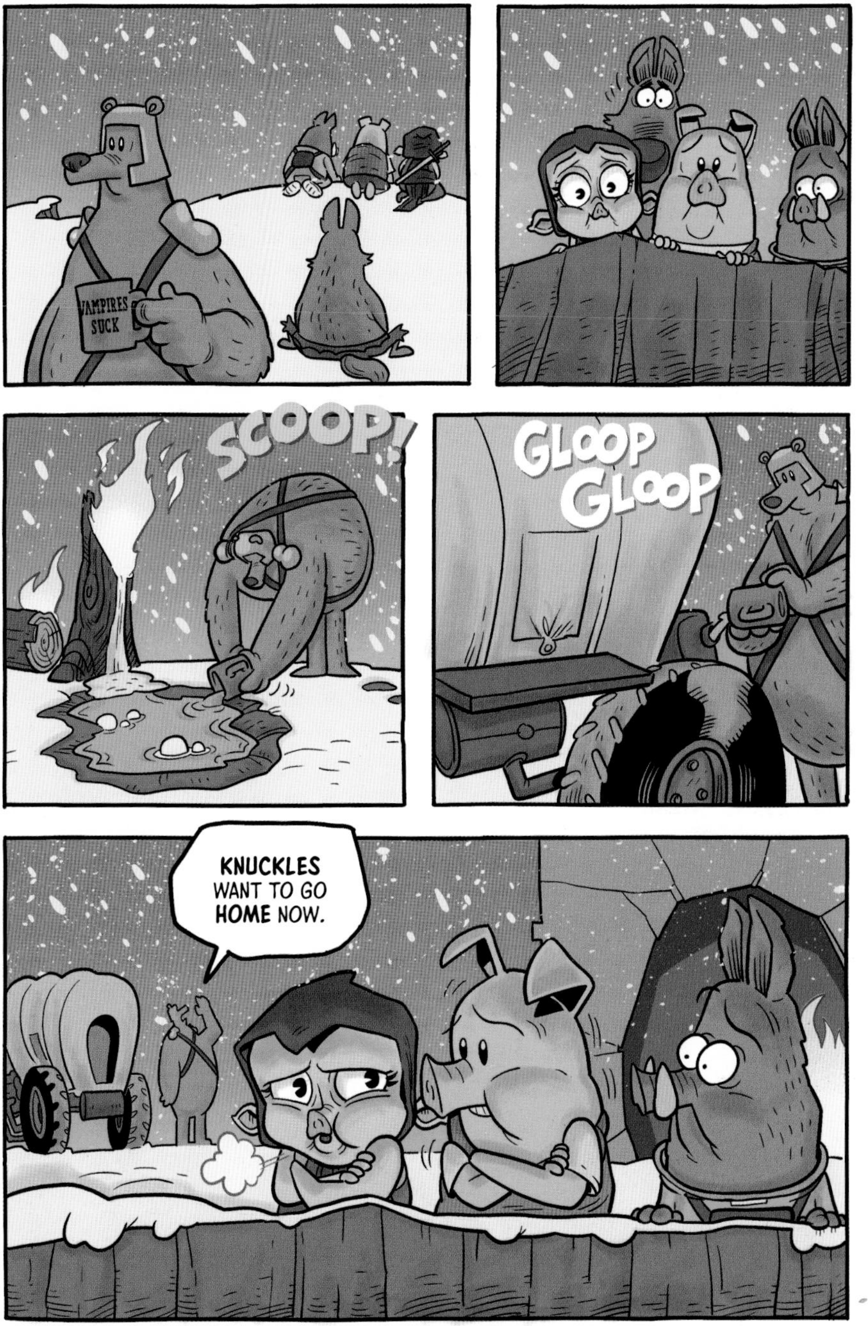
VAMPIRES SUCK
SCOOP!
GLOOP GLOOP
KNUCKLES WANT TO GO HOME NOW.

CHAPTER NINETEEN

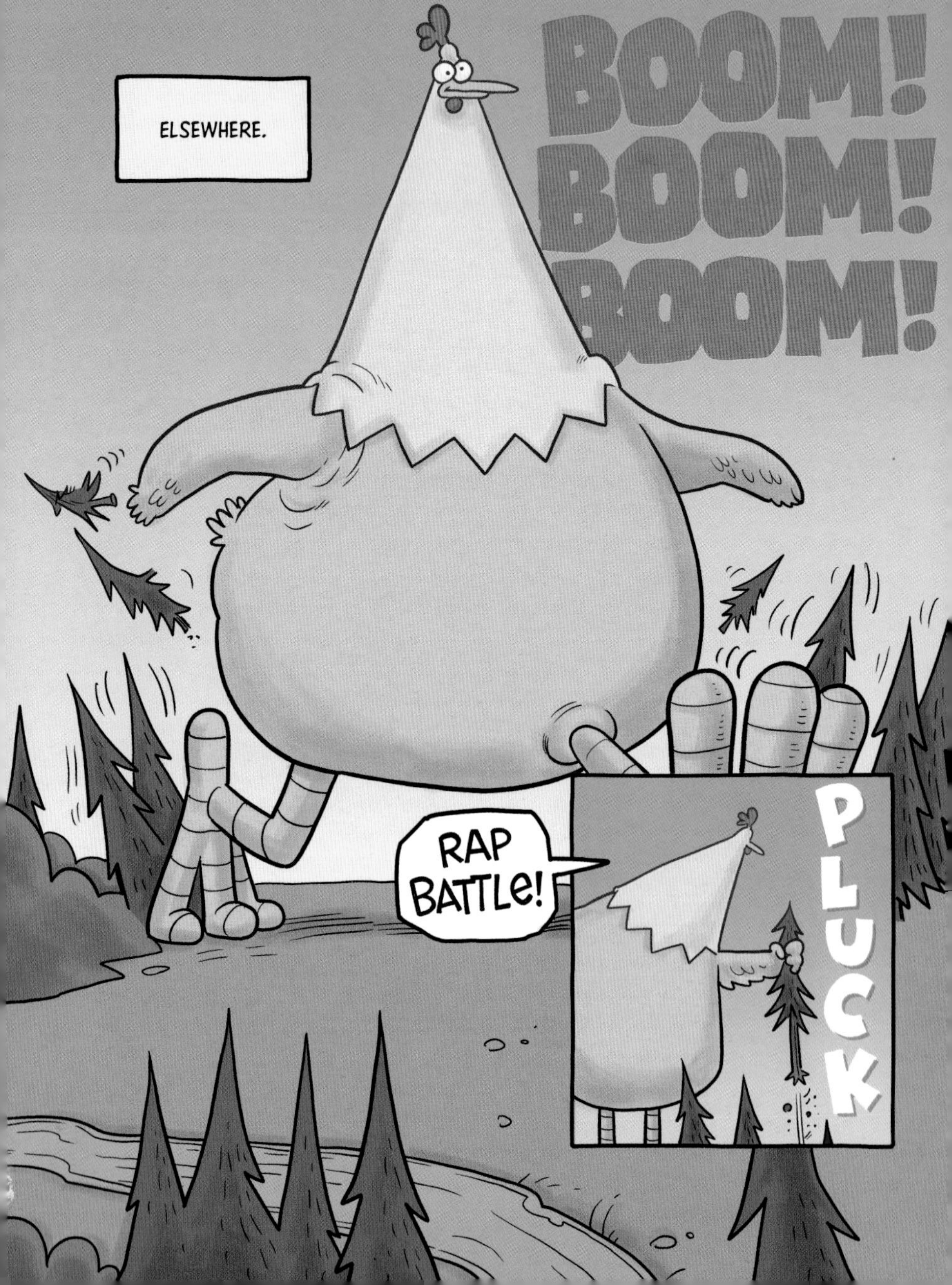

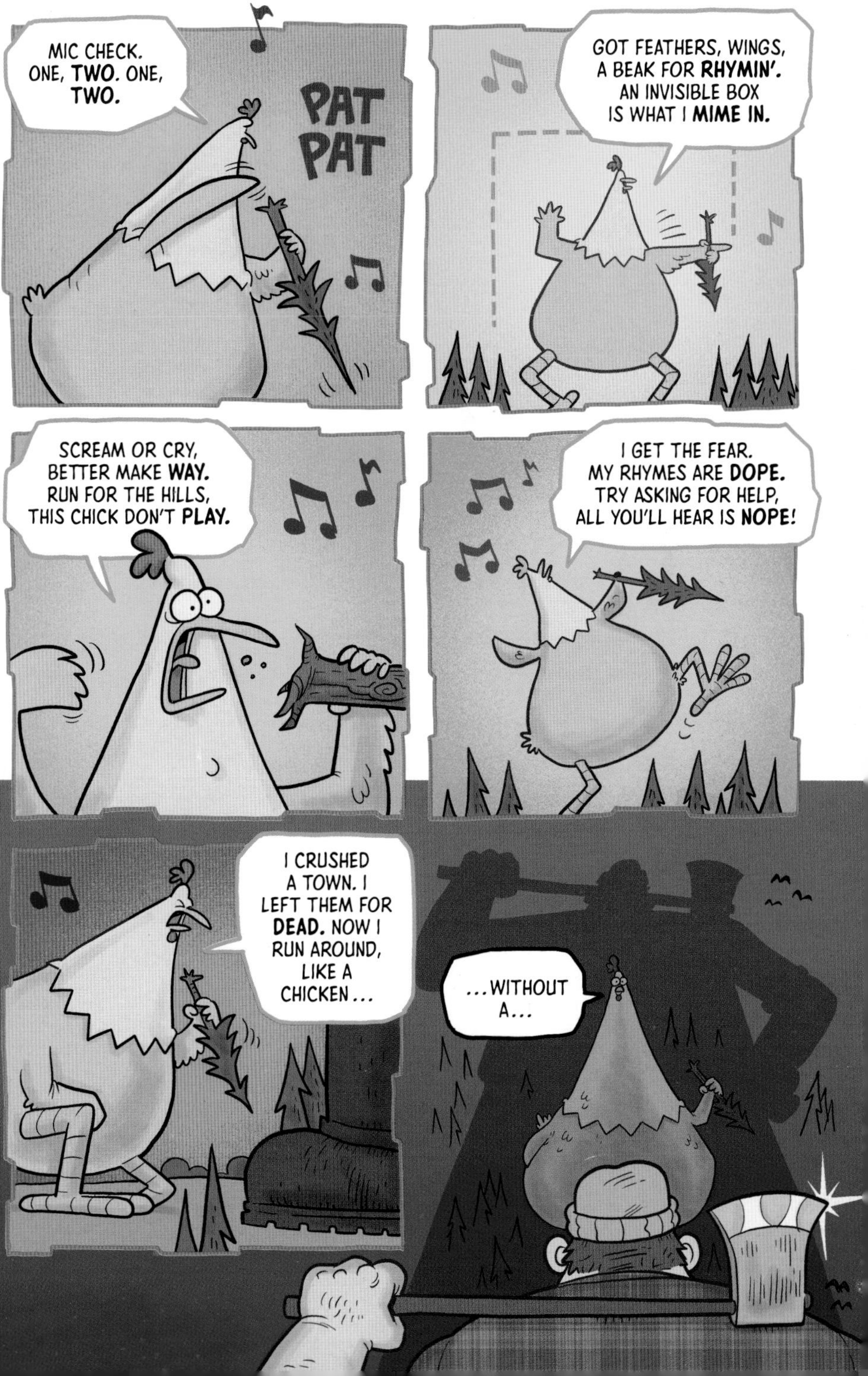
MIC CHECK. ONE, TWO. ONE, TWO.
PAT PAT
GOT FEATHERS, WINGS, A BEAK FOR RHYMIN'. AN INVISIBLE BOX IS WHAT I MIME IN.
SCREAM OR CRY, BETTER MAKE WAY. RUN FOR THE HILLS, THIS CHICK DON'T PLAY.
I GET THE FEAR. MY RHYMES ARE DOPE. TRY ASKING FOR HELP, ALL YOU'LL HEAR IS NOPE!
I CRUSHED A TOWN. I LEFT THEM FOR DEAD. NOW I RUN AROUND, LIKE A CHICKEN...
...WITHOUT A...

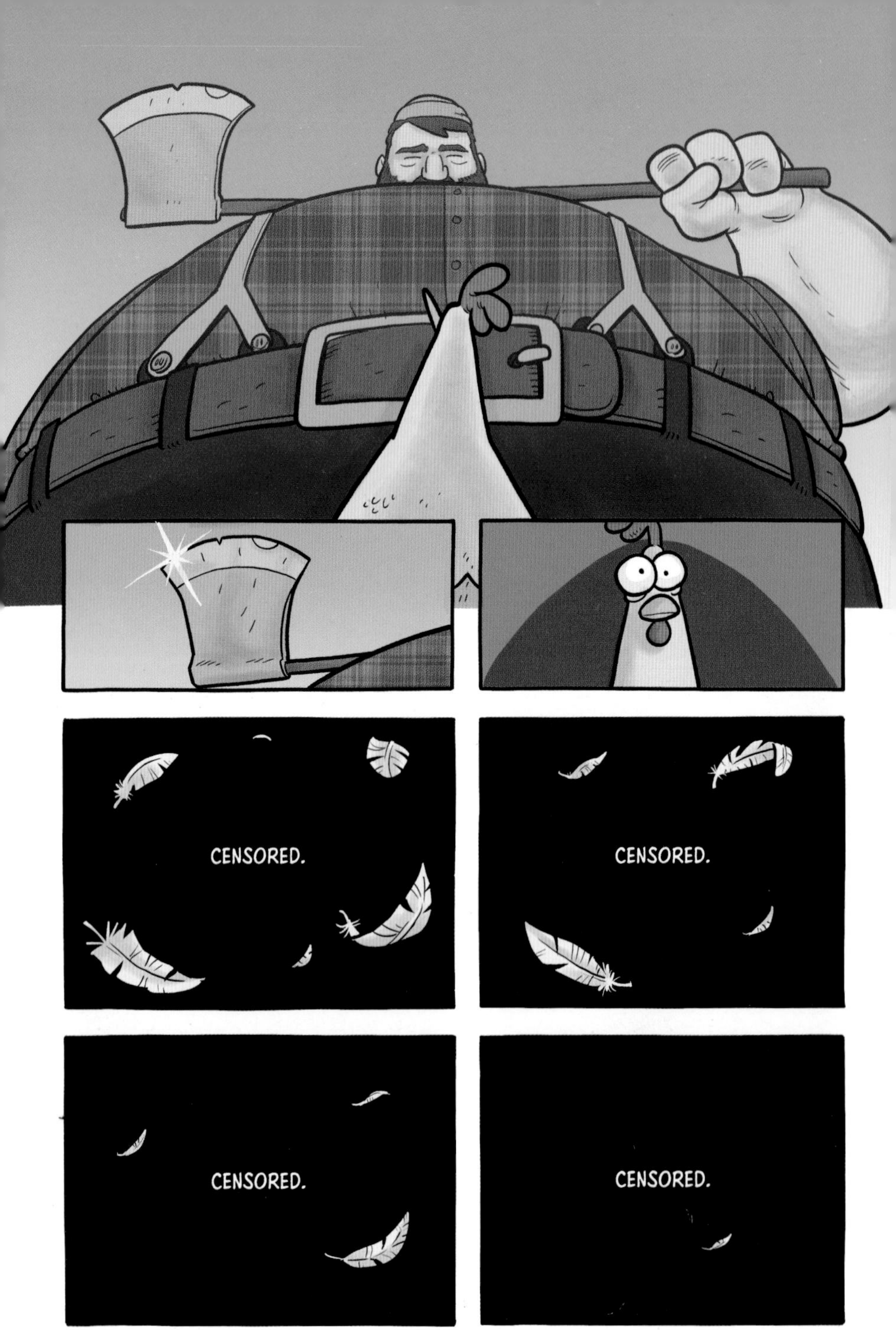
CENSORED.
CENSORED.
CENSORED.
CENSORED.

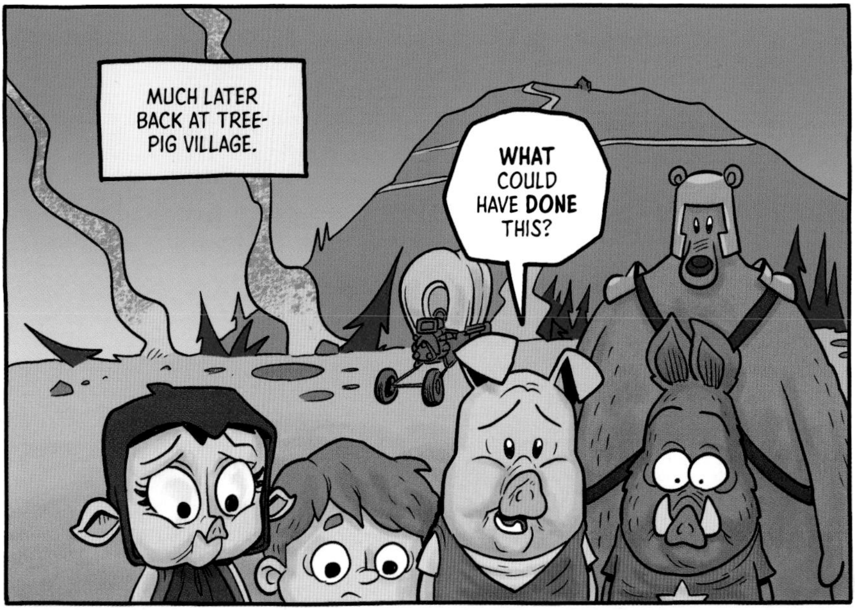
MUCH LATER BACK AT TREE-PIG VILLAGE.
WHAT COULD HAVE DONE THIS?

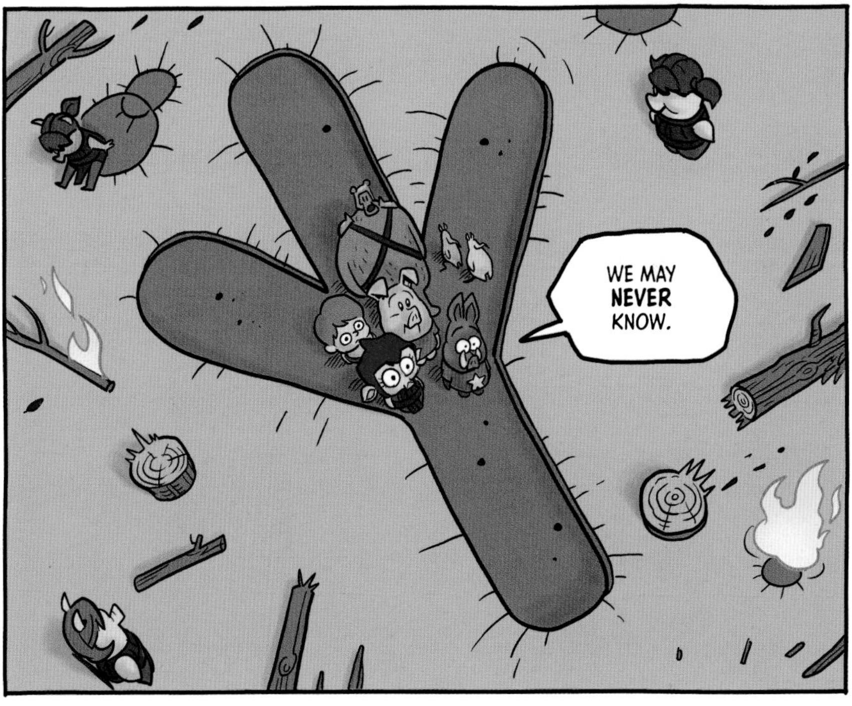
WE MAY NEVER KNOW.

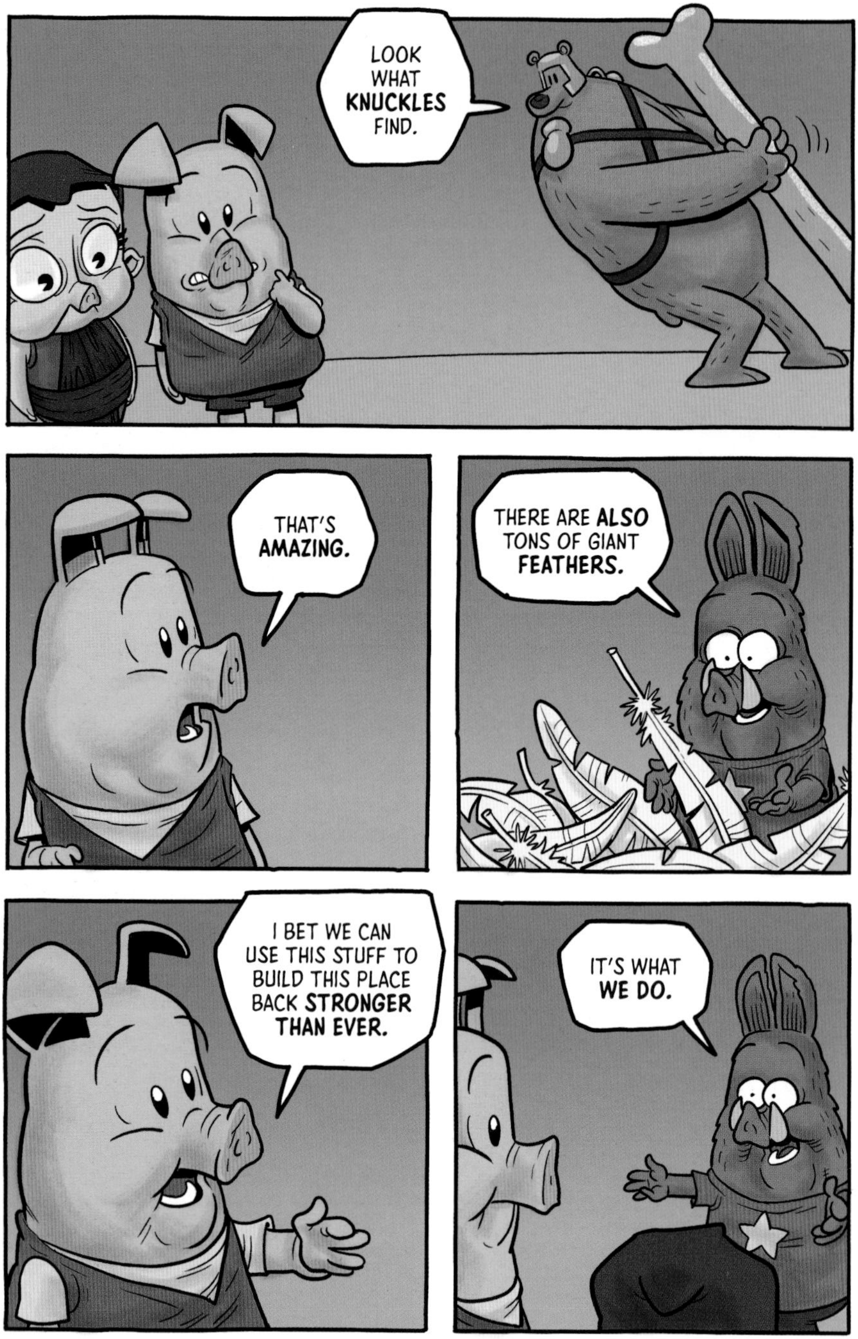
LOOK WHAT KNUCKLES FIND.
THAT'S AMAZING.
THERE ARE ALSO TONS OF GIANT FEATHERS.
I BET WE CAN USE THIS STUFF TO BUILD THIS PLACE BACK STRONGER THAN EVER.
IT'S WHAT WE DO.

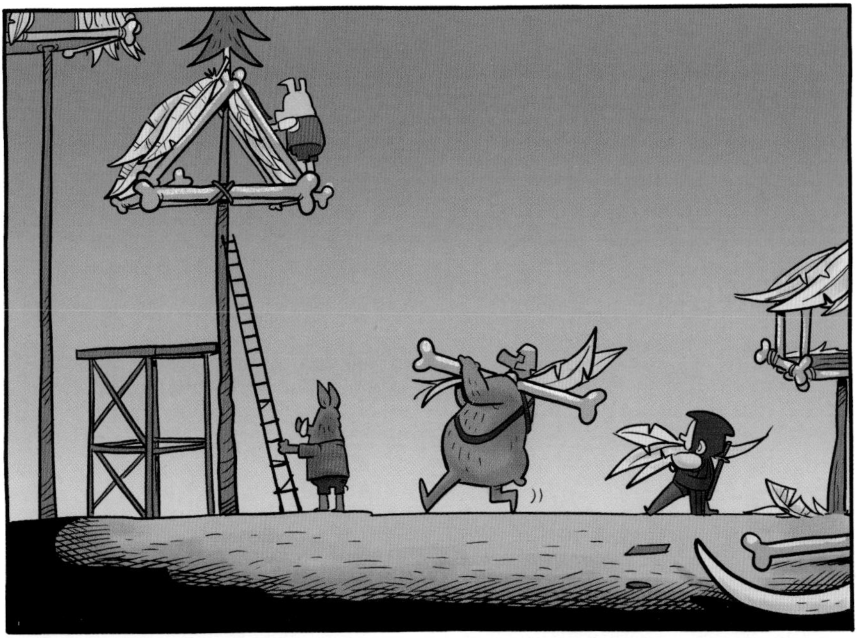

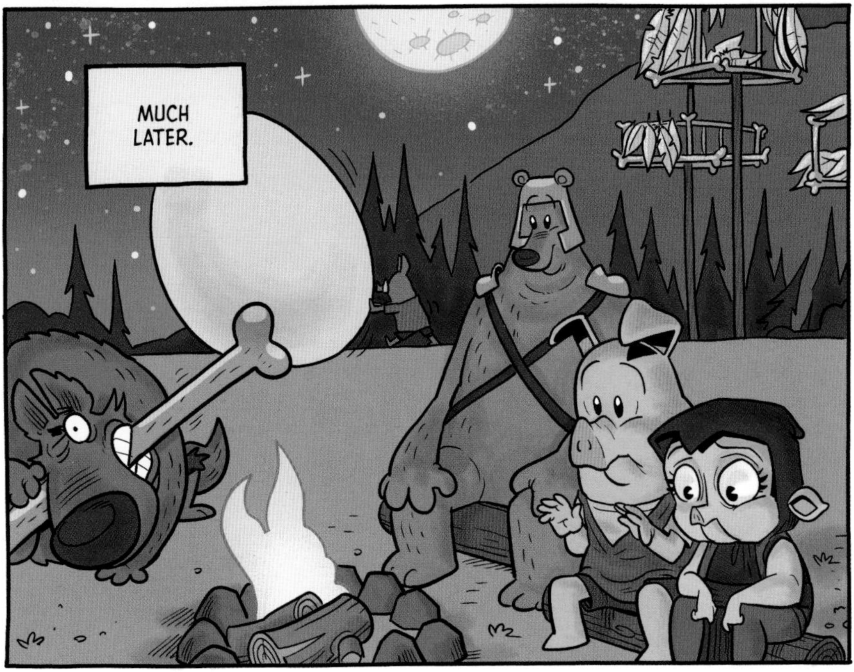
MUCH
LATER.

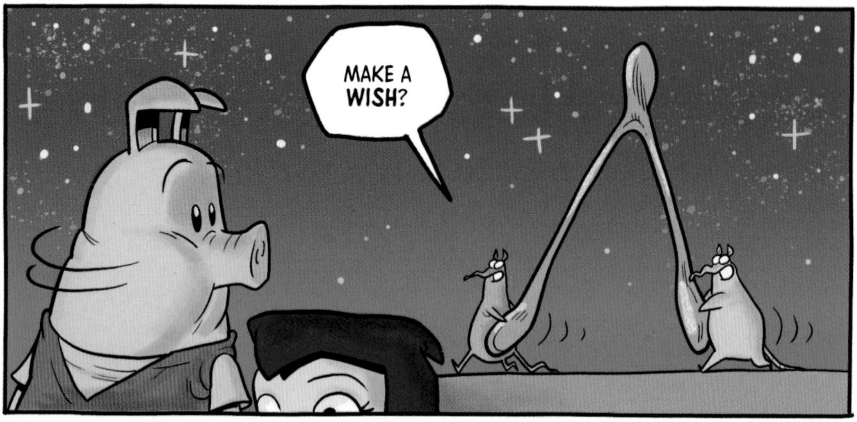
MAKE A WISH?

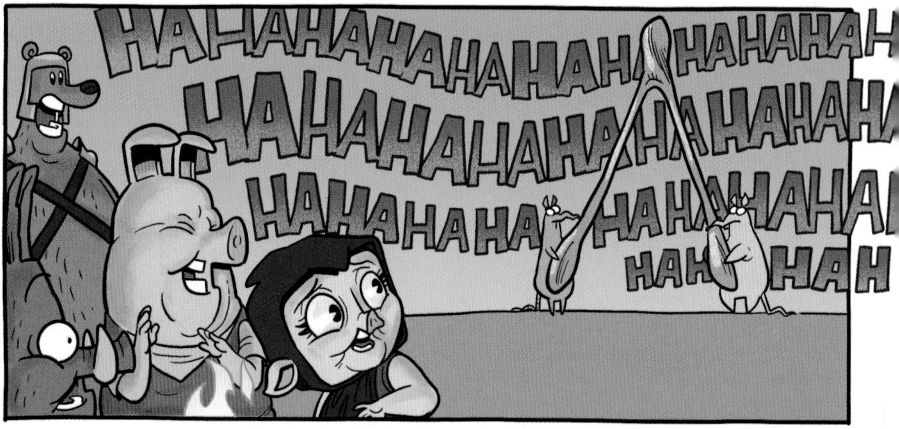
HAHAHAHAHAHAHAHAHAHAHAHAHAHAH
HAHAHAHAHAHAHAHAHAHAHAHA
HAHAHAHAHAHAHAHAHAHAHA
HAHHAH

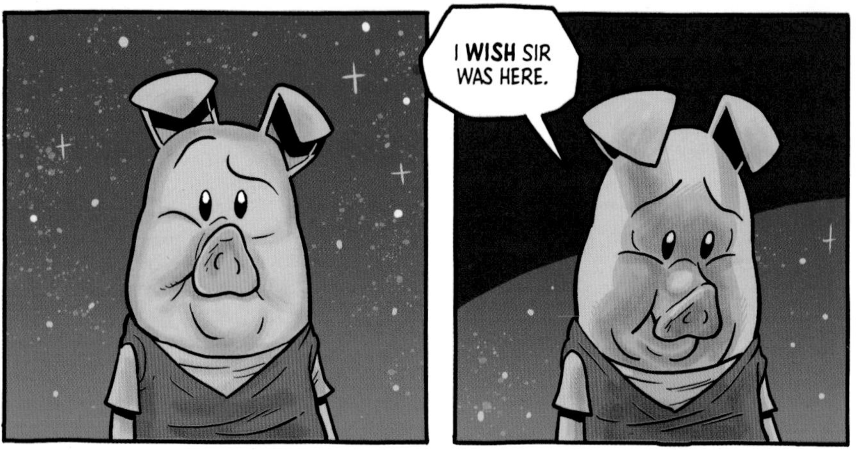
I WISH SIR WAS HERE.

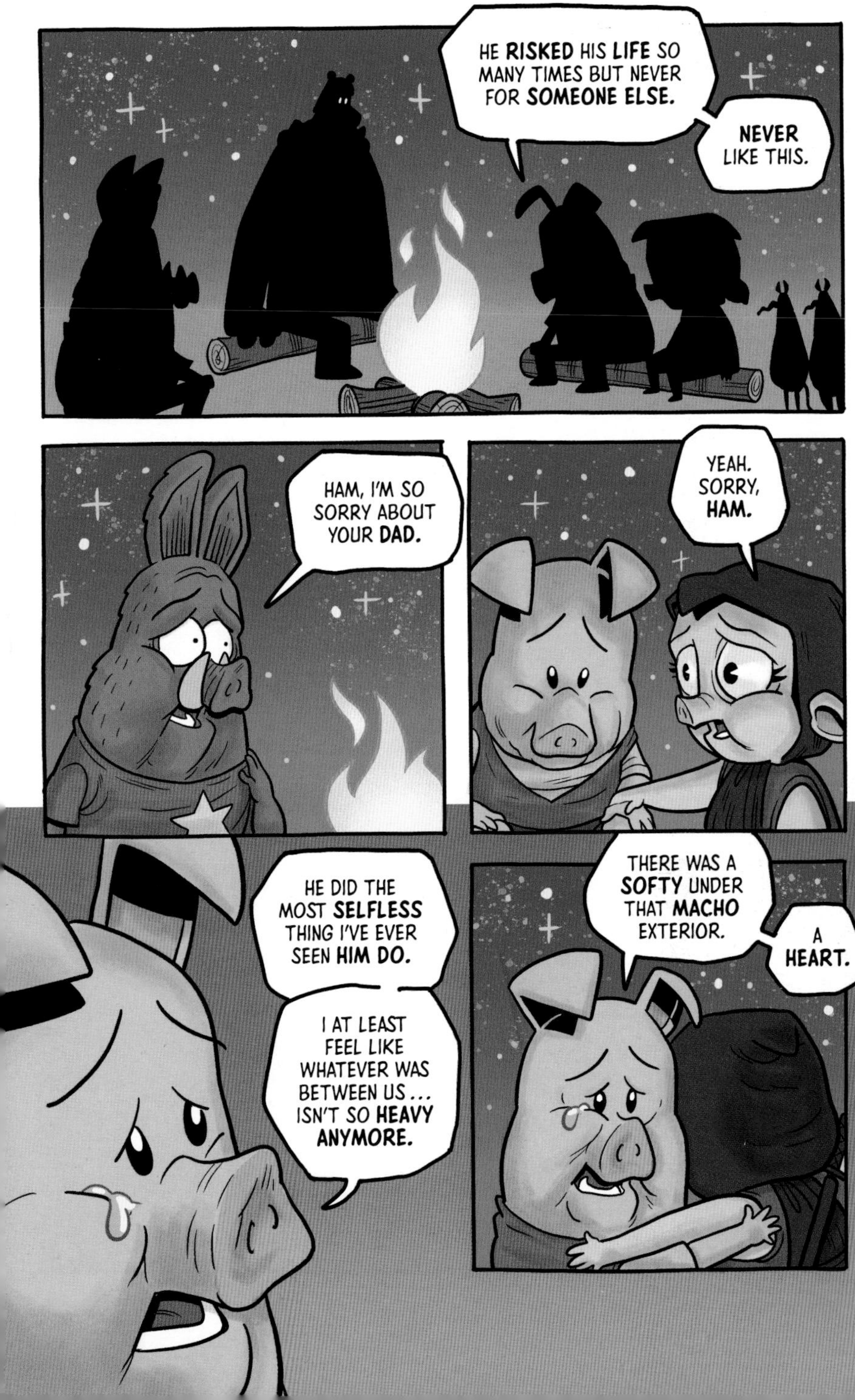
HE RISKED HIS LIFE SO MANY TIMES BUT NEVER FOR SOMEONE ELSE.
NEVER LIKE THIS.
HAM, I'M SO SORRY ABOUT YOUR DAD.
YEAH. SORRY, HAM.
HE DID THE MOST SELFLESS THING I'VE EVER SEEN HIM DO.
I AT LEAST FEEL LIKE WHATEVER WAS BETWEEN US... ISN'T SO HEAVY ANYMORE.
THERE WAS A SOFTY UNDER THAT MACHO EXTERIOR.
A HEART.

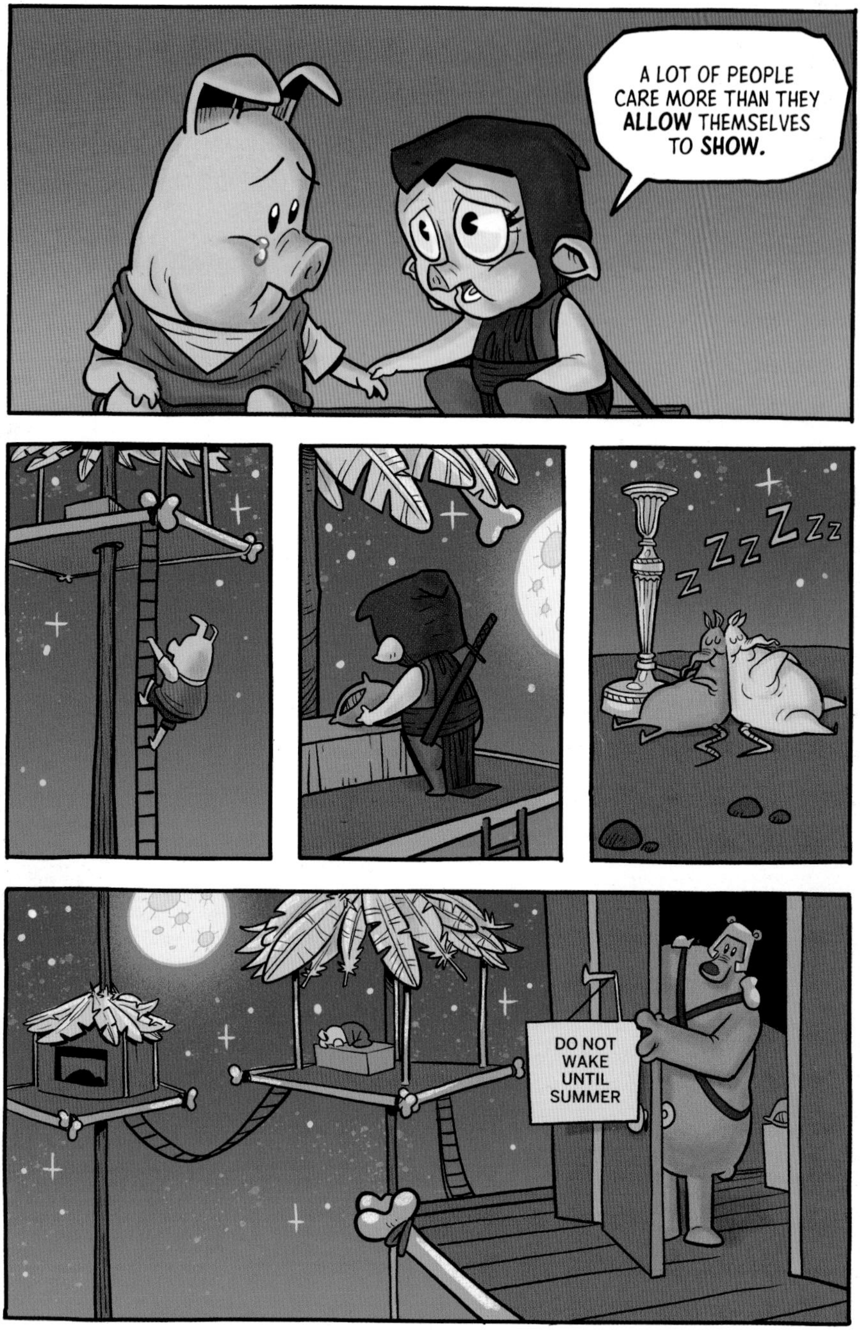
A LOT OF PEOPLE CARE MORE THAN THEY **ALLOW** THEMSELVES TO **SHOW.**
ZZZZZZ
DO NOT WAKE UNTIL SUMMER

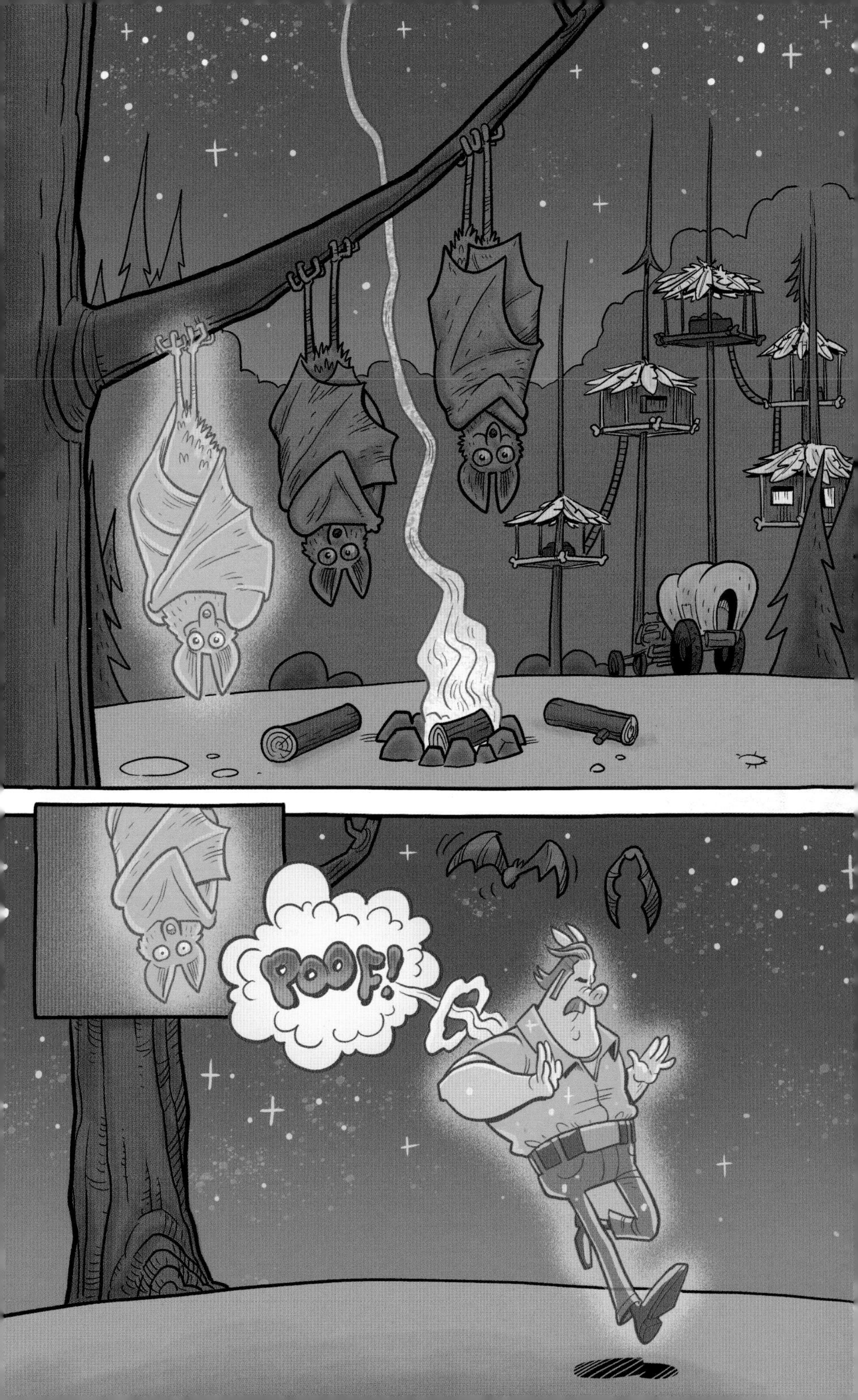
POOF!

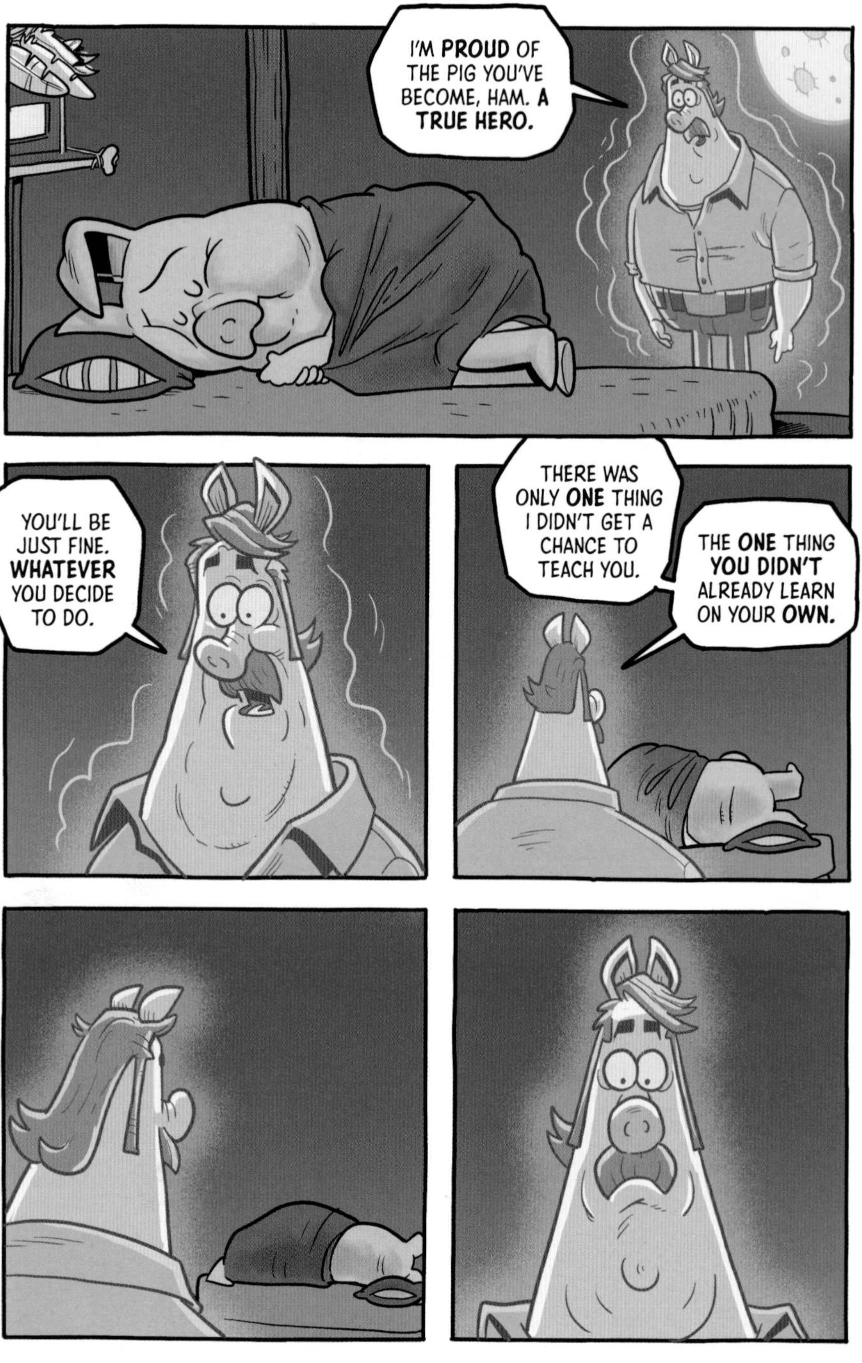
I'M PROUD OF THE PIG YOU'VE BECOME, HAM. A TRUE HERO.
YOU'LL BE JUST FINE. WHATEVER YOU DECIDE TO DO.
THERE WAS ONLY ONE THING I DIDN'T GET A CHANCE TO TEACH YOU.
THE ONE THING YOU DIDN'T ALREADY LEARN ON YOUR OWN.

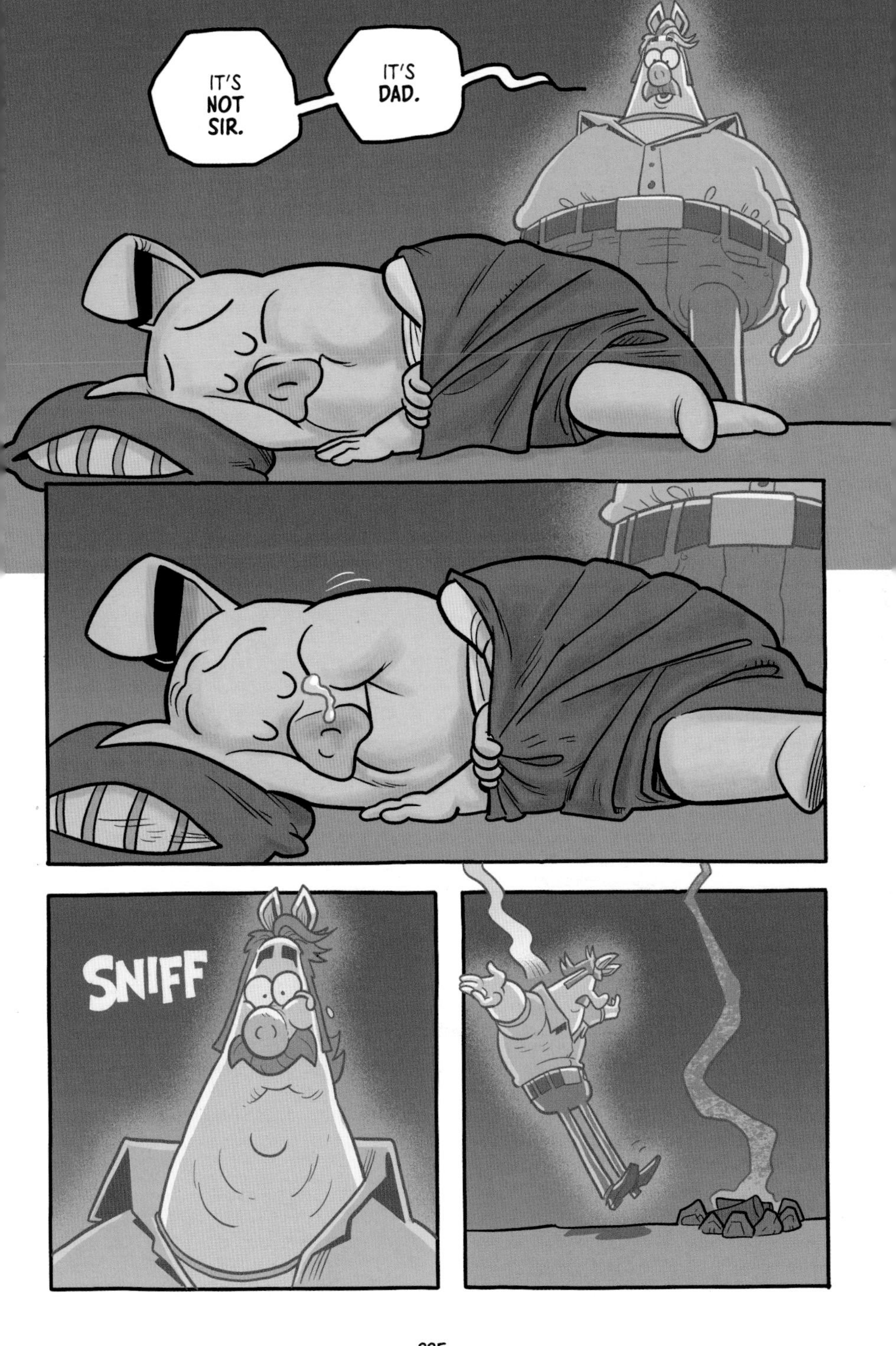
IT'S NOT SIR.
IT'S DAD.
SNIFF

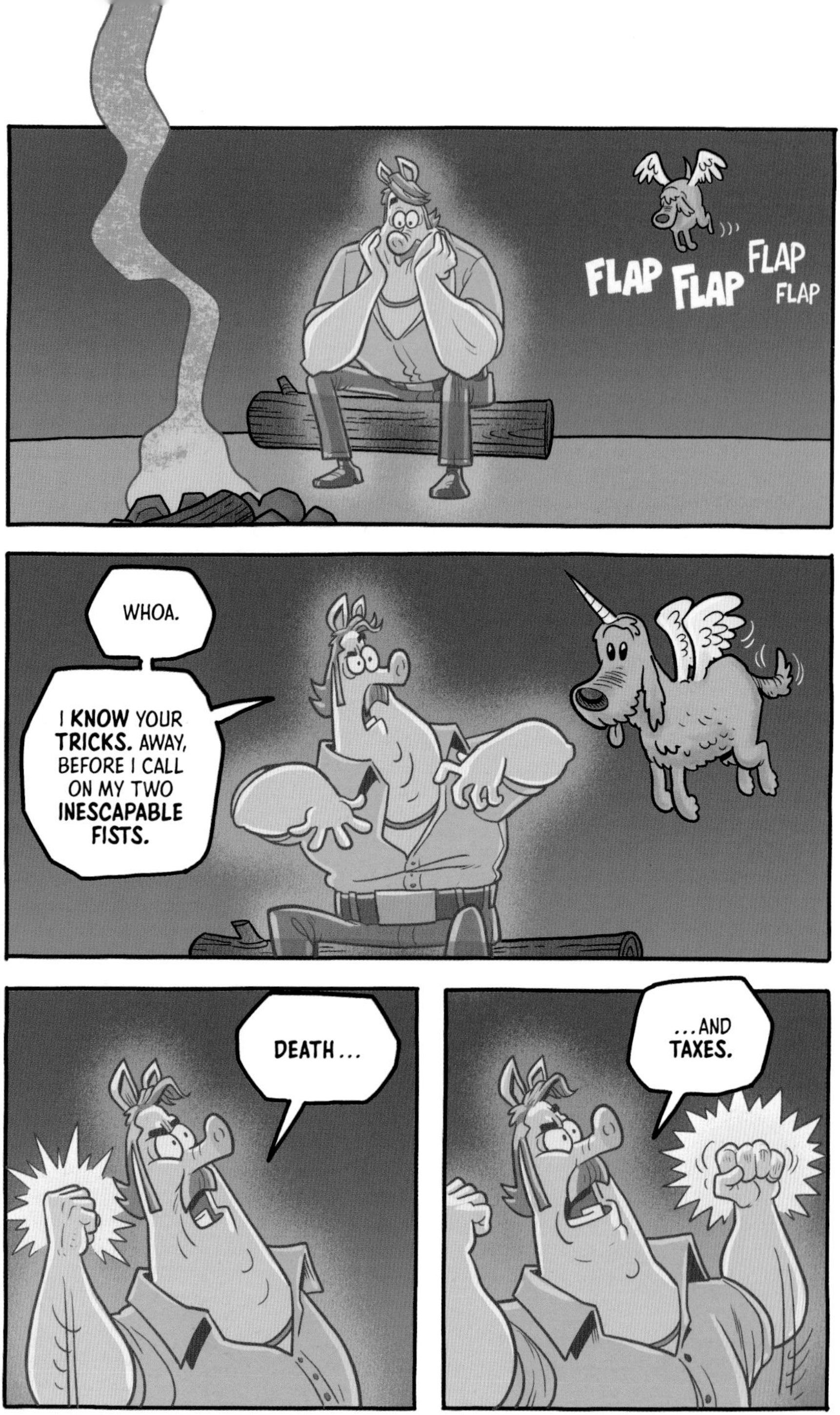
FLAP FLAP FLAP FLAP
WHOA.
I **KNOW** YOUR **TRICKS.** AWAY, BEFORE I CALL ON MY TWO **INESCAPABLE FISTS.**
DEATH...
...AND **TAXES.**

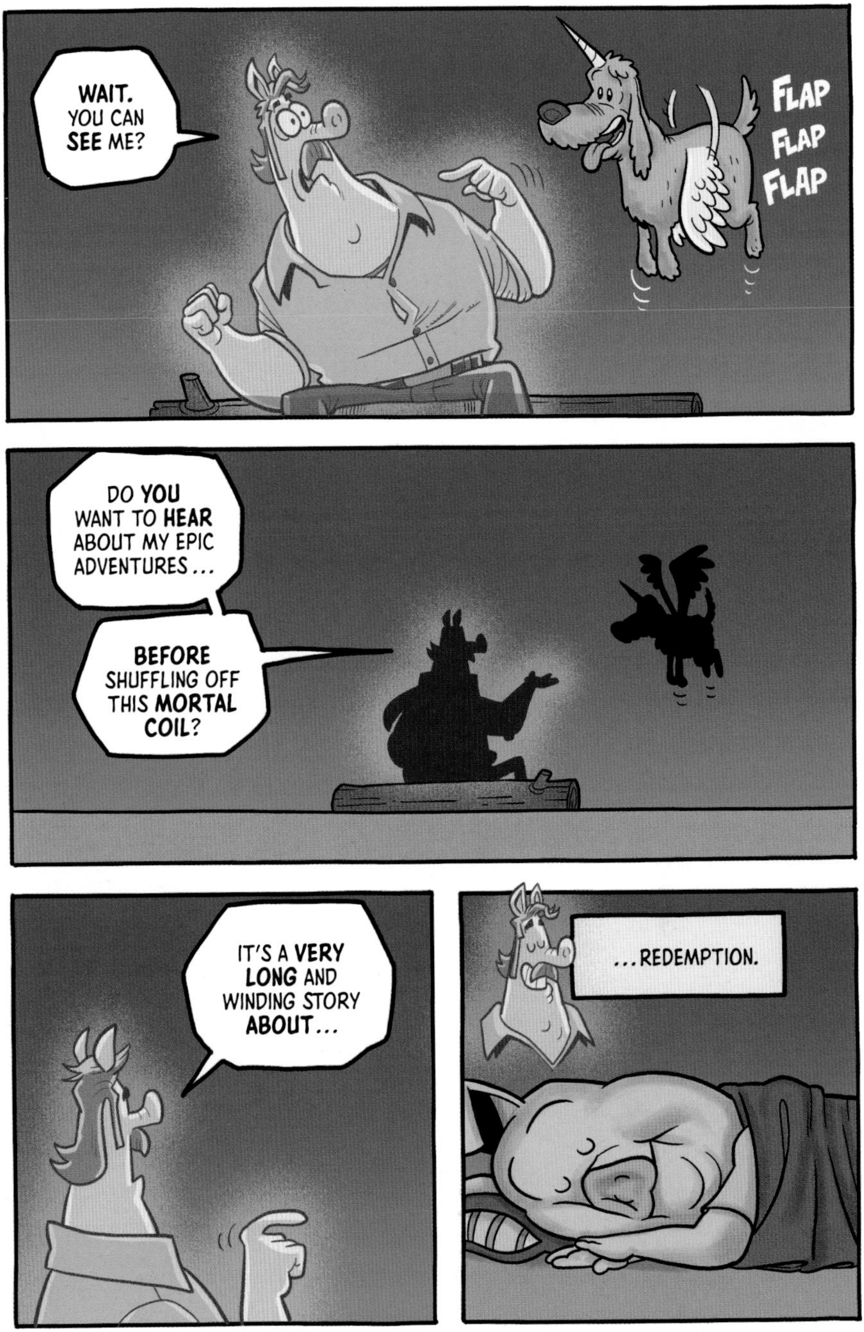
WAIT. YOU CAN SEE ME?
FLAP FLAP FLAP
DO YOU WANT TO HEAR ABOUT MY EPIC ADVENTURES...
BEFORE SHUFFLING OFF THIS MORTAL COIL?
IT'S A VERY LONG AND WINDING STORY ABOUT...
...REDEMPTION.

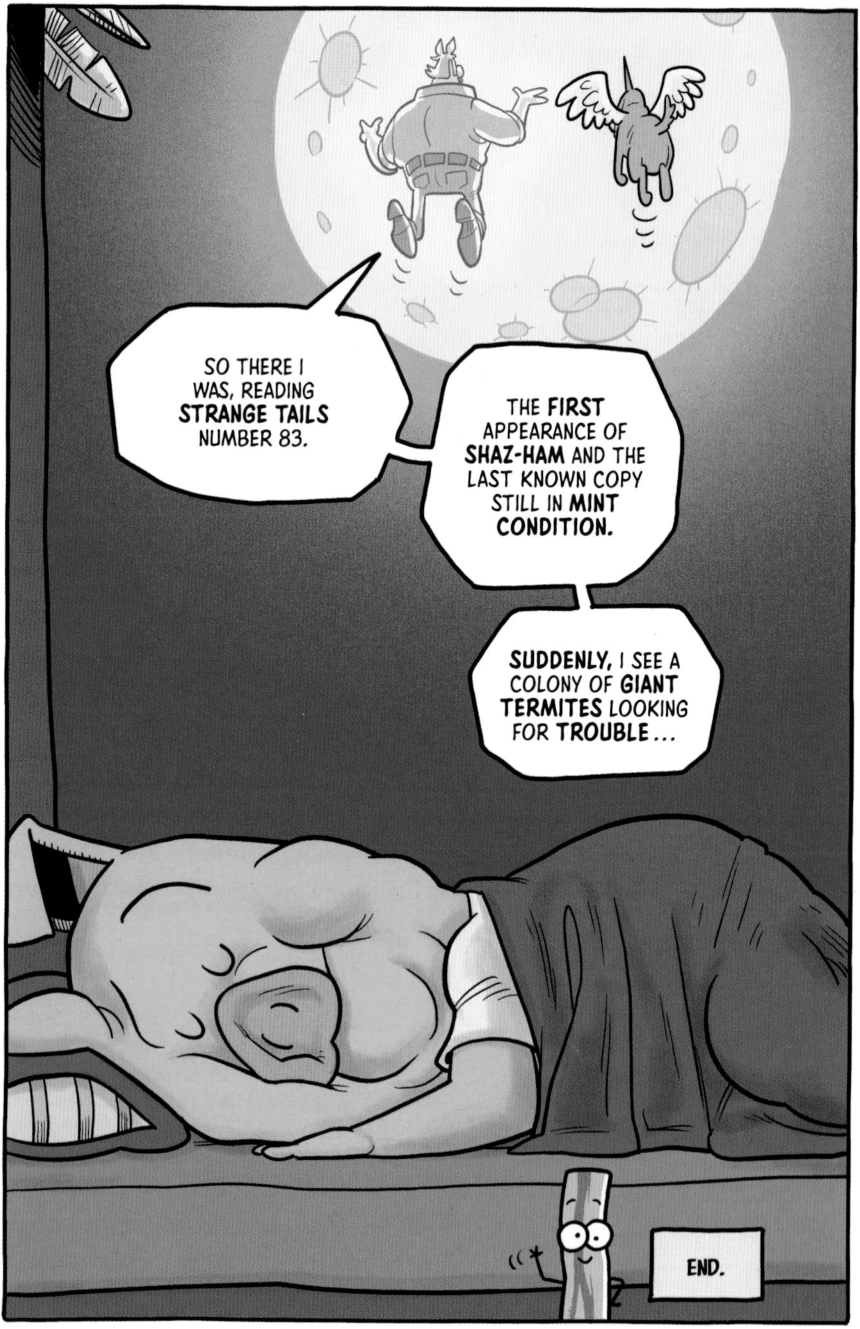
SO THERE I WAS, READING STRANGE TAILS NUMBER 83.
THE FIRST APPEARANCE OF SHAZ-HAM AND THE LAST KNOWN COPY STILL IN MINT CONDITION.
SUDDENLY, I SEE A COLONY OF GIANT TERMITES LOOKING FOR TROUBLE...
END.

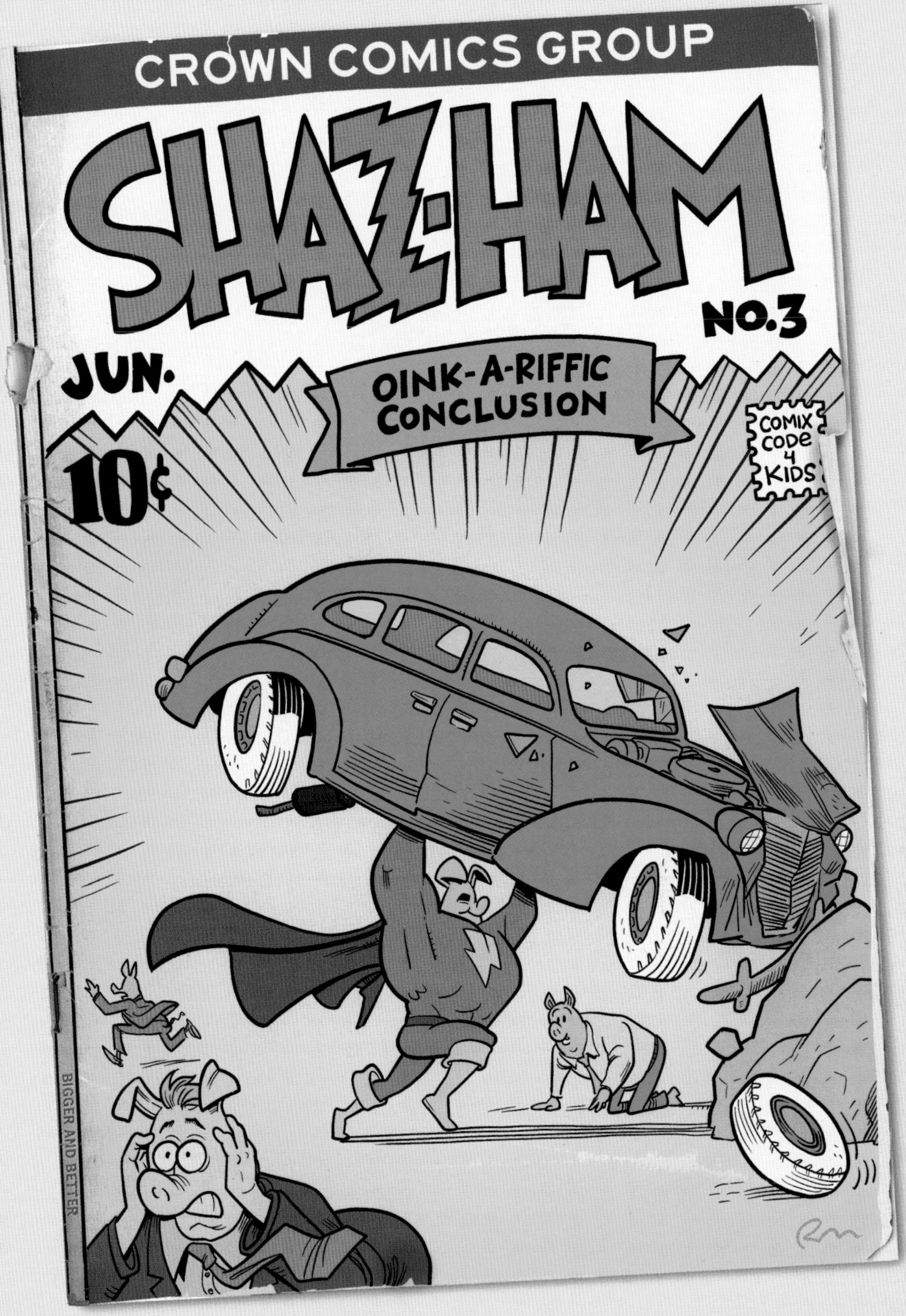
CROWN COMICS GROUP
SHAZ-HAM
NO.3
JUN.
OINK-A-RIFFIC
CONCLUSION
COMIX
CODE
4
KIDS
10¢
BIGGER AND BETTER

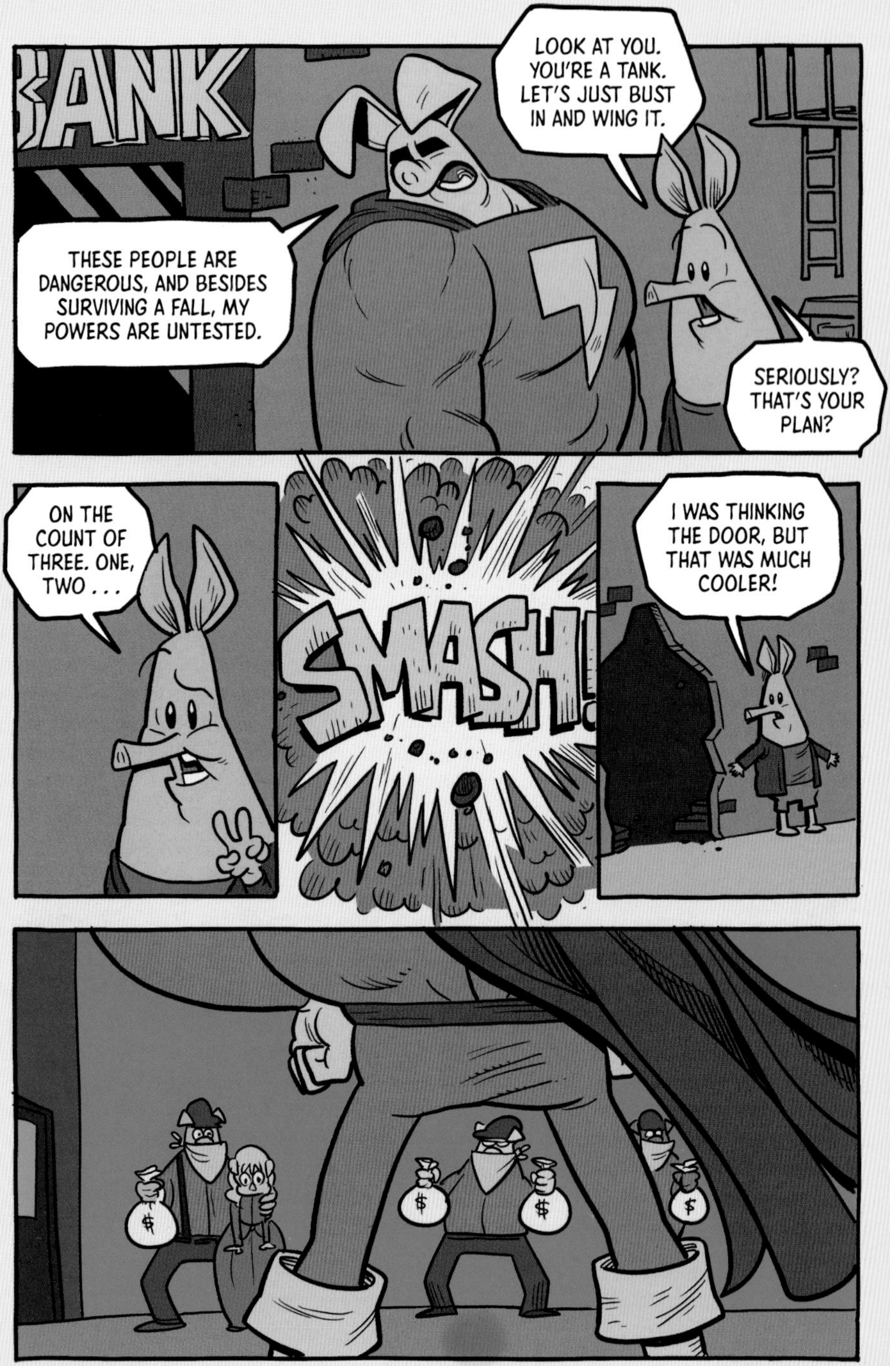
BANK
LOOK AT YOU. YOU'RE A TANK. LET'S JUST BUST IN AND WING IT.
THESE PEOPLE ARE DANGEROUS, AND BESIDES SURVIVING A FALL, MY POWERS ARE UNTESTED.
SERIOUSLY? THAT'S YOUR PLAN?
ON THE COUNT OF THREE. ONE, TWO . . .
SMASH!
I WAS THINKING THE DOOR, BUT THAT WAS MUCH COOLER!

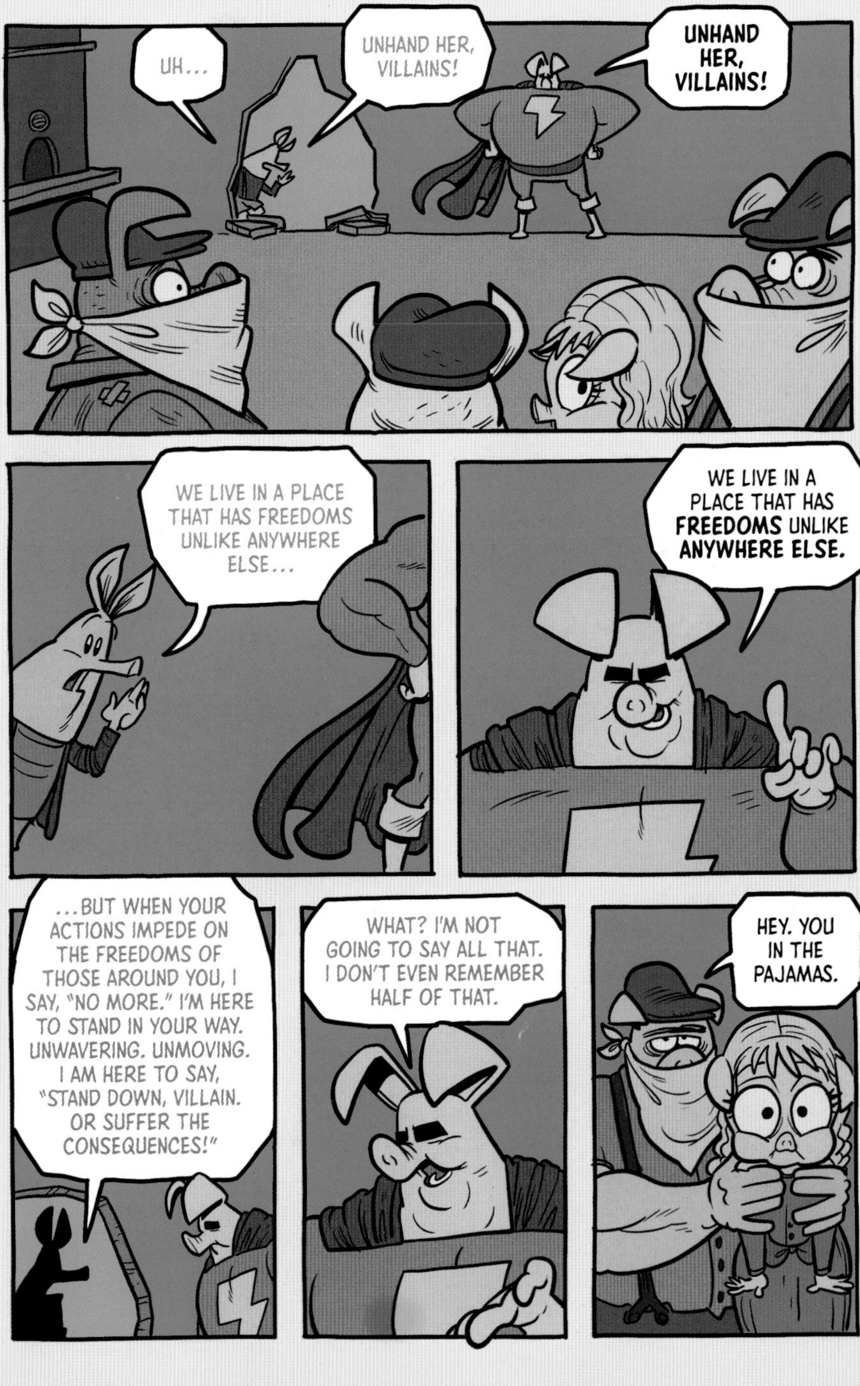
UH...
UNHAND HER, VILLAINS!
UNHAND HER, VILLAINS!
WE LIVE IN A PLACE THAT HAS FREEDOMS UNLIKE ANYWHERE ELSE...
WE LIVE IN A PLACE THAT HAS FREEDOMS UNLIKE ANYWHERE ELSE.
...BUT WHEN YOUR ACTIONS IMPEDE ON THE FREEDOMS OF THOSE AROUND YOU, I SAY, "NO MORE." I'M HERE TO STAND IN YOUR WAY. UNWAVERING. UNMOVING. I AM HERE TO SAY, "STAND DOWN, VILLAIN. OR SUFFER THE CONSEQUENCES!"
WHAT? I'M NOT GOING TO SAY ALL THAT. I DON'T EVEN REMEMBER HALF OF THAT.
HEY. YOU IN THE PAJAMAS.

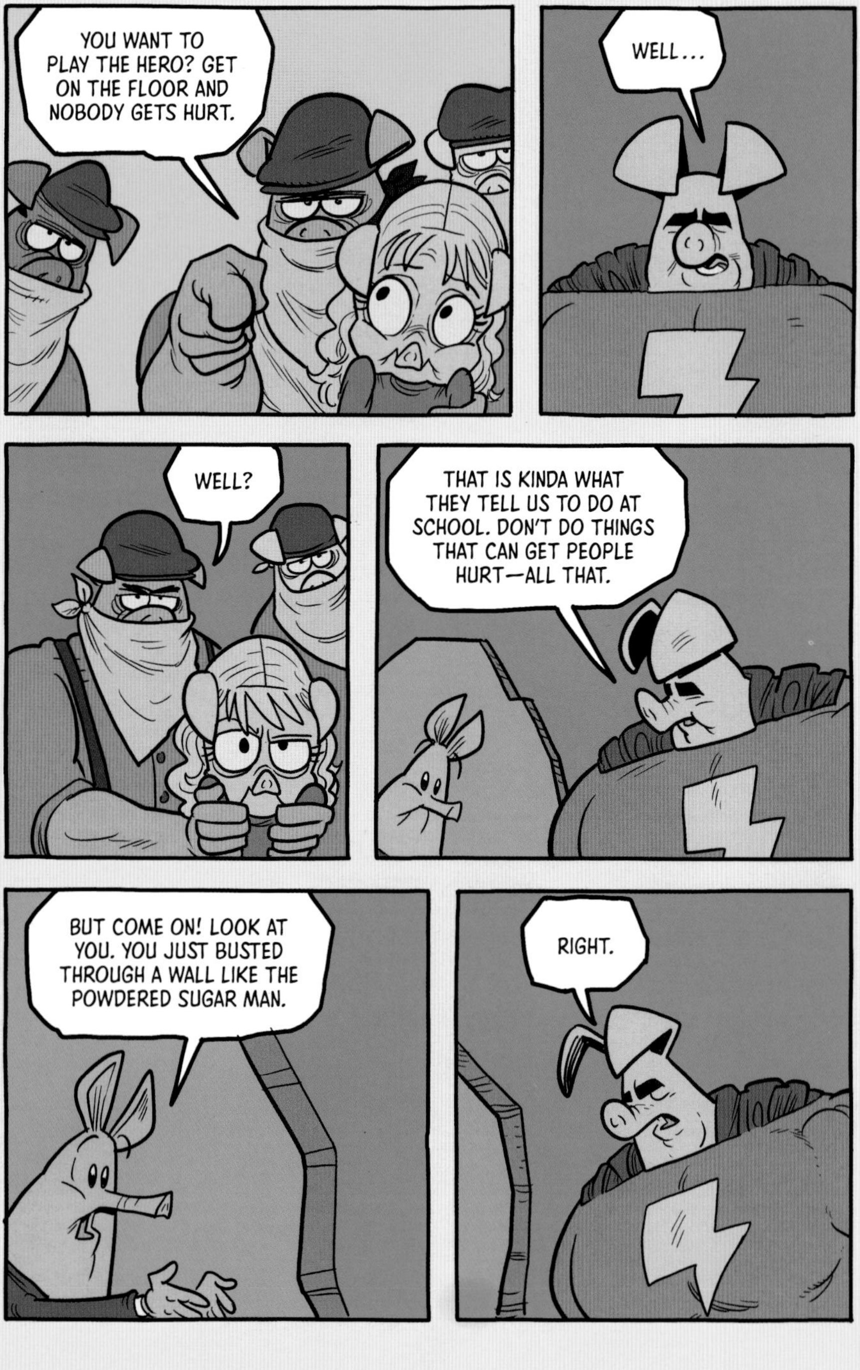
YOU WANT TO PLAY THE HERO? GET ON THE FLOOR AND NOBODY GETS HURT.
WELL...
WELL?
THAT IS KINDA WHAT THEY TELL US TO DO AT SCHOOL. DON'T DO THINGS THAT CAN GET PEOPLE HURT—ALL THAT.
BUT COME ON! LOOK AT YOU. YOU JUST BUSTED THROUGH A WALL LIKE THE POWDERED SUGAR MAN.
RIGHT.

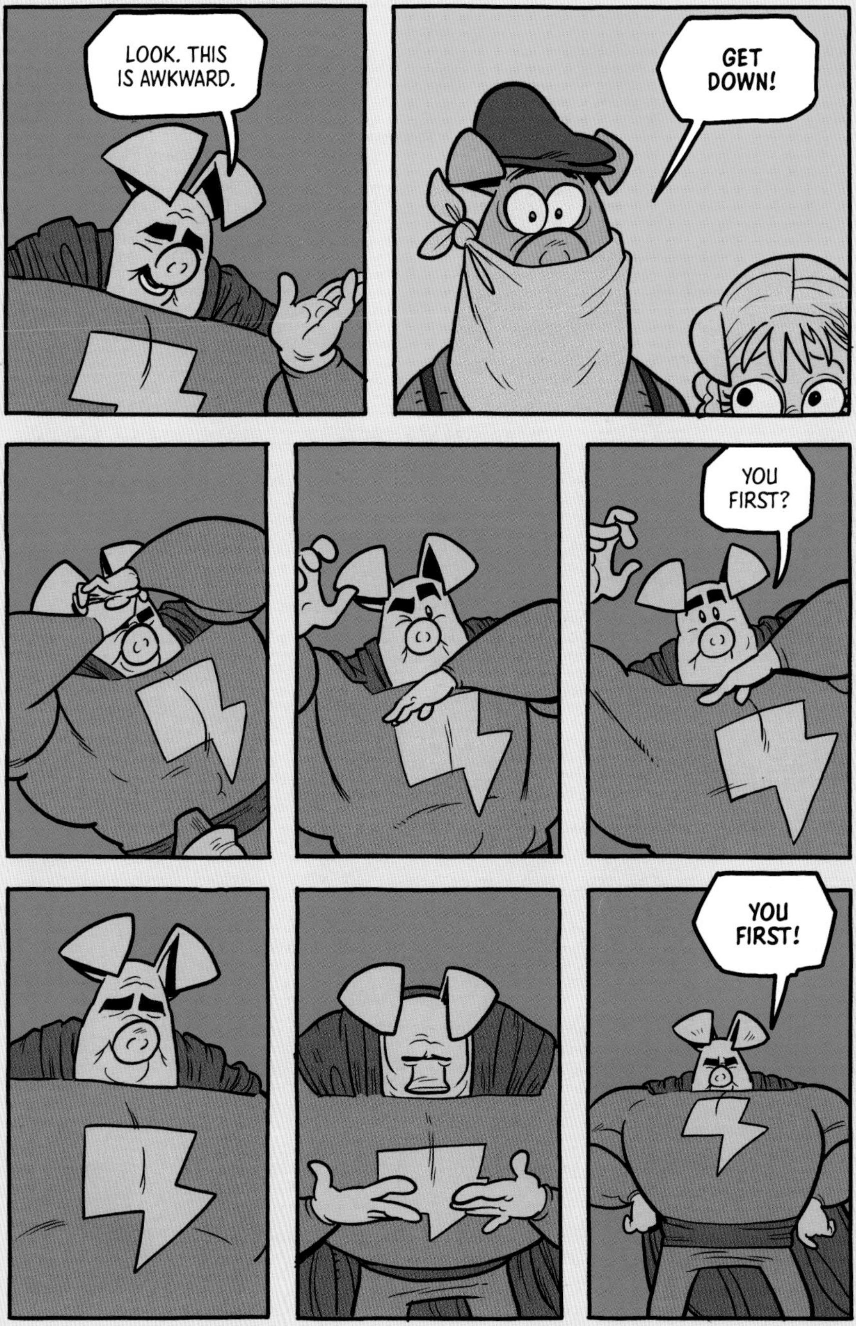
LOOK. THIS IS AWKWARD.
GET DOWN!
YOU FIRST?
YOU FIRST!

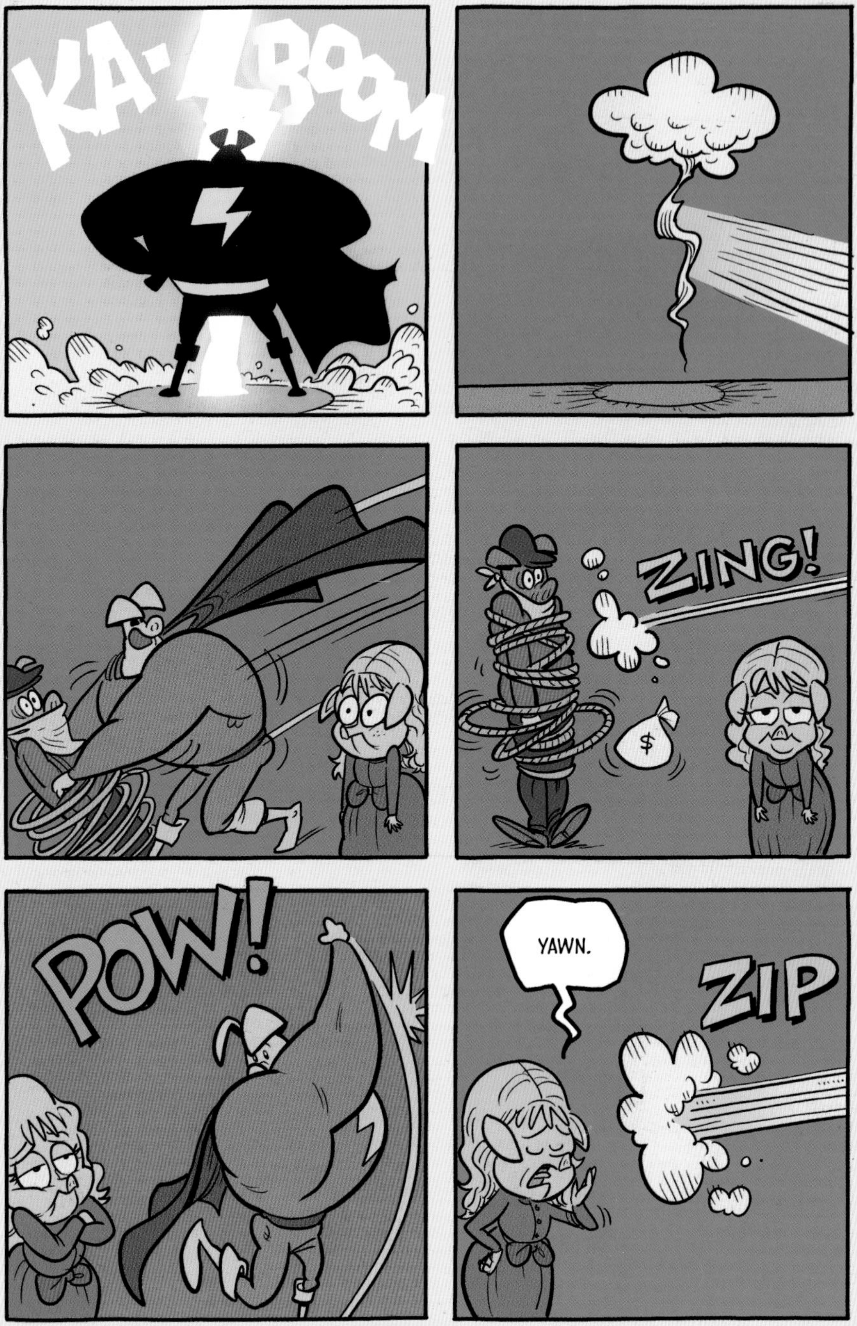
KA-BOOM
ZING!
POW!
YAWN.
ZIP

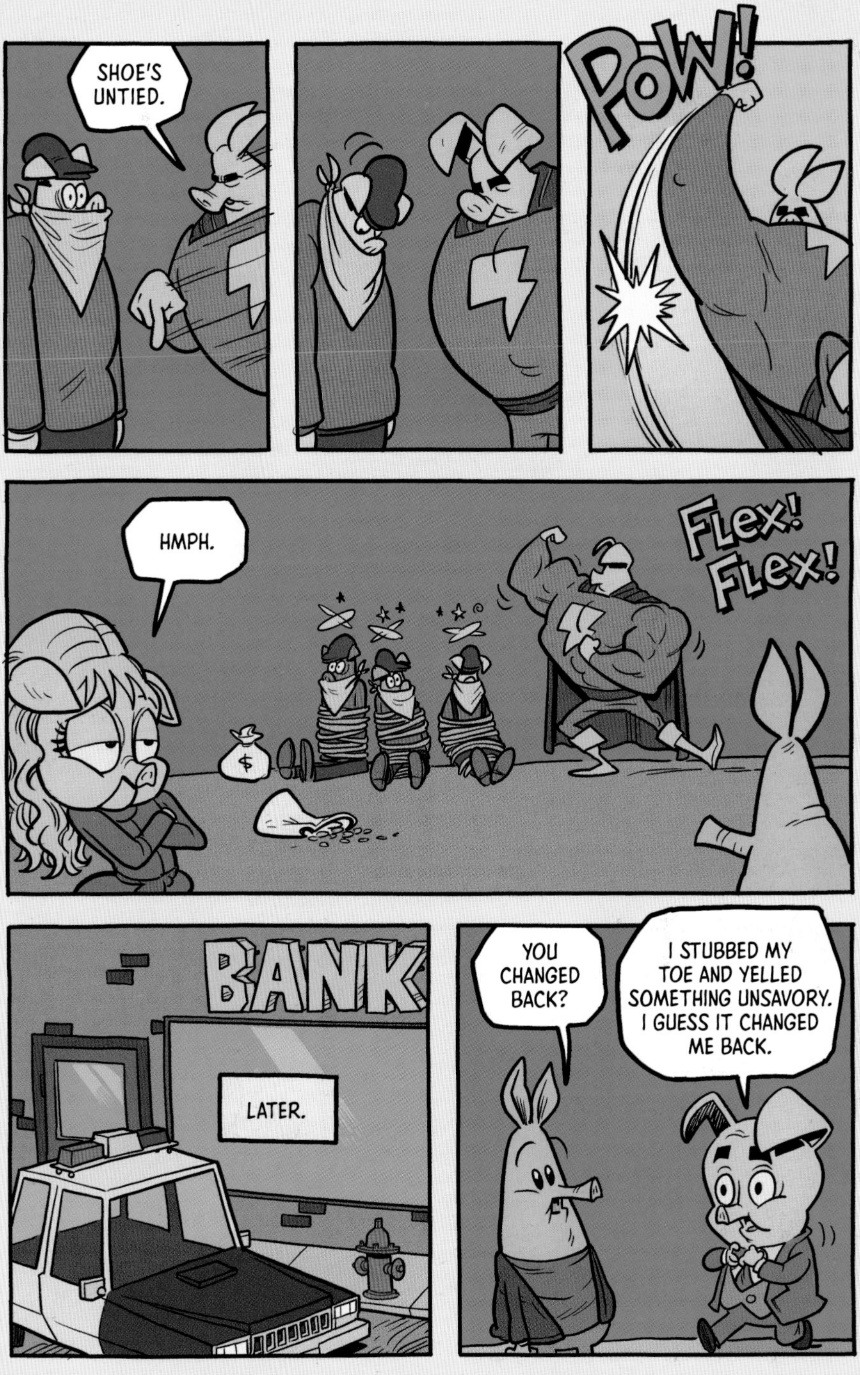
SHOE'S UNTIED.
POW!
HMPH.
FLEX! FLEX!
BANK
LATER.
YOU CHANGED BACK?
I STUBBED MY TOE AND YELLED SOMETHING UNSAVORY. I GUESS IT CHANGED ME BACK.

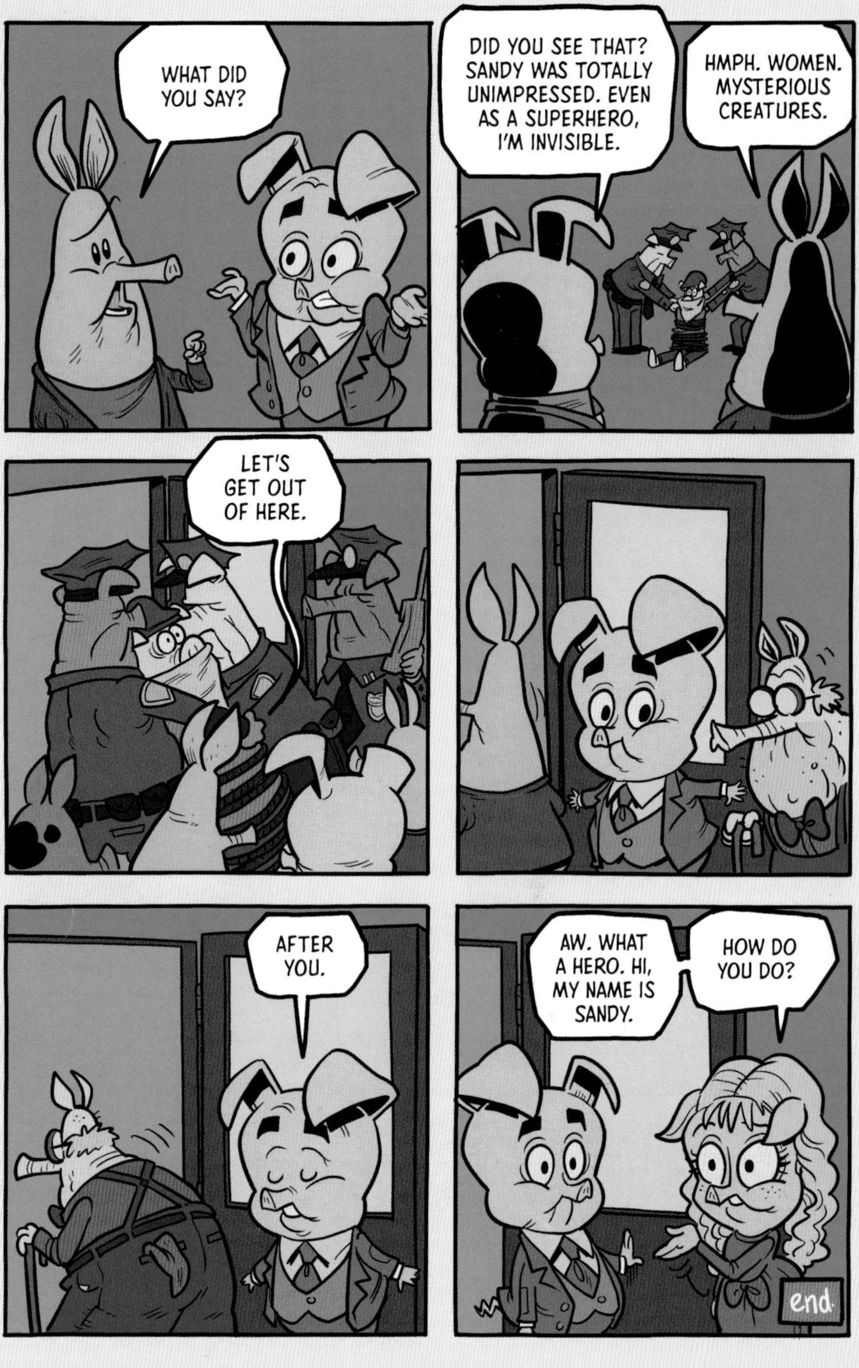
WHAT DID YOU SAY?
DID YOU SEE THAT? SANDY WAS TOTALLY UNIMPRESSED. EVEN AS A SUPERHERO, I'M INVISIBLE.
HMPH. WOMEN. MYSTERIOUS CREATURES.
LET'S GET OUT OF HERE.
AFTER YOU.
AW. WHAT A HERO. HI, MY NAME IS SANDY.
HOW DO YOU DO?
end.